THE TARGET BRIDE

A FORBIDDEN LOVE MAFIA ROMANCE

ENDANGERED BRIDES
BOOK ONE

R. R. NIGH

REDWOOD
PRESS

PROLOGUE

Rocco

FUCK VITO.

One hard flick of my coarse finger, and the vintage Italian coin twirls on the tabletop in front of me for fifteen seconds at a time.

I've been counting.

It's all I can do to keep my nerves in check.

Assignments like these always put me on fucking edge.

Exactly the way Vito likes it.

Me, in the dark, unaware of what's really going on, and the last to fucking find out.

Every. Single. Time.

Ever since that little prick came of age, my life as an enforcer for the Balboni crime family has turned into the tenth circle of hell. Since before Vito was tall enough to whisper in his father's ear, he's been gunning for the position of the don's right hand.

Don't get me wrong. I don't fault him for being ambitious. If my father were Don Jacopo Balboni—the feared and revered head of one of the most notorious organized crime outfits in NYC—I'd be jockeying for position within his inner circle myself.

Long story short, the minute Vito successfully wormed his way into his father's cabinet was the same minute I wound up with a target on my back. The kid has it out for me. Always has. He's eight years younger than I am, and because I've always been a favorite of his father's, he treats me like the older brother he never wanted, like I'm some kind of threat to *his* position in his own family.

Me. The old orphan outcast.

Fucking ridiculous.

The kid is a butt-hurt loose cannon, out to make my life a misery. And unlucky for me, it's one of the few things he's truly gifted at.

Sitting here in this strange hole-in-the-wall café is just one more case in point.

This morning, he slapped me with another spur-of-the-moment assignment, and today *really* isn't a good day for it.

My head is murdering me. *Fuck.*

I've got a migraine for the ages pounding through my skull, like a stampede of angry elephants. Broad daylight and city noise only make it worse.

Still, I should be grateful.

Thankfully, today's out-of-the-blue assignment is simple. Not like the time Vito's go-to assassin caught a bullet between the eyes trying to do a hit, and I got called in to finish the dead guy's job.

All I have to do is meet with a person of interest on the family's behalf.

But why the fuck did Vito pick *this* place for a meeting with a person of interest?

The place stretches long, like a galley kitchen. Exposed brick walls. Ugly, buzzing fluorescent lights cover the vaulted ceiling, at

With his voluminous hair, streaked with silver, and the matching gray stubble, gruff and gripping his chin, the man looks like an old wolf in a designer suit.

He strides into the place as though he owns it, his sharp, inquisitive eyes instantly falling on my face. Staring directly at me, sure and unflinching, he approaches my table with intention and lowers himself into the chair across from me with deliberate control. Saying nothing, he continues to search my face with his eyes.

Now, I'm unnerved.

My brain is ripping itself apart, I'm in desperate need of a truckload of aspirin or the gun holstered against my chest, but does it show? Is that why his eyes trace my face as though my skin is a book he's reading?

I can't tell if I'm hallucinating or disassociating yet, so I drop my eyes to the man's hands, folded on the table between us.

That's when I spot them, some of this man's tattoos.

Ice-old surprise breaks open in my chest.

On the back of his left hand. Unmistakable.

The asp viper. Mouth open wide, short sharp fangs poised to strike. Kill.

The Dalla Porta...

What in holy hell has Vito gotten me into now?

The Dalla Porta are the Balboni's sworn enemies. Vito sent me out here to meet a viper envoy and didn't give me even the slightest heads up?

My brain hurts even worse.

The Dalla Porta Crime Family is a high-profile international smuggling operation headquartered in NYC and Sicily. Lots of money. Lots of security. Lots of power and political cache in the criminal underworld. They're the go-to for people looking to smuggle art, humans, weapons, and drugs from one place to another.

I serve the Balboni Crime Family, the longtime rivals of the

Dalla Porta. We're what the police would call a racketeering outfit, highly skilled in intimidation and exploiting the vulnerable. We're good at stealth operations, finding out secrets, and exploiting them for financial and political gain. Most of the family's operations involve blackmailing people to keep their secrets hidden.

We have footprints in both New York and Sicily as well, but we don't have nearly the capital the Dalla Porta boasts of.

Not anymore.

Not since those vipers nearly wiped the entire Balboni family off the face of the earth, a decade or two ago.

On a regular day, fraternizing with any member of the Dalla Porta mob, or even their *allies* and associates, is grounds for murder within the Balboni. So why the fuck did Vito give me this assignment?

Even more concerning...

Judging by this man's tattoos, he's not just anybody. He's high up...

"I'm being rude." The man pulls a cigarette from his lapel. "Not introducing myself. My name is Orazio Di Rienzo."

Holy fuck. I'm talking to the Dalla Porta's spymaster.

Inner circle. Top rung. Alarm bells peal through my already aching head.

What the hell is a man this powerful doing trying to meet up with someone in the Balboni family?

"Rocco De Carlo." My name falls out of my mouth, robotic and rough.

"You're not what I expected." He admits, exhaling a trail of smoke. "I remember a young man. You're far from it."

Confusion clangs through me. "We know each other?"

A wry smile comes to his face, eyes deepening with something that looks remarkably like kindness. "No. I suppose we don't."

Just what the fuck is going on here?

Orazio Di Rienzo isn't acting like a man meeting an emissary for a crime family. He's talking to me like he knows exactly who I am, as though I'm exactly the person he was hoping to meet today.

Almost as though he and I go way back.

But I would most certainly remember meeting this man, if I had before.

Orazio sits up straighter, nodding, as if he's finally confirmed something, and then he rises from his chair. "Excuse me a moment, Rocco. I need to make a phone call."

Almost as soon as he entered, Orazio hurries out of the café and across the street to where his Bentley town car is parked, leaving me staring after him in pained curiosity.

I still don't know what the fuck this meeting is supposed to be about, but now there are some questions I want to ask the man as soon as he returns—

BOOM.

A sudden detonation pierces the air, a blast the size of a city bus shattering the café front's windows and shaking the foundation of the store. Tables and chairs blow back, my own body expelled on impact, fire, heat, smoke, and dizzying amounts of pain and disorientation claiming my awareness—I black out.

For minutes or hours, I'm lost in darkness, until my eyes peel back, the noise of fire truck sirens in the distance coming ever nearer.

I'm on my back, lying on the floor of this café, small chairs and tables pinning me to the ground.

My senses return to me in such dizzying waves of sight and sound.

As soon as I scramble to my feet, adrenaline moves my muscles until I've thrown everything off me and I'm standing up, nicks, scars, and glass crumbles all over my person.

Wide-eyed. Ears ringing. Consciousness fragmented.

I climb over the rubble and through the open rectangle cut out, where the door to this shop used to be, stumbling out into the carnage of this city block.

Pungent, acrid scents stab the inside of my nostrils, smoke in the air bringing an itch to my eyes.

The Bentley town car parked at the curb is now a blackened, burned-out husk. Still-crackling flames dance on its hood. That mess in the driver's seat must be the obliterated corpse of Orazio's chauffeur.

Car parts and melted flesh decorate the cement, darkened now with ash and other residue from the explosion.

And chunks of Orazio Di Rienzo's body—dismembered, badly burned, and partially melted in the blast—litter the street. The outline of what must be his head, left shoulder, and arm, completely severed from the rest of him, are unrecognizable.

All that's left of the man is a thick, smoking, leather wallet lying near my feet.

A half-singed family photo peaks over the rim. Ash obscures Orazio and his wife, while his twin daughters smile up at me.

Nora

"IF YOU GET scared or you need to come down for any reason, just hold onto the rope like this, and we will help you. Okay?"

An affirmative chorus follows my question.

With a smile on my face, I grapple down from the bright orange beginner's rock climbing wall to the applause of a small group of eager fourth-graders.

We've had several school groups today, and it's been kids everywhere, nonstop since nine a.m.

Absolutely, it's been hectic and chaotic. But I also love kids.

And there's something about The Rock—the climbing gym where I work—that seems just perfect for little ones. Maybe, it's all the colored walls that seem to extend forever up to the ceiling. Or the funky-shaped hand and foot holds that look like they were molded from Play-Doh. Maybe it's the random geometric shapes the walls are bent into. I have no idea.

All I know for sure is that I've loved rock climbing since I was a kid, and seeing all the elementary schoolers here, their excited eyes wide with wonder—it just makes me feel like my five-year-old self is hugging me tight.

School field trip day is one of my favorite days to come into work.

Hands down.

Wouldn't miss it.

Everyone who works here knows this about me.

Including Micah Hayes and Eli Wong. The pair of them mill nearby, helping me out with this newest crop of kids.

Micah's tall, gangly frame is easy to pick out of any crowd, let alone a crowd of kids, all of whom seem convinced he's a giraffe in disguise. Warm green eyes peer out from his vacant, smiling, nice-guy face. His pretty boy looks, coupled with his sinewy, athletic build, usually make him a hit with kids of all ages and genders, not to mention adults.

And Eli is similarly lovable, though short and compact. His bulging, sculpted thighs are the envy of bodybuilders the world over. His easygoing, talkative demeanor is soothing, and he's got a dimple so deep, a small child could drown.

Eli kneels on the ground, helping the second group of kids with their helmets and harnesses, while Micah leads the first group of students to the chalking station, and then over to the beginner's wall to pick out their starting footholds.

The parent chaperones stand around the perimeter, snapping photos and waving at their own children, peppered in amongst the class.

Echoes of chattering, laughing, clinking carabiners, and rope lines slapping against the practice walls...All of it is music to me somehow.

I can't stop myself from smiling.

Once the students begin their climbing adventure, Micah finds his way to my side, flashing a quick smile at me.

He's been doing this a lot lately.

I give him a little smile back, though inside, my anxiety teeters up a few notches.

Micah hasn't said anything yet, but his intentions are rolling off of him in waves. Like loud cologne.

Lately, he's been shining with that *I want to ask you out* glow.

The one that usually makes me run for the hills.

And speaking of running…

"Bathroom." I mouth to him the first chance I get, before retreating around a nearby corner toward the staff lavatories.

In the cool, quiet of this well-lit washroom, I balance my hands against the sink and catch my breath. I do love kids, and I'm fine with crowds, but still, that doesn't change the fact that I'm an introvert on the inside.

Being around lots of people for extended periods of time zaps my energy like I've been free-climbing for four hours straight without rest or water.

After a few deep breaths and two splashes of cold water to my flushed face, I'm starting to feel closer to center.

Then the washroom door swings open, and Mia Quentin strides in, her tall, built frame on full display in her black sports bra and form-fitting leggings.

Mia is a club regular and a tangential friend of mine who works part-time for the gym coordinating climbing schedules for groups, like the ones here with us today. We've run into each other a lot in recent months. She's one of the very few women who like to spend their nights rock climbing, like me, after the workday is long over.

"Hey, nightbird." She beams with that twinkle in her eye whenever she uses her nickname for me.

"Hey yourself!" I drop my hands to my waist.

Mia's a CrossFit queen, a master-level free climber, and a *total* womanizer. Her sports bra has the word LESBIAN printed across it in bold, block letters.

I know she wears stuff like this so that other gay women can pick her out easier, but really, I think she loves creating chaos when men find themselves staring at her perfect boobs, only to realize they have no chance in hell with her.

"Hiding again?" She arches an eyebrow at me.

"Guilty."

"Knew it. Micah's still on your tail…" She pulls open one of the neon pink lockers against the wall and tosses her bag inside. "Look. Don't pay the kid any attention, or hey. Even better. Tell him where you're going this fall."

Mia's the only person at the gym I've told about my September plans.

The ones that involve me leaving the US to join my sister in the south of Switzerland and get my Master's in Tourism and Hospitality.

Mia's spot on, as usual.

Even if I were interested in Micah in a romantic way, I'm not looking to connect with anyone right now. I'll be gone for good in five short months. What's the point in starting something real?

I'd honestly be happy to drop the news on Micah so he won't embarrass himself by asking me out. The only reason I haven't so far and don't feel I can is because I haven't told Aggie yet, our boss.

Agatha Jean-Gerard is the owner and operator of The Rock. She founded the place about a decade ago. She's an outdoorsy, tough mama, and my personal mentor of many years now. To say that I love her like family would be an understatement. With the exception of my sister and my parents, I love Aggie more than I love a lot of my biological family members.

I love Aggie so much that I've been agonizing over how to break the news to her.

After five years of working here, I'm leaving…

My heart falls in my chest.

Aside from my dad, working at The Rock is the only thing about New York City I'm going to miss...

Mia pats my shoulder, surprising me. "Ready to get back out there?"

"Almost." I give her a half smile, probably badly disguising the sadness pinching me on the inside. "I need another minute."

"Whatever happens, you got this." Mia has this uncanny ability to give me a pep talk in five words or less. She should go into marketing.

The woman goes, and I'm left on my own again.

My fingers fly up to the pendant around my neck for support whenever I'm anxious, and this moment qualifies. The gold cross I always wear is cool to the touch and has a translucent seeing stone in the center of it.

I take the cross, then pull it up toward my eyeball, peering into the stone.

If someone watched me do this, to them, I'd probably look crazy.

But that's because they wouldn't be able to see what I'm seeing.

Displayed deep inside this tiny little stone is a photograph of my family.

In the garden on the terrace of our childhood home, my parents smile at the camera, while my twin and I, in sun dresses, squeeze each other tight, grinning ear to ear after all the ice cream had been eaten.

This picture grounds me until I'm calm enough to face my life again.

Everyone in my family has this picture in their possession.

Mom, Sis, and I all have matching cross necklaces with the photo inside. They were a gift from Dad, who carries the same photo in his wallet. Even though we're seldom all together anymore, knowing that we each carry this memento makes me feel connected to them.

The thought of that doubles my strength.

"Let's get back out there," I cheer myself on, retying my tawny brown waves and curls into a fresh ponytail.

As soon as I'm out of the lavatories, Aggie's the first thing I see.

She crosses my sightline, tension and fear in her well-defined muscles, striding up to Micah and Eli, a hard, unreadable look on her face. "Where's Nora?"

Her demanding tone makes me freeze where I stand.

Micah and Eli spot me and point this way. Aggie turns to me, eyes alight with concern. Cold streams of foreboding drip down my spine as my mentor approaches me with fire under her feet.

"There's a call for you. From your mom."

My mom? My heart slams at my ribs.

Mom never calls the gym.

Something's wrong. I can feel it.

Aggie nods toward her office, and I rush that way, jogging on uncertain legs into the warm, quiet darkness of The Rock's administrative suite.

Heart shaking in my chest, I grab the phone. "Mama? I'm here. What's going on?"

On the other end, my mother sobs uncontrollably.

She's...*wailing.* Distraught.

Broken, grieving cries rip from her throat, cutting my ears, striking deep at my racing heart. *Oh God.*

"Mama, what is it?" I try again. "Put Dad on the phone. Put..." My own sobs begin. I choke on the words, my eyes blurring with hot, heavy tears.

My mother doesn't even have to say it.

She's not a woman who cries or breaks down.

If she's in this state, it can only mean one thing...

The day has finally come that my father's dangerous work has killed him.

CHAPTER 1

Nora

IN A WOOD-PANELED vestibule off the main sanctuary of Saint Anthony's Cathedral, an enormous catholic church overflowing with flowers and members of the Dalla Porta mob, I wait in plaintive silence for the arrival of Nico, my sister.

Sitting by a large gothic window in utter silence, a grimace of grief plastered to my face, I might as well be one of the gargoyles on the cathedral's roof. Right now, my brain is a still pond full of black, angry water. Grotesque, heartbroken thoughts swim beneath the surface like mythical sea creatures.

My heart is in a darkness so deep, I fear light will never break, ever again.

How could it?

My dad was my best friend, the person who knew me the best, the person who cared most about my happiness and dreams...And he's gone. Forever.

Murdered. *Slain.*

The police report says a gas leak is to blame, but we know better.

It was a car-bombing that ripped him apart, tearing him from our lives too soon.

My jaw trembles with the strain of holding my wretched sobs inside, while silent tears streak down my cheeks.

At least, I'm alone in here for now.

Instead of *out there* with everyone else.

To my right, there's a side door that leads outside to the road, where Nico's car should pull up any minute now. But a big part of me wants to push through it and run, as far as I can, as fast as I can.

Because I can't do this. Going to Dad's funeral is like accepting that he's gone, and I don't accept.

I don't accept.

The only other door in this room leads back into the sanctuary, where the shuffle of mourners speaking and gathering in lowered voices washes over me in waves, even through the wood and stone barrier between us.

I try not to focus on anything.

If I try to think even one thought, the weight of my world crashes down on me afresh, eviscerating me so thoroughly, I can barely stand.

My soul lays prostrate on the floor in front of me, even now.

Outside the window, a town car pulls up, and I spring to my feet. I shove through the outside door, the second Nico steps out in her seven-inch black stilettos.

My sister has a life rule. The worse you feel on the inside, the more devastating you should look on the outside.

The lower she feels, the higher her heels. I just barely understand the sentiment, the lower I feel the higher I climb too.

Into the buzzy April air, I run at my sister, and she runs at me.

We slam into each other, tears flying, as we squeeze each other for dear life. I can barely breathe. There's so much I want to say, but all I can manage is nonsensical blubber. She kisses my cheek four times in a row. *"Ciao, Bella."*

"Me?" Pulling back to stare at each other, I give her another once over. "Look at you!" God, she smells expensive and amazing, looks *gorgeous.*

Even dressed for mourning, Nico looks like a million bucks. Her unique sense of style was an early indicator of her future career, working in fashion. She is quite literally fresh off a runway in Milan, in her sleeveless, sweetheart-cut jumpsuit, a silk patterned shawl slung over one arm.

She laughs, despite the tears rolling down her cheeks. Then her face crumples up, and mine does too, because...we haven't seen each other face-to-face in twelve whole years. The last time we were in the same timezone, we were teenagers.

And these are the circumstances that reunite us?

We squeeze each other close again, a fresh wave of sobs washing over us.

"I'm so glad you're here." I hiccup, the moment my strength returns to me.

"Where else would I be?" We release each other, sharing a knowing look.

I can't stop looking at her. She has my same oval-shaped face, hair texture, and height. Aside from the subtle color differences in our eyes and hair, we have all the same features. We're both twenty-five.

Except Nico looks stunning, cultured, and so grown-up, and I look like I fell out of college five minutes ago. Familiar pangs of jealous longing echo through my empty, cavernous chest. But I stuff them down with guilt.

As much as I want to envy my sister's style, aplomb, freedom, and career success, I can't forget the reason we've been separated all these years. Nico was banished by our parents when she was only thirteen. They separated her from our family and sent her abroad.

All because she tried to save me from danger.

Losing Nico was the first time I ever lost my best friend. Losing Dad was the second. *Is the second.*

Oh, God...

Nico catches the tears water-falling from my eyes with warm, delicate fingers, before she folds my arm through hers. We hold tight to each other, clinging close, as we enter the church.

Thank God she's with me. There's no way I could have done this on my own.

The cathedral is dressed to the nines. Fat, overflowing white lily flower arrangements are stationed every four feet around the sanctuary's perimeter. On the altar, two big bouquets sit on either side of the large frame, showing our father's face. I can barely look at it without losing it.

We cross in front of the altar, and to our left the central aisle opens up. Thick ivory candles line either side, smaller clusters of blooms in between their bases, and dominating the the middle of that walkway between the sanctuary's grand doors and the altar behind us is the closed casket, covered in roses and carnations.

What's left of our father's body...

I have to look away.

Tatiana Di Rienzo, our aggrieved mother sits directly in our path, slumped in the front row, inconsolable. I've never seen her like this before.

Eyes puffed, swollen and damp. Hair pulled too tight up into pillbox hat, a small, fishnet veil covering her flushed face.

This can only be the unimaginable grief of losing the love of your life...

Nico and I go to Mama, and as soon as she slowly lifts her head and sees Nico beside me, she pulls my sister down onto the pew beside her. A small tearful reunion unfolds, and I back up a little to give them some space.

Standing here at the front of the sanctuary gives me a perfect view of everyone in attendance today. My eyes skate around the room, surveying the showing of mafia folks who've come out to honor my father.

The most prominent among them is Don Sabatini Calzavarra.

Head of the Dalla Porta crime family, he's the textbook definition of wealth and power, all mixed up in one tall, imposing, terrifying man. He clears six feet easily, his thick silver hair slicked back over a square forehead worn through with lines. His deep brown eyes have long looked black from up close and at a distance. Not that anyone can see them through the shades he's wearing, mouth fixed into a firm line.

Unfailingly dapper in a designer suit, he's the last to enter the sanctuary, flanked by his security detail and his only son and heir, Ciro Calzavarra.

His diamond-shaped head is brightened by his exacting blue-eyed gaze, above which his dark, salt-streaked hair sits coiffed to the left.

Ciro isn't as tall as his father, but he carries himself like he is. In his forties, he's well-dressed in fittingly somber attire. The expression he wears is the only problem.

Ciro is known for his poker face. At all times, his puckish mouth makes him look smug. Even now, at a funeral for a high-ranking member of the family.

Looking at Ciro Calzavarra is like tempting bad luck to bite you. The second before he turns his head and catches my eyes on him, I look the other way entirely—

My heart misses a beat and stumbles against my ribs.

Standing tall at the back of this church is a man I don't recognize.

A twinge of heated surprise flushes through my chest, as I find myself suddenly locked within his dark liquid gaze, across the distance of thirty pews.

He's...striking, I must admit.

Dark curls cropped short above his regal rectangular face,

studded with glowing brown eyes. A straight, elegant nose directs my attention to his mouth...

Those lips were definitely designed to kiss...

Horrified by my own invasive thoughts, my face warms. I want to look away from him, but I can't tear my eyes from the intensity of his gaze.

Fine cuts and nicks mar his handsome face. They look fresh, not faded, which means he came by them recently. Doing something dangerous.

Definitely a mafioso. I'd bet money, even though I can't see any tattoos from here.

God, I don't know how this man does it, but I swear, he's wrapping himself around me with his eyes. The longing in his rich brown irises captures me like mountain vista, his gaze fathoms deep, so potent and powerful that I can't look away—

Not until I'm interrupted by the invasion of my personal space.

The sharp, unmistakable custom cologne of a certain pig I know creeps up my nose. I jerk left, and there he is, approaching me with all the arrogance of any overindulged, spoiled brat anywhere.

Gianfrancesco Calzavarra.

Frankie, as his friends and family call him.

He's Ciro's son. Don Sabatini's one and only grandchild.

Gianfrancesco is the son of the Dalla Porta's future don, and an up and coming enforcer, though his "work" for the family usually includes a truck full of hard liquor and the strippers who pour it, according to my dad.

A head taller than I am, Gianfrancesco intimidates me with his thick, muscled, frame. Except for one curl resting on his square forehead, he's slicked the rest of his chestnut waves back across his meaty head. Clearly, his grandfather has inspired his style. His stubbled face and cruel mouth hide two rows of vicious white teeth, and don't even get me started on his eyes.

The ones that assess and appraise me whenever I'm in his vicinity.

Ugh.

His left eye is a muddy sort of green, and the right eye appears pitch black most of the time. Above and below his right eye are two jagged scars, brown and faded from time, but still distinct. Flashbacks dance at the edges of my mind whenever I glimpse those scars, but I don't want to think about that now.

Frankie drifts up to me, his uptight mother fastened to one arm.

"Eleanora." His tongue curls around my name. I hate the way he says it, like I'm meal he's hungry for. "I've come to offer my condolences."

"Thank you." Wow, my voice sounds lifeless. Even to me.

"Your father was a good man," his mother adds, shocking the hell out of me.

Donna Calzavarra is a woman I've never been able to pin down. It's clear she loves her son more than anything on Earth, but honestly, she seems to hate everything else.

Her husband.

The whole Dalla Porta family.

Me. *My mother.*

I've never seen her smile at anything or anyone other than Frankie, let alone praise someone. I'm stunned.

I'm even *more* stunned when Donna releases Frankie's arm, wraps her tense fingers around my forearm, and leans over to plant a kiss on my cheek.

Like she's one of my aunts or cousins.

Then she walks right past me, leaving me alone with her son, while she pays her respects to my mother.

Donna's always cordial, but freezing fucking cold with us.

This is the warmest she's ever been. And it's honestly frightening.

"We were shocked to hear the news." Frankie picks up our

nonexistent conversation thread, preventing me from getting away from him without looking rude. "Losing a parent is hard."

Not like you would know.

Frankie steps in closer to me, and I instinctively back up.

Irritation flickers in his eyes.

Guess he noticed.

"If you need a shoulder to lean on..." The threat in his voice hides between his seemingly kind words. "I'm—"

"Intruding where you aren't wanted?" My sister—*my hero*—steps between us, protective and strong, as she always, always have.

The change in mood between the three of us is immediate.

Frankie's freakish eyes narrow at my sister, his lips tightening into a frown. Just the tension in his severe jawline sends my shoulders tensing up too.

Jesus, I hate conflict.

That's one of the many differences between me and my twin sister. I do everything I can to keep the peace, and she does everything she can to disrupt it.

And she's great at it, I must say.

Nico's beautifully manicured hands fall to her trim waist, as she cuts her eyes at Frankie, giving him a glare just as good as the one he stabs her with.

"*Nicoletta.*" He says her name with enough menace to raise the hairs on my arms.

She spits his name off her tongue. "*Gianfrancesco.*"

They look each other over, slow, unbothered, yet brusque, like two cowboys in a duel about to shoot each other or die trying.

It's the first time they've crossed paths in many years.

And the last time they met...Nico put those scars on his face.

That's right.

Gianfrancesco Calzavarra is the *real* reason my sister was sent away.

Frankie's mouth curls into a sharp, sarcastic sneer. "Over a decade of exile has done wonders for you."

Nico scoffs under her breath. "Wish I could say the same. Unfortunately, ten years of people kissing your ass has only made *you* uglier."

Frankie bristles, almost imperceptibly. "You're still insolent, I see."

"And you're still sniffing around my sister."

"My *fiancée*, you mean."

Yuck. A chill zips down my spine. Frankie has long been under the strange misapprehension that one day I'm going to be his wife.

Even though I'd rather die.

Nico just shakes her head at him, like he's a sad, sad sight. "Ugly *and* delusional. How depressing."

"You'll see." Frankie grins at my twin, eyes humorous and bright, like he's enjoying some private joke. "I'm so excited to disappoint you."

"Mission accomplished."

Before Nico and Frankie take any more shots at each other, our father's funeral grinds to a start. My sister and I seat ourselves on the pew beside our mother, and then, Nico squeezes my hand tight and whispers to me. *"It's going to be okay."*

The five little words take me back.

Nico said the same thing to me on the day everything fell apart the first time, all those years ago.

We were thirteen then. Frankie was fifteen. We'd only recently gotten home from living abroad, my sister, my mother, and I...

The Dalla Porta crime family is a big deal in New York City and in Sicily, where it began. Our father, Orazio Di Rienzo, was the family spymaster, in charge of finding, gathering, and utilizing important information to the family's benefit. When we were small children, he and our mother decided to send us to live abroad, for our safety.

My sister and I were told it was a vacation. But in reality, we weren't allowed to return to New York for about ten years.

When we did get home, we soon encountered Frankie.

He was fifteen then, and already an asshole.

It was hard not to notice the way he watched me. He was always watching me. And it wasn't long before we gleaned why. Rumors had spread throughout the family that I was his intended bride.

When my parents got wind of the idea, they were furious. Nothing angered them more than the idea that I would be wed to that idiot.

And for once, all four of us agreed on something.

But even my family's full resistance to the idea didn't stop Frankie from harassing me. He used to grab my wrist and drag me around the Dalla Porta estate. And every time I tried to pull away, he'd only squeeze harder.

He'd tell me in lurid detail all the things we'd do once we were married, regurgitating all the vile, vulgar, sexual slang he'd likely overheard from enforcers in the family, who were old enough to spend time in strip clubs and brothels.

It was nauseating and deeply uncomfortable for me.

But I was always told to tread carefully with him. He may be an asshole, but he's also the don's grandson, a protected prince of this mafia. Angering him would come with consequences.

Nico was the one who didn't care. Whenever we were together and Frankie appeared, she protected me from him, antagonizing him until he stormed away. She was so good at it, that it got to the point where if Frankie saw the two of us together, he didn't bother coming over to annoy me.

If he wanted to harass me, he waited until he could get me alone.

And one day, he did.

He caught me by surprise walking down a hallway, and dragged me outside into the estate gardens. Around several hedge corners in the shade of a secluded tree, he threw me down in the dirt and got on top of me.

He tried to take things too far, but Nico saw him haul me off, and came running. When she got to us, she shoved him off me, and cat-clawed him across the face. She slapped him so hard, one of her nails scratched his left cornea and injured his eye.

I'll never forget his grunts of pain, hand over his eye, drips of blood rolling down from beneath his palm.

This is why his eyes are so freakish.

His right eye remains the greenish brown he was born with, and the other eye looks black all the time because his pupil can't retract anymore.

As soon as we could see how hurt he was, Nico and I ran for the hills.

Attacking a Dalla Porta prince is an offense punishable by death.

Our parents knew that banishing my sister before any worse sentence could be handed down was the best way to go. So, they sent Nico away to Europe to save her life, even if separating the two of us broke our hearts.

And still does.

I squeeze my sister's hand back, fresh tears rolling down my face.

I've missed her more than words could ever say.

Dad's funeral slogs by, but it's over in about ninety minutes. I don't remember a word anyone said, nor a single hymn that was sung. I spent the entire time lost in my own thoughts, spiraling through my own grief.

By the time a pair of church attendants usher us, the family of the deceased, out the cathedral's side entrance to a waiting limo by the curb, I'm feeling more drained and exhausted than I did when I woke up this morning.

We help our mother inside, who seems little more than a corpse, she's so silent and ghastly thin. Nico climbs in after her, settling her sleek black clutch purse in her lap. Then, a faraway lightbulb blinks on in the back of my mind.

My purse.

I left it in the vestibule earlier, while I was waiting for my sister to arrive.

After murmuring this to Nico, I jog back inside the church, cutting through a crowd of mourners, fighting the outflow of traffic, and ignoring the pitying looks people throw me. Desperate to get away from it all, I throw my whole weight against the vestibule door and push inside—*Holy shit.*

My feet freeze, and I lurch on the inside, feeling it all the way in my kneecaps.

It's him. The man from earlier. The unspeakably gorgeous one...

The one I locked eyes with from across that crowded church.

He's here in the vestibule.

We're alone in here together.

His gaze flies to me the second I'm inside, and the same surprise I'm feeling is evident on his face.

"Um..." Since my mouth's already hanging open, I might as well speak. "I came in here to get my purse."

His bright brown eyes flick to the bench where I was seated hours ago, my little bag slumped against the wood. Robotically, I march over and reach for it, at the same moment he does. In the process, our hands brush.

The heat of his skin presses into my own.

An electric shock transfers between us, making me jump.

He draws back too. I watch his Adam's apple dip low in that thick, graceful neck.

"Here." He offers my purse to me.

Just that one syllable, and I know how buttery, rich, and deep his voice is.

The man must be a whole two heads taller than I am. If he fell on me, he'd crush me flat, so why am I fully convinced that he knows how to be gentle, just from the softness in his deep voice?

My heart clammers, as I take my purse back from him. "Thank you."

I might stand here staring at him all day if I don't leave right this moment. With difficulty, I tear my gaze from his striking face.

Only to be ensnared by him again.

"Please—" He takes a heavy step toward me. "Allow me to tell you how sorry I am for your loss."

Wide-eyed and full of unexpected tears, I blink at him.

The sincerity in his voice arrests me. Concern glimmers in his eyes.

I can only nod, too choked up to speak. He takes another step toward me, almost as if to shake my hand or give me a hug, but in the same moment, I turn on my heel and dash from the room.

Before I *completely* shatter into a million pieces, never to be put back together again.

CHAPTER 2

Nora

"SO WHAT NOW?" Nico whispers to me, as the limo pulls away from the curb.

My heart still thundering from my five minutes in heaven with the mystery man, I fight to swallow down the lump of emotion in my throat. "The repast."

"Guess it was silly of me to think this would be a sprint instead of a marathon." Nico gives me a cheering little smile, though sadness hides in the corners.

Nico was always the strongest of the three of us, the one who made the rest of us laugh in the face of horrific tragedy.

"It's been so long since you were home..." My eyes keep tracing her face.

"Has anything changed at the estate?"

I almost laugh. "Absolutely nothing."

The Dalla Porta estate—the official headquarters of the mafia, where Don Sabatini lives, as well as his immediate family, and most of his circle too—is a vertical gilded age mansion in New York City, squished between two other buildings. The Dalla Porta own the entire block that the mansion sits on though, so it's entirely secure.

All the buildings adjacent to and across from the estate are property of the family. Multiple spaces in multiple different buildings are used to conduct the family's various business ventures. And Dalla Porta soldiers litter the surrounding streets, often posing as pedestrians, when really they're security.

Before my father died, we lived in the Hurst building, it's the left-adjacent building of the Dalla Porta estate. Dad was Don Sabatini's oldest, closest, and most-trusted friend, so he had the option to live wherever he wished, and he chose the top two floors of the Hurst building next door.

His official office was in the Dalla Porta estate, and he and Don Sabatini even had a passageway built between the two buildings to shorten the already minuscule commute.

But since my father's passing, it was decided that my mother and I would be relocated to a suite on the Dalla Porta estate. This decision was apparently made for our safety, but in actuality, it means I find myself in Gianfrancesco's crosshairs at least once every single day.

As the limo pulls down the avenue, the estate comes into view. Nico leans against me, ducking her head to see more from my window. "It's bigger than I remember...wow."

The estate itself is about seven floors, five above ground, and two basement levels.

The don and his immediate family live on the top floor. My mother and I were allocated a suite on the fourth. The entire place is lavishly decorated with master-painted ceilings, antique chandeliers, and carpets big enough to hide an SUV under.

Much of the place's splendor and gilt is hidden though by the warehouse-amount of flowers covering every flat surface. Condolences from relatives, associates, and business partners, have poured in from all over the world, honoring our dad.

Stepping into the mansion transports us to a rainforest full of forget-me-nots, white roses, orchids and lilies. Not to mention the rainforest *animals*, which include at least a hundred mafiosos and their wives.

A mass of people surround my mother the minute we're inside the grand foyer, standing beneath the first of several frescos adorning the ceilings in this place.

"Come on." My twin throws me a mischievous look. "I want to see your cell."

Nico bends her fingers through mine and tugs me toward the triple-wide staircase that folds through the center of this gilded age monstrosity all the way up to the top floors. We hasten up the enormous steps until the symphony of guests has shrunk down to a dull roar.

In the expansive fourth floor hallway, I take my sister down the hall to pair of locked double doors, and let us inside. The suite where they have me and and mom is a two-bedroom-two-bath-room apartment in and of itself with giant den, a kitchenette, and small study, and a veranda that boasts a mediocre view of the city. I'm sure the fifth floor is better.

Nico strides into the room like she's in a luxurious hotel and spins around a few times. "They're keeping you caged in style, I see."

"Don't joke." I drop my purse on the coffee table and flop down onto the lush couch, closing my eyes. "I'm so ready for today to be over, I don't know what to do."

"Well, you could start by telling me about *the guy.*"

"W-What?" The man from the vestibule burns bright in my memory, but...how did Nico know about him? I didn't say anything.

When my eyes snap open in alarm, I find her standing by one of the huge windows in this place, reading a card she swiped from a condolence bouquet—one of a few—seated over there.

All too slowly, I realize she's found the arrangement that was sent by my coworkers at the Rock. They all wrote and affixed cards in the bouquet and she has one of them between her fingers.

"This is the guy, isn't it?" She waves the card at me. "The one who has a crush on you. Micah, right?"

"Oh." I relax against the cushions, once again letting my lids droop closed. "Him."

"I can tell the feeling's *so* mutual."

"He's nice and all, but I'm leaving the city in a few months—"

"Hallelujah."

"—Plus, you know me. I'm not that concerned with dating. And even if I were, I'm really not that attracted to him."

"I suspected as much from your letters." Nico says. "Ah, well. Poor guy."

She puts Micah's card back with the bunch, and comes to flop down onto the couch beside me.

Since our separation as teenagers, my sister and I have been writing each other letters, a few every month. I bore her with all the monotony of my life, and she heartens me with the excitement of her own.

"It's not his fault." I exhale hard. "Honestly, I haven't been attracted to anyone in a really long time."

I trip over that last sentence, the mystery man returning once again to mind.

What is with me?

Heart reacting over a stranger I met at my father's funeral?

Am I a member of the Addams family or what?

"Anyway," I maneuver around, so I can smile at my sister. "How are things going with you and *Massimo?*"

I exaggerate his name, I can't help it. If my sister's life is a soap opera I've been watching, he's definitely the romantic lead who brings all the spice and *drama*.

There's no disguising the way the color comes to her face when I bring him up.

"Things have been...good." She supplies me a coy smile, but is obviously hiding far more juiciness underneath.

"You're not going to get off that easily." I give her a stern look, that makes both of us break into grins. "I can tell how much you like him just from the way you write his name on a piece of paper."

"*Excuse me?*" She balks at me, cheeks pink.

"Like you're making love to him with the just tip of your pen."

Nico covers her face to muffle her embarrassed giggles and I playfully poke her side until she comes out from her hiding place.

"Okay, okay!" She drops her hands, eyes quivering with unmistakable joy. It lifts my heavy heart. "Things with Massimo are *amazing*. I've never been so in love in all my life. Is that what you wanted to hear?"

"You have to ask?" I scoot closer to her, as though someone downstairs might overhear us. "*So?*" I lift my eyebrows at her. "Does this mean there's a Valentino wedding dress in your future with strappy little Manolo heels?"

My twin melts into the couch, her eyes rolling up to heavens in imagined ecstasy. "I would honestly love that."

Our catching up is interrupted by a bell on the wall, ringing out through the apartment. I think every room in this entire mansion has one of those bells. On a normal day, the ring of that bell means it's time for dinner in the grand dining room on the first floor. Today it signals the beginning of the repast, honoring our fallen father.

"Ready for some five star dining with a side of forced human interaction?"

Nico's off the couch before I am. "Oh, good. I'm *starving.*"

We make our way to the Dalla Porta dining room, and as good as the food smells, the scent is nauseating when mixed with the stench of cigar smoke and too much cologne, brought to us by the collection of made men eager to stuff their faces.

Members of the serving staff guide me and Nico to our seats at the mile-long dining table. We're about a quarter of the way down from the head, where Don Saba and his family are already seated.

Trying to look at anything other Ciro, Frankie, or our mother's lifeless expression, I work my eyes over the luxe design and furnishings in this absurdly big room. A sprawling red carpet lays flat beneath our feet. The red carpeting matches the rouge velvet upholstery of each of these deluxe dining table chairs. Deep red curtains overhang the large windows surrounding us.

Security guards in shades with ear pierces stand in front of every window and exit. They could be statues if not for the occasional drift of their heads, as they crack their necks and eye the guests for anything suspicious.

In one corner of the room, a marble fireplace the size of a walk-in closet dominates. And lined around the perimeter of the room are tables of food, that the serving staff piles onto fine china and bring to us with smiles on their anxious faces.

Steak and lobster are a treat. Almost like a reward for getting through the shittiness of that funeral, but still...

Gourmet food does nothing to close the yawning, aching void in my heart that the absence of my father created. I haven't eaten anything all day, and even now, I don't feel hungry. I haven't had an appetite for anything...not since we got the news he was gone. For several minutes, I chew very little, pushing excellent food back and forth around my plate.

My pathetic display is only stalled by the clinking of a glass at the end of the table.

Ciro Calzavarra has something to say, standing at the right hand of his father. That man loves to hear himself talk, so I'm not surprised that he's taken it upon himself to give some sort of speech—even though he and my father hated each other.

What I don't understand whatsoever is why our mother is standing beside him.

"Thank you all for coming here today." He opens, that smugness coloring his whole face. "While we've gathered on a somber occasion, we do want to take a moment to share a bit of good news that will honor Orazio Di Rienzo, a dedicated member of this family of many years."

"What is he talking about?" Nico demands under her breath.

I give my head a little shake. I haven't the faintest idea.

"A month from now in May, on the second to be exact, Orazio's oldest daughter Eleanora and my Gianfrancesco will be married."

Both my jaw and my sister's must hit the table in front of us, we're so gobsmacked.

What the fuck is that crazy man talking about?

Applause spreads through the room like a virus.

My internal organs are failing, one by one. I regret glancing toward Gianfrancesco who has the most wicked, triumphant look on his evil face.

Nico grips my forearm under the table, alarm rearranging her features into a thinly-veiled grimace.

"Orazio, rest his soul, always desired that our children—and our families—be joined in a marital union, and in the wake of his tragic death, we felt it was finally time to honor his wish."

THAT'S A LIE! My throat aches to scream.

Nico viscerally bucks against the table when that crock of shit falls from Ciro's treacherous mouth.

Our father hated *nothing* more than he hated the idea of my being forced to wed Gianfrancesco. Part of the reason he was excited to send me abroad this fall was so that any hope of our being married could be curtailed.

In fact, the only person who hated the idea of this marriage more than our dad was our mom. The woman who's currently standing beside Ciro, saying *nothing*, while he announces this unspeakable travesty.

"What the hell is she doing?" Nora grits out only loud enough for me to hear.

I'm not even breathing anymore.

My mother stands there at Ciro's side, despondent. Doing nothing. Saying nothing. As though there's nothing to object to.

The nanosecond Ciro's done with his little announcement and the room has devolved into cheers and guests have risen from their seats, Nico and I fly from our chairs, hurry through the applauding throngs of family members and friends to rend the truth from our mother.

We each take one of her arms and all but bounce her out of the party into a secluded alcove on the first floor of the estate.

"Just what the hell is going on here?" Nico presses, as soon as we're alone.

"Lower your voice." Our mother lowers herself onto an ancient settee. The thing creaks between her small amount of weight.

"*Mama!*" Nico's offended by this as though *she's* the one who was just announced as his bride. "How can you act so calm? Ciro thinks he's going to marry Nora off to that...that..."

"Close your mouth and know your place." The fight our mother puts into those five words seems to use up every remaining ounce of her strength.

"Understand *what*, Mama?" I sit down beside her, searching her distance expression for some semblance of the woman I know and love. "You and Dad always told me that I would never wed Gianfrancesco, no matter what anyone else said."

"It was true then, but it isn't now."

Stunned silence drops between us like an anvil from the sky.

"What?" I gasp on a shaking breath. "What are you saying?"

"I'm saying your father isn't here to protect us anymore." Our mother's eyes drop to her hands, laying pitifully in her lap. "He was murdered. And they still don't know who was behind it. Who's to say the perpetrators won't come after us next?"

"What does that have to do with marrying Nora to that arrogant brute?" Nico paces before us one way and then the other, frustration lining her every limb.

"Marrying Nora into the Calzavarra family ensures that we'll be protected and well taken care of for the rest of our lives." The hopelessness in our mother's voice is crushing.

"Mama, that's ridiculous!" Nico kneels in front of her, taking Mom's hands in hers. "Come back with me. Both of you. We'll stay with Dad's family in the south of Switzerland. They'll give us all the protection we need. Nora's already scheduled to come and stay. All we have to do is move the trip up—"

"Nora's not going anywhere." The finality in Mama's tone might as well be a bullet in my heart. "And neither am I. Everything has already been decided."

I have to cover my mouth with my hands to keep the distraught sobs of horror from ripping out of me. Even my sister is at a loss for words.

"Nico, go back to your hotel and pack your things… You'll be on a plane back to Italy in the morning." Then Mama turns to me, adamant and clear. "Nora, you *will* wed Gianfrancesco. You won't go abroad. You will stay here, support him as his wife, and have his children. End of discussion."

Our mother pushes up from the small settee and starts to leave the alcove. Before she goes, she gives me one final order, as I sit here shaking with uncontrollable dread and despair.

"Now, go and pay your respects to your fiancé and his family. They're your family now too. "

CHAPTER 3

Rocco

WITH EVERY PASSING SECOND, my ability to focus rips apart at the seams.

Just standing here with my mouth shut is a high bar.

In the living room of the Balboni warehouse—a luxurious, sprawling Manhattan loft-style condo—Don Jaco holds court, surrounded by his inner circle.

Jacopo Balboni is a thick, round man with a laughing face. He's bald, fond of hats, covered in tattoos, and his thick strangulating fingers are lined with big, gaudy rings, each more significant than the next. Jaco's dark eyes crinkle around the edges like he's amused, even though he rarely is.

His son sits beside him. Vito's elbows balance on his knees, his fingers steepled ahead of his vulgar mouth while he, and everyone else in this room eagerly watch the television screen affixed to the chimney of the fireplace to my left.

Vito, Jaco, Fiero, the underboss of the family, and Lancini, our capo, gathered in here to review the covert body cam footage I collected this morning at the funeral of Orazio Di Rienzo.

They're watching it on the television, but I'm watching it my mind.

I can barely stop reliving the day's events over and over.

Glancing up at the tv screen every now and then, seeing my memories up there in HD? It's uncomfortable at best, damn near invasive at worst.

But why?

I've been assigned to record many events in secret, and never before have I felt so tense about sharing the footage.

Why this time?

My shoulder muscles are coiled up so tight, any sudden movement and they'll crack right off my body. Don't tell me all of this is because of that woman...

From earlier.

One of Orazio's daughters.

Even all dreary and distant, in that flowing black dress, she could have turned the head of any man in any bar in the city. I was deep under cover on a fucking mission and she turned mine.

No woman's ever distracted me so thoroughly that I can recall.

What a horrible time for it.

I picked her out of the crowd at once, almost. She, her twin, and their mother...I recognized them from that singed photo in her father's wallet.

The one I swiped from the ground before sprinting away from that grisly scene.

Which reminds me.

I'm still fucking pissed at Vito for his latest attempt to get me killed.

My eyes linger on his dumb baby face, twisted up into a mean pout. His curls sit atop his forehead, chaotic and unruly, almost like he rolled out of bed to be here tonight. And still, this is the way he looks when he's focused...

I could throttle him for getting me into this.

And I've been so preoccupied thinking of that woman that I've all but entirely forgotten how I feel about this situation as a whole.

This assignment creates conflict in me as I have never before experienced.

Luckily, I'm good at hiding my emotions. Because on the inside, chaos reigns.

It's one thing to murder someone.

I've done it before. I don't enjoy it, but there's a kind of morbid resolve that settles over me when I'm assigned to take someone out. Especially when I'm aware of their crimes, against the family or otherwise.

It's quite another thing to be used as hit bait.

To be tricked into leading a man to his death.

And that's what happened here.

I was the last person to see Orazio Di Rienzo alive, just before Vito and his goons blew the man up. Vito had me completely in the dark about their plans to murder him. My instructions were to meet a person of interest on the family's behalf, nothing more. But *this?*

A man who interacted with me like he knew me...To see his blackened corpse in pieces across the pavement? Then, to be assigned to go to the man's funeral and see all the faces of the people most affected by his death?

Even having a small moment with one of his daughters, who happened to be the most stunning creature I've encountered in many years?

Unimaginably strange. All of it.

Remorse snaps at me, rabid and wild.

For the first time, a small voice in the back of my mind insists that I've taken a wrong path. Which is terrible news. It means the tiny sliver of a conscience I've carried with me all this time has gotten a size bigger.

I shouldn't have to explain that a job like mine requires apathy. And the kind of loyalty that's stronger than any feelings of altruism or benevolence.

I've always had the stomach for it. But something about this particular assignment has me feeling off my game. In more ways than one.

My heart actually knocks at my ribs while Vito eagerly watches the body cam footage I collected. The sight of him eating it up yanks open all of the various drawers full of Vito-inspired anger.

Honestly, he's been looking for the perfect opportunity to kill me for years. A week ago was the closest he's ever come to offing me. I almost want to clap.

Dumb prick.

At least, he's consistent. I'll give him that.

Vito's hated me from the very beginning, which has always made for a stark contrast to his father, who's always loved me, by comparison.

Jaco took me under his wing when I was relocated to New York City around the age of nineteen. He began nurturing my talents, as an up and coming enforcer. He did this, much to Vito's disdain and jealousy. My talents showed themselves early, and Jaco kept me close, all through my training years with the Balboni family.

I was promoted to full enforcer before long, and quickly worked my way up the ranks into Jaco's inner circle. I'm efficient, thorough, and unflappable. That made me an asset, so Jaco wanted me around.

But Vito did his best to isolate me from the other members of the family, and his best was more than enough. I'm sure he made up every reason in the book for them to hate me, and best of all, he likely threatened to excommunicate anyone who allies themselves with me when he becomes don. So the other enforcers and foot soldiers of this mafia resent, avoid, and revile me too.

All in all, I've been set apart from the riffraff of the family, and by necessity and also my own nature, I've become a loner in all of it.

Standing alone on a small pedestal.

And of course, now that Vito's all grown up, and he's positioned himself as his father's right hand, he's also become my direct superior, which means I have to follow all of his instructions, no matter how dangerous or asinine.

And this time around...those instructions led me to Eleanora Di Rienzo.

That's her name.

Listening to the chatter of invited guests, I was able to pick up on it.

Eleanora...Her amber-eyed gaze, shining out from her oval face framed by dark, voluminous curls. Well-shaped limbs, crafted with care. Her delicate sloping curves...

Obviously, still in her twenties.

Jesus, I feel old just *thinking* about how long ago that decade was in my own life.

I'm still thinking of her when the tape gets to the part of the morning where our eyes locked across the church.

No one in this room knows she was looking straight at me, but I do...

The unexpected electricity that crackled between us then is still palpable, snapping and pulsing beneath my skin.

Even on tape.

The moment is broken, and then she begins talking with the Calzavarra family. Ciro Calzavarra's wife and son engage her, the former kissing her cheek before attending to Orazio's widow.

Left in the frame are Eleanora and Ciro's brat, facing each other, when Vito stops the recording.

"Her." He stands from his place on the couch. "She's the one."

Alarm clangs through my scattered mind. Why the hell is he referring to Eleanora? What can she possibly have to do with this?

"Who is?" I blurt out, hoping to God I'm wrong.

"The little princess Ciro Calzavarra covets so much."

"He...wants her?" My muscles flex for a fucking fight.

Just the thought of that shitstain Ciro Calzavarra turning Eleanora into one of his whores puts me in a homicidal mood, for some reason.

"My intel revealed that Ciro's turned down mergers with other families because he wants his son to marry her," Vito illuminates.

My first thought is *why?* What's so special about her?

But then I remember the way she looked at me.

My heart kicks hard at my ribs.

"We've left Ciro in peace for too long." Jaco glares. "It's time we repay him for all the blood he's spilled."

Next to Jaco on the low leather sofa, Fiero crosses his legs and smirks, lighting a cigar. "Let's see what happens when we steal his treasured jewel."

"Once again, you've done well, Rocco." Jaco lifts his whiskey glass in my direction, which is *high praise* coming from that man. A vein pops out of Vito's forehead whenever his father commends me. "My son will give you your next assignment."

Oh joy.

Vito stabs me with his soil dark eyes, then jabs a thick pointer finger at the screen. "Your next job is to *kidnap that woman.*"

CHAPTER 4

Nora

IN A LUSH MANHATTAN WEDDING BOUTIQUE, I stand on a big round block. Before me, a mirror, and reflected in the glass is...me, wearing an insanely gorgeous wedding gown.

My shoulders and collarbones are left bare from this sweetheart neckline. Down to my knees, this lace wedding gown sheaths me like a second skin, and then trumpets out in every direction, obscuring my bare feet with sparkling ivory tule.

As though in a dream, I run my fingers over the soft textured fabric. Every time I look up and see myself in the mirror, my tawny hair piled into a pineapple bun on my head, a tiara at the crest and an ivory veil flowing behind me, I'm surprised by my appearance all over again.

Behind me is a chic, modern, and peacefully quiet show room. From the ceiling, poles extend, supporting an enormous kidney-shaped rack, where over a hundred wedding dresses are hung, curving around one way and the other.

On a plush cream-colored couch, my mother sits, flipping disinterestedly through a wedding catalogue. Every now and then she looks up at me, her lip trembles, her entire face souring at my reflection, and then she looks down again, like it's too much.

I wish I understood what was going on in her mind, but I don't.

My approaching nuptials don't seem to bring either of us any joy, but today, at least, I'm happy.

Just to have this time with her.

I've honestly never once considered the prospect of getting married. Just wearing this gown makes me feel as though I've stumbled into a parallel universe.

But that's okay.

Now that I've decided to kill myself, I'm actually glad I got to try one of these on once before the end. There really is a magical beauty to an immaculate white dress and soft, gauzy veil cascading from my head.

Who knew that even I—a mountain woman trapped in New York City—could look so pretty?

Not that my mother's noticed.

It's been two weeks since the funeral, and still, Mama looks on the outside the way I feel on the inside—entirely despondent and detached from life. In some ways, my mother's entire personality change following my father's death has made my decision to die an easier choice to make.

I thought long and hard about it and can't see any other way through.

There's no way I can marry Gianfrancesco Calzavarra, and there's no way out of the family or the arrangement.

My dad, in many ways, my best and only true friend, wanted to protect me from this, but now that he's gone, the life I imagined for myself and dearly dreamed of having are gone too.

All my plans to leave America and join my sister abroad have been cancelled. I won't get to go back to college and study tourism, let alone open my own resort in the alps one day. My sister and I are as close as two separated twins can be, but given her history with Gianfrancesco, it's entirely possible he will forbid me from seeing or corresponding with her for the duration of my marriage to him.

Without her letters…there's no way I'll survive.

I asked my mother if I would at least be able to keep my job at The Rock, since I wouldn't be leaving, and she said no.

No Calzavarra wife is permitted to work.

A full-time wife and mother would be the only path open to me.

Which means that I would spend my days as a prisoner on the Dalla Porta estate with nowhere to go, nothing to do, and no one to see, except my violent, forceful, wicked husband.

The horrors that await me, so long as I'm alive, are worse than death. Worse than any bleak future I could have ever conjured for myself. And the one person who should care most doesn't seem to care at all.

In the weeks since my father's death, my mother has morphed into someone I don't even recognize anymore. She's unreachable now, eyes far away, her spirit lost in a world of unceasing sorrow, and Nico…*God bless her.* Nico is safe a thousand miles away with a man she loves. Beyond my reach.

In other words, there's no one for me to turn to. And no place for me to run.

There's no way forward or back.

Which means this can only be the end.

This is as far as I can go.

And since this is my last day on Earth, I'm determined to enjoy it.

Mama and I are scheduled to spend the day together, tending to wedding preparations, and everywhere we go, I do everything I can to have a good time.

I try on more than one wedding dress, twirling around in each one, like I'm a little flower girl instead of the bride.

This high-end wedding parlor also has a tea room, where guests can taste test cakes and other hors d'oeuvres to be served at their wedding receptions.

It isn't long before Mama and I are seated at a small circular table, tiny adorable plates covered in wedding cake petit fors seated before us. Moist vanilla cakes frosted with sumptuous butter cream, followed by decadent chocolate squares and an indulgent mint icing. The coconut cake with the rich chocolate sauce quickly becomes my favorite.

I'm not even a huge sweets person, but just for today, I savor every flavor with mindful intention and gratitude. We shouldn't be hungry after the cake tasting, but the tea room staff bring over steak, potatoes and roasted asparagus afterward that I can't resist either.

Meanwhile, my mother seems barely able to force a few bites here or there. It's as though she's lost her desire to eat altogether, and even going through the motions is a struggle. Still, I smile at her and make conversation, even when she doesn't engage. I treat her the way I did before Dad's death, as though she's still the same person, even though in reality she's a hollow shell.

After lunch, we're ushered by our security detail to our next appointment. A meeting with the florist to decide on the wedding flowers. A chipper, bouncy attendant in the shop with a neat apron tied trimly around his waist plies my mother with poetry about the different flowers they have in the shop and what each bloom represents, and which particular arrangements send the most romantic messages at a wedding.

I admire the attendant for his passion, despite my mother's total lack of encouragement. While he converses and she tolerates it, I float through the rest of the shop, admiring the many colors and unique scents. Roses and hyacinths, baby's breath, dahlias, tulips, and daisies in every color...

If I didn't know better, I'd think spring was invented right here in this shop.

At one point, I step outside onto the sidewalk and just take everything in.

New York City in April.

Across the street, a park smiles at me, its trees flowering with pink-petal blossoms and some of the brightest greens I've ever seen. People walk the streets with a hopeful bounce in their step, everyone thankful to be done with snow and arctic cold for several months, before the oppressive heat of summer bears down on us all.

My final spring…How lovely.

Mama meets me outside when she's done with the florist, and even though she barely seems here with me, I fold my arm through hers while we walk and pretend that I'm a kid again, out for the day with my mom…

But no one day can last forever.

In a few short hours, all our wedding errands have been run, and I know in my heart, it's time for us to part ways.

As we approach the luxury SUV idling at the curb, waiting to pick us up and return us to the Dalla Porta estate, I slow my steps and grab my mother's hand.

"Mama."

She looks at me, eyelids at half-mast, like she could fall asleep standing right here. "What is it?"

"I want to spend the evening at The Rock." I give her my warmest smile. "May I?"

"We're expected back."

"I know, but I'll be quitting next week." *To be a full-time wife.* "If I could have a little time to say goodbye to everyone, I'd really love that."

My mother exhales with softness and squeezes my hand. "Don't be out too late."

I nod, and she begins to turn away.

But before she can, I fling my arms around her and squeeze her tight.

I know it'll be the last time.

On her cheek, I leave a kiss. "I love you, Mama."

She pats my back, and I release her. Nodding, eyes suddenly full, she climbs into and shuts the door behind her.

Watching the SUV disappear down the block, along with the security detail that's been shadowing us all day, I'm finally able to breathe.

Though I'm a wreck on the inside.

Oh God, how did it all come to this?

Swiping at tears of anguish, I square my shoulders and head to The Rock for the last time. I want to make my final goodbyes before leaving this earth.

As I walk the pavement, the back of my neck tickles.

All day, I've felt the same sensation over and over. Like someone's watching me.

I imagine that it's my dad, waiting patiently for me in the afterlife.

CHAPTER 5

Rocco

AFTER DOING reconnaissance on Eleanora Di Rienzo for two weeks, the day to kidnap her has finally come.

I almost snatched her from the back room of that wedding parlor earlier—one stab of my pen would have tranquilized her, and I would have carried her out the back in an oversized wedding dress bag—but as soon I as I saw her in that dress…

All the fight fell right out of me.

There isn't a word for that amount of gorgeous.

For fuck's sake.

What really laid me out was the expression on her face.

Eleanora almost seemed happy? Relieved?

Which doesn't make sense to me at all.

Because I've been watching her, I know with all certainty that she's been death on a stick, day in and day out, for the past two weeks.

Pangs of guilt and regret about what happened to her father stab me every time I glimpse that broken look on her face.

But today...she's different.

Like something's changed. Like things are looking up.

Don't tell me she's actually excited to be marrying Ciro's hideous offspring.

No, that can't be it.

The file Vito gave me for this assignment—the first file he's bothered to hand me in months, I might add—made it clear that Ciro's wanted the match between Eleanora and his son for years, but Orazio was staunchly against it. He always stopped the engagement from happening, whenever Ciro pushed for it.

My fingers produce the picture I have of their family...I've only pulled it out of my pocket and traced the lines of the Di Rienzo's faces a hundred times.

The unmistakable love in Orazio's eyes as he holds his family near.

In some deep dark corner of my heart, that look makes me ache for the family I've lost, the people I can't remember...

Moving the fuck on.

It's obvious to me that Orazio was close with his daughters.

All to say, if Eleanora really wanted to marry Gianfrancesco, why would her father have opposed the match so strongly? And if she *doesn't* want to marry that shit-for-brains, as I suspect, why did she look so happy trying on wedding gowns?

I still can't square it, watching from a rooftop, as Nora and her mother walk toward a sleek black Escalade parked on the corner. An April breeze ruffles my hair, as I focus my binoculars, zeroing on their faces as they converse.

Reading their lips, I'm surprised to learn that they're separating.

Eleanora wants to go by her job at The Rock, and her mother seems to be headed home, security detail in tow.

Is it my lucky day?

This is excellent.

No guards tailing her makes my job seventy-five percent easier. At least.

I watch her, following on the rooftop as far as it'll go, as she walks the block below and finally hails a cab.

Folding my binoculars down and sliding them into my pocket, I head for the fire escape I used to get up here, and climb down into the alleyway behind the wedding boutique.

I already know my way to her job, so I don't have to follow her too closely.

In fact, I may just beat her there. My midnight-blue Jaguar XF is parked one street over from here. Thirty long strides and I'm there, sliding into the driver's seat and turning over the engine.

Cutting the wheel hard, I whip out of my parallel parking space and drop my foot on the gas. Better not dally. Based on the shift calendar I swiped from her job's administrative office, she's not on the schedule for this evening. Which means she's making a special stop. And there's no guarantee how long she'll be.

I've been following her to and from work a lot the past several days, and as a result, I've found a few covert ways to get inside The Rock rock climbing gym. Observing her while on job had its perks. Now that I know she's headed to the rock climbing gym, my next best opportunity to grab her is already taking shape in my mind.

Only takes ten minutes of my crazy driving to get over to The Rock and park nearby. There's no easy inconspicuous place to spy on things from below, so I go high.

From a catwalk almost two stories above the bottom floor of the gym, I perch in the shadows, waiting for Eleanora to arrive and then eavesdropping, as she chats warmly with her coworkers. The same night that I snuck in after hours to make a copy of her shift schedule, I placed bugs around the facility, so I could hear the conversations going on far below me.

Every word said in earshot of my listening devices is audible now, loud and clear.

"I can't believe you're leaving us," one of her male co-workers says. He touches her forearm in that borderline way that immediately tells me he wants to fuck her, but hasn't gotten a single chance.

Sucks to suck...

After a few minutes of listening to various overlapping conversations happening below, Eleanora breaks away from everyone and starts to put on a harness and chalk up. Anticipation drums in my chest, as she approaches the advanced rock climbing wall. It's the one that stretches all the way up here to the catwalk I'm standing on...

Up until now, I've only seen her scale the three different intermediate climbing walls. Though, she's been so sad and out of it, I know I've never witnessed her go for it at full strength.

Tonight is different. Eleanora marches up to the lavender climbing wall, with all its different complex outcroppings and smaller, more difficult hand and footholds. She's unperturbed by the level of difficulty. I don't pick up even a hint of trepidation in her purposeful strides.

She chalks up her hands and attaches herself to the wall, beginning her ascent.

All I can say—though I'd be hard pressed to ever admit it out loud—is that Eleanora Di Rienzo is mesmerizing to watch. I could watch her climb all day, and I have, a few times before now.

My focus is swallowed up by her nearing presence, as she mounts the wall, working her way up to me—Up to the top, I mean! *Shit.*

Despite remaining hidden in the catwalk's dark shadows, my heart bucks in my chest when Eleanora climbs all the way to the top of the advanced wall, getting close enough to my position for me to see how graceful, strong, and gorgeous she is from up close...

Sweat trickles down her face and neck, giving her olive-tone skin an alluring glimmer. While her hair dangles from the neat ponytail at the back of her head, her amber eyes brighten with triumph and satisfaction. The muscles in her thighs and calves strain and work, pronouncing themselves against the otherwise perfect smoothness of her legs.

I can't take my eyes off her, as she tops the wall, groping with one hand over the upper edge for...something. *What is she looking for?*

She slams her hand on whatever it is when she finds it, and then a happy-sounding alarm blares through the gym.

I tense at the sudden noise, my nerves tender and high strung.

Far below, her coworkers, who've gathered around to watch her climb, cheer and clap. The happy exhaustion on her face has her smiling, a light from deep within further illuminating those eyes I find myself drawn to, over and over again.

I swallow hard as hell, watching her from these shadows...

Remorse for her father's death claws at me, and it wasn't even my doing. How will I handle hurting her? Hauling her off to a Balboni safe house, when I haven't a clue what will be done to her?

My fingers ball into fists.

I withdraw down the catwalk until she's no longer within my direct sight line.

Putting physical distance between us seems to strengthen the control I have over my thoughts and emotions.

Now, I lurk by the door that leads onto the catwalk, a good fifty paces between me and that dangerous woman.

Permitting myself to study her only a few moments longer, I observe her freedom, as her hands come to the ropes attached to her harness. Her muscles slacken.

Victorious, joyous even, Eleanora lets herself relax into her suspension, looking as though she could sing. She drops her head back, closing her eyes, and gives the ceiling a smile any man would be jealous of.

She hangs up there like that, swinging slightly, for several minutes.

What can she be thinking of?

Does she really get so much joy out of climbing a wall?

Envy tolls through me.

The void in my chest calls to me again. To see someone so full of life reminds me of the emptiness that pervades my own existence...

Oh, wonderful. I'm getting all dark and philosophical again. It's probably time I pay Tanya another visit. Maybe, Saint Mary's too.

Eleanora cables down from her high place, and I force myself not to watch her anymore. Instead, I listen through my earpiece for the conversations that follow.

Below, she's saying her goodbyes.

Inside, my muscles tense and release, anticipation flooding my limbs. She's about to leave. If she's leaving, then that means it's almost showtime for me.

At the end of the day, no matter what she does to my mind, she's just another assignment. So what if she's the first person I've ever been assigned to abduct? So what if her father seemed to know me? So what if I'm mixed up inside about it all?

My duty is clear. My will is iron.

I wouldn't be here otherwise.

"Come here, sweetheart." It's the voice of her boss, a woman named Agatha, based on my research.

The rustle of two people hugging comes next.

"This...will be the last time I'm here for a while," Eleanora explains.

"Since you're getting married." Emotion rises in Agatha's voice. "I know..."

Unable to take it anymore, I glance over the catwalk's railing and find them far beneath me, saying their farewell.

After they've released each other, Nora hugs all of her cowork-ers. Even the men. Both of whom hold her too tightly and for too long. And then she disappears toward the locker rooms to get changed, which based on my estimations from previous shifts of hers, should leave me fifteen minutes to get downstairs and get in position.

On the other days I've been here, she always heads right out of the building and walks back to the Dalla Porta estate. If I wait in the alley on the perpendicular street, I should be in perfect position to snatch her.

Well. There's no time left to waste.

In minutes, I've made it to the correct alley. A traffic mirror high on the brick wall in front of me offers a reflection of the block, the one she should be walking down any second.

I lean flush against the bricks, a cigarette between my teeth to take the edge off. I've never hated myself so much for something I haven't even done yet...

There. I straighten up.

Eleanora appears in the mirror. All she has to do is turn right, as she always does—

She dips left, and strides off in the other direction.

Fuck! The one day she chooses to be unpredictable...

I whip out from the alley and book it down the block, tailing her on foot, close but not too close.

Where the hell is she going?

My mind races through different scenarios.

I've mapped out every place she's been in the past two weeks. I even have her typical walking routes memorized. Wherever she's headed tonight, she hasn't been there one time in the past fourteen days.

Shit, shit, shit, and *shit.*

Now, I'm at a disadvantage.

Buzzing with anxiety on the inside, I stalk her through the dwindling evening light, confused by the strange spring in her step, mind ping-ponging through different scenarios of where she might be headed.

Dusk casts hazy shadows across long Manhattan avenues, as we walk, pedestrians passing both of us by.

There's a stop light up ahead. Shit. If she stops and turns her head this way, she'll see me. What if she recognizes me from the funeral? What will I say if she comes up to me? My heart dribbles thinking about it.

But before she reaches the corner, Nora ducks down a dark alleyway I don't even *see* until she's gone.

What the fuck?

Suspicion clangs through my brain.

Now, I'm beginning to think this might be a trap.

Did Vito set me up again? Am I walking into something dangerous?

Quickening my pace, I zip into the alley behind her. She's several paces ahead of me, and then...stranger still, I see her grab a back door, one that doesn't even have a handle or a doorknob, and yank it open, disappearing inside.

Maybe Ciro and the rest of the Dalla Porta crime family have realized I'm out to abduct their prized bride, and I'm walking to my death, but now my curiosity is too intense to repress.

Just where the fuck is she going?

Dark alleys, back door exits?

I get to the door and enter what appears the basement level of an emergency staircase. Several floors above, her soft footfalls carry into my ears.

Cloaking my steps as best I can, I hurry up the stairs after her. This would be the perfect place to subdue her. Dark, lonely, quiet, isolated.

If I can catch up to her in time...

Jesus, she's fit.

Several minutes later, after I've rapidly climbed sixteen flights of stairs, I need a second to catch my breath, but she's already through the door at the top of the case. This stairwell must be at least twenty stories high... *Fuck.*

All that rock climbing is good for something.

Can't stop now. Not when she's presumably all alone on a rooftop, ready for the fucking taking.

Now, that I'm alone in the stairwell, I don't have to mask my pursuing footsteps any longer. With a big breath, I ready myself and then sprint up the rest of the floors, four at once. It's hard and my muscles ache by the time I reach the top a few minutes later, but all the HIIT training I've done in my life prepared me well.

I push through the stairwell door out into the crisp April night air and find myself on an industrial Manhattan rooftop, lit only by a series of tented glass skylights and the apartments directly below. They give the whole roof a warm glow, but it's nothing compared to the view of the New York City skyline sparkling over that ledge—

The one Eleanora Di Rienzo is standing on, facing the boulevard below.

My heart slams down to the pavement.

She's going to jump.

Panic sandbags me, sending my entire nervous system into overdrive. I damn near blackout, my protective instincts surge so hard and strong through me in the speed of a millisecond. The world drops into slow motion, my heartbeat pulsing through my entire body at once.

"NO!" I roar, as Eleanora bends her knees and leaps from the edge.

On the inside, I'm crushed by an avalanche of neurological mayhem. My eyesight blurs with shadows from the past. A vision breaks the moment in half. I see Eleanora in the air, but I see the back of another woman standing in front of me, before bullets pierce her center tearing through her shoulder and torso—

I lose all connection to reality for several seconds.

Body radiating with distress, I fly at the ledge like a bat out of hell. Arms clawing through the air, they clamp onto her body and rip her out of the sky with the force of an industrial crane.

The next thing I know, I'm falling backwards onto concrete, Eleanora's body boxed in my embrace. We hit the ground hard, all sense of time, space, and sensation swirling to black.

Slowly, my wits return to me.

My ribs feel close to cracking, as hard as my heart's pounding.

Pain blossoms in my back, followed by the strain in my arms and shoulders, still in a rigid position around...Eleanora's body.

My eyes fly open, and there she is, body tangled with mine here on the ground, her gorgeous eyes alight with surprise and bewilderment. The adrenaline inside me—and probably her too—dies down hard and slow, until my head is pounding as hard as my fucking heart.

"*You...*" She whispers, breathless and astonished.

Static electricity cracks through me, everywhere our bodies press together. I'm...still crushing her to my chest, like she's some precious treasure.

What the fuck is going on here?

Without another thought, I clamber to my feet, tearing her from the ground along with me. Her body is dense, likely from her well-toned muscles, but still light enough for me to throw around.

When I've steadied us both on our feet, the moment between us turns awkward almost immediately. Eleanora holds herself like she's cold, eyes filling with tears.

And for some reason, irrational rage spurts through me like bile and flies right out of my reckless mouth.

"What the fuck were you thinking!" My eyes bulge at her. I'm actually shaking, I'm so angry. "YOU COULD HAVE DIED." My fingers ache to snatch her shoulders and shake the stupid right out of her, but they coil to trembling fists while I near scream at her. "If I hadn't been here, you'd be a pile a guts on the fucking sidewalk, you psycho! *Is that what you want?*"

By the time I've gotten all my shouting out, I'm gasping for breath, my pulse still flying beneath my skin.

Eleanora drops her eyes to the pavement between us, quiet and unflinching.

Then, she astounds me. "I don't know what you're doing here or why you saved me, but...this is my life. It's mine to do with what I want. If I want to die, that's none of your business."

The words are barely out of her mouth before she brushes past me, marching toward the rooftop exit doors.

My fingers clench hard around her arm. "And where do you think you're going?"

Her wide-eyed gaze snaps to my face, this time irritation coloring her flushed cheeks. "Let me go."

"Why? So you can try again somewhere else? I don't think so." I close her soft hand in my fist and stalk back to the rooftop door, dragging her along behind me.

Eleanora jerks her hand, but doesn't get free. Not even close. "What the hell do you think you're doing?"

"Taking you home." I rip the emergency door open with my free hand, then yank her through it with the other. "It's what your father would have wanted."

Those two crazy-ass, entirely thoughtless, ridiculous sentences that just fell out of my mouth shut her up for all of about thirty seconds, as we begin the long climb down to the bottom floor, entirely in the dark except for the temperamental motion-sensor lights that buzz on at their leisure or not, while we tromp past.

"You don't even know my name!" She insists, tone sharp and demanding. "How the hell do you know my father?"

I halt, rounding on her without a thought. "I know your name, *Eleanora.*"

Her distractingly beautiful mouth pops open, like I've caught her off guard.

The thought of sliding my tongue between her lips attacks me, and I'm so destabilized by it that I launch into the alibi Vito gave me before sending me behind enemy lines to infiltrate her father's funeral.

"I'm an old family friend of the Dalla Porta mafia." The lies tumble from my mouth like drool from a Pitbull. "Your father helped me when I first got to this country twenty years ago. Just because we've never met doesn't mean I don't know who you are."

She blinks hard at me, voice softening ever so slightly. "Doesn't change anything. Whatever connection you have to my father doesn't give you the right to interfere."

"Maybe not, but I'm not the kind of man who asks for permission." That's all I can come up with, while emotions war inside me.

"So you're a brute." I keep walking, pulling her along behind me, and after several flights, she stops resisting the iron grip I have on her lithe fingers.

"A brute who just saved your life."

"You mean, *ruined my death.*"

Fuck, this woman's stubborn.

We bicker all the way down to the ground floor and up the alley we came from. She has a quip for every line that leaves my mouth, refusing to back down whatsoever.

Needless to say, Eleanora Di Rienzo isn't what I expected at all.

I thought she was demure and deferential, introverted and interesting. I've got her completely wrong, I realized by the time we make it back to my car.

She's stubborn, brash, and outspoken. Tough. And obviously, ballsy as they come.

The worst part is that I like her the more for it.

She provokes me, using her quick, sarcastic mouth to poke me in places I didn't know I had.

I'm thoroughly exhausted and invigorated by the time I've stuffed Eleanora into the passenger seat of my car. She glares daggers at my dashboard all the while, though I know they're meant for me.

The thought of that almost makes me smile...*Just what the hell is wrong with me?*

Sliding into the driver's seat, it dawns on me. My assignment.

I'm supposed to knock her unconscious and take her back to the Balboni safe house. Now would be the perfect opportunity. But I'm not going to do that at all.

I really am…about to take her home.

My brain isn't thinking about work at all. Instead, it's completely occupied, imagining all the sick, twisted *sinful* ways I could make use of her sharp tongue…

"There's no need to say anything else." Nora sits back in her seat, but doesn't relax. "You're a brute *and* a busybody, I get it."

"No, you don't get it. Pulling a stunt like that…" *Now, I'm lecturing her?* "Listen to me. Whatever you're going through? It's not that bad. Definitely not so bad that you should die over it, understand?"

Eleanora makes an exasperated sound that simultaneously irritates me and intrigues me enough that I want to find out what other sounds I can get out of her.

"You don't know anything about me *or* what I'm going through." She folds her arms tight across her chest, like a child. "And if I wanted the opinion of some random, pushy, nosy *stranger*, I would have asked for it—"

"Rocco."

"What?"

"My name." I glance over to her, as I turn the engine over and pull away from the curb. "It's Rocco De Carlo."

Eleanora looks at me like I'm nuts.

And that's exactly what I am.

Right now, I'm operating so far off the deep end, I have no explanation to offer myself, let alone her, or *Vito* when I get back empty handed in an hour.

"Well, *Rocco*, your *overreaching* concern is duly noted, but if you're expecting some sort of thank-you for tonight, you can forget it."

"Are you always this stubborn?" I ease to a stop at a red light and grill her with my eyes. She jerks her petite little chin at me, raring to quip, but as soon as her gaze touches mine, we're locked in another stare down, intensity pulsating in the air between us.

Her antagonistic expression falls just slightly, giving me a peek under her armor.

She swallows, almost like my undivided attention unnerves her. It's definitely doing something to me...

Do I scare you? I ache to ask but don't.

Because...of course, I scare her. I ought to. I'm going to hurt her eventually.

Aren't I?

"The light's green," she murmurs.

She's so mesmerizing, mumbling at me like that. *You're going to break her, if you're not careful,* my conscience warns.

My only defense is dropping my foot on the gas, and squeezing the steering wheel for dear life.

After the heat of our melded gazes breaks, we fall into a pensive quiet. And it's not long after that disappointment tolls through me, hard and solemn.

We're approaching the outer limit of the Dalla Porta estate and adjoining properties. This is enemy territory, and I'll have to drop her off without getting too close, if I don't want to be seen or arouse suspicion.

Which means my time with this woman is drawing to a close.

Why does that reality make desperation break open inside me like watermelons smashed with baseball bats?

A little pissed about it, I screech to a halt by a nearby curb, somewhere close enough that she'll have a short, well-lit walk back, and far enough that no one will notice that she got out of my car.

She reaches for the door handle—like she's planning to leave without so much as a goodbye, after all we've been through—but I'm quicker. I engage the child lock, which makes her scowl at me so good, I could kiss her, right here.

Her cellphone pings, and she pulls it from her pocket. I glance at it when she does. It's a text from her mother.

"Look..." I pour all the sincerity I have into my voice, and snatch her unlocked phone in the milliseconds of her distraction. "The next time you think about doing something that stupid, fucking call me first."

I toggle to her Contacts, and add my name and number in, but then, pretending as though I'm still inputting information, I connect her phone to my private server and add an app to her phone that will transmit all her whereabouts directly to me. She won't even know it's there.

"Done yet, *Grandpa?*"

Now, that hurts. My fingers tense hard enough around her smartphone to dent the stupid thing, as I slap it into her waiting palm. "Just how old do you think I *am?*"

"Does it matter?"

Of course not. Wow, Rocco. As if she'd ever be attracted to you.

Facing her lack of interest in me—when nearly all my thoughts for the past three weeks have revolved around her—devastates my already chaotic mind.

I don't have a ready reply to that one.

Instead, I unlock the door and she climbs out, pausing to meet my eyes one last time. Tension stirs between us.

"Nora," she finally says. "Call me Nora. Only my parents call me by my full name."

Then, she slams my passenger door and disappears down the street, leaving me reeling in her wake.

CHAPTER 6

Nora

WELL, suffice it to say my night took an unexpected turn.

I've been laying here on this palatial queen bed for hours, and I still can't fit all the pieces together quite right.

When I left home this morning, I never thought I'd see this giant offensively red bedroom ever again. What is it with this mansion anyway? Why is red the official color of every room? It's like the Calzavarra's are bragging about all the blood on their hands.

Red carpets, red drapes, red bed skirts, blankets, chairs, and walls...

I expected to leave all of this behind, but here I am.

Back from the dead.

Because of that man.

Rocco.

Somehow, it seems a huge weight has lifted off my body. It's not that I'm relieved to still be alive, but more that the gravity of my actions was fully upon me. I'd made peace with it, and when he pulled me back, literally seconds before the free fall, the weight of my actions was displaced...Postponed, almost.

It's a strange in-between, beyond-description sort of feeling.

Maybe, I didn't free-fall to my death, but I've definitely been free-falling in the hours since our encounter.

I can't forget the urgency and concern in his dark, hypnotic eyes.

Or the sensation of being caught in his tight, muscled embrace as he squeezed me to his chest....

The vice grip of his meaty man hands when he dragged me off that rooftop and brought me home, like it was some deeply personal offense against him that I, a total stranger, tried to jump to my death.

Why did he care so much?

And what the hell was he even doing there? How did he find me?

That rooftop is Dad's secret stargazing spot. So far as I know, I'm the only one he's ever taken up there. How did Rocco find his way there?

And more importantly, just who the hell does he think he is?

Yelling at me.

I don't like conflict. Even now, the leftover adrenaline from sparring with him sparkles in my veins. But the one thing I like less than conflict is being spoken down to, like I'm a kid.

Rocco's a friend of the family...an old acquaintance of Dad's?

It's hard for me to imagine Rocco De Carlo sharing a cigarette with my dad, but maybe that's just because I can't figure him out at all.

Not his actions, motives, or thoughts. Certainly not the words he said.

Blowing a breath out, I sit up, shaking my head until thoughts of that bizarre, infuriating man disappear altogether, like an Etch-a-Sketch.

I rise from the bed, climbing through the red curtains that hang from the enormous, *ancient* mahogany bed frame that extends above and around me, like a wooden mouth ready to snap closed and devour me.

Despite my lodging here for the past few weeks, this big, fancy room still feels entirely foreign to me. I miss my old room in our family apartment in the Hurst building next door. I still don't know why we had to move onto the Dalla Porta estate proper, but after Dad's death we were rehoused here against our will. Now we eat, sleep, and shit under the close watch of Ciro Calzavarra and that son of his.

Ugh.

I can't seem to get any peace, no matter what I do.

I feel on edge in a bedroom down the hall from my fiancé's. Especially knowing that he has the key to my room and takes it upon himself to stop by at any time of the day or night, according to his whim.

How can I relax?

I don't feel like I belong to myself anyone. I don't belong in this massive suite either.

It's like I'm locked up in the beast's castle, my life having been bargained away.

No matter what I do, nothing feels right. Most every night, I sit awake, nervous and agitated, staying up too late, until restless exhaustion drags me under.

Tonight won't be any different.

Knuckles slam against my locked bedroom door.

I about jump out of my skin, yanking a pillow to my chest and squeezing hard.

Shit! Who is that?

A shard of ice pricks my heart. What if that's Gianfrancesco out there?

Case and fucking point.

Frankie has been keeping close tabs on me since our engagement was announced. It's horrible. Most of the time, he stops by at some random hour of the day to engage me in bland, yet suggestive conversation that makes my skin crawl. So far, he hasn't attempted to lay a hand on me, but...

This is the first time he's ever stopped by at night.

I gulp hard.

Deep in the pit of my nauseous gut, I've been waiting for the night when he shows up like this, drunk on alcohol or something stronger like *lust,* and tries to have his way... *Oh, please God, help me.* My fingers fly to the cross around my neck.

I almost drop to my knees in prayer.

Avoiding Frankie will only make him knock harder, I know that. So I force myself to go to the door and answer it, pulling the heavy wood back a crack—

Relief crashes over me like a tidal wave.

It's not my fiancé after all.

Completely amazed, I find instead Hugo Raffanelli standing at my door.

The man in tall, polite, brown-haired and warm, his kind blue eyes peering at me with intention and focus. Even though it's almost ten pm, he's still wearing a suit, like he just got back from some business function for the family.

Hugo was my father's apprentice all the way up until his death. He's also the most likely candidate to become the family's new spymaster.

I'm so relieved to see him that for a second, I consider throwing my arms around him the way I used to when I was a kid, and he was still the kindly older brother I never had. Instead of the intimidating, successful grown man he is now.

Hugo is pretty wonderful actually, as mafiosos go. In fact, the only strike against him is that he's my fiancé's best friend.

"Hugo? What are you doing here?" I pull the door further open. "Working late?"

"Something like that." For the first time, I notice he has a brown paper package tucked under one arm. "May I come in?"

"Of course." I step back entirely, drawing the heavy door wide enough for him to enter my ridiculously red bedroom. I fight every impulse not apologize for how horrid the place is. "What's going on?"

"I have something for you." He holds the parcel up. "This came in the mail today...It's from your father."

"From...Dad?"

He gives me a solemn nod. "It came with a note, requesting that I deliver it to you in the event of his untimely death."

"You mean..." A few seconds of stunned, incredulous silence, and then I drop into a chair before I choke.

I can't believe this.

My father sent me a package from beyond the grave?

And I almost missed it?

Only one thought swims through my disbelieving mind.

Thank you God for Rocco De Carlo.

That handsome nosy bastard did me a favor for which I need to find some way to repay him one day.

"I've spent the past few hours checking it for any listening devices or explosives residue...you know, in case it was a trap." Hugo offers it to me. "But it's completely clean. It checks out entirely. It really is...from your dad."

Heart trembling in my throat, I reach for the box and set it down in my lap with shaking fingers. "Thank you," I warble to Hugo.

"It's the least I can do." He strides back to the door. "I'll leave you alone now...And Nora. You don't know how sorry I am. About what happened to him."

I nod, but I've lost all power of speech, as he lets himself out, and my teardrops sink into the brown paper wrapping this mystery box, seated in my lap.

As soon as Hugo's gone, and I've stopped shaking a little, I dive into the package. There's a part of me that's afraid of what I'll find, but considering I could have been dead and missed my chance to find out just a few hours ago, I know it can't wait.

The weight of the small package is uneven and when I get it open, I immediately find out why. In one side of the box sits a brown leather journal and on the other side is a neckless, with another seeing stone embedded in the cold silver pendant.

I recognize the stone at once, since it's the same kind that's embedded in the cross I always wear. Grabbing the necklace, I hold the pendant up my eye and squint inside.

Naturally, I expected to find another photograph, but instead I see numbers and letters. Almost like a product number, as though Dad forgot to specify what he wanted to go inside the pendant.

But my father isn't like that.

He doesn't miss small details like this.

I know what I'm looking at is exactly what he wants me to see.

4APCGA47R.

It's a code. More specifically, it's probably one of my father's cyphers. The man loved things like this. Secret, coded messages.

He used to make me and Nico memorize different types of coding systems when we were kids. He'd test us by leaving us secret messages around the apartment. Instructions. Like code that meant *meet me in the park,* or *book case, third shelf.*

If we were able to find him or whatever he wanted us to look for, he knew we were getting better at deciphering his meanings.

But God, I never thought all that practice would come in handy at a time like this.

I set the necklace down and grab the journal. When I open it, each and every page looks blank. But still, I know my father better.

Rising from the chair beside the bed, I cross the room to the vanity, where my open suitcase lays, overflowing with random articles of clothing and necessities from my old room. I dig through it until I find what I'm looking for.

A blacklight flashlight.

I hate turning off the lights in this cavernous, uncomfortable place, so instead, I climb into the horrible princess bed they've got in here—the one they stole from the Palace at Versailles—and draw closed the curtains on either side, closing me into darkness, with slivers of light peeking through the bed's drapes.

Opening the journal in my lap, I click on the flashlight and the second its purple UV beam hits the page, the satisfaction of being right washes over me.

Words. Lots of them.

Written in invisible ink.

Exactly something my father would do.

Eyes welling up once again, at the sight of my father's familiar handwriting, I take a deep breath and read the note he wrote for me, through bleary eyes.

My dearest Eleanora,

If you're reading this, I'm gone, and not from old age.

Under normal circumstances, I wouldn't be afraid to die, but these days, I am afraid. I'm afraid that I may be forced to go before my work here is done. And that's why I'm writing to you.

Much is at stake, my darling. The work I'm doing involves the family, yes, but more importantly, it involves our family.

If I'm gone, then you and your sister are the only ones

who'll be able to uncover the truth of what happened to me and why...

Look into it, I beg you. For all our sakes.

Everything you need to know about the work I've been doing you'll find in my secret office. I've left you a necklace with a cypher to help you find it.

Some of my work is written in code to protect it from the naked eye. The rest of this journal contains several keys and legends that will help you decipher things.

I know you can do it.

And lastly, my darling, even though I won't be around to remind you, please know you'll always have my love.

ODR

I TRACE over his three-letter signature with shaking fingers, speechless and frozen in this pocket of darkness.

My mind is in free-fall once again, careening through this new reality I find myself in, colliding with rocks of new information all the way down.

I barely know how to believe my eyes.

Processing what this means is another story altogether.

*Wait, wait, wait...*I need the universe to slow down.

If my dad took care to make all of these messages and clues for me, it means that he knew for a fact or heavily suspected that he would be killed the way he was.

But this is the sticking point.

My father was part of the upper echelons of the cosa nostra in this city. He had friends, but he had far more enemies. If he'd been killed on a mission for the family, like any soldier slain in the line of duty, there would be no mystery about that. And even if we, the family, wanted to investigate his death in that case, we wouldn't be told much.

The business operations and casualties thereof are largely confidential in the Dalla Porta mafia. At least, they are to women. Women aren't allowed to hold positions of power within the family or be privy to what goes on politically. We're just the shiny ornaments that decorate the lives of these deadly, dangerous men.

And my father knew that.

If he's asking me to investigate his death, it means he didn't die in the line of fire. He wasn't murdered in some acceptable way.

He had to have been tricked. Betrayed. Double-crossed.

It had to have been carried out by someone he considered a friend or ally.

Why else would he beg me to investigate the truth, unless someone we both know was behind it?

Does this mean someone within the Dalla Porta had my father killed?

Faces of the men in this mafia flash through my mind, like a crazy carousel of potential suspects. Hugo, Ciro, Gianfrancesco, Sabatini, Lazzarato, our capo, Marcello, Gessi, advisors to the family...

This little journal in my lap.

It changes everything.

I'm still not going to marry Gianfrancesco. I will kill myself, if it comes down to it and there's no other way out. But before that happens, I'm going to do everything within my power to investigate my father's death.

Resolve hardens inside me, like I've been pumped full of wet cement.

I have to. It is quite literally his dying wish.

I owe it to him. He was my best friend.

And if I find the motherfucker who stole my father from me, I'm going to kill us both or die fucking trying...

I slam the journal closed and climb out from the curtains

beyond my darkened bed, thoughts racing almost too fast for me to catch them.

Everything you need to know about the work I've been doing you'll find in my secret office. I never even knew Dad *had* a secret office, though I'm not surprised.

That man was full of secrets.

And apparently, even the way he died makes the list...

For a few heavy moments, I'm overwhelmed by all that I don't know, all that I can't understand yet. So, I bring myself back to the hard facts and try to find solutions to the smallest and most concrete of my current problems.

One thing I do know for sure is that I'm being closely watched now, as the prospective bride of the Dalla Porta's one and only prince. *Gianfrancesco...*

Everywhere I go will be reported to *someone,* and probably him too, which doesn't bode well for my intended sleuthing.

If I'm going to investigate who or what got Dad killed—especially if those responsible are part of the Dalla Porta—I'm going to need cover.

Privacy.

And as much as I hate to say it, I'm also going to need back up.

Where is my sister when I need her?

I pace for several minutes, puzzling through it.

My first instinct is to ask Hugo for help. I practically grew up with him, and I trust him completely. I'd never suspect him of something like this, not for a moment. He respected and admired my father too much to be part of his murder, but...Hugo is nothing if not loyal. And he is under oath and obligation to the Dalla Porta, so I doubt he'd be able to keep my investigation efforts a secret, even if he wanted to.

And if by some horrible twist of fate he *is* responsible for my father's murder, going to him for help would only put me at the top of his hit list.

The faces of my coworkers at The Rock briefly traipse through my mind.

Even if someone among them could help me, I don't want to endanger any of their lives by getting them involved.

I need someone who's familiar with the workings of the mafia world.

Someone who could look out for me a little, but also whose life I don't care about protecting in all of this.

Anyone I care about, I wouldn't ask, and anyone connected to my family could be the culprit, so...I guess I need someone tangential and expendable to me.

The handsome face of the man who yelled at me earlier tonight blooms bright behind my eyes...

Luckily or unluckily—I can't decide—Rocco's the only man I can think of for the job. It's entirely a long shot.

But I do have his number...

CHAPTER 7

Rocco

I'M ONLY a few minutes from the Balboni warehouse when my phone vibrates hard against the console.

Vito. I know it's him. Who else would call me this late at night?

Though I'd be lying if I said there wasn't a small wild hope somewhere deep inside me that it might be Nora Di Rienzo...

Why? So she can put you in your place again, **Grandpa***?*

Irritation rips through me once fast, as I answer Vito's call.

"Where the fuck are you?" He growls over the line. "Why haven't you arrived at the secure location with the target by now?"

Despite the hell I know is coming for me, there is something deeply satisfying about pissing Vito Balboni off.

"I'm almost back to the house." I swerve my Jag around a tight corner, barreling toward the underground entrance to the building. "The mission didn't go as planned."

A coarse, sinister chuckle. "Oh, I can't wait to hear about your failure."

Shocking.

Vito can't resist an opportunity to make me look bad. A sick sort of glee simmers in his acidic tone. He's clearly seething, but also excited for me to look bad in front of his father. "Get your sorry ass up to the conference room. *Now.*"

The line goes dead.

I pull into the garage, parking my car on the smooth industrial cement in a short row of other luxury vehicles.

Good thing I've been practicing what I'm going to say.

By the time I make it up to the post-modern conference room in the Balboni warehouse, I've already got a pretty good script outlined in my achy head.

I let myself inside and find everyone waiting, like I'm the guest of fucking honor.

Just perfect.

A long cedar meeting table dominates the center of the room. Jaco sits at the head of it. Behind him on the far wall, an enormous television hangs. Scattered and standing around the room are Vito, pacing, eager for the show to begin, and a few of the family's top enforcers—a.k.a. Vito's cronies. The ones he brings with him whenever he hopes to seem intimidating.

Since my ass is the one in trouble, I do everything not to roll my eyes.

"Vito tells me tonight's mission failed." Jaco eyes me across the long table, gaze pointed but not nearly as hungry for vengeance as Vito's.

"Well? Don't keep us in suspense," Vito cuts over me when I try to reply.

"As you know, I've conducted recon on the target bride for the past several days." I hold my fist behind my back, standing tall. "Today, I was prepared to abduct her—"

"But you didn't." Vito can barely keep the smirk off my face. "Care to explain what the fuck happened?"

"She tried to kill herself." *Is that what he wants me to say?*

"Pardon?" Jaco raises a bushy eyebrow.

"Eleanora Di Rienzo made a suicide attempt this evening." I squeeze my own fist hard, hoping to banish some of the senseless pain and helpless anger I feel, knowing that she tried to harm herself.

The memory of it sends my head pounding even harder.

In fact, my skull's been hurting steadily ever since I had that crazy vision...the one triggered by seeing her up on that ledge. I was so distracted by her I didn't even notice the pain until she was gone...

"You're saying she's *dead?*" Vito claps slow and sarcastic. "Good work, dipshit. Except we can't fuck over Ciro Calzavarra with a dead bitch. A dead bargaining chip is as good as trading dirt—"

"She's not dead." I interrupt his tirade just to stop myself from throwing a punch. "I stopped her in time."

"Did you?" Jaco brings a thick cigar to his mouth. "Good job."

Here comes that vein from Vito's forehead. "If she's not dead, why didn't you bring her here?"

"There were witnesses," I lie. "The best I could do in that situation after making contact with the target was gain some of her trust. I did manage to bug her phone which will enable us to keep even closer tabs on her and the Dalla Porta in the coming days."

Vito's jaw drops open.

"So it wasn't a total loss." Jaco sounds pleased, much to my surprise, and everyone else's. The other enforcers stab me with resentful looks. "Sounds like you managed to salvage things."

"I did what I could, sir."

"Good. Your quick thinking kept us in the game." Jaco adjusts in his seat, making the small thing creak beneath his weight. "We still have time to do what must be done."

"But—" Vito jerks his face toward his father, still hoping for a good fight.

"Calm down, Vito." Jaco taps his cigar, ash falling down into the tray on the table. "No war was ever won without persistence."

Vito glowers at me, even angrier than before.

I don't blame him.

Even I'm a little impressed with myself. I presented my case well, especially considering what a car wreck I am on the inside.

This splitting headache and the flashback I had on the rooftop, seeing the silhouette of who I'm sure was my mother...

That was the fullest memory of my childhood I've seen in *years.*

Why did that flashback come over me when I saw Nora up on that ledge?

Why then? Why did that memory come back at all?

These many years I've been without clear recall of my childhood, I've grown to accept the impossibility—at least, the *improbability*—that I'll ever regain what I've lost, but tonight... Something changed.

And that's a fucking understatement.

Why did every protective instinct inside me awaken with vehemence when I tried to save her? The experience overwhelmed me, in a way I'm unfamiliar with. It's like I was out of my own control.

That's never happened before.

Thankfully, Jaco dismisses me, despite his son's obvious urge to cross-examine me for several more hours.

I make my exit from the conference room swiftly, grateful to be free to pop my migraine pills, take a shower, and get to fucking sleep. Today's been a damn rollercoaster, and I need to recharge. ASAP.

Striding the few hallways over to the corridor where I and the other top Balboni enforcers quarter, uneasiness returns to my exhausted body.

I can lie to Nora Di Rienzo. I can lie to Vito and Jaco.

But I can't lie to myself.

I know good and damn well that I didn't save Nora or take her home because of my job... I've been thinking about that confounding woman nonstop since we met at her father's funeral. That's a fact.

How is it possible that I have such complicated emotions toward a woman I barely know? And a woman I've been assigned to capture, at that?

Surviving Vito's inquisition is enough for one day, I decide. I'll save my own tough questions for another time.

The coal-gray door to my suite comes into view. I've never been so ready to retire to my room for some well-needed rest, but when I enter my suite, I find an invasion in progress.

Lounging in my dark leather armchair, like a lazy house cat "guarding" the place while I've been away, is Anunziata Balboni.

Jaco's only daughter and Vito's younger sister.

The girl who's been selected as my future wife.

Zia.

She looks up the moment I'm through the door.

Detaching herself from my furniture, and reattaching herself to me, she slings her long, slender arms around my tired neck. Like a serpent. Or a cruise-ship anchor.

"You're home." She smiles, eyes alight with happiness.

Anunziata is excited to see me. She usually is.

"Zia. To what do I owe the pleasure?" I try to be nice to her without being too encouraging, but her eyes spark anyway, full of suggestion.

"We haven't had any pleasure yet..." She all but purrs.

Here we go.

Zia has loved me all her life.

Which might be romantic if I weren't twice her age.

Instead, when I look at her, I see her wailing at four years old, the night her mother was murdered. The way she stared eerily at me as I carried her to safety.

Then her seven-year-old persona comes to mind. The withdrawn bratty little short-haired thing who didn't even come up to my waist, wearing some red and white private school uniform, clinging to the back of my pant leg. Back when I was still a rookie enforcer assigned to her security detail.

Once, when she was around twelve, she overheard me tell someone I like women with long hair. To this day, she refuses to cut it more than a trim's length. Even though she'd insisted to the point of temper tantrums to wear it cropped and short up until then. Well, now she's twenty-seven—only two years older than Nora—and her tresses fall in long, rippling waves down to her waist, dark as espresso.

Zia is someone I will always care about, but not someone I can desire.

I have no bad opinion of her. She's the only person in the whole of this mafia, beside her father, who doesn't actively hate me for one reason or another.

But that's not the same as being attracted to her.

I'll be forty-fucking-five in July. That's nearly two decades of difference between us.

It's not that age matters all that much to me.

But marrying her, after watching her grow up? The whole idea makes me feel like a pedophile. And even if I hadn't body-guarded all her birthday parties or followed her through shopping malls, she reminds me too much of Vito.

They're nothing alike personality wise, but their features are similar. Same dark hair and candescent blue eyes. Similar smiles and mannerisms. Though they take after they're mother, they're definitely both Jaco's children, no doubt about that.

Gently detangling Zia's arms from me, I move to the alcove by my floor-to-ceiling windows where I keep my coats. "What are you doing here?"

"Can't I come to see you?"

In recent weeks, Zia's been trying to escalate our relationship.

She's even gone so far as to press her father to shorten our engagement, and get on with the business of planning our wedding... Even if I'm entirely reluctant, I can't stop her.

That I marry his only daughter is Jaco's wish, and his wish is my damn command.

I'd marry an old shoe, if he wanted it.

Honestly, it would probably be better for morale around here if I *did* marry an old shoe. Part of the reason the other top enforcers despise me is because they've all been drooling over Zia since she hit eighteen, dying to drag her down the aisle and into their bedsheets. I could say less.

"You can." I put my coat away, taking my time. "But I'd still prefer advance notice."

"You never pick up when I call."

"You always call me when I'm working." When I turn back to face her, she's standing closer than I thought, hands settled on her hips.

"Rocco, you can't use that excuse forever, you know." She drifts closer, and I brush past her, headed for my medicine cabinet, the one located in my kitchenette.

"I know..." Grabbing myself a glass of water, and three extra-strength horse pills, I knock them back and pray for migraine relief.

"Your head's hurting again?" Zia guesses. She's one of the few people who knows about my horrible brain issues.

I give a small nod, but don't saying anything more, while I gulp back the contents of my water glass.

She comes my way and folds my fingers through hers. Then she leads me by the hand back to my seating group, and guides me into my arm chair by the window, overlooking Manhattan. Only a moment passes, before she climbs into my lap, the same way she used to when she was four.

I usually stop her right here, but tonight I can't be bothered.

God, I feel old.

Probably because I am old.

But I'm not stupid.

Zia tries to lure me into intimate encounters every chance she gets.

And she's good at it, I hate to say, though I doubt I want to know where she got her experience. The way she slides her hand across my shoulder and chest, while gently massaging the back of my neck with the fingers of her other hand? It drops my eyes closed involuntarily.

Despite my qualms about our engagement, moments like these erode my resistance a little bit. Lately...however I feel I about it, I've been on the verge of giving in to her a little more. And why not?

After all, marrying her is an inevitability. I can't escape it.

I'll have to kiss her eventually.

And...more than kiss her.

But my willingness to accede to her sexual suggestions came to a screeching halt the day of Orazio's funeral.

The day I met Nora.

Her defiant, amber-eyed gaze makes me tense in my seat, even with a beautiful young woman draped around me like a damn blanket.

"What is it?" Zia whispers, when I open my eyes.

"Nothing," I tell her, but in my mind, I still feel the shape of Nora's body pressed tight against my own. Lying on the ground with her weight on top of me...A sensation I'm already craving a sequel of.

Fuck.

Anunziata is attractive in her own right, but her eager youth doesn't compare at all to Nora's understated maturity.

Not that I should be comparing them.

As if it matters that Nora gives me temptation. She's clearly uninterested in a man my age. And even if she weren't, what would that change?

I'll still have to hurt her in the end.

My eyes find Zia's in the warm dimness of my bedroom lighting. She's gazing at me in an expectant quiet, asking me to kiss her without her words.

For the first time ever, a thought comes to me.

Maybe, letting off some steam with Zia is exactly what my body needs...

For once, I don't refuse her when she nestles deeper into my lap, brushing my cock as she settles her waist over mine, her long legs straddling my hips.

She presses her warm lips to my neck, kissing up over my jaw, onto my cheek.

I let my eyes fall closed again, relaxing into the sensation.

But all I'm really doing is arguing with Nora in my mind.

Zia's about your age, and she's all over me. What's your excuse? The pettiest part of me puffs up in my chest.

But when Zia bends toward my mouth, my phone shrills.

I turn my head at the sound, forcing her lips to land next to mine instead of on them. "You're supposed to be off the clock, remember?" She leaves a few more kisses on my cheek.

Ignoring her, I check the number, but I don't recognize it.

Zia continues her advance, as I answer, holding the phone to my ear.

"Rocco?" The voice on the other end of the line shoots me straight out of my seat, catapulting Zia onto the floor at the same time. "It's me. Nora."

A few seconds of astonished silence elapse, me standing there in utter disbelief that she's called me.

"One moment," I manage.

Then, I proceed to haul an offended, partially-embarrassed Zia up off the floor and into my armchair. I pace the length of my room to my en-suite bathroom, and quickly lock myself inside, bracing against the contemporary sink.

"Yes..." I clear my throat. "Hello. This is Rocco."

Jesus fucking Christ, I sound so uptight over the phone.

Nora clears her throat too, both of us acting awkward as ass.

I'm 110% floored that she called me. After all, I only gave her my number as an excuse to bug her phone. I never imagined that she might actually use it.

What can she be calling me about?

"Um..."

"What is it?"

"Is now a good time—"

"It's fine. Please go ahead."

I hear shuffling on her end, like she's moving around. "Are you...? Well, are you doing anything tomorrow?"

Nora Di Rienzo is calling to check my schedule?

"My day is open." *Or it very soon will be.*

"I was wondering if...if you might be willing to go somewhere with me, if you don't have any other plans."

"Yes, I'll go with you." I agree without giving it a single thought.

"Really? You will?" Nora sounds shocked. "You're not even going to ask me what it's about?"

"Tell me tomorrow." I squeeze the counter with my free hand. "What time should I meet you?"

"Ten am."

"Where?"

"I'll text you the location."

"Okay."

"Okay," she repeats.

We're back to awkward, and my head's about to explode, so I rush to the end, even though hearing her voice against my ear is an experience I find absurdly intoxicating.

"Good night, Nora."

"Night...Rocco."

We hang up, and I feel so amped inside I might bounce up to the ceiling and concuss myself. Can't recall the last time I felt this way...

What is this bubbly shit in my chest? *Excitement?*

In the back of my mind, I rationalize away. I know I'll have to kidnap Nora sooner or later. What's wrong with tomorrow?

Considering how absolutely *ridiculous* I'm acting around this woman, I definitely need to get this assignment over with quick.

Preferably before I get her or myself killed...

After I've splashed scalding hot water on my face to get the smirk out of my cheeks, I unlock the bathroom door and re-emerge into my bedroom.

Zia is pacing in the center when I arrive.

"I hope it was important," she snaps.

"It was." My hands find her shoulders, as I gently steer her toward the door. "And now it's late. I think, we'd both better get to bed."

"I'm not tired!" she insists, but I've already got the door to my suite open.

"Well, I am." I give Zia my sincerest apologetic look, which only earns me a glare. And *man* does she look like Vito when she does that...

Without a goodnight, she stamps off down the hallway back to her own room.

Hate to kick her out.

She's a good kid and she doesn't deserve to be held at arm's length by the likes of me, but I've got to get some rest.

And by *get some rest,* I mean I need to lay awake for hours, pondering the question which keeps me from sleep:

Why is it that I want to keep my time with Nora Di Rienzo a secret from every single person I know?

CHAPTER 8

Nora

I BARELY SLEEP a wink all night.

Instead, I lay in my bed for close to eight hours, pressing my dad's letter tight to my heart and making plans.

There's no way I'm going to get through this without a plan.

By the time Mama and I head down for breakfast the following morning, I know what I'm going to do, just not exactly...*how* I'm going to do it.

Kicking off my sleuthing operation requires me to...speak up during a meal in the grand dining room, when I'm seated around a table that consists of the head of the Dalla Porta mafia, his son, his daughter-in-law, his grandson, and my mother.

How the fuck am I supposed to do that?

I don't speak to these people when I see them in a hallway on their own, let alone *together* in a group over a meal. Every particle of shyness in my body is dying in lava.

But I can't let the discomfort stop me from talking.

This will be my one and only chance.

I should also mention that breakfast at the Dalla Porta estate is still a new and completely horrible experience for me.

Seated at this double wide mahogany table that's more than a hundred years old makes me feel like I'm trapped in a historical drama. The serving staff bring out platters covered with eggs, breakfast meats, and pastries, all of which are delicious, but if I have to eat them under the leering looks of Gianfrancesco, I barely taste a bite.

I'm too nervous.

Sitting here with this complex and undesirable mix of very important men is like trying to eat a meal while sitting in a hot frying pan.

But I do everything within my power to cling to the bit of courage I have left.

Thinking of Dad and his letter, his plea for my help…

His belief that I can do this.

The man strengthens me, even from beyond the grave.

My opportunity comes when Ciro puts down his coffee cup long enough to announce, "Tatiana and I have wedding details to go over today." The way he says it, chewing on a smile, turns my fucking stomach.

One glance at my mother, and I know she's even less enthusiastic about the idea than I am.

Don Saba nods, but doesn't say anything in reply.

The man is a tight-lipped enigmatic business machine, even at the breakfast table surrounded by his family.

For a sickening moment, I imagine Ciro and my mother need to discuss dowry preparations, like I'm some kind of cow my mother is selling to Calzavarra family. I swallow the sour thought down with a dry piece of toast.

The only person who seems to hate the sound of this more than myself and my mother is Donna Calzavarra, who looks positively *ill,* her clawed, manicured hands squeezing a short glass of orange juice hard enough to shatter it.

The subtext in my prospective mother-in-law's case is clear.

She'd rather die than see her only son married to me. I desperately wish I could tell her the feeling is mutual. Maybe then, she and I could be on the same side.

But today, unfortunately, I realize I'll have to upset her even more than usual...

To clear the air after Ciro's announcement and to change the subject altogether, I gather all my strength and get started with Operation Spa Day.

"That's perfect," I chime in, drawing several pairs of eyes to my face. "Because I've...got a busy day planned myself."

"*You?*" Gianfrancesco spears a sausage, eyeing me over a stack of pancakes. I can't tell if he's shocked that I've spoken or that I've found a way to be busy.

"Yes, in preparation for the wedding, I've scheduled a series of spa treatments for today." My mother's looking at me like she's never met me before. Donna looks offended that I, the outdoorsy one, might deign to get a manicure without her permission. Gianfrancesco looks gobsmacked.

I know why.

It's obvious why I have the attention of almost everyone in the room.

This is the most enthusiasm I've ever shown for this wedding, though *feigned* is much closer to the truth.

"Which spa will you go to?" My mother mutters to me in disbelief.

Before I can tell her about the place I picked out, Ciro interrupts with, "That's wonderful. A woman should do everything she can to be beautiful."

Eat shit, you rotten bastard.

I smile brightly. "That's exactly how I feel."

My mother's depressed demeanor isn't so thick that she can't tell something's wrong with me. Remarks like Ciro's make me cringe.

"We'll have the usual security detail escort you there and back," Ciro decrees, just as I expected.

I nod. "Thank you."

My fiancé studies me with his razor-sharp eyes, but doesn't say a word. We all return to our plates, though I'm so shocked and relieved I actually made it through that without incident that I want to run all the way up to my room.

Later, after breakfast adjourns, and I've gotten dressed, I say my goodbyes to my mother, who looks even more down today than she looked yesterday. I know that no one is taking my father's death harder than she is, but my gut tells me something deeper is wrong with her. And I just don't know how to ask her what it is.

She still seems far away, like a walking, talking shell.

I'll find out what's going on with her after I look into Dad's death, I promise myself, hurrying down a palatial amount of stairs in this giant place to the underground garage when my security detail is waiting to take me into the city.

After giving them the address, we're off to the Faraday Spa and Salon, a ultra-luxurious high-brow rest and rejuvenation destination near Central Park. When I get out, two guards position themselves outside the place.

To the one who's in charge, Jackson—a big burly linebacker type with scarred hands and a mean face—I say, "I've got treatments lined up back to back today. I should be done a little before the spa closes today at five pm."

He gives me a nod. "We'll be here all day."

"Thank you." *For falling for this nonsense.*

I head into the spa, the guards don't follow me through the glass doors.

The reason I picked this location is because it's located in a sprawling multipurpose plaza, one that has multiple entrances and exits. It looks like a small shopping mall in here honestly.

I walk like I'm headed to the spa as long as I'm within the security detail's sightline, and as soon as I round a marble corner, I'm gone.

Striding the length of the building, I exit on the east side. I was dropped off on the west. I check my phone. It's 9:55. I'm right on schedule.

I jog two blocks and cut over one street, and that's when I spot a deep indigo Jaguar idling at the curb. He's really here, waiting for me, just as he said he'd be.

I feel like a criminal striding up to the passenger side of Rocco De Carlo's sports car. All the windows are completely tinted black. For all I know, I've got the wrong guy.

But when I give the door handle a tug, it opens, and there he is, unbothered and imposing behind the steering wheel, glowing brown eyes hot on my face.

He's dressed in all black—a designer suit, if I had to guess— well-fitting dark slacks sheathe his grasshopper-long legs, while a sleek leather belt stretches around his waist. On top, he wears a black-button down shirt, sleeves rolled up over his thick, veiny forearms and cuffed beneath his elbow.

Basically, he's a GQ cover model, and I look like a hopeless fashion shoot assistant dressed in comfy cotton parachute pants with drawstrings at the ankles and a plain white razorback athletic tee I've worn a million times. He's probably wearing Italian leather shoes, and I'm wearing Converse high tops.

I've never cared about the way I dress before, but right now, I'm so self-conscious about it, I can barely get my mouth open.

"Good morning," I peep.

"Get in."

I do as he says, and soon find myself seated comfortably in the lush brown-leather interior of his car. Last night was so frantic and strange I didn't notice a single thing about this vehicle, but today, the fine details stand out to me.

Or maybe I'm just stalling.

Because it's crazy that I'm here right now. That he is too.

We're total strangers and I'm about to ask the impossible of him.

"Nora—" My name in his mouth makes me squeeze my legs together.

"Thank you for meeting me here," I cut him off with a genuine smile.

He seems taken aback. Slowly, he exhales hard, as though giving up on what he was initially going to say. "How are you feeling today?"

"You mean, am I planning to jump off any buildings later?"

His eyes fly to mine, that anger from last night still simmering low. "Are you?"

"No. Not today, anyway."

"Not *ever*." He presses hard.

"*Anyway...*" I tuck some of my hair behind my ear. "I know, last night we probably got off on the wrong foot—"

He scoffs. "You mean, *ledge.*"

"Oh, *you're* allowed to joke about it?" I meet his angry eyes, but the uninterrupted eye contact seems to be a lot. For both of us.

We mutually turn away, facing forward toward the windshield.

"No one's joking." Rocco clears his throat. "Continue. Please."

"Fine." I clear my throat too, folding up my argumentativeness and putting it away.

"As I was saying, I assume you're wondering why I asked you here."

"You assume correct." His long, powerful fingers tighten around the leather on his steering wheel. "Why did you call me last night?"

My cheeks get hot for some reason, even though that's a perfectly reasonable question. Why was I calling a strange man in the middle of the night?

"Well, you did tell me to call you first if I was planning to do anything stupid..."

"Nora." He grills me with his eyes. "Enough riddles. What's going on?"

Sitting this close to him has my heart slapping around in my chest. I'm hot in all the wrong places, and painfully aware that if I grab a fist full of the button-down he's wearing and tug hard, his mouth will be on me—*Nora! Holy Jesus, get it together.*

I shake my head a little. "Sorry. Yes."

God, I hate the way being alone with Rocco in his car brings back that same electric energy from last night.

Just as potent and palpable as before.

It's a lot to ignore, but I'll have to if I'm going to tell him the truth.

"You said you knew my father."

The line of his jaw hardens, and he gives me a nod.

"Last night, I got a package from him."

"A package?"

"From beyond the grave, yes."

Rocco's eyebrows climb his regal forehead.

"I know it sounds crazy, but it's true." I rush on. "Long story short, my dad was murdered under mysterious circumstances, and in the package he sent, there was a letter telling me that my sister and I are the only ones who'll be able to figure out what really happened to him."

"You mean…he knew who was after him, expected the hit, and left a trail just in case they got away with it?" Rocco's up to speed, just like that.

I nod. "I would have gone to my sister for help, but she lives in Milan. You're…oddly, the only person I could call."

"Let me get this straight." He casts his heavy gaze out over the dashboard. "You want me to help you find out why your father was killed."

"And who was behind it, yes."

"What makes you think I can help?" He covers his mouth with one of his massive hands, taking a gravely pensive stance.

"Well…you're a mafioso. I'm assuming you know how to work a gun."

"Nora, this is serious." His eyes dart back to mine, which puts more heat in my cheeks. "What exactly are you asking me to do?"

"I need someone to have my back." I fold my hands in my lap. "Figuring out what happened won't be that hard. My father loved puzzles, clues, and secret codes, and he spent years training me to crack them. I'm sure with the everything he's left me and whatever I find at his office, I'll be able to put it together. But…"

"But what?"

"In case the people who were after him are still around…" I can't help the way I swallow hard. "In case they may be after me and the rest of our family, I'll need someone to have my back. You know, someone who doesn't mind shooting a few people, if it comes down to it."

"You're asking me to be your personal bodyguard?"

"Just for today." I hold up both my hands. "Promise."

"But why me?" There's an unreadable hardness in his voice that puts me on edge. What am I going to do if he refuses me? "The Dalla Porta has hundreds of soldiers. Why do you need my protection?"

"Because there's a very real possibility that someone within the family had my father killed, and now that I know that could be the case, I can't trust anyone. Not until I've learned more about the truth."

"What if he genuinely was killed by one of his enemies?"

"Doesn't matter." What Rocco doesn't know is that I was up all night pondering these tricky questions. "Someone was after my dad. Whether they got to him or not, he wants me to know who that someone is. And I…need your help."

"Last night, I pull you off a ledge, and this morning, you want me to help you charge into some kind of blood feud you know nothing about." He throws a hand in the air between us. "What's next? A heist? Deep space?"

Understanding slams into me.

The answer's no.

Why did I think he'd want to help me? Anyone would be crazy to agree to something so wild on short notice. And we don't even know each other.

I'll be lucky if he doesn't mention this to anyone within the Dalla Porta camp…

"Sorry for asking so much of you." Defeat settles through me. "You're right, I know it's insane. There's no reason for both of us to risk our lives. I'll figure this out on my own—" Eyes prickling with ridiculous tears, I reach for the handle to get out, only to hear the chirp of Rocco engaging the car's locks.

Another hard exhale.

Slowly, I turn back to look at him.

This time when our eyes lock, the feeling of it is snug and intimate. A ripple of heat travels the length of my body, as he fixes me with that sensual stare.

"What *exactly* do you propose to do?"

"Is that a yes?" I whisper, hope bouncing between my ribs.

"I already regret it, but…"

Now, I really could kiss him, just out of pure gratitude. But I won't.

Because that would be bad.

Entirely bad.

"First, we've got to find my dad's office."

"You don't know where your own dad's office is?"

"Not his professional office." I pull the special necklace from my pocket. "His *secret* office."

Rocco puts the car in drive and whips out onto the road. "Where are we headed?"

I look hard into the seeing stone one more time, though I spent at least two hours checking and double checking the code before breakfast this morning.

4APCGA47R.

"Fourth avenue."

Rocco revs through a intersection as the light turns yellow, and we're off, flying through the city toward what I hope will be more answers.

My father left a mystery for me to solve and the next step is most definitely to find whatever the code in the necklace he gave me leads to.

Luckily, I've solved enough of my father's cyphers to decode this one.

Each part of the code has a different meaning, a different interpretation style.

The first two characters are usually an indicator of the place.

For a while, I wracked my brain trying to remember if I'd ever been to an apartment with him that was unit 4A, in case this necklace was meant to lead me to someone. But no luck. Finally, I decided he must be talking about a street.

4th Avenue. 4A.

"Where on Fourth Avenue?" Rocco asks, as we turn onto it.

"Not sure," I admit. "Pull over here and I'll look."

"Look for what?" Rocco dips against a red-marked curb, flashing his hazards.

"PC."

"Excuse me?"

"It's the next part in my father's code." I must sound like a total crank, I know, but many years of experience has taught me to go with my gut when it comes to solving one of my father's riddles.

PC, PC, PC... My eyes scan the road around us. I search high and low, everything from street signs to shop fronts to engraved plaques, stuck to the sides of buildings.

Nothing.

Next, I whip out my phone and google "PC 4th avenue." The results are numerous, random, and inconclusive, until a facebook page catches my attention. It's for a place called *Pete's Cafe...*

When I tap the address of the place, I learn it's on 4th avenue, and it's actually...Wait a minute.

"I'm going to get out."

"And go *where?*" Rocco gives me a look of concern.

"Have a little faith, Mr. De Carlo." I climb out of his jag and hit the bricks following the directions on my phone, the necklace safe in my fist, deep in my pocket.

I head for the crosswalk and keep searching my surroundings for any sign of a—Holy shit. I see something. It's a tiny mom-and-pop shop tucked into half a corner of a building across the street.

Pete's Cafe. PC. Is this the place my father meant?

There's only one way to find out.

I wait for the light, then jog across the street to Pete's Cafe. I race up the few steps to the entrance, fingers snatching for the front door handle...Only to find that they're closed. The door's locked.

Great. What the hell am I going to do now?

I return down the steps and find myself facing this intersection once again.

If this is the wrong PC, then trying to solve GA, the next part of code, will be useless. But if I am right and this darkened sandwich shop is what my father intended, then I should start searching for anything that might spark the answer to the riddle...

But it's several minutes of standing there without a single inspiration.

Rocco can see me from his car across the street, and God only knows what that man must be thinking.

It's not that his opinion of me matters or anything.

It's just that...I'm trying to maintain a belief in myself that I can do this, and it would be a lot easier if he didn't think I was insane.

Nora, he pulled you off a ledge last night. That ship's sailed.

I'm looking hard at a big office park building, rising high above the curb where Rocco's parked, when a giant garbage truck rumbles to a halt at the curb blocking my sightline and clogging up my nose with that acrimonious Manhattan refuse stench.

I cover half my face with my hand, enduring this awful garbage smell—

Then, like tripping up a staircase, the next answer to the code comes to me.

Garbage.

Garbage Alley! GA.

Pete's Cafe, Garbage Alley!

The truck groans and hisses out of the way, and I see Rocco's gotten out of his car. Now, he's leaning up against the side. I swiftly text him what I've found, and then jog around past the front door of Pete's Cafe.

Sure enough, about fifteen steps past the shopfront is the entrance to a long narrow garbage alleyway. It's definitely the one Pete's Cafe uses. I can tell because there's a back door with a sticker of their logo affixed to the rusting metal.

I'm in the right place.

Thank God.

The best part is the last portion of my father's cipher is already solved.

47R is the easiest part of the riddle, doesn't require any sleuthing at all.

It means *forty-seven steps on your right.*

Dad used to hide things from me and Nico when we were kids and use the number of steps and directions to train us to find things this way.

Counting my steps, I stride down the outdoor corridor, brick walls rising on either side of me, big green dumpsters parked at fixed intervals along the way. I try not to jump when a family of rats scurries past.

I jump over the nasty looking puddle of trashy water, and all the while continue counting. *Thirty-two, thirty-three, thirty-four...*

I'm almost there, when the back of my neck starts to tickle.

Someone's behind me.

I turn back, expecting Rocco—A tall, lanky muscle bag towers over me instead, cracking his tattooed knuckles.

How can a man this big be so silent? I didn't even hear him coming and now, it's far too late. Heart clattering between my ribs, I back-step on shaky legs, colliding into someone thick, stocky, and hard as granite.

A small involuntary shriek of surprise escapes me.

I whip around, getting my back to the wall.

Now, I can see them all, five in total…

Mafiosos. For sure. Each of them more gruesome and carved up than the one before. And that's not all I pick up.

Holy shit.

All of them have at least one tattoo in common. On the ring finger of their right hands, a thick red stripe is etched into their skin.

Oh, God, they're Pezzullos.

Dad must have made us memorize over a hundred different signifying tattoos, each of them an unmistakable identifier of the mafia families of New York City.

The thick red ring is the signet of the Pezzullo clan.

Their crime family runs protection rackets. They kidnap people for fucking money, and even worse, they're allied with the Balboni crime family…The sworn enemy of the Dalla Porta. The worst, most brutal, heinous, and hated of all our rivals…

If they find out who I am…

Or worse, if they already know who I am, it's *Goodnight, Eleanora.*

They've got me surrounded, and Rocco's nowhere in sight—

"Well, what have we here?" A sixth Pezzullo soldier saunters in, the rest of the pack parting around him. The ringleader is only a few inches taller than me, with a toothpick stuck in his mouth, and a neck tattoo that comes all the way up to his jaw.

His left eyebrow has a permanent nick through the middle of it, and his hair is disheveled, like he's run his hands through it one too many times.

With his right hand, he tosses his toothpick at the ground.

Blood tinges his disgusting fingernails with a rust color.

"Found a little alley rat." The towering lanky one responds, voice low as fuck.

"Now, the question is..." He saunters toward me, bending slightly, so we're eye to eye. He smells awful. I flatten myself against the bricks behind me, just trying to stay as far back as I can. "Is she in the right place at the wrong time? Or the *wrong* place at the wrong time?"

The short stocky one I backed into flicks a butterfly knife out from his fist, flashing his discolored gap-tooth smile at me. "We could cut her until she squeals."

"She definitely looks like a squealer," another adds, making kissy faces at me, to the laughter of his comrades.

Fuck. Violent sex crimes swirl through the back of my mind. Even worse, I know I'm not the only one imagining it.

"I hate to cut the pretty ones." The ringleader loiters ever closer. There's no more room for me to back up.

"Are you the ones who killed my father?" My question comes out hard and breathless. Scanning their sick, excited faces, not a single one makes a move to answer me.

Not before the ringleader slaps his gruff hand against my face, gripping my chin and cheeks in his filthy palm. "We ask the questions here, *bella*—"

The ringleader's voice cuts off mid-sentence.

In a flash so fast I almost miss it, a bullet skates through his skull, right behind his eye sockets. I swear to God, it looks like a pinball flying beyond one eyeball then the other, followed by a tiny black projectile exiting his left temple in a spray of red-black blood. My body constricts, horror stunning me into a hyperventilating statue.

His body goes slack, falling right out of the frame of my

eyesight, as I stand panting and petrified against the wall. Mouth open and gasping, I shake, unable to make a single move.

The rest of the Pezzullo soldiers reel back, cursing in English and Italian. Their heads rip to my left, gaping in anguish at the ringleader's killer.

Holy shit, it's Rocco!

He strides down the alley, his firing arm outstretched, a gun with a silencer tight in his fist. *"Touch her, and you die."*

CHAPTER 9

Rocco

ASIDE FROM GETTING to spend time with a beautiful woman, so far, today is *really* not my day. Five Pezzullo foot soldiers charge straight at me, wild with wrath.

That's fine.

I could use the fucking workout.

This morning, I had to skip mine in order to meet Nora on time.

I fire on the tallest one, putting a bullet through his thick neck. He grabs at it with both hands, blood spraying beneath his giant fingers.

The thickest one barrels straight past him and catches my elbow to his fucking face. He stumbles back a few feet with a broken nose, then wildly hacks in my direction with his butterfly knife, snarling at me.

My bullet flies straight into that ungodly craw of his and down he goes, taking two of the smaller men with him. Before they can scramble out from beneath his enormous dead weight I nail them both between the eyes.

I've only got two rounds left.

Thank God, there's only one more fish to fry—"HOLD IT!" The final foot soldier roars.

Rage eats me up from head to toe, when I look up and see that filthy fucker with Nora in his grip. One of his grubby palms bends her arm behind her back, while the other balances a gun against her head.

Oh, I'm going to make his death painful.

Immensely painful.

"Let. Her. Go." My voice always drops lower when someone's pushed me over the edge. This fucker's about to find out.

"Oh, no. She's coming with me."

I stalk forward, stepping over the fresh corpses of his former comrades.

"*She's mine,*" I growl at him. "And unless you want to end up like your friends, you'll take your dirty flea-invested paws off of her."

"Don't take another step!" This dumb fucking kid is shaking.

What is this? His first mission? I almost don't want to brutally murder him.

"Rocco…" Nora whimpers.

My eyes slide to hers. "It's going to be okay."

"Not for you." The Pezzullo boy removes the gun from Nora's head and fires straight at me. I dodge right and take off like a damn jet plane, rushing him with the full speed and force my body's amassed in the past twenty years of mafia life.

The boy yelps, as I close in, forgetting about Nora completely, who has the good sense to leap out of my way as I ram into that motherfucker and slam him against the nearest dumpster. His skull snaps against the dark green metal, disorienting him, but that's the least of his fucking problems.

After knocking his gun from his hand, I wail on him.

I beat his his face with my gun, until he's dizzy and thoughtless. Then, I holster my gun and do the job with my bare fucking fists.

One heavy punch. Another. Another.

I don't stop until my knuckles are red with his blood and his teeth go flying onto the rough pavement.

"I told you—" I grunt, knocking his head against the dumpster for the second time. "—what would happen if you touched her, didn't I?"

He groans, bloody drool dripping from his mouth.

With a fistful of his shirt, my knuckles digging into his sternum so he can't move, I rip my favorite fountain pen from my lapel pocket, flick the cap off and stab it into his neck. It only takes a few seconds for him to stiffen up like the corpse I'm about to make out of him.

I release his chest and he slides straight off the dumpster and hits the ground, on his back, eyes wide open, his swollen bloody face a multicolor mass of bloody flesh. Leisurely, I step closer and squat over him.

"You know what I love about this particular blend of toxins?" I know he can hear me. I gaze right into his frightened gray eyes. "It paralyzes a person, but it doesn't stop them from feeling pain..." I rise to my full height. "There's something poetic about that, I can't explain it."

Retrieving my gun, I aim for his groin, then fire two bullets straight into his moldy dick. He's not going to need it where he's going.

The kid unleashes a howl that echoes through the alleyway.

Guess his vocal cords are the only part of him the paralysis hasn't reached yet.

"Don't worry." I tuck my gun away. "The paralysis will kill you in a few hours. It'll only hurt until then."

When I turn back, I see the full picture of the carnage I've unleashed, and more to the point, I see Nora hunched at the wall, yanking at one of the bricks with shaking fingers. I approach her.

She nearly jumps into my arms, she's so freaked out when I appear over her shoulder. "What are you doing?"

"T-This is it." Both her hands are tight around a loose brick.

"*This* is your father's secret office?"

"No. It's a clue." Finally, she yanks hard enough that the brick comes free, but the force sends her toppling backwards, straight into me. I catch her with my left arm, the one that isn't covered in Pezzullo blood.

The proximity of her body does something to me.

Something it shouldn't do.

For a moment, we can't look away from each other. And then Nora rolls her lips together and gets back to the wall.

Damn. Nora was right.

Behind the loose brick is a folded piece of paper and a big silver ring with several different keys on it. She snatches them up, replaces the brick and then turns back to me, looking a bit queasy. "Let's get out of here."

"Couldn't have said it better myself."

The fingers of my good hand wrap tight around hers, and we're gone, hurrying out of the garbage alley before anyone on the perpendicular streets notices the trash we left for pick up. We're back at my car in a matter of minutes, and before a word is spoken, I book it away from the curb and drive hard through the Manhattan streets. We're miles and miles away before we hear a single siren.

There's still so much adrenaline coursing through me, I actually feel buzzed.

Totally wired. Taking corners too fast, barely slowing down at red lights.

Nora's right beside me, but I almost feel like I can't look at her.

A strange anxiety thumps beneath the surface of my skin.

She knew I was a mafioso when we met. She was the one who asked me to come today, and fuck, am I glad I did. When I imagine what the Pezzullos might have done with her, I get close to ripping my steering wheel right off the console.

But that doesn't mean I didn't terrify her back there.

Or that I'm not still doing it, right now.

"Pull over up there." Her voice is small. And when I finally dare a glance at her, I can see she's a bit green.

"What's wrong?"

"We need to take care of your hand." She's talking about my right fist, covered mostly in Pezzullo blood, but probably a bit of my own too. I really let loose on that fucker back there…

"It's fine." I swallow hard. "I'm fine."

"I'm not," she clarifies, covering her mouth.

This is the part where she tells me to drop her off anywhere because she's too disgusted to continue in this quest with me. Things got too real back there.

My heart sinks lower with every thought—

"Sorry," she mutters, as I dive into the first open parallel parking space we come across on this road. "I just…I'm not good with blood."

Without another word, she gets out of my car and walks a few paces down the block, before heading straight into a Duane Reades.

Great. She's probably gone in there to puke her guts out.

I nauseate her.

Of course, I do.

I shot a dude's dick off back there. Definitely not my most civilized moment.

Christ…I need to stop by confession.

I'm not saying Nora Di Rienzo had any wonderful opinion of me before now, but whatever she thought of me, I'm certain I just took it down several pegs.

It's not even eleven am.

I tense my right fist, sending a hissing, aching pain through my hand.

Maybe I went harder at that guy than I thought.

Why I went totally ballistic just because he held a woman I barely know hostage?

No idea. *God damn it.* What the fuck am I even doing?

Alone in my parked car, I finally have a moment to breathe. Just sitting here, Nora's scent filling up the air, I'm conflicted as hell.

I agreed to meet her today, assuring myself I'd use this opportunity to nab her as I'd been instructed to do, so why am I chauffeuring her around the city and playing Dark Knight? Why am I getting so comfortable playing the part of a family friend she's never met before?

She just caught you off guard, that's all, my pride insists.

I don't know what I expected Nora to say when she got into my car this morning, but *help me uncover the truth about my father's murder* definitely wasn't it.

That whole conversation we had about it earlier planted ample amounts of chaos in my gut. Guilt chews the edges of my mind, even now. But I'd be lying if I said my curiosity isn't also hella piqued.

Orazio Di Rienzo is a bigger mystery than I could have imagined.

I thought Vito ordering me to meet the man in secret was strange. I thought Orazio interacting with me as though he knew me was even stranger, but now it turns out, the man sent his daughter messages from beyond the grave?

Somebody call fucking Sherlock Holmes.

Like, what the hell?

This just gets weirder and weirder.

Her father knew someone was trying to kill him...

I know Vito and his boys were behind it. The Balboni and the Dalla Porta are sworn enemies. The number of bodies we've caught, on both sides, is enormous. The mutual animosity is obvious. So why would Nora's father want her to look into a feud that goes back decades?

He was an incredibly sharp, *shrewd* man who loved his family more than anything. Why would he send his daughter into danger?

She seems to be under the impression his death was an inside job, but I know it wasn't, which means...her father's messages have only set her up for a wild goose chase. A damn dangerous one at that.

But I couldn't tell her that. All I could do was agree to help her.

Even though *helping* endangered mafia daughters isn't in my job description. It's not even in my character. Or at least it *wasn't*. Not until I met her.

It's just guilt. Good old fashioned Catholic guilt.

That's the only reason I resolved to help her like this today, I pretend.

I was the last one to see her father alive. Even though Vito kept me in the dark about it, technically, I still aided in Nora's father's death.

If I blow my cover...If she finds out who I actually am or the role I played in Orazio's murder, things are going to get dicey. In ways I don't even want to consider.

No. I won't let that happen.

I'll just have to tighten up and get this mission over with, however I can. The sooner, the fucking better.

Now, my foot's tapping. Can't keep my eyes off the sliding glass doors of that convenience store. *Should I go in after her?*

Is she hurling into a toilet right about now?

Is she hurt at all? I got there in time to take them out, but that doesn't mean they didn't shake her up in the ninety seconds it took me to get into that alley.

My muscles tense up all over again, remembering the way I saw men swarming onto that backstreet after Nora.

I sprinted across the street with everything I had, darting through traffic while car horns blared, whipping out my gun in broad daylight. And then, just my fucking luck, I get there and I recognize the men crowding her.

Pezzullo soldiers. The red rings tattooed on their right hands, and the fire-bitten crosses on the backs of their necks gave them away.

They're Balboni allies.

But something I still don't understand?

What the hell they were doing there to begin with...

I know I should have handled the situation differently.

But if even one of them had survived and told their administration that I was behind the killings, Vito would have had all the ammo he needed to get me gone from the family. In the body bag sort of way.

Killing allied soldiers usually costs the ultimate price.

But I had to take my chances. As soon as I saw them giving Nora trouble, their lives were over. Even if they hadn't pissed me off like that, I couldn't risk blowing my cover by acting chummy with them.

It would have tripped a wire with Nora.

Likewise, if the Pezzullo's had seen me with her—and been smart enough to know who she was—and opened their big mouths, it might have gotten all the way back around to Vito that I haven't been following his fucking orders.

So I... acted like I was protecting Nora from danger. The way she asked me too.

But was I really acting?

The fear that zapped through me, hot as lighting, realizing she was in danger...That wasn't fake. My killer instincts, activated and in full force, triggered by a surge of protective desire...I didn't make that up.

And that's not a good thing.

I'm so engrossed in my own thoughts that I jolt on the inside when Nora suddenly reappears, drawing my passenger side door open and sliding inside.

Now, she carries a brown paper bag, which she sets down on

the floor between her legs. Digging into it, to my great surprise, she pulls out...a First Aid kit?

Maybe, she is hurt.

"Did they cut you?" I blurt out, my eyes scanning her beautiful body for any scrapes I missed in the scuffle back there.

Her eyes rest on my face. "Let me see your hand."

"My—" Eyes wide, I blink at her. I glance down at the sticky, bloody knuckles of my right hand. Like frigid ice water's been dumped on my head, I realize what's happening.

Nora is trying to take care of me.

Me.

I'm dumbfounded by it. So flabbergasted by this small act of kindness, I just sit there staring at her, unable to say a single word.

"May I?" She reaches slowly for my hand, as though I have any power to resist her, when she's shining so brightly before me.

Gingerly, she lifts my heavy hand and places it on her left thigh.

Dear God, it takes an Atlas amount of strength to leave my hand limp. My fingers ache to squeeze and rub the softest part of her leg, hidden from me only by the thin cotton slacks she's wearing.

Desire gongs through me like the damn bells of Notre Dame, but I force myself to freeze. I'm so still beneath her touch, I'm barely breathing.

She sets to work with a quiet focus, cleaning my stinging hand with antiseptic wipes that burn the fuck out of my slightly wounded knuckles. Wiping away blood, applying ointments...She even bought a special box of bandages made for hands, the kind that can wrap around my knuckles better than the standard band-aids can.

Honestly, this moment is so surreal, she's like a movie I'm watching.

She gently returns my hand to me, a small sheepish look on her face.

And I've forgotten how to talk, but the silence is dragging

between us, so I force myself to open my mouth. "Where did you learn to…"

"Use a first aid kit?" Her eyebrows rise, a warm humorous expression on her face. "Believe it or not, I've been in my fair share of fights with…carabiners and rope burns. I've learned a thing or two about patching myself up."

"Thanks." It almost comes out like a cough.

"You're welcome." In my periphery, I notice Nora's fingers, playing with each other. "And *thank you* for…what you did earlier."

"Offing those guys, you mean?"

Well, I feel like a fucking idiot, but Nora doesn't seem to notice.

Instead, she glances at me, sidelong and sincere. "For…having my back."

CHAPTER 10

Nora

AND I THOUGHT *yesterday* was a whirlwind.

It's not even noon yet, and already Rocco's saved my life twice.

My cheeks are hot and achy, like I've been trying not to smile for hours. Self-consciousness does this to me.

It's hard to relax with this giant, gorgeous, insanely loyal man sitting next to me with his eyes on mine, which is why I know I've got to forge ahead with my plan.

Just because today doesn't feel real doesn't mean it's going to last forever. I have a mystery to solve and only a few hours to do it.

"So...where to next?" Rocco clears his throat. "What did your father's note say?"

From my pocket, I retrieve the keys and slip of paper I found in the alley wall. "Nothing really." I unfold the paper. "It's a map."

Holding it up, I lean a little toward Rocco so he can see it.

That's when the scent of his expensive cologne, subtle and

divine, sneaks up on me. *God, what is that?* It smells like something spiced and a little sweet mixed with petrichor. I could lose myself forever in that scent—*Nora! Mission!*

"At the corner of Deal and Rosevine, huh?"

I set the map down, and Rocco busies himself typing the address into the oversized tablet this car comes with. As soon as the navigation's set up, we're on our way once again.

My only refuge against the attractiveness of the man beside me is to focus hard on why we're here today. And the bigger picture...

The one that's making less and less sense.

"Those were Pezzullo soldiers back there...I'm sure of it," I murmur aloud. "What do they have to do with this?"

"I have the same question."

"Hell of a coincidence." My fingers trace the rough edges of the keys on the ring, seated in my lap. "Them lurking around the exact spot my dad left a clue for me."

"I don't believe in coincidence."

"Neither do I..." My brain applies itself to this conundrum, but to no avail. "If they were the ones who killed my father, why would they be hanging out in an old alleyway that he used to use as a message fence?" I shake my head. "That's almost like a perpetrator returning to the scene of a crime."

"The Pezzullo family definitely isn't known for any kind of strategic or tactical finesse, but if they were behind it, this would be a stupid move. Even for them..." Rocco muses. "I agree. It's strange. Felt more to me like they were keeping an eye on the place."

Now, there's a thought I hadn't considered.

"You mean, like monitoring it?"

"That would put them there on purpose."

On purpose...

"You don't think..." Something like trepidation trembles in the pit of my stomach.

"What?"

"There's no way they could have been waiting there for me, right?"

Rocco's expression darkens, until he's glaring at the road. "Anything's possible."

"But even I had no idea I would be there today, how could they have possibly known or predicted it?"

"Doesn't add up." Rocco tightens his left-handed grip on the wheel. "I don't know what they were doing there either, but one thing's for sure. You were right to ask for my help. Something bad could have happened if you'd gone there on your own."

The leering faces of my attackers flash through my mind. "I know."

We fall into a pensive quiet, sounds of the city in the background muted by Rocco's nearly soundproof windows and doors.

His perspective in all this is valuable, I'm starting to realize. I haven't seen his resumé or anything, but it's obvious what a skilled enforcer he is.

He knows a lot about our world.

Everything he's said so far today has been spot-on, and the fact that he shares my apprehension about this situation validates my own sense of what's normal and what's off. Really off.

Thinking about that is all I can to do to ignore that rough protective edge in his voice, the same one from last night...Almost like my safety matters to him.

I know I'm being dumb. It can't be that he cares.

Not when we barely know each other.

It's honestly a wonder we're able to be even this civil to each other, when all we seemed capable of last night was arguing, back and forth.

In fact, until Hugo showed up at my door with the box from Dad, I completely resented Rocco De Carlo for ruining my suicide attempt...

Now, I'm grateful he intervened.

My feelings toward someone have never done such a wild one-eighty in the course of just twenty-four little hours, but here we are, wending through Manhattan toward some unknown destination, allied instead of antagonizing each other.

I wonder if we'll encounter anymore uninvited guests.

My stomach clenches at the thought. I think I've had my share of guns, blood, and violence for the moment.

Traffic in the city is maddeningly thick today, a parade or something is going on. So it takes a good ninety minutes for us to finally make it uptown. When Rocco pulls to a stop, I think we've reached another red light, but then he puts the car in park.

"This is it." He nods toward the intersection ahead of us.

I scan the crossroad, unsure what we're looking for, and then a wave of nostalgia claims me like a rough tide. Recognition hits.

"This is…"

"What?"

I can't breathe. My hand flies over my lips to keep my heart from flying up my throat and out my mouth.

"Are you all right?"

Nodding, I work to get my breathing to slow down after this emotional sucker punch. Looking blearily down at my knees, I try for words. "My dad…he used to bring me and my sister here when we were kids."

I haven't been here in years, but it's just the same.

The Purple Palace movie theater.

It was built in the 1930s, when grand, lavishly decorated theaters began to crop up all over the city.

Dad used to bring us here to see matinees of black and white films like *Sabrina* and *Funny Face*. Watching Audrey Hepburn movies is probably what got Nico into fashion in the first place… Meanwhile I could never take my eyes off the stunning architecture, the wonderfully ornate detailing of the walls and ceilings, all of which were too pretty to climb. Still, I yearned to.

The joyful afternoons of our childhood return to me, hard and poignant. But now is hardly the time for sentimentality, so instead,

I climb out before Rocco can ask me another question, swiping at my damp eyes as I go.

Out in the early afternoon light, squeezing the key ring in my fist, I look both ways.

My heart jumps when Rocco materializes at my side.

The look on his face says it all. *I'm coming with you this time.*

"Come on." His giant, warm hand curls gently around my left forearm. "We can make it."

Traffic won't let up, so we jog across the street in between clusters of speeding taxicabs and groaning inner city buses, jaywalking swiftly to the other side. Rocco tugs me along.

It's disorienting being here, one foot in the past and one in the present.

But at least I'm sure we're in the right place. If my father was going to have a secret office somewhere, it would definitely be here.

Once we're across the street, I pull out the keys and examine them more closely. Each one has a number imprinted on it, random numbers ranging sporadically from 1 to 25. Rocco and I aren't exactly sure what it means, but the theater has a side door with the number 1 carved into it, and when I try the key, it fits the lock, like magic.

The first door leads to a staircase somewhere deep within the bowels of the Purple Palace. Another wave of deja vu bowls me over, as soon as we step inside and begin the climb. The place smells like burnt popcorn and the old, purple velvet the theater is full of.

Next, we find our way down a long curving corridor with old seats leaned against one wall, and dim, restored, art deco lighting fixtures buzzing above us. Checkered black and white tiles extend beneath our feet. The muffled noise of movies in progress drift through the walls, but the voices and action sequences are so muffled we can't hear enough to identify anything.

At the end of the hallway is a spiral staircase, the kind made of iron, almost like an old fire escape, except it's indoors. Rocco and I share a look of trepidation before ascending the cramped, spiraling steps. The metal creaks beneath our joint weight, as we follow the stairs up into an unlit darkness.

A locked door awaits us at the top, and I try the next key in the sequence.

The door opens, and we push into another dark space.

Before I can do it, Rocco gropes a hand against the nearest wall until he finds an old light switch and then, the room comes to life around us.

It's a vintage projection room.

My heart swells up all over again.

I've never seen a place that matched my father so well in my life.

The room looks like him. It even smells like him.

Like he was just here a few minutes ago, like he'll be right back...

Tears roll down my cheeks, as I step further inside.

It's a small square room with red painted walls. An old projection screen dominates one wall, about my height. On either side of it are small curtained windows, with the drapes drawn closed. On the next wall is a world map with North America and Europe in the middle, lines and lines and *lines* of red thread zigzagging across it, held in place with pushpins.

On the back wall of the room are another pair of curtained windows, mirroring the two on either side of the screen. In between them, a massive desk is pushed flush with the wall. The desk is piled high with papers and notes, and around those, framed photos of our smiling family.

Pictures of Mama, Nico, and me.

The same family photo hidden in the cross around my neck.

Packs of Dad's favorite cigarettes, stacked next to a stash of coconut covered chocolate bars, his guilty pleasure of choice. A coffee mug. An engraved lighter. Journals. Notebooks. Fountain pens.

And the last wall holds the sole entrance and exit to this place, on either side of which, old movie posters hang.

One from *The African Queen*, another of *The Maltese Falcon*.

In the center of the room, an old projector is stationed, surrounded by a small collection of old chairs.

The clipped, lilted dialogue of a silver-screen masterpiece softly invades the silence of the room. I drift over to the curtained window beside the projection screen, Rocco close behind me. We peak out through the curtains, and find ourselves high above one of the main viewing theaters of the Purple Palace.

Below, a thin crowd of movie goers munch on popcorn watching *Casablanca* on the enormous screen before them.

"Was your father a cinephile?" Rocco's deep, velvety voice crawls gently into my ears. He's so quiet, I almost forgot he was standing behind me.

"The biggest," I whisper back, my eyes tracing the line of Ingrid Bergman's stunning features. To say I've seen this movie hundreds of times is no exaggeration. And most of the iterations, I saw with my dad.

The movie tugs hard at my heart strings, so I have to let the curtain fall from my finger tips and move on.

Before I break down totally and completely.

Rocco glides toward the wall covered in maps and red threads. I didn't notice it when we first stepped inside, but that wall isn't just maps and yarn. There are also photographs and notecards pinned up and around them, giving additional context. Rocco examines things more closely, while I take in the room for the second time.

Another thing in here I missed? Hanging from the ceiling are more photographs. Gruff scarred faces glare out at me from the Polaroid frames, the names of mafioso members scrawled in my father's unmistakable handwriting across the bottom.

There must be more than thirty faces attached to the ceiling by thin threads.

"What *is* all this?" I murmur to myself, fingers connecting with a worn old photograph of a woman I don't recognize. The name written beneath her portrait is *Rossana Facci.*

"Seems like your father was looking for someone." Rocco runs his finger tip along the yarn connecting two points. "Or...tracking the movement of something."

"Maybe the people who were trying to kill him." I can't take my eyes off this photograph.

"Maybe."

I pinch Rossana's picture between my fingers, examining her dark soulful eyes and long tangled curls. She wears a simple white dress with a flower pattern around the hem. On a rooftop, she stands for the picture. And behind her in the distance is a range of mountains I've seen before.

She's in Sicily...

Who are you? I wish I could ask her.

Some of the old-world, wooden theater-style chairs in the center of the room are piled high with fat, overflowing files. Folders. Dossiers.

"I don't get it." Lifting up a dossier, I glance at Rocco, who's staring right back at me. "This office is nothing like the office my dad has at home."

"What do you mean?"

"The man was organized. To a fault." I glance around this small projection room. "I feel like we're standing on the inside of his *brain* or something. Like, what is all of this doing here?"

Rocco grabs one hand with the other, behind his back. "He seems like a man who liked his privacy."

"He was..." I shake my head. "But it's not like the Dalla Porta lack strong security measures. Dad was *in charge* of the security measures. He should have had more privacy than anyone. So why this place?"

Rocco's eyes drift around the room, like he's deep in thought.

Setting the dossier back in its spot, my gaze falls to the projector a few feet away, a hopeless feeling beginning to sprout in my chest. "Who was he trying to keep all of this a secret from?"

Rocco seems to zero in on the projector at the same time I do.

I'm so on edge in here, I'm almost afraid to touch anything, but Rocco seems fearless. He maneuvers between two of the small theater chairs so that he's standing directly over the projector, and then he turns it on.

Achingly bright light cuts through the room casting an image onto the projection screen. An image that's laying on the stage glass beneath the condenser lens.

Another old photograph.

It comes into focus and...

The gasp that escapes me is deep, loud, and involuntary.

It's an old family photo. A man, his wife, and their three sons, but—

"That's Sabatini Calzavarra..." Rocco's just as taken aback as I am.

Don of the Dalla Porta crime family. It's him, much younger than he looks now, standing next to the same woman whose picture caught my eye, hanging from the ceiling. Rossana Facci.

She's...his wife?

But the most shocking part about this photograph by far is the boys, standing in front of them in their Sunday best.

This doesn't make any sense. Those five words swirl around my head, faster and faster as I examine their faces, the resemblance between them and their parents undeniable.

The oldest son is the tallest with dark curls like his father and a soft, warm smile on his face. The middle son frowns, glaring at the camera, hair cropped shorter, fingers fixed around a toy airplane. And the youngest one with that smug look on his impish little face...That's Ciro. My future father-in-law.

119

"Saba has three sons." The words fall out of my mouth in disbelief.

"Not one." Rocco leans against the chair in front of him, eyes wide.

"So why is Ciro the only son anyone knows about?" My dad was Saba's oldest and most trusted friend, and he's talked to me about the Calzavarra family many times, but he's never once mentioned that Saba had three sons.

"There are two other Calzavarras that have been, what? In hiding all this time?"

"That's what I'd like to know…" My voice sounds hoarse. "What the hell happened to them and what does this have to do with…with…"

Fuck, I'm all choked up, I can't…

The tears I've barely held at bay spring free, sobs bursting from my chest.

I have to hide my face with my hands, it's just all too much.

I'm such an idiot. An idiot in way over her head.

Whatever my father's been looking into, clearly he's been at it a long time. This secret office is obviously the work of several years.

Did I really think I'd be able to waltz in here and solve a mystery I've known about for less than twenty-four hours?

Why did I think this would be easy?

I thought I'd find my way here and there'd be a great big sign saying, *Nora, the person who killed me is…?*

Of course not.

My own father didn't know who was responsible for his murder. It's a mystery he hoped I'd be able to solve, but how can I?

I'm falling the fuck apart without him, and there are only two weeks before I'll be forced down the aisle with Gianfrancesco, hardly enough time to solve a mystery of this magnitude and make some kind of escape.

Helplessness and defeat ravage me on the inside, as ugly tears of grief pour down my face. Even with shaking shoulders, a throbbing head, and a hiccuping voice, I'm overwhelmed by how much this office reminds me of my dad.

His scent tinges the air, engulfing me.

Everything he loved and everything he questioned all thrown together in here like a blender-full of his deepest passions and curiosities.

He's everywhere.

Everywhere and nowhere.

And I'm so lost without him.

God, I wish I were—A large warm hand appears on the small of my back.

The hand pulls me, *guides me* with gentle force straight into the massive, muscled embrace of Rocco De Carlo. He wraps both his big arms around me and holds me tight, while I cry.

I'm amazed by his tenderness.

The man holding me as I sob is the same man who brutally murdered my would-be attackers just a few hours ago? Just to protect me? The same man who yanked me off a ledge and reprimanded me like a child for endangering my life?

No man has held me as close as this, so firm and still gingerly.

Not since my father, a decade ago, the day after my sister was exiled to Europe.

Rocco's heat envelops me. His big wide hand rubs up and down my trembling back, while I bury my face and my hands into his hard, dense chest.

In the same moment, I simultaneously feel so pathetic, I could die and also...so moved by the selfless actions of this one man that I...I...

My heels rise on their own while my hands glide up and over his chest, arms fastening around his neck. Then I ply my damp tear-stained face to his, mixing his lips with mine.

CHAPTER 11

Rocco

Sweet Jesus Christ.

Nora's warm lips press mine hard, urgent and giving. She tucks her beautiful face against the line of my own, our noses dipping against each other as she angles her head at my mouth. Volts of electricity fry me to a crisp just from this single kiss.

Flung into a frenzy, my heart reacts in my chest, shaking like an atom, too fast for me to catch. I've been kissed by women before. I've also kissed my fair share, so why does this feel so different?

Like I was pretending all those other times, and this is my first taste of the real thing? With her arms wrapped secure around my neck and my arms lassoed tight around her waist, it's like we're trying to get inside of each other through our torsos...

My body locks around her, squeezing her so tight to me, she'll pull away gasping before long. As for me, I would happily never breathe again if her kiss were there to entice me into suffocation.

I'm semi-frozen, stalled between the overwhelming desire to devour her with my mouth, hypnotized by the pleasure of it, and bewitched by the heady, deeply satisfying scenario I've found myself in.

This woman wants me after all...

Despite our prickly beginnings, Nora's infected with the same fever that has a hold on me. Deep, dark possessive pride crackles and dances within me like sweet bonfire flames. On the inside, I'm grinning ear to ear, like a cartoon wolf headed for a picnic.

The pettiest part of me wants to stand here and measure her lust. Let her take the lead and show me with that pretty mouth just how much she wants this.

After all, we've only just met. She's dealing with tragedy and a mystery on top. Wanting me can't be part of any plan.

No, for her, it must be real.

This hot, searching kiss of hers must come from some hidden well of desire deep inside her. And I want to drink from it, every single drop.

But stronger than any pettiness or yearning for dominance in the depths of my soul is the animal, roaring and thrashing wildly in my chest.

I want Eleanora Di Rienzo madly. *Horribly.*

So badly that restraint hurts me, now that I know she wants me even a little.

I want her more than I've had the strength to admit to myself up until this point, and now that she's in my arms, the floodgates have exploded open, unable to hold back the high monsoon waters of my carnal greed.

Hot blood courses through me, pumping hard as I open my mouth against hers, daring to deepen her incendiary kiss.

I taste her tender mouth, sliding my tongue against hers.

The sensation wakes my dick up faster than the speed of light.

Our tongues lap at each other, creating a heat exchange that threatens to melt away all of my remaining resolve. The more I get of her sensuous mouth, the more my hunger for it multiplies, my appetite expanding like water claiming paper.

Against her back, one of my hands makes a fist around the fabric of her shirt. The other rises to the back of her skull and into her soft, luscious waves, my fingers plunge like Olympic divers.

She follows my lead, her strong, lithe fingers raking through my hair then gripping the nape of my neck in a way that makes me thirst for the sensation of her fingers, dragging down my back. Nora intoxicates me like this for several minutes, tangling her mouth with mine, pressing her heated body against me with all her might.

Later, when she breaks the kiss to fix her crazed eyes on mine, panting at me in surprise, I can only mirror her blank, flushed expression. Breathing hard, I hold her here, preventing her from moving even a centimeter away from this heat we've made, though I can see her flight reflex twinkling at me with the light bouncing in her amber-eyed stare.

"I..." Her breathless voice arouses me all over again. "I'm sorry, I...got carried away. I just wanted to thank you."

Her eyes fall to my mouth. I feel her fingers unlocking from around my neck, as though she plans to let me go.

"Thank me for what?" I squeeze her a little tighter, which brings her eyes right back to mine.

"You came with me today, protected me from those guys, and you even..." Her sentence trails off, her eyelids drooping low.

"Is this how you thank every man who does you a favor?"

She shakes her head no. "I've never thanked anyone like this before."

A possessive intensity mows me down inside. My fingers tense around her body. "So this is something special you've done for me?"

Nora mottles her lips together, like she's too embarrassed to reply.

Shaking her head again and squeezing her eyes shut, she brings her hands to my shoulders, like she means to push me back. "You probably have a wife or a girlfriend or something. I shouldn't have..."

"I'm not married." I nudge her mouth with mine. "And I don't have a girlfriend."

And I am most definitely going to hell for *this*.

Anunziata's on another planet, she's so far from my mind right now.

So what if I have an arranged fiancée?

It's not my fault. Nora has one too, and neither of them offer us what she and I have just experienced together.

If we had this kind of chemistry with the people our families picked out for us, Nora and I wouldn't be in this compromising position, contemplating another meeting of our tongues.

"You don't?" Nora's eyebrows raise a little and so does her pretty little voice.

What I don't say is that it probably wouldn't matter if I had a wife *and* a girlfriend. Nothing would make me strong enough to resist what I feel about Nora in this moment.

That's perhaps the most damning part of all.

Guilt thunders through me, remorse stabbing into my conscience with a pitchfork. Just because I'm going to hell doesn't mean Nora is. What the fuck am I doing, trying to corrupt her like this?

I shake my head no, and even though it kills me, I also begin to release her.

She won't take her eyes off mine, something like hope mixed in with her beautiful features. *God, I want her so bad.*

"No one's ever kissed me like that," she whispers, gazing at my mouth again.

Dark, possessive fire rips through me, overtaking every ounce of my better judgment. The last of my restraint snaps.

"Oh, damn it all." I pounce on her, a growl barreling up my

throat. A breathy gasp of surprise escapes her as my mouth gloms onto hers, ravenous and demanding.

With my hands, I grab her rough around the waist, ripping her against my body as I step between her legs, forcing us backwards.

I drive our shuffling bodies, a tangle of eager mouths, hands, and arms, until we collide with the desk, Nora bracing against it and me, hunching over her, extracting savage kisses from her open, moaning mouth.

You're mine now. **All mine.**

I tell her with my fingertips, digging my teeth into her delicate neck. Murmurs and gasps of pleasure echo through this small room, setting new fires in my already burning blood.

Fuck, it's over now.

There's no way I'll be able to hold back the deluge of desire gushing through me.

My rough hands grope her thighs urgently, squeezing them, stroking up and down the length of them, pulling them apart around my waist, so I can feel the heat between them against my stiff cock.

She's got me hard as a telephone pole, just from her hot, giving mouth and her hands grabbing my chest and pressing into my shoulders.

My hands skate up over her midsection and under her white shirt. She gasps against my lips the second we make skin to skin contact, my hand on her soft, smooth midriff.

The fabric of her top sits ruffled against my forearms while I work my fingers under the cloth lining of the bra she's wearing, and then her perfect breasts are in my hands, like some kind of supple, sexy dough.

Her nipples harden against my hot palms, and I want to suck them into my mouth so bad, I'm probably drooling. I want to knead them into submission until she's panting, wild-eyed and fixated on nothing and no one but me, ever again.

Gallons of possessive lust swirl through my system, inebriating me. This woman is a feast for every single one of my senses, and the more of her I get, the more of her I *crave*.

But then, I open my eyes.

I see her, flushed and hazy with heat, her legs open, her top half in disarray. From the waist up, I've got her nearly naked on her father's desk.

Ans suddenly, it's too much.

Knowing that my brakes are going to bust, and any second I'm going to tear her clothes off and fuck her right here, on the desk of a man I helped kill, the man she loved and admired most?

Guilt collides with my conscience like a 16-wheeler.

For all the unspeakable things I've done in my twenty years as an enforcer, I know I'm already going to hell. But I'm not so bad a man as *this*.

I will not ravish a woman I've betrayed in her father's office.

Nora opens her eyes when I freeze. The lust shimmering in her amber eyes simmers down to earnest confusion. My mouth hangs open, but I don't know what excuse to give her.

And I don't even get the chance to try.

Into our breathless quiet, a disco funk ringtone spurts to life, filling this small room with Walter Murphy's *A Fifth of Beethoven*.

Somehow, it's ominous.

Nora's eyes widen like a wave of horror's just washed over her.

I release her at once, unhanding her breasts, gingerly removing my palms from her body and stepping back, despite the crushing disappointment that befalls the lust-bitten beast, still snarling inside me.

"Shit." Nora stands up from her father's desk, hurriedly smoothing her shirt down. "That's my alarm."

Crossing the room to the chairs in the center, she grabs her small purse off one and retrieves her phone. Whatever she sees on her screen brings even more horror to her face.

"What is it?" My voice sounds thick and strange.

"We've got to go. *Now*." She holds up her screen, the display reads four pm. "Everyone thinks I spent all day at a spa in Manhattan, and the place closes at five. If I don't get back there in time, my security detail is going to find out I snuck off."

Nora's in the same boat as I am, spending time with me that no one else can know about. I completely understand.

It's honestly perfect timing. If I don't get this woman away from me as soon as humanly possible, I'm going to do things to her with my cock. If not for my deeply ingrained Catholic guilt, I'd have started already.

I'd be doing right now...

God, I want her.

"Let's get out of here." The words are almost a cough. Traffic was murder coming this way. I only hope a bit of crazy reckless driving will get her back in time. "Good thing you set an alarm."

Nora shakes her head as we exit her father's secret office and lock it behind us. "It may already be too late."

"Not if we hurry."

I race down the steps ahead of her. Just standing too close feels dangerous now.

Now that I know what happens when we touch.

Attraction and desire run wild inside me, as we speed-walk back the way we came, hurrying down the long checkered hallway. One kiss got us carried the fuck away, almost. *How is that possible?*

I've had quite a few sexual encounters up until this point, but none that I wasn't fully in control of. None that I could not have detangled myself from at any moment, if duty called.

Meanwhile, the only reason I am finding my way through the underbelly of a gorgeous old movie theater with this stunning woman and not actively hammering her to a desk is because of God. My restraint up there was toast.

Nothing would have stopped me. Nothing could have stopped me.

Divine intervention is the only explanation.

Her kiss thinned my self-control down to fucking *nothing*.

No woman alive can say the same.

Gruff, horrified at myself, and so desperate for more, it's embarrassing, I throw myself into driving, barely allowing myself so much as a glance in Nora's direction as we speed back into the heart of Manhattan.

All the way back into the city, one question wallpapers my mind: *What the fuck was that crazy makeout about?*

The energy between us is hot and charged now, scorched almost, like the earth after lighting strikes.

Jesus, is this what people call sexual tension? I had no idea anything so awkward and uncomfortable really existed.

I almost miss it when Nora points out a curb.

"Over there is good." Her voice draws my eyes to her face, as I dive against the curb and stamp the brakes.

What do I say now? I'm fighting everything inside me that wants to kiss her goodbye, especially since I don't know when or if we'll see each other again.

Another thing I'm unsure of?

How I'm ever going to hurt this woman, now that my body wants hers this much.

CHAPTER 12

Nora

HEART CLAMORING IN MY CHEST, I race back to the spa on foot, spurred partially by the butterflies raving through my body after that kiss...

I can't stop experiencing it in my mind.

A horn screams past, as I dart out into traffic without a care.

I'm going to get hit by a car thinking about that kiss.

What the hell is wrong with me?

Why'd I do it in the first place?

I didn't give it a single thought. My body acted on its own. And it felt so... So...

Good is an insult to how incredible it felt.

Just yesterday, I was ready to end my life. And today I learn I've never experienced real pleasure before. Not like that.

My world has been on its side from the moment I got Dad's

message from beyond the grave, but after my day with Rocco, everything's shifted all over again.

Now, my world is completely upside down.

I'm almost back to the Faraday Spa and Salon. The business park stretches high into the blue sky above me, I'm just steps from the west entrance—

Out of nowhere, a big coarse hand clamps around my forearm, wrenching me back until I've turned to face my attacker.

I damn near scream bloody murder, right here in broad daylight.

Like an ice cube down my shirt, fear streaks down my spine.

"Hello..." I gulp, staring straight into the scowling face of Jackson Giamatta.

The head of my security detail.

To say that he looks displeased would be a very white lie.

He doesn't even address me, he's so furious. Instead, he grumbles into his earpiece. "I've got her. Release the spa personnel. We're headed back to the landing."

Release the spa personnel? Oh God.

"Please tell me you didn't hurt anyone."

"The Faraday closed at two o'clock today. They had a private event." Jackson grits out the words. "You were nowhere to be found. We did what we had to do."

Shit. Due to unforeseen circumstances, I misjudged the timing, and the spa closed hours before I expected it would. Which means Jackson and the others know I pulled a fast one on them.

Without another word, Jackson turns on his heel and proceeds to drag me down the block with one hand, while pulling out his cellphone with the other. He dials someone and holds it to his ear.

Oh no, he's phoning the estate. Has to be. "Yeah, get me Frankie."

He's going to report me to Gianfrancesco?!

Double shit.

"Yes, sir. We found her. She'll be home within the hour."

No, no, no. My heart bangs at my ribs. This is bad. So very bad.

At the curb, a blacked-out luxury SUV pulls to a halt. Jackson rips open the back door and all but tosses me inside, slamming it shut behind me.

Whoever's driving engages the locks, to stave off any thoughts of me diving out into traffic. *God damn it.*

The SUV accelerates away from the curb and I'm left alone in this XXL backseat to contemplate my fate.

The horrible thing is that…if I'd known it was already too late, I would have tried to spend more time with Rocco. To think I broke up our steamy montage just turn myself over to a bunch of jailers.

But was I really the one to break it up?

A few droplets of doubt drip from my mind.

Rocco was all over me. Having his big hot hands all over my chest…I melt a little against the plush leather seat I'm strapped to. I can feel the ghost of his touch on me, even now… But what was that at the end?

He stopped. He pulled back. He was staring at me with this tortured look on his face. I could tell he was about to say something, but he didn't get the chance.

I should have asked him about it on the car ride back here. The thought crossed my mind more than once, but I couldn't get myself to open my mouth. Not when I was free-falling through the aftermath of his kiss.

Slapping my hands over my reddening face, I shake my head hard. He's miles away and still, I'm entranced by him.

God, I feel jealous of every woman that's ever touched him.

How could anything make me feel so good? Let alone one man I just met and barely know? Nothing about it makes sense.

No, I don't have all the romantic or sexual experience in the word, but even I know, it's not supposed to be like *that*. Not with a relative stranger. Not with someone who doesn't mean anything to you or vice versa.

Rocco held me and touched me, affirmed my life somehow, just with his mouth and his hands. After spending weeks detaching from the idea of being alive, connecting with him like that was... out of this world. It's like he stuck my feet on the ground, firmly planted me back in the earth I was ready to leave.

I'm actually shocked how much everything's changed for me in just twenty-four hours. Because of him. If I had gotten my way, I'd be dead and gone right now, and instead...

Well, I'm still dead. When Frankie's done with me for duping my guards, who knows what I'll be? Thoughts of Rocco are pushed off by my impending dread, as the SUV transports me back to the Dalla Porta estate to face the fucking music.

This is so awful.

Just because I'm his fiancée, people report to him about my whereabouts, like I'm a child under his supervision? I want to barf from the wretched taste of toxic masculinity, all over this scenario.

The tension in my throat only tightens as we near the outskirts of the Dalla Porta's enclave in the center of the city. We turn onto the main block, and other security personnel dressed in street clothes take notice of us, rolling down the road. The window's are tinted pitch black, but all of them watch us drive past like they know exactly who's inside.

They probably do.

God only knows how many of them were deployed to search the city for me once my personal detail realized I was missing.

So this is what it feels like when an audience gathers to watch someone be put to death. My fingers squeeze the cross around my neck, while I send up prayers that I'll survive Frankie's wrath.

I've never faced it before. I've never had to answer to this man about anything in my life. My father was always here to protect me from it, but now...

Hot tears prick at the back of my eyes.

I snuck out to find out what happened to Dad, but all I found was more questions and more reasons to stick around for this horrible time in my life. That's all I have to show for whatever confrontation I'm about to be thrust into.

All too soon, the SUV stops at the curb in front of the Dalla Porta mansion, tall and imposing between the buildings on either side.

I'm in so much trouble, the guards don't even let me walk into the house by myself. One of them cuffs his big meaty hand around my left bicep, and two more crowd me, one in front, one on my right, escorting me up the front steps and straight upstairs.

Not to my own suite, which for the first time, I desperately long to hide in, but to Gianfrancesco's all the way on the fifth floor of this enormous mansion.

The security guards don't even give me the courtesy of a moment to collect myself before knocking on Gianfrancesco's door. They just haul me straight in, where the man himself is waiting in the center of his sprawling quarters on a brown patterned Persion rug, with his back turned to me.

His suite is luxury from top to bottom. Sixteen-foot ceilings. A chandelier lights up the whole floor plan, encrusted with jewels and crystals. There are two vanities on either side of the painted-black double doors we've just come through, one full length so he can admire himself, and the other a half-length, probably so he can get a better look at his oversized head.

The whole place is bedecked in black or brown wood and leather with royal red upholstery and accents everywhere else. It matches the rest of this horrid house. But right now, the furnishings only remind me of blood and my desperate hope that he doesn't plan to spill any of mine.

"Leave us." Gianfrancesco's commanding voice carries through the room, and the bodyguards boxing me in disperse at once.

In seconds, I'm alone in the den of the beast I've been ordered to marry.

All I can do is stand there in silence, aching to flee.

"*Well?*" My fiancé's menacing voice, edged with ire, makes me flinch. "What have you to say for yourself?"

"I h-hope you've had a pleasant day?"

Gianfrancesco whips around in my direction, a vein standing against his forehead as he glowers at me with one green eye, one dark. "You're lucky they called me, and not my father."

I shiver at the thought, but try for a little smile. "Why's that?"

"I have a better sense of humor."

Swallowing down a lump of fear, I inch backward toward the door and hope he doesn't notice.

"Where were you?" He growls.

Ah yes, the question of the hour. I had at least thirty minutes on the car ride back here, but I didn't spend one second of it thinking about how I would answer this very obvious question. *Way to go, Nora.*

"Out. In the city." My eyes flick away, a nervous habit. "Exploring."

"*Alone?*"

Eep. My heart flops, Rocco's face flashing in my mind. But I manage to stay calm enough that I nod, a plausible story thankfully taking shape on my tongue.

"I wanted a day to myself." Gathering my courage, I meet his gaze again. "Things have been so busy with the wedding preparations, I just wanted some—"

"What did you do?" He demands taking a heavy step toward me. "Where did you go?"

My jaw clenches.

I'm supposed to be appeasing him right now, I know that.

I'm in the wrong, and I've been caught out.

But God, he pisses me off, acting like he's entitled to know anything about me that he wishes to know.

"What does that matter?" I ask carefully.

"*It matters if I say it does,*" he snaps at me, barely hiding the snarl in his throat. "Now tell me, Nora."

"No." I say, surprising us both. "I'm not your prisoner."

Gianfrancesco's eyebrows rise high, and then lower down into an even deeper frown. I've made him even angrier.

This is going just wonderful.

"You're right." He sneers at me. "You're not my prisoner. You're my *property*. There's a difference."

My mouth drops open, I'm so insulted. Bright hot sparks of anger glisten beneath my skin. "I don't belong to anyone. Least of all *you*," I snap back. "No matter what you may *think*, if we can even call it that."

I've done it now.

Gianfrancesco marches straight up to me, invading my personal space the way I *love* so much. Any other day I would have backed up to the door, but now that he's pissed me off, I'm just mad enough to stand my ground, even when he's close enough to headbutt me.

"I hope you enjoyed your day on the town, Nora, because you aren't going to get another one," he snaps. "I forbid you to leave the estate without my express permission and an escort of my choosing. *Until further notice.*"

Shock spreads my features wide, red-hot ire melting down my ribs.

Just who the fuck does this overgrown brat think he is?!

"*You're grounding me?*" I can barely breathe, I'm so angry.

"Looks that way." Gianfrancesco smiles, like he's enjoying the rage eating me up from head to toe. With an extra smirk, he nods his chin toward the door behind me. "You're dismissed."

I storm out of his room without a moment's delay. Mostly to get away from that oppressive stench he calls a cologne.

In the freedom of the fifth floor hallway, I fume. Put me in a fireplace and I'd keep this mansion warm for the winter.

How dare he...

Why did I try to kill myself when killing him is obviously the answer?

I march downstairs to the fourth floor and stamp all the way to my bedroom.

All I can do is pace the floor, I'm so pissed.

He's forbidden me from leaving the estate without his consent?

I let out a loud, exasperated groan, and then toss myself into bed.

It's not until I've stewed about it for several hours, turned out all the lights and laid myself into an angry rest that I realize that his stupid would-be royal decree isn't even the worst part.

The worst part is that taking away my freedom means I won't be able to investigate my father's death or... see Rocco again.

Desperation and disappointed angst boil me alive.

How did these two things become the most important pursuits in my life overnight?

All I know is that I'm in a bind.

The straight-jacket, no-escape kind.

What the hell am I going to do now?

CHAPTER 13

Rocco

"Forgive me, father, for I have sinned."

"What have you to confess?"

"I… have kissed a woman." *A woman I've been ordered to abduct.* "An engaged woman."

"Against her will?"

"No, she started it." I clear my throat because I sound like an asshole. "I mean, she kissed me first."

"Under what circumstances did this contact take place?" Father Thomas's voice is worn through with age, but warm. He sounds the way a father should, I've always thought. It's not like I can remember my own.

"It was earlier this evening…" My memory caresses the image of her face. "She was crying at first. She's been grieving the loss of her father the past two weeks."

"Were you offering comfort to her?"

I close my fists tight, all my muscles tensing up in this dark confessional stall, built for a man about three sizes smaller than myself.

"Yes," I answer with difficulty. Offering someone comfort isn't a bad thing, but it is when you're a bad person. Like I am. "But I still shouldn't have allowed myself to get carried away. She probably only did it to thank me."

"What was she thanking you for?"

I shrug, exhaling hard. "I saved her life, I guess."

"When did this happen?"

"Last night, I pulled her off a ledge, and this afternoon some men came after her, so I shot them all and poisoned one." I wince on the inside. "I'm not proud of it."

A moment passes while Father Thomas soaks up my sins of late. "Have you told anyone about these events?"

"My employer knows about last night." I swallow hard. "No one knows about this afternoon. Or the kiss."

"Salvation is possible through repentance, prayer, and supplication, Rocco. You know this."

"I know."

Father Thomas gives me the usual diagnosis he gives when I come in and tell him that I've murdered some folks. A hundred Hail-Mary's, and the heavy suggestion that I turn myself over to the police, and find a new profession.

And at the end, he suggests I try to save a life, for every life I've robbed.

After I've thanked him for his time, I roam the dark, empty pews of Saint Mary's. I'm usually on my own when I come at this time of night. Which is perfect. There's no one to distract me when I kneel down and pray to God.

What have I done?

Involving myself with a target?

The lust I bear Eleanora Di Rienzo cannot be ignored, but neither can the truth. Pursuing her means going against the

Balboni family, and precious few people live to tell the tale of that. Not even Jaco's irrational approval of me would survive defiance of this magnitude.

And Nora...if she finds out who I am and what I've been an accessory to, she'll sic the full force of her fiancé and his family on me. It'll be a race to find out who can destroy me first. The Balboni or the Dalla Porta.

I won't be able to outrun them both.

But the idea of hurting Nora gets more impossible by the second.

I exhale hard, rising from my place of prayer.

There's only one place where guilt this heavy finally eases off my shoulders. And it's where I usually go after a rough day at work.

After I've had to kill some people.

Tanya's.

In about half an hour, I've dragged my sorry ass all the way across town to the Covered By Grace Veterinary Hospital. It's a small two story building on the east side of Manhattan with a blue awning out front illustrated with a napping dog and kitten, cuddled under an umbrella.

They're one of the few vet hospitals in the city that are open twenty-four hours, and the place is run by a pair of sisters, Grace and Tanya Greer. Grace is in her early seventies and covers the hospital during the day. Tanya, her much younger sister, is in her fifties and works the night shift.

Tanya's something like an older sister to me.

I breeze up the steps and through the front door, that poignant clinical hospital smell colliding with the odor of animals, all of it muted under the waiting room air freshener.

When I first started coming here, I found it off-putting. But now it puts me at ease.

Especially when an old friend rises from his dog bed and lumbers over to me, balancing on his hind legs to tell me hello.

I scratch behind his soft, expressive ears. "You look old as hell."

He barks, as if to say, *Back at you.*

"I hope that comment was directed at Moon." Tanya lays the magazine she's reading flat on the check-in desk in front of her, while I scrub Moon's shaggy head, his tail wagging nonstop.

"What are you doing up here?" I give her half a smile.

"Kiki has the night off." Tanya shrugs one shoulder.

Her usual night-receptionist comes to mind, a perky someone in her early thirties, who's usually wearing lavender scrubs and a suggestive smile.

At least, while I'm around.

"Good for Kiki."

"She'll be sorry she missed you." Tanya's eyebrows hop in that annoying way. "She does so enjoy your visits."

"Now, I remember why I usually come in the back door."

"Ha ha." Tanya ropes her sandy-blond hair up into a ponytail. "Now I remember why you usually can't get a date."

The sensation of Nora's open mouth on mine charges through my brain. I have to run a rough hand through my hair just to comb that insanely hot memory right out of my head. I swallow back a gulp of lust, and force myself to breathe. "Please give me something to do."

"Hard day at the office?" She fixes me with a knowing, caring brown-eyed stare.

One reason she and I get along so well is because we both have the kind of jobs where death constitutes a hard day at the office.

I nod.

"Come on back." She whistles at Moon and he trots her way. I follow.

Tanya and I met years ago after I came across an injured stray dog, lost in Manhattan. A scruffy little mutt with brown and black fur. I couldn't take care of him, but I needed to find someone who could, and Covered by Grace was open.

Tanya had to do emergency surgery to save the little guy's life, but she worked a miracle, as she often does, and he lived. I named him Moon, she ended up adopting him, and he's been the hospital's unofficial mascot—and guardian, as I like to think of him—ever since.

We follow Tanya into the back area of the hospital. She opens her office door, so Mutt can go inside and get comfortable on his *other* bed. It's bigger and cushier than the rest. This is where he stays when Tanya has work-work to do, the kind he can't be lumbering about for.

She tosses him a bone and he wastes no time, happily gnawing away as she closes the door. Her office has two enormous rectangular windows in it on opposite walls, one of them that faces the operating room and the other that faces the shelter area of the hospital, so she can keep an eye on Moon and he can watch her work.

Tanya and I head into the shelter room, where animals recover from surgery, wait for their owners to pick them up, or await adoption.

"Louie here could use some love." Tanya nods toward a small Pitbull with bandages around his left and right front legs. "He got out of surgery early this morning."

"On it." I climb out of my coat and toss it on a nearby bench, before settling myself on the floor, unlocking Louie's cage and bringing the sleepy fella into my lap, careful of his sore front legs. He settles easily into my lap and closes his eyes, soon after I've begun petting him.

Most of the time, I spend my nights off here, decompressing.

Truthfully, I come here to make sure I'm still human.

Dogs are excellent judges of character, and if dogs ever stopped liking me, I'd know for sure I'd completely lost my soul.

"You with your magic hands." Tanya leans in the doorframe of the shelter area, giving me a satisfied look.

Meanwhile, her words trigger another memory, this time of my hands digging into Nora's perfect thighs... My cock stirs beneath the hem of my pants.

Jesus Christ.

Thankfully, Tanya leaves me be.

Another reason we get along is because she's great at recognizing when I need some time by myself. And tonight, I definitely need that.

I can't stop thinking about the kiss. About Nora.

No woman's ever had this effect on me before. I'm beyond my depths, floating out in the open ocean, miles away from the shores of my comfort zone.

I'm agitated.

Restless.

Kidnapping her for Vito is the farthest thing from my mind.

When I'm nothing thinking about the fire-starting power of Nora's touch, I'm thinking about her father's death and that secret office of his that we were able to find.

Messages from beyond the grave. Keys and directions hidden in a wall.

A secret room in an old movie theater.

I'd expect smoke and mirrors from the longtime spymaster of the Dalla Porta, but even I'm awed. The man was clearly formidable.

So much so that it doesn't seem real that Vito with his bean-sized brain could have conceived of a way to kill the man...I just can't square it.

I didn't want to say too much to Nora while we were in Orazio's office. I was so fascinated by everything we found there, I might have blown my cover if I'd allowed myself to say everything I was thinking.

But one thing was clear as daylight.

Orazio Di Rienzo was definitely tracking the movement of something. I'm sure about that. The maps on his wall, the threads, the notecards with dates, start locations, ending locations... He was definitely tracking, all right. The old fashioned way too. He was working on something on his own, instead of using the Dalla Porta's databases or technology. Which he easily could have done.

It means that whatever he's searching for is completely off the grid.

What could be so well hidden from a man with so much power and influence?

And more importantly, what could he have been up to that Jaco and Vito determined themselves to take him out? I'm not buying that they were motivated by a general, nonspecific hatred for the Dalla Porta. My gut tells me this runs deeper than a decades-old blood feud.

This cannot be categorized as a tit-for-tat either.

I'd bet my life on it.

Orazio sent his daughter clues from beyond the grave. This has to be bigger than a rivalry between families. Her father must have been investigating a secret. Something Vito and the others need to stay buried.

But what?

What could be so important?

Later that evening, after I comfort the animals in recovery and shoot the shit with Tanya for an hour or so, I return to the Balboni warehouse. I park my car in the garage and climb up the steps to the lofty warehouse-style first floor—

A bone-shattering roar shakes the walls.

The surprise sound drops my body into high alert. I duck into the shadows, flattening myself against the wall beneath the stair-case that leads up to the second and third floors, hand flying to my gun.

On the far side of the room, the big metal doors that punctuate the foyer burst open, slamming straight into the soldiers behind them on guard duty. The two of them go down, as Pasqual Pezzullo thunders into the place in a murderous rage.

"*WHERE IS HE?*" Pasqual erupts like a frothing, angry volcano.

His flat wide face always reminded me of a bulldog. Especially when he's like this, practically foaming at the mouth. With one meaty hand, Pasqual hauls one of the Balboni soldiers up off the ground, while a few others—one of whom is definitely shot in the arm—storm through the doors after Pasqual.

"Who?" The soldier in Pasqual's grip asks before catching a fist to the face.

"*VITO!*" He explodes, his rough, ragged voice bounding through the place.

I've never heard someone bellow Vito's name like that before. Must be important.

Still, I don't move an inch.

And it turns out, I don't have to. Descending the steps above my head with a leisurely gait is Vito himself.

Unsurprising.

People in Norway probably heard that yell.

"Pasqual." Vito's voice is a little looser than usual. Probably means he's on his second bottle of whiskey for the evening. "You storm in here? It's the middle of the night—"

"I do you a favor, *and you get my son killed?!*" Pasqual fires off like a canon.

I cannot hide my surprise.

"Disperse." Vito snaps his fingers, and the Balboni soldiers, wounded and all, shuffle off in their different directions.

Not a single one notices me, and Vito doesn't either, as he swaggers down the rest of the stairs, amazingly unafraid of the seething, vengeful father on the other end of the room.

"Now, what's this all about?" Vito asks the moment he thinks the pair of them are alone. "What's going on with Gino?"

"I'll tell you what's going on, you fuckface!" Pasqual slaps his fat hand around Vito's throat. Vito's fingers jump to Pasqual's forearm, prying helplessly at his release.

My God, I don't have any popcorn.

"*An easy job*, you said." He seethes, squeezing Vito harder.

"Good practice for up and coming enforcers." Pasqual spits the words, hopefully spattering Vito's dumb face with his tepid saliva. *"Watch an alley for me, that's all there is to it."*

"What are you saying happened?" Vito chokes out.

"I'm saying my son and four of his friends were murdered today watching your lousy, godforsaken back, now you're going to *pay.*"

As enjoyable as this dinner theater is, I'm not paying attention anymore.

Lights keep clicking on inside my head, too many of them and shining too brightly for me to overlook.

In the span of thirty seconds, it seems I've stumbled upon a few very important pieces of information.

Number one. Vito Balboni is the one who ordered those Pezzullo soldiers to watch the alleyway where Nora was ambushed earlier today.

And number two. Turns out one of the men I put down in the ensuing standoff was the son of the Pezzullo clan's capo.

Whoops.

Before I can glean anymore from their conversation, Jaco arrives. The soldiers Vito sent off must have alerted him.

Jaco, flanked by Fiero, and quite a few more Balboni soldiers enter the room then and usher Pasqual and a slightly-shaken Vito into the conference room at the end of the hall, leaving me alone, unnoticed, still perched beneath the stairs.

Once they've all gone, I remove myself from my hiding place and race up the stairs to the upper floors, eager to get to the privacy of my suite so I can think.

I'm intrigued by all I've overheard.

How could I not be?

I knew the Pezzullos were allied with the Balbonis, but I had no idea they were watching that alley at Vito's request.

Why?

Why did Vito request it? Why did the Pezzullos agree?

I don't have the answers, but the more I think about it, the more I begin to realize that the death of Orazio Di Rienzo must have more significance than I ever thought.

Why else would Vito go out of his way to hire security for a dead man's hangout?

Doesn't make any sense.

Not unless he's trying to keep more than bones buried...

CHAPTER 14

Nora

AFTER MY GIANFRANCESCO-DIRECTED rage thoroughly exhausts me, I fall into slumber and spend the rest of the night drowning in dreams of Rocco's touch. Tossing, turning, tangling myself in my covers, remembering his mouth and his hands, all the heaven I may never have again until the horrible scrape of old curtain rings against an even older rod claws through my heated slumber.

Achingly bright midday sunlight stabs my closed eyelids, forcing me to scrunch them further closed in discomfort.

"Get up this instant." The unfamiliar razor's edge of my mother's voice cuts through my stupor in seconds.

My eyes peel back and there she is, hands on her hips staring daggers at me from one side of my bed.

"Mama?"

"You heard me." With an angry hand, she snatches a fistful of my covers and whips them back, leaving me cold and exposed in my pajamas. *"Den.* Now."

She marches out of my bedroom through the adjoining suite door that leads to our little living room, leaving me alarmed and interrupted in her absence.

What's going on? Why's she so upset?

I climb out of bed, yawning, and catch a glimpse of the bird's nest on top of my head. *What if she's not the only one waiting for me out there?*

Quickly, I wrestle my hair into a top-knot and shrug on my bathrobe. Then, I pad with bare feet after her into the den, where she stands on the carpet, furious and beyond speech.

I scratch my fuzzy head, deja vu tingling low on my spine.

She looks shaken, wearing a dress I've never seen before. It's not the kind of dress she would have picked on her own. She hates form-fitting clothing. For a moment, she paces one-way before turning back to me, and for just a moment, I notice her zipper's not all the way up in the back. Like she was in the middle of getting dressed to leave.

Even her hair is more disheveled than usual.

It's clear she's angry, but the deep, untouchable despair on her face is still there. Where it's been every single moment since the news came.

"Mama?" I finally venture, when she still hasn't come out with it yet. "What is it? What's wrong?"

She folds her arms tight across her slender chest. "I've just learned from Ciro that you're forbidden from leaving the house."

Shit. Fuck. Damn.

"Uh…"

"Frankie gave the order because you snuck out yesterday?" She demands, her voice teetering up an octave. "You lied to each and everyone of us at breakfast, including Saba, the man who makes our lives possible, and ran off on your own?"

"Mama, I just—"

"What the hell were you thinking?!" She shrieks.

Actually shrieks, throwing her arms up to the sky.

My heart clangs around in my chest, sorrow and embarrassment and discomfort tumbling around too. I don't know what to say.

All my life, my mother has been on my side. But since Dad died, I've been on my own. I'm so unused to being on opposing sides that I don't even know how to handle this right now, her being mad at me.

Especially over something like this.

"Would you have let me go if I said I needed a day to myself?" I throw the question at her, tears brimming in my sleepy eyes.

"Of course not!" She paces toward the door to our suite, and then whips back once again. "You're not a teenager anymore, Eleanora. You're twenty-five years old. You've got to be smarter than this. Didn't I raise you to be smarter than this?"

Hurt rams into me, shocked tears rolling down my cheeks. "What's that supposed to mean?"

"It means there are *rules*, Nora! And you're too old not to know what they are."

"Oh, all of sudden, it matters what they think?" I throw my arm aside, like the Calzavarra family is standing right here in the room. "Since when have you bowed to them over nonsense like this?"

My mother shakes her head. Actually, her whole frame is shaking. "Watch your mouth. Don't speak about them that way—"

"Why not? You always have!" I want to scream.

"*Watch your mouth*, I said!" She shouts back at me, as if to silence me forever. "The Calzavarra family is the most powerful cosa nostra in this city. We are not going to find ourselves on their bad side because you need a day to yourself. Understand me?"

"Who are you?" My voice is a trembling whisper. "All this hysterical Dalla Porta worship... How can you take their side? I'm your daughter!"

"No, you're not!" She cuts me again with words she's never said before. "Not anymore, Nora. You're not mine anymore…"

My heart breaks.

Just when I thought it couldn't be shattered any more.

My own mother is breathless, tears pouring fresh down her face.

"You're a Calzavarra daughter now," she warbles through angry tears. "You became one the moment the wedding date was set. Understand? It's not about what I think. It's not about picking sides. There are no *sides*. There's only one. And we're both on it now, whether we want to be or not."

"Well, you're not my mother anymore." My expression mottles with rage. "So I don't have to listen to *you*."

I can't believe I've said such ugly words to the woman who raised me. I'm breaking my own heart, this is such an awful moment.

"Eleanora—"

"I don't even recognize you anymore." I cut her off, my own voice rising above the wobble in my throat. "You have never kowtowed to those people out there. Not once in my life. What the hell happened to you? I don't get it. I don't understand how Dad's death could have changed you so entirely."

This hollow, obedient, subservient creature my mother's become is completely foreign to me. In every way.

"Why are you so afraid of them?!" I shout at her in disbelief.

Roaring back at me, her wet eyes sharp as butcher's knives, my mother's voice becomes a low growl. *"You have no idea what they're capable of."*

"Dad's not going to let anything happen to us!" I burst.

But then silence falls between us.

I realize now that I've betrayed my own weakness and proven my mother's horrible point all at once. And at the same time, I feel the full force of it.

Just how big a void my father left…

All this time, I really did think my family and I were untouchable so long as Dad was around, and now? Without him?

Maybe, it really is as my mother says.

"I am only going to say this once." My mother's voice stabilizes, as she swipes an angry hand across her eyes. "So get it through your head here and now."

Inside, I brace for more pain. I know whatever she has to say is going to hurt even worse than everything we've said in the past few minutes.

"Your father is gone." She swallows hard. "Without him, we are castoffs in the Dalla Porta mafia. Our survival now depends on the charity and good opinion of the Calzavarra family." Her expression darkens. "Especially Ciro. Even if it makes us subject to his every whim…"

"No, Mama." Now, I'm begging. "There has to be another way. Let's go abroad again. We'll stay with Dad's family, like we did when Nico and I were young. We'll—"

"There is no other way." The finality in her tone pulverizes me. "There will be no going abroad. We will stay here under the Calzavarra's roof, and carry ourselves as well-mannered guests. In two week's time, you will marry Gianfrancesco to secure our futures. And until then, you will not step foot outside this house unless I am with you and we're attending to preparations for your wedding. Is that clear?"

I can't speak, I'm so depressed and horrified by this entire conversation.

This discussion was clearly meant to grind down any remaining fight or resistance inside me toward the prospect these people have designed for my life.

To be a bride of the Dalla Porta.

And I would be lying if I said this confrontation with my mother hasn't hurt and humbled me in unexpected ways. But what's also true is that my mother's declaration of the way things are going to be from now on only makes me more determined to discover the truth about Dad's death.

I will escape this family and the path they've laid out for me, one way or another. And before I do that, I want to honor my father's final request.

That's all there is to it.

Deep in my heart, it's simple.

If I can't go out to investigate, then I'll have to start sleuthing from within.

Beginning with Dad's official office on the Dalla Porta estate.

CHAPTER 15

Nora

I LET myself into Dad's old office, careful not to trigger the silent alarm, or any of the booby traps set up in here. The place is an old gilded age study with an intricate woodworked ceiling, dark hardwood floors, bookshelves on every wall, a large curtained window Dad always kept closed, an imposing desk right in the middle of the circular room, a fireplace behind it, and an antique chandelier strung from above.

The silent alarm is triggered unless you know the security code and where to punch it in—on a small nearly imperceptible keypad on the wall to my left. The booby traps can be deactivated by punching in a second code.

Otherwise, the room sprays ink.

Not kidding. My father was relentless when it came to security. If anyone entered his office without his express permission, they'd set off the silent alarm, which would bring armed guards to the room, and they'd get splashed with ink. The kind that marks your skin for at least a week, showers be damned. It never comes out of clothing.

I like to mark my enemies, Dad once told me. *Makes them easy to track.*

Truthfully, in the weeks since his death, I've avoided coming in here.

Too painful.

I can't count all the times I wandered in to bug him about one thing or another. Or the afternoons I spent lounging in the armchairs by the fireplace, flipping through comic books or old Victorian novels.

All while he sat quietly at that huge desk, reviewing reports, typing on his computer, researching, checking, doublechecking... And he could always feel it when I was staring at him, even if there was no way for him to know it.

When we were young, my mother used to scare us saying, *your dad has eyes everywhere.* He'd see if we didn't eat our vegetables or cheated on a test. Even during the days when my mother, sister and I lived apart from him in Europe for a few years, separated by an ocean.

Before the move, when Nico and I were still tiny, we used lay out on the carpet with our coloring books and toys, playing while he worked. As a teenager, I used to curl up in the seat by the window and do my homework, while he poured over video feeds he had set up all over the city.

I know the man's office by heart, I've been in here so many times...

But I don't allow myself to reminisce too long.

I know I'll cry again, and then I'll just wind up thinking about Rocco. The way he comforted me in Dad's secret office, and the heat that followed.

Rocco and that unfinished kiss...

Intent on staying focused, I try not to be too overwhelmed by the nostalgic scent of my father all over this place, while I look through his things for clues about the matters I discovered yesterday.

That picture of Don Saba, his wife, and three mysterious sons...

If Dad really thought someone other than his enemies was responsible for his death... If it really was someone connected to the Dalla Porta, perhaps it's connected to the secrets of that photograph and the family it depicts.

The one I apparently don't know all that much about...

The same one I'm being forced into.

Well, my father's office is big, and teeming with information, but if I'm looking to uncover a secret, I need to start with the information that's most protected.

I need to check his desk drawers. The ones he keeps locked.

He taught me how to pick locks when I was in middle school, soon after Nico was exiled. A questionable parenting decision, I agree, but it was one of many things he taught me to keep my mind off the heartbreak of being separated from my sister.

Not sure if he knew I'd be using those skills like this one day, but here we are.

I pull my pocket-sized locksmith kit from my pocket, about the size of a smartphone, kneel on the backside of the desk and get to work. It's a complicated lock, but not too complicated for the daughter of Orazio Di Rienzo.

A few minutes of careful work, and the biggest of his locked drawers is open. I'll work my way through all of them if I have to.

If I have to come in here every day for the next two weeks in order to solve this mystery, I will. *Anything for you, Dad.*

The biggest drawer, I soon discover, is full of files, organized alphabetically. Most of them seem to be old business records. But there's one file that's out of place. It doesn't follow the A-Z pattern the others do, and it's been put all the way at the very back of the drawer, as though he didn't want it to be found.

It's thicker than the other files too.

It takes a few tries for me to get my hand around it well enough to haul it out from the depths of the drawer and into the light.

Seating myself in my father's big office chair, I finally have a good look at the file's name. *The Red Years.*

Well, that's not ominous at all...

Sounds like some dark depressing Russian novel from the 1800s...

I open the file and find inside a stack of pages that might as well be a manuscript, there are so many pages and chapter titles.

Typed in a cold official font, like a military report, the first page I touch has another ominous heading at the top...

Scared but adamant, I settle myself deeper into the chair and prepare to read whatever comes after such a gruesome title.

The Beginning of the 40-Year Blood War

In Sicily, circa 1970, the Balboni and Dalla Porta crime families were only two generations into their inception. They soon entered a period of rapid expansion, including their immigration to America, where their business exploits would flourish and live on in cosa nostra history for decades to come.

Jacopo Balboni, Jaco as he was known, was in his late 20s at that time. He was the presumed heir to the Balboni crime family, and when it came time for him to marry, he chose a girl he'd long favored. Rossana Facci, age 17, the only daughter of the Facci crime family, a long time ally of the Balboni.

MY EYES about pop out of my skull.

Rossana Facci! That woman whose photograph I found yesterday, the woman who turns out to be Saba's late wife... She started out as the arranged fiancée of Saba's sworn enemy?

I'm only on paragraph two of this report, and already this hidden history has stunned me. Eager, I keep reading.

The Facci family was all too happy to arrange the match between her and the future don of the Balboni, even though Rossana cared nothing for Jaco and had always despised him. Against her will, the two were engaged.

A few months into their engagement, Jaco forced himself on Rossana.

She ran away into the woods before the wedding to escape the marriage, and days later, she was found hurt, sick, and newly pregnant in the wilderness of the Calzavarra family's land by central members of the Dalla Porta mafia.

Sabatini Calzavarra, in his early 20s then, found Rossana himself, and not knowing who she was, convinced his family to take her in. Rossana's mental and physical health weren't in good condition, and soon, a doctor determined that an abortion was necessary to keep her alive.

In the months that followed the procedure, her health improved and she and Saba came to love each other. But to marry the intended bride of the Balboni family meant war. Many members of the Dalla Porta were against the marriage. No one wanted war.

But Saba overruled them and determined to marry her, even at the cost of making himself an enemy of the Balboni family and their allies.

Jaco Balboni never forgave Rossana's rejection or betrayal, and when he learned about the abortion, he additionally felt that Rossana had robbed him of his first born child. Soon after the wedding, the Balboni declared war on the Dalla Porta, vowing to revenge themselves on the Calzavarra family a-thousand-fold for their treachery.

Report transcribed from the Sabatini tapes, 1979.

I COME to the end of the first page, *just the first page,* mind reeling. This report was transcribed from words Don Saba said himself. It must be true. Dad's signature sits under the transcription notice.

Dad might have been the one who interviewed him, all those years ago…

Following the first page are more pictures.

Images of Rossana when she was younger, probably during the period when she was sick and recovering from Jaco's attack… There's one of her sleeping in a small, spare bedroom, looking gaunt and close to death. It makes my heart ache.

There's a photo of Rossana and Saba on their wedding day.

I'm shocked by how handsome, open, and kind Saba seems then, when he's young. In all my life, I've never once seen Saba smile the way he does in this picture… He's always been a big, dark shadow, leading the Dalla Porta with a steady, unshakable power. I never would have guessed he had a story like *this* underneath his veneer of deadly disinterest in the world…

Past all the photo pages and notes my father scribbled, dating the pictures and noting their locations, the next page of the report has a different heading.

Moving to America & Jaco's Revenge

Circa 1974, New York City.

Soon, the success and reputation of both the Balboni and Dalla Porta families necessitated that they expand their reach to the United States. Both mafia families resettled in New York City.

Saba and Rossana began expanding their family. They had three sons together, born in quick succession. Quirino Calvzavarra, their first born. Azeglio Calzavarra, their middle son. And Ciro Calzavarra, their youngest.

The next major conflict between the Balboni and Calzavarra families wouldn't take place for many years. Sickened by the success of his rivals and likely still stewing over the betrayal of Rossana, Jaco and the Balboni enacted their greatest revenge at the turn of the following decade.

Saba had to make a trip back to Sicily to handle a business matter one summer, and during his brief absence, they attacked. The Balboni abducted Quirino, the Calzavarras' eldest son, as payback for what happened with Rossana and her subsequent abortion.

Rossana did everything in her power to stop the Balboni from abducting Quirino, but it lead to her death, all the same. Jaco killed her himself.

The Red Years

When Saba learned of all he lost and what the Balboni had done, his grief and fury sent him into a years-long killing spree. During a period of ten years after Rossana's murder and his oldest son abduction, he indiscriminately murdered anyone connected to those responsible out of rage. His search for Quirino and his quest to avenge Rossana was unstoppable.

His reputation as a lethal, indomitable force within the mafia world elevated the Dalla Porta as a family never worth crossing.

Many of Jaco's friends, family members, and allies were slaughtered during the Red Years, including his own wife. Jaco allowed all of it to happen, evading his own demise as best he could.

The Rise and Fall of Azeglio

Despite the unceasing search and siege Saba laid to New York, Quirino was never found. Eyes turned to Azeglio as the presumptive heir to the Dalla Porta mafia. Once he was old enough to join his father in the killing spree of the Red Years, he did so, and quickly gained a reputation for himself as a brutal, violent, unhinged assassin, capable of anything.

In 1986, only a few months after Azeglio's marriage to a protected daughter of the Dalla Porta mafia, the Balboni family struck again out of revenge for everything they lost during the Red Years. They broke onto the Dalla Porta estate and executed Azeglio as yet another act of vengeance.

Saba was forced into raising further hell. And over the next five years, he nearly wiped the Balboni family off the face of the earth.

I SET the pages down on my father's desk, mind working so fast I'm actually a little dizzy. What the hell am I reading?

I knew the Balboni were the Dalla Porta's greatest rivals, despite the fact that the Dalla Porta crime family is far more successful than they are... I knew that there was a long and dark history between our families, but I had no idea just ugly that history was.

The Balboni are responsible for the slaying of Saba's wife, the abduction of one son, and the murder of another?

The amount of loss that one man has suffered...

No wonder he doesn't smile anymore.

Leaning back in Dad's chair, I let my head fall back, so I'm staring up at the intricate carvings of the wood ceiling. The zigzags and geometric patterns stare back me, while I ponder...

Well, I guess this explains why Ciro's the only son I've ever heard of... and why people who know the history don't bring it up.

But the strange part is that Dad circled, underlined and heavily annotated the section of the report talking about Azeglio's death.

Scanning the lines of his cramped handwriting, I find cryptic questions all stacked up together. It's clear to me that he was suspicious about the facts concerning Azeglio's death. Maybe, he even doubted some of the facts recorded in the report.

Is this what got him killed? I can't help but wonder, looking at all his pen marks. *Was he investigating the death of the middle son? Did someone kill him because he found out something about the murder? Something he wasn't supposed to know?*

The sound of a door unlocking nearby startles me from my deep thinking.

My sleuthing is about to be interrupted.

It's coming from upstairs.

Technically, my father's office has an upstairs and a downstairs. Until about five years ago, upstairs was just more bookshelves, but since my father took on Hugo as an apprentice, the upstairs part of this office was given to him.

I have about sixty seconds to close up the file I found, put it back in its place at the back of my father's deepest drawer, safe behind a lock.

When Hugo's face appears over the railing, high above my head, all he sees is me sitting at Dad's desk, looking the part of a bereft daughter.

"Nora." He greets me with my name, never hello.

I give him a little wave. "Come to do your work for the day?"

He nods. "How are you?"

I shrug. "You know."

He gives me a curt nod.

Thankfully, I was able to put everything away before he caught me snooping. Relief sighs through my chest. If he'd caught me, he probably would have been obliged to report it to Gianfrancesco or worse, his father Ciro. Though I'd like to think Hugo wouldn't have, out of respect for me.

"Take all the time you need." He gives a small smile.

"Hugo…" Looking up into his kind eyes, I'm suddenly very tempted to ask him if he knows anything about the Red Years… But I can't quite get myself to do it. He's not old enough to remember anything about it, and I'm not sure if Dad would have told him. And I can't risk outing my research interests. Not at this time.

Still, he raises his eyebrows, and says, "Yes?"

"Nothing." I rise from behind the desk. "I'll get out of your way."

"All right." He braces both arms against the railing. "I'll see you tomorrow then."

"Huh?" I toss him a blank expression. "What's tomorrow?"

He chuckles, but I barely hear it from down here. "Your engagement dinner?"

"My…" A idea explodes in my mind, like someone nailed me in the face with an egg. "My engagement dinner!"

"I'm looking forward to it."

"Thank you, Hugo!"

I dash out the door without another word.

Hugo's just given me a brilliant, wonderful, terrifying idea.

CHAPTER 16

Rocco

GETTING information out of Vito Balboni is like getting candy out of a piñata.

It requires goading with a stick.

He'll break open easy if I apply the right amount of pressure. And antagonizing him isn't all that difficult, seeing as how all I have to do is *exist* in his general vicinity.

In fact, I already know exactly how I'm going to do this.

Vito Balboni typically arrives home late in the evening, around eight or nine.

I'm usually out doing my work at this time of night, but it pays to know his schedule so that on the occasional day that our free time overlaps, I don't run into him.

As soon as he's climbed the stairs from the garage basement, he heads for the liquor cabinet in the kitchen, his usual first stop.

He doesn't see or expect me to be here, waiting for him.

But tonight, I am.

The kitchen is spacious and spare with a lone island in the middle where I nurse a glass of Scotch.

Vito cuts his eyes in my direction the moment he recognizes that it's me.

And I know exactly what that ugly look means.

Of course, Vito knows I live here, he just hates to be reminded at times like this.

His espresso dark curls are coiffed into his preferred shape, and his suspicious, icy blue eyes slice around the room like laser beams. Vito isn't as tall as I am, but he's thicker, and definitely in the head. He's wearing one of his nicer suits, and if my eyes don't deceive me, there's a smear of lipstick on the collar of his black oxford shirt.

I smirk at my Scotch.

Perfect.

"What are you *smirking* at?" His voice is low and ragged, like he's already turned his throat to sandpaper with too much whiskey. There's more menace in it than usual, *and* I didn't even have to be the one to speak first.

All of these facts add up to one thing.

Vito's in a foul mood.

Which means he's looking for a fight.

Basically, I couldn't have picked a better night to poke at him, if I'd tried.

"Long night?" I sip my Scotch, keeping a close eye on Vito in my periphery.

He scoffs at my sarcasm. "*Bastard.*"

Glass clinks against glass, as the heir to this mafia messily pours a fifth of whiskey and proceeds to down it all in one gulp. He slams the empty glass down on the counter like he's trying to break it, and then marches away from the cabinet like he means to stagger upstairs to his bedroom.

But he's not getting away that easily.

"Out whoring again?" I toss the question at his back, and watch him freeze, the muscles in his shoulders puffing up. "Remind me, which place is your favorite? The Black Shanty downtown or—"

Vito rounds on me, eyes boiling with rage. "Was someone talking to you, you orphaned fuck?"

"It's nothing to be ashamed of." I drop my head a little to the left. "What others get with charm, you get with money."

His eyebrows shove down deep into a scowl of volcanic proportions. "What did you just say?"

"I understand. After yesterday, you probably need to blow off some steam." I shrug. "Hopefully, Pasqual wasn't too rough on you—"

Vito charges me like a raging bull, and just for good measure, I let him.

He slams my back against the titanium refrigerator, the force of our combined weight making everything in the kitchen shake.

"What do you know about it?" He snarls through gritted teeth.

"Nothing." I hold up my hands in mock compliance, even while the prick has a fistful of my shirt and his acrid breath in my face. "I may have overhead something from the guys about an alleyway and a favor gone wrong, but that's all I know."

"*Who* was talking?" Vito's spit flies dangerously close to my chin.

"Nobody." I analyze the desperation on Vito's face. He seems close to edge.

Now's my moment. If I double down, I may be able to get him to spill whatever secret he's hiding.

It's time to get some answers.

"But what was Pezzullo doing here anyway, Vito?" I venture, keeping my voice low and steady. "This doesn't have anything to do with the Di Rienzo job, does it?"

Vito's eyes hop wide with recognition, and even drunk and damn-near drooling, he shoves a knife to my throat with impressive accuracy.

"You know what I always hated about you? You ask too many goddamn questions." A sharp pinch of pain announces itself near my jugular, as Vito presses the tip hard at my skin. But I don't wince. Not in any way that he can see. "You know what you're supposed to know. So, shut that disgusting mouth of yours and do what we pay you for."

Vito rips his body away from me, stalking toward the staircase against the far brick wall, and stomping up into the darkness of the higher floors.

Silence falls in the kitchen as I spiral through my own surprise.

Vito actually had the balls to pull a weapon on me, that's interesting. But what's even more noteworthy is that Vito didn't break.

It's not often that I have to break him, but on every occasion in recent memory when I attempted it, I got through his defenses rather easily.

But not this time.

Why?

Am I losing my edge?

Vito was clearly threatened by the questions I asked...

His ability to keep me out of his pea-sized brain only intrigues me more.

Vito's not that great at keeping secrets, and if he's suddenly developed a flair for it, it can only mean that what's going on here has something to do with his pride or his shame.

For only pride and shame keep men in silence.

Even stupid men, like Vito.

What the hell is he up to? And how did Orazio Di Rienzo and his oldest daughter get tangled up in it all?

The alleyway, Vito hiring the Pezzullos to watch it. Vito using me as hit bait for Orazio's murder, now the operation to abduct Nora before her wedding day?

All of these pieces connect, I just have to figure out how.

After a few more seconds of puzzling, I brush down my ruffled shirt and examine my neck for any bits of blood. Next, I make a beeline for the stairs.

It's time I get to work.

I want to do more research on Orazio Di Rienzo.

Through the cops in Jaco's pocket, we have access to a few different online databases that are off limits to the public. I should be able to find more information about the man there. Maybe I'll find something that can create sense out of the chaos Vito's thrown me into.

In my suite, I hole up at my desk, pulling open my laptop with too much force and navigating to the Balboni's private, untraceable back door entrance to the police database. This thing has all kinds of stuff. DNA evidence. Criminal records. Birth certificate copies. Real estate listings. The list goes on.

With heavy fingers, I type *Orazio Di Rienzo* into the search bar and hope.

In a matter of seconds, a list of matching and related documents as long as my arm populates before me. Everything from immigration records and a copy of his passport to newspaper clippings and articles about the Dalla Porta empire.

Apparently, he's been on the cops' radar for many years, even though he's never been charged with anything. On paper, he's one of a few C-suite members of Dalla Porta Enterprises, the import export conglomerate the Calzavarra family owns and runs. He's been listed under many titles including Chief Security Officer, Chief Operations Officer, and others.

Only been married once. To a... Tatiana Loretti.

My mind slowly conjures the image of his grieving widow, folded onto a pew at the funeral. She looked like a punching bag all the stuffing had been punched out of.

Guilt pings through me.

When I click on her name, nothing comes up. There are no records in the database about her, despite the numerous records about her husband.

Hmm. Wonder if he had anything to do with that.

I keep reading.

There are photographs of him, taken all around the world, at various business summits and high profile meetings of the minds. I know I should dig into this, but a nearby hyperlink snares my eye, and then my cursor.

Children.

I click the link, and two photographs appear, one of Nora and the other of her twin, Nicoletta. The pair of them are definitely identical twins in the technical sense, but Nora's irises are bright amber brown, and Nicoletta's are darker, richer. They're both brunettes, but the shades are a bit different, matching the same variety that they get from their parents...

Just seeing Nora's name hyperlinked before me sends rabid, desperate curiosity cascading through my system.

It shouldn't.

She's just a job.

But I click anyway. I can't help myself.

It's not like I've been able to stop thinking about her. Or about that kiss.

Not since the moment it happened.

Everything else that's transpired in the meantime has been the longest fucking commercial break in the world.

Fuck, I want to touch her.

See her. Squeeze her against me until she fucking pops.

Lust burbles up to the surface of my consciousness, but I force it down with everything I have. Instead, I force myself to read the words that appear before me, even if they do nothing to take my mind of the woman.

There isn't much in her file. Why should there be?

All I find are a few different copies of her photo ID.

Two different passports. There are even JPEGS attached of each of the different pages. First, I check the expired one. It's actually the first passport she ever had, if I'm not mistaken. It looks like it was first issued to her when she was about elementary school aged. Stamps on the pages indicate she spent quite a lot of time in Europe back in those days and didn't return to the states until middle school.

She's been here ever since.

Apparently, she studied anthropology and tourism at Columbia...

I read over the few records the database has on her multiple times. I don't know if I'm trying to memorize these random bits of information or if I'm trying to be closer to her by learning whatever I can.

Whatever the reason for my insane choices, I'm acting like a fucking stalker.

If I thought for one second there was another man or mafioso on earth sitting around looking through her personal records with half a boner in his pants, I'd put a bullet through that sick fuck's brain.

But here I am, not suicidal in the least.

My eyes flick away from the screen to the clock, ticking on my desk. It's almost ten. *Christ.* I've been at this for almost two hours and seventy-five percent of that time was spent reading and rereading the few tiny files they have on Nora.

Pushing away from my desk in my rolling office chair, I lean back, placing my palms over my tired eye sockets. The chair creaks beneath my weight, but doesn't falter as I stay in this semi-reclined position, deeply questioning whatever morals are left after twenty years' involvement in organized crime.

Once my mind's cleared some, I return to upright and glance down at my phone, sitting quiet on my desk.

All over again, I'm agitated.

I want to call her.

But that would be bad. *Worse* than every idiotic thing I've done up until now.

No. I can't stoop that low. Even if I'm dying to hear her soft, steady voice.

What am I? In *withdrawal* for her sass? Her adorable awkward allure wrapped up in feisty, foolhardy—My phone vibrates against my desk.

My eyes snap to the screen, and then I shoot straight up out of my seat.

Here I was hoping she'd call me, and miraculously...She is.

CHAPTER 17

Nora

AT LEAST HALF of me was hoping he wouldn't pick up, but he does.

Rocco De Carlo answers so abruptly on the first ring, I jump where I'm seated in the middle of my giant horrible bed.

Stomach in boy-scout-knots, I keep shooting anxious looks at my door, like a crowd of people might be eavesdropping on the other side.

Like someone might barge through at any second and accuse me of talking to a man on the phone alone in my room.

Ugh. What the hell is wrong with me?

I'm nervous as *hell* to talk to him. So nervous I barely know what to say. Forget being able to breathe normally.

"Rocco?" My voice is barely above a whisper.

"Is everything all right?" The deep, rich tone of his voice caresses my ear. It's so visceral a tingle travels down my spine at the speed of a rollercoaster.

I almost laugh at that. "Nope. Everything is still awful, but no worse than a few nights ago."

Surprise surprise, *that* didn't put him at ease.

"What's going on?" The intensity in his voice strengthens with urgency.

"Nothing. I just…" My voice trails off.

I hold the phone away from my ear and hope he doesn't hear it when I slap my hand over my face, because *what am I doing??*

"Nora?"

"Yes, here. Sorry. The reason I'm calling is because I need to see you."

I don't realize how fucking incriminating that sounds until the stupid words are off my tongue. *Oh God.* My fingers itch to toss my phone across the room like a football.

The silence that follows only solidifies my own idiocy, so I've got to say something.

Attempt *some kind of* damage control, even though I should never be allowed to speak again.

"That didn't come out right." My cheeks roast in this *beyond* awkward moment. "Let me start over. I…found something today. In my dad's office."

"You went back to your father's office by yourself?" Incredulous concern amps his voice. "Are you okay? Did anyone try to—"

"No, no, no." I try to overpower the alarm in his voice with my inner calm. "Not his *secret* office. His official office. Here. At the estate."

"Oh." A relieved exhale snuffles the line. "What did you discover?"

"It's…" I swallow, glancing again at my locked bedroom door. "More than I want to tell you over the phone. Can we meet up again? In person?"

"Yes. Where?"

I take a deep breath. Next comes the crazy part. "Here."

"Where is 'here'?"

"The Dalla Porta estate."

Another pause from Rocco gives me the opportunity to contemplate how ridiculous a request I'm making.

"If it were up to me, I'd prefer to meet you somewhere else, but..." Bitterness seeps into my tone. "It's not up to me anymore."

"What are you talking about?"

"Yesterday, I didn't make it back in time..." I'm still punching Gianfrancesco in my mind. "Long story short, I'm grounded until further notice, and I can't leave the house without an escort or express permission."

"But you're allowed to receive gentleman callers?"

This time, a giggle actually escapes, despite the suckiness of my reality. "Maybe."

One good joke and all the awkwardness tangled up between my ribs eases away to nothing. Who knew this dangerous and deadly serious man had a sense of humor?

"I'm listening." Rocco actually sounds intrigued, as opposed to entirely against it, which surprises me, I must admit.

Setting foot on Dalla Porta property is an ominous proposition, even for friends of the family, but he doesn't seem the least bit cowed by it.

"Tomorrow night, there's going to be a big party, and lots of associates and friends of the family will be there." I gather my knees to my chest in the crook of one arm. "You could come."

"Define big party."

"It's..." My heart sinks a little. "An engagement party, actually."

And then my heart sinks a *lot*, so far down it crashes through the floorboards underneath my bed and my head jerks up in realization.

Holy shit. Yesterday, I kissed a guy, even though I'm completely engaged to someone else. Yes, it's against my will, and no, Gianfrancesco has no affect on my heart, mind, or body besides my gag reflex, but that doesn't change the fact that I am still technically engaged.

I made a whole point of finding out from Rocco whether he had a wife or a girlfriend, but didn't stop to mention the colossal cancerous tumor hanging off my own love life... What if it matters to him that I'm not single? Even though...

Oh God.

This time, I'm the force behind the awkward silence.

But in a moment, Rocco's voice reappears.

"*Your* engagement party, I presume?"

My jaw drops open, but the gasp is silent. "How did you know?"

"Let's just say your marriage to Ciro Calzavarra's spawn has been...decreed far and wide."

That sentence kills any leftover humor in Rocco's voice. And mine.

"Ugh." I hang my head. "I'm sorry you didn't hear it from me. And I'm sorry that I did *that* yesterday without telling you the truth first."

"Stop apologizing, Nora." His voice is hard. "Besides...I'm not."

"You're not what?"

"Sorry." I hear him take another big breath. "I'm not sorry you kissed me. And I'm not sorry I kissed you either..."

"What?" Hope spears me clean through my chest. "You mean... it doesn't bother you that I'm...?"

"Being forced to marry someone against your will?" The disdain in Rocco's voice comforts me, like he hates the whole idea. Almost as much as I do. "It *does* bother me, Nora, but probably in the same way it bothers you..."

Unexpectedly, my eyes well with tears.

Rocco is the only person other than my sister to act like this whole mess I'm in is a tragedy. I hear it in his voice. Real anguish hidden beneath his carefully chosen words.

I have to pinch the bridge of my nose and cry a second in silence. The words just won't come. And then I hear shuffling on Rocco's end of the line, like he's changing positions.

"I apologize." Those two words seem hard for him to say. "I shouldn't put words in your mouth."

"What?" I blubber, voice thick.

"I'm assuming." He makes an annoyed sound. "I should be asking. How *do you* feel about that fiancé of yours?"

I blink at my room, full of momentary confusion and then… unchained affection.

Rocco's leaving room. For how I really feel.

Even though he hasn't said a wrong thing yet.

"You were right the first time." I make a pathetic sound, something akin to a watery laugh. "Rocco, I tried to kill myself a few days ago. You think I did that because I'm madly in love with my fiancé? I hate the man. Always have. I would literally rather die."

"Oh, thank God."

That makes me laugh full out.

That, followed by Rocco's hilarious backpedal attempts.

"I mean…" More shuffling and throat clearing. "I'm not thankful you tried to harm yourself, but I…"

I keep laughing until he gives up entirely.

His uncensored relief has given my face a cheek-aching sort of smile.

"I suppose you could do far worse," he finally recovers. "The youngest Calzavarra is worth his weight in sapphires, emeralds, priceless paintings, you name it."

"He's an ass."

Now, it sounds like Rocco's trying not to laugh. "At least, he's close to your age."

That comment tickles me. It's almost like Rocco's fishing to find out what I think about *his* age. Or should I say, the age difference between us…

"Yes, he's two years older than I am. A magnificent achievement." I rock back until I'm laying flat on my bed. "Honestly? Age doesn't really matter to me."

"Really?" His tone is gravelly, more serious somehow. "Why not?"

"My parents."

"They're open minded?"

"Maybe." I smile, remembering my parents as they were. "The age gap between them was more than twenty years... But they were madly in love."

"Always?"

"Always." I remember them dancing in our living room, when they thought Nico and I weren't watching. "Age never seemed to be a problem for them."

"So the youngest Calzavarra doesn't get any points for his youth."

"None." *And you don't lose any for your maturity,* I'm too shy to say.

"Well, what else is wrong with him?" Rocco's tone is again buoyant and light. "I understand women find him attractive."

"*Hardly.* Where do you get your information?" I roll onto my side, still grinning ear to ear. "He thinks he's God's gift, that's for sure."

"Arrogant?"

"Who do you think went on a power trip and forbade me from leaving the house?" My own question drags the smile off my face.

"Sounds like Frankie wants to keep you all to himself." Unexpectedly, a gruff, sensual edge comes to Rocco's tone. "...He's not the only one."

My heart leaps for joy at those words.

The irrational giddiness that bursts beneath my sternum forces me to roll onto my face and silently scream into the duvet beneath.

Rocco surges on. "I can also understand why he wants to marry you. What baffles me is why he's so dead set on marrying a woman who doesn't want anything to do with him."

I toss back onto my side, beaming at the far wall. "Is there another kind?"

"Touché." A moment passes, and then Rocco's solemn voice returns. "Nora, you already know I don't approve of your methods... but I don't blame you at all for trying to get away from your situation. And regardless of how you did it, I shouldn't have blown up at you like that the other night."

My heart's always been a boulder stuck in the mud, but Rocco moves it with just the touch his finger, with just the sound of his warm, gravelly voice. Wow.

This one apology is somehow more than I've ever received from a mafioso.

"I..." Every single logical thought falls right out of my head. "Rocco De Carlo, I really want to see you again."

This is what the sound of his voice does to me.

Turns me into a over-honest blabbering mess—

A sharp intake of breath invades my ears.

Followed by a deep, heavy exhale.

I can almost feel the heat of his breath on my skin.

God, just the sound of his breathing gets my heartbeat spastic and wild.

"I also want to see you again..." His voice is a low-level growl. A smaller version of that sound he made when he pushed me down on that desk. "Very much."

If my heart can twirl, it's doing that right now. Spinning between my ribs, like a little girl in a brand new dress.

Until Rocco spoils it all.

"But that's a very bad thing, Nora." He's deadly serious.

Doubt smothers the excitement fizzing inside me. "What do you mean?"

"I mean you're not the only one with an arranged fiancé." Another hard exhale. "Not to mention, a powerful family-in-law-to-be who wouldn't be pleased to learn about this."

So...I'm not the only one with a betrothed.

It's hypocritical as fuck, but this one small admission does make me feel a bit betrayed. I asked if he had a wife or a girlfriend, and he said no.

How artful. Misleading me like that.

"You're engaged."

"Unfortunately."

"Why didn't you say anything?" I sit up on my bed. "Yesterday, you let us—"

"Get carried away. Yes. I did." He makes a sound I haven't heard, almost like he's trying to come up with what to say next.

"Well?" I try to keep the smidgen of irritation out of my voice. "You know all about my fiancé. So, let's hear it. Who is she?"

"Her name is Anunziata."

How quickly my smile has transformed into a petulant little pout.

"She sounds beautiful."

"She is."

"And she's got to be young." Passive aggressive, party of one.

"Why do you say that?"

"I've never heard of an arranged marriage between two forty-year-olds."

"I resent that."

She's probably nineteen, twenty. I roll my eyes hard. Just when I was starting to convince myself he was different.

"Look, Rocco. If you've already got a pretty young thing with your name on it, what does that make me? An appetizer?"

"Nora…" He blows out a long breath that makes the line snap. "The marriage isn't my idea. It's what she and her family wants. She's known me all her life. To me, she's still that kid I used to take to school, just all grown up."

"Well, that's not creepy or gross at all."

"Now, you understand my resistance to the match." He sounds sincere, despite the wave of pettiness crashing against my rocks. "I've been trying to resign myself to it for weeks, but…something keeps getting in the way."

"Let me guess. She's too perky?" I exhale. "Too bouncy? She doesn't get your references? What? What could be so wrong with her?"

"She's not you."

That shuts me up fast. I'm frozen stiff, completely speechless.

Is he saying what I think he's... What the hell is he saying?

"Eleanora Di Rienzo...ever since I saw you in that church on the day of your father's funeral, I haven't been able to think of anyone else."

My whole face goes slack with wonder. He's saying all these beautiful words, and I'm just sitting here mute and overflowing with more emotions than I ever knew I had...

"In other words, you've changed things for me." He swallows, hard enough that I hear it over the line. "In ways that I can't ignore...Can you, Nora?"

"No." I release a shaky breath. "It's not like I've...ever felt this way about someone before." Squeezing my knees to my chest once again, I rest my chin on top. "Something's definitely happening. Something new."

"For me, too."

Oh, God. It's like this man has me dangling by a thread.

A second ago I was pissed at him for hiding his fiancée from me, and now I'm throbbing beneath my pajamas. I didn't even know I *could* throb.

Jesus, am I in trouble...

"I want to kiss you again," I blurt out. Why am I breathless, just from sitting here doing nothing? Why the fuck is my heart beating so fast?

His sultry voice roughens. "Is that all you want?"

I squeeze my legs together tight, flopping over on the mattress, cheeks on fire. "What do you want me to say?" I whine, slapping my free hand over my face.

"That you're wet and waiting for me..."

I melt with the heat of his scorching hot words.

No man's ever had this affect on me before. Blushing, throbbing, rolling around on a mattress, all to the soundtrack of his hot, hypnotizing voice.

"Rocco..." His name leaves my lips like a moan.

"Yes, sweetheart?"

If I were standing up, I would have fallen onto something when he said that...*Swooned.* It's criminal the way *sweetheart* sounds on that sexy, sexy tongue of his.

"So will you come tomorrow? To the party?"

"Wouldn't miss it." With three words, he slays me with excitement all over again. "But you'll miss it, if you don't get some rest."

"What?" I glance at the out-of-place-in-this-old-palace digital alarm clock on my nightstand. Four a.m. stares back at me. FOUR AM? "We've been talking all night?"

"I didn't notice either."

Rocco and I say our goodbyes. He wishes me a good morning, and I try not to sound like the phone-a-slut operator, moaning at him over nothing, and then I scramble underneath my covers and turn off the lights.

Holy fuck.

I've been nervous about the engagement dinner because I know I'll be glued to Frankie's side, at least for part of it.

For any of it is already too much.

But now, I'm even more nervous.

Because all I want to do is be alone with Rocco De Carlo.

And as fate would have it, he feels the same way.

CHAPTER 18

Rocco

I SLEEP LIKE SHIT, the gift of another restless fucking night.

Dark, murky nightmares of things I can't remember mixed with swirls of Nora's voice and imaginations of her body beneath my greedy hands.

My heavy eyelids tug open around 10:00.

Rocco De Carlo, I really want to see you again.

I smash a pillow over my head, as the echo of her voice sends my eyes curling back into my skull.

Jesus Christ, that woman...

She's going to be the death of me. I'm sure of it.

I try to roll over onto my stomach, and immediately regret it. My cock's up, standing tall and defiant, and doesn't wish to be laid on.

Not by me anyway.

Can't remember the last time I woke up with a rager.

I was probably a fucking teenager.

Dropping my hands over my tired, exhausted face, I breathe deep.

I need to get up, pound some protein, meditate, then hit the gym like I mean it. Or I'm going to completely unravel before the day's done.

And there's far too much to do today for that. For starters, if I'm going to keep my word and show up tonight—and see Nora the way I've desperately wanted to for the past forty-eight hours— I'm going to have to pull off the hack job of my life.

Somehow, I'm going to have to engineer some way to get my name onto a Dalla Porta guest list. If I'm not on the list, security won't even let me go for a stroll down their block. At least, my name won't give my affiliation away.

Goes without saying I've never set foot on the Dalla Porta estate.

No Balboni member ever has.

It's behind enemy lines. Entirely.

Even attending Orazio's funeral in Saint Anthony's Cathedral, the patron church of the Dalla Porta, felt dangerous. Only God could protect a man in there.

Getting onto the official estate *proper* will require finesse.

I'll have to find out how Vito got me into the funeral and use the same inside track to score an authorization for Nora's engagement party. *Without* Vito finding out about it.

And while I'm at it, I'll just sneak onto a NASA base and score a trip to Mars.

I squeeze my already aching forehead.

Just how the fuck am I going to pull this off?

Vito again bobs to the surface of my mind. As impossible as it is for me to believe, especially considering finesse is not Vito's forte, obviously he must have some kind of *in* with the Dalla Porta somewhere. A mole on his father's payroll. How else was he able to get me into a funeral that high profile?

Therein lies my problem.

If I show up at that engagement dinner without his input, whoever Jaco's paying is going to report back to him. And how would I explain it?

More reconnaissance?

What happens if the spy sees me with my tongue in Nora's mouth?

I'm sure I should be more concerned about what'll happen if *Gianfrancesco* sees me manhandling his bride, but the thought gives me more pleasure than not.

Still, I don't have an answer to my question. How the fuck am I going to get into that engagement party without telling Vito or tipping off Jaco's spy?

I'm already on Vito's bad side. And after our little chat last night in the kitchen? I'll be lucky if he doesn't blow me up the way he did to Nora's father.

Guilt bears down on me, hard and heavy at that intrusive thought.

What are you doing, Rocco? What are you doing?

I'm barely awake and already, I'm on pins and needles.

Sleep was elusive. Visions of Nora, her body...

The idea of getting to see her tonight generates this bone-deep anticipation, an excitement I can't seem keep at bay...

My cellphone shrills on the nightstand next to me. I rip it off the small square table, heart pummeling my ribs, expecting Nora's number.

To my great disappointment, it's Vito.

He's calling early. Earlier than usual.

Oh, goody.

I answer without a word, and Vito doesn't wait.

"Jaco wants you. Get up here. *Now.*" The line cuts dead.

Something's definitely up.

Ominous premonition buds in my stomach as I detangle myself from my bedsheets and march to the bathroom. Stripping out of my clothes, I notice that even the disturbing sound of Vito's voice this early in the morning has done nothing to deter the hard-on I have for Nora.

I heave a heavy breath, turn on the faucet in my granite-tiled shower, and resign myself to doing what a pubescent boy would do in my situation.

Jack off.

Under the high-pressure water flow, I let my hand drift down to my adamant cock. My eyes drop closed in defeat. I can't even watch myself do this.

Choking the crown of my cock one stroke at a time, I brace myself against the wall in front of me with my free hand, Nora's form appearing behind my eyes.

Her scent.

The smooth, clear cadence of her voice.

The softness of her breasts returns to my eager memory. Even clothed, the sight of her opened thighs bending around my waist welcomed me, hardened me, *haunts me* even now...

The way she threaded her strong, lean arms around my neck and kissed me, like I deserved her...As though I could ever deserve something so good, after all the horrible things I've done—

A cross between a grunt and shout claws out of my throat, an orgasmic shift tearing through my core. I shoot, semen splattering the post-modern granite slab I'm balanced against. My cum drips slow down the shower wall, mixing with the rain.

Still breathing hard, a frenzy of activity happening under my skin, I lean my forehead against the cool stone, letting the hot water wash away the sins I have yet to commit. The next time I get my hands on that woman, I swear to God.

I don't know what I'll do, but I do know that I won't be able to stop myself.

Deep inside, I want her. So much that I've already claimed her as mine.

That's the scariest fucking thing of all.

185

I climb out of the shower, fresh and clean, yet feeling dirtier than ever.

A towel slapped around my waist, I exit and nearly drop the thing in surprise.

Anunziata stands in front of my floor to ceiling windows with her back to me.

"Zia?" She doesn't turn. "To what do I owe the…" *Inconvenience.* *"…pleasure."*

I head straight for my kitchenette, while I wait for her to respond.

I'm definitely going to need coffee to get through this.

Meanwhile, she's still giving me the silent treatment.

I blow out a breath. "Whatever this is about, can it wait? Your father wants to see me right away." After pressing a few buttons, my espresso machine begins to drip Sicilian coffee into a small ceramic cup.

She scoffs. "I don't even get a *good morning* before you blow me off?"

"Good morning." I snatch my cup the second the machine's done. "And yes, by all means, blame me for your bad timing." I meant to say that under my breath, but judging by the way she whips around to face me with a sharp, unamused look on her face, I'm guessing she caught every word.

"You owe me an apology, Rocco."

After taking a big sip of my scalding hot espresso, I place it back on the counter and meet her eyes across the twenty feet between us. "I apologize."

Then, I go to my closet to grab clothes.

"You don't even know what you're apologizing *for*, do you?" She throws the question at my bare back.

She's right. I don't.

"You wouldn't ask me for an apology if I hadn't done something that merited one."

Without another word, Anunziata marches straight up to my

backside and rips the towel away from my waist, leaving me naked in front of my suits.

"*Zia...*" Now, I'm angry. "Give me my towel back."

"Not until you apologize for throwing me out like that."

"I don't have time to play childish games. Your father expects me upstairs—"

"What about what I expect?" Her voice teeters on the edge of shrill.

I'm just angry enough that I don't care if she sees my dick. Pivoting back, I face her. She stands a few feet from me, my towel dangling from her fingers.

"How long are you going to treat me like a child?" She demands, face pinched together in rage.

I stalk toward her, grilling her with my eyes. "As long as you keep *acting like one.*"

The moment I'm within range, I snatch my towel back from her and wrangle it around myself without breaking irritated eye contact.

Her eyes parry mine like sharp, lancing blades.

A bit of nudity didn't faze me or her at all, apparently.

"Just tell me the truth." Her lips tremble, eyes reddening with emotion. "You love someone else. Right? That's why you pay so little attention to me."

And with that, Anunziata Balboni knocks me flat on my ass.

Of all the things she's ever said to me, this is the one that gut punches me into next month. My eyes widen, but my mouth seals shut.

Usually, I can manage an excuse. A cop-out. Something.

But not today.

Not when I feel like she's crashed a hole in my heart, and all my emotions have begun to spill out of their container, like fish-filled water from smashed aquarium glass.

What the hell am I supposed to say?

I've never gotten off on my *memories* of a woman before, but did I or did I not just bust a nut thinking about Nora? She's obsessed me for weeks now. All of that crazy shit I said to her last night on the phone was the truth.

I've been able to think of no one and nothing else but her, ever since we crossed paths at her father's funeral.

Not once have I summed all these facts up to...love.

But Anunziata's staring me in the face, and so is that fucking terrifying, incriminating little four-letter word.

Another moment of this passes, us in this speechless confrontational showdown, and then Zia flutters her eyes up to the ceiling, tears slipping down her cheeks.

"I knew it." Her voice gets small and shaky.

More guilt tolls through me, solemn and deafening. "Zia—"

"Save it." She holds up a hand to stop whatever I might have said, and all but sprints to my door and disappears.

Well, fuck.

My morning just went from bad to cataclysmic, and I haven't even seen Vito yet.

And in addition to being inwardly shaken by what just happened with Zia, now I'm late. Rushing into my clothes, I head out, mind in chaos, as I navigate up to third floor of the Balboni's warehouse-converted loft, all the way to Jaco's office.

The place is a long rectangular room outfitted in mahogany furnishings with two walls of exposed brick and an old world painting of Sicily hung above the mantle. Jaco sits behind a massive desk, Vito scowling over his shoulder. Fiero and Lancini smoke cigars in low, leather armchairs, a game of chess splayed out between them.

Everyone looks up when Jaco's security team lets me into the room.

"Our match will have to wait," Fiero blots the end of his cigar. Lancini raises an eyebrow at me but doesn't say anything. He rarely does. Our capo is known for his lethal silence. Almost as well known as Fiero is for being a master of the long game.

"What the fuck took you so long?" Vito snaps at me like a poorly trained Rottweiler.

Jaco holds up a hand to silence his son, while taking a sip from his brandy glass.

Drinking before eleven am? My first guess is that Jaco was up all night.

That's typically the only time I catch him drinking hard liquor this early in the morning. And if he was up all night, he had reason to be.

Which worries me.

That ominous premonition is still there, simmering beneath all the emotional chaos that Zia unleashed on me.

"We have another mission for you." Jaco gives me a mirthless smirk.

"Something new?"

"Of course not," Vito sneers. "You've got to *complete* an assignment before you get a new one, remember?"

My stomach hits the deck. I was afraid he'd say that.

This must be about Nora.

Amusement lifts Jaco's twisted features. "It's come to our attention that fuckstick Ciro is having an engagement party for his little boy and our bargaining chip this evening." His words send my heart shattering against the crags of rock bottom.

Please, God, don't let this go where I fear it's going.

"Let's just say we fashioned you an invite," Fiero chimes in, folding his fingers together in his lap.

"The new plan is so simple, even *you'll* get it," Vito insists, voice leaking with sarcasm. "Kidnap that girl *tonight.* No exceptions."

CHAPTER 19

Nora

ATTACHED to my obnoxiously red bedroom is an en-suite *parlor* that's a cross between a lavish bathroom and an oversized walk-in closet, full of clothes that don't belong to me. Tags hang from designer dresses, all draped on racks. A glass case at the back of the room displays different pairs of high heels, all in my size. A low cabinet sits covered in jewelry options, all lovely.

All horrible.

This is my nightmare.

I feel like I'm trapped in a miniature department store.

On a regular day, my idea of a great outfit is cargo pants, a sports bra, and a light breezy activewear tank that leaves my shoulders and arms out so I can climb easy, free, and uninhibited to my hearts content. If I'm not barefoot, I'm wearing *climbing shoes.* Sneakers for running. Or Converse high tops, if I'm feeling sassy.

I can honestly count the number of times I've worn high heels in my life on my hands. It's less than ten times.

Nico would have a ball in here playing dress up, and in that scenario, I'd be somewhere nearby reading a graphic novel without a care.

But today, no such luck is mine.

At the enormous vanity in the bathroom side of the parlor, I fuss with my appearance, the way I've been doing for the past several hours straight. For the first time ever, I've spent almost an entire day worrying about what to wear.

To this goddamn engagement dinner.

I don't even want to go. I'd completely repressed the reality of its happening until Hugo brought it up last night. And even then, the only excitement I felt was about the opportunity of inviting Rocco to the estate.

Rocco.

The face I make in the mirror *horrifies* me.

I've never tried to impress a man before, so why am I desperately giving it my best shot for *him*? A man I barely know.

An engaged man at that.

She's not you.

Why do those three words somehow make up for everything wrong about the fact that we're both entangled with other people while…doing whatever we're doing with each other?

I don't know what to call it.

We're sleuthing together? Sort of.

We're not dating. We're not flirting.

We're kissing, but… Killing people to protect me and holding me while I cry? What category do those fall into? Definitely not just plain old primal lust. Right?

This whole experience with him has shown me just how little I understand human contact. I know I've always been a socially-reserved deep thinker. Nico was the headstrong outgoing one, and

191

without my sister by my side...almost from the moment she was exiled, I became withdrawn and closed off.

My world has always been small. Only myself, my family, and my dreams were in it.

Making friends and other connections has always been a shit-show. I'm usually completely lost in romantic situations. Typically, I can fathom what's happening, but never what to do about it. In other words, when someone takes an interest in me, I notice, but it doesn't move me.

Definitely not to any kind of action.

And even on the extremely rare occasions when I find myself into someone, it's not like I've ever known how to flirt or reach out. I often end up hurting someone's feelings really badly.

Goes without saying, I've never been in a serious romantic relationship with anyone. Maybe I've run into a guy or two at work who thought I was nice. Maybe I've kissed a few people, had a fondle here or there, but for the most part, I've never met anyone who was able to deeply draw me out from my shell.

I've never known how to open up to others.

But with Rocco...everything's different.

And I'm going to see him again very soon.

On that anxious-excited note, I resume tugging at the hem of the dress squeezing my body together. It's a cocktail number in a deep blood orangey color. Only, half of it is missing. The hem stops at my upper thigh. If someone so much as looks at me too hard, they'll get a flash of my ass.

And the top of it wraps around my neck, almost like a dog collar.

Who picked out these clothes? And why did they pick fucking everything from the same slut couture boutique?

Another no.

Part of the reason picking out a dress for tonight has taken so long is because it takes me fifteen to twenty minutes to extract myself from each of these dresses. A carnage pile of them, all brightly colored and expensively patterned, lays on a long ottoman nearby, at least ten deep.

Next to the giant vanity is a hook, where I've hung all the potential things I might wear. Riffling through them for something less form-fitting and tight, I wrestle a blue number from the pack.

I hold up to my body in the mirror.

This one might actually work.

Knock knock.

I jump, backing away toward the closet side of the room. I'm completely naked and unsure who to expect, banging on my door.

"Who is it?" I call, hiding myself behind a rack of dresses.

"Your mother."

I heave a sigh of relief until I remember that I'm still angry with her about everything that's going on, not to mention that horrible fight we had... We haven't spoken a word since. She even sent one of the housemaids to remind me about the engagement dinner tonight instead of doing it herself.

What does she want now?

"Are you dressed?" Her voice sounds defeated, even muffled through a door.

"Almost," I lie.

"Hurry," she adds. "It's time."

Yikes! Already?

"O-Okay." I gulp. "On my way."

How can that be?

I dart out from my hiding place and snatch up my phone. 6:51.

Fuck. She's right. The engagement dinner starts at 7:00. Guests have been arriving for the past hour at least, which means...

Rocco could already be downstairs, waiting for me.

My heart guns it in my chest.

Maybe this wasn't such a good idea, inviting him. I do want to see him, and I definitely need to talk to someone about everything I discovered yesterday, but I already hate parties. Knowing he's down there too does nothing to calm me.

Only makes anxiety jump up and down inside me like concert-goers at a rave. My legs are genuinely a little shaky.

In just my bra and underwear, I force myself to sit down before the vanity, meeting my own gaze. "Breathe." I coach myself. "You've run down the clock, and now it's time for you go. Keep your chin up. You can do this."

It's finally time for me to attend my engagement dinner.

What I should be most anxious about is the reality that I'll be stuck on my idiot fiancé's arm most of the night, but instead, all I can think about is seeing Rocco.

I know I can't waste any more time deliberating, so I climb into the deep blue dress. Its fitted top and graceful scoop neck are elegant, and it hangs longer on my leg and not quite as tight as the torture trap before it.

There's no way I'm going to get away with a pair of flats, not that this closet comes with any. I pick the shortest pair of diamond crusted shoes I find that match the color of this dress. Thank God the work the hair and makeup team did earlier still looks nice.

When I emerge back into my bedroom, my mother paces, waiting for me in yet another dress that fits her all wrong. It's black and shimmery, uncharacteristically tight, and cut far too low in the front for her to have picked it out herself. Maybe she's stuck with the same slutty wardrobe options as I am…

Her dark, exhausted eyes travel the length of my body, and back up to my face.

"Come on," she murmurs without comment on the outfit I've picked out.

I nod, but say nothing else.

We feel like strangers now…and the cold sensation of it breaks my heart so thoroughly, I know I'll start sobbing right here if I focus on it.

Together, she and I navigate to the exit of our joint suite into the fourth floor hallway. Even all the way up here, we can hear the echoes of footsteps, laughter, and clinking glasses. Invited guests wait below, and we're soon to join them.

In silence, my mother and I climb down from the fourth floor to the second, pacing the long red-carpet marble hallway expanding before us toward the extravagantly grand foyer on the first floor, now crawling with mafiosos, their wives, and adult children.

A cloud of cigarette smoke mixed with the chandelier light below gives the first floor a sort of warm haze, and through it, as I walk near, but not too near, the bannister, I search the throngs of people for Rocco.

I can't see everyone from up here. Not by a long shot, but...my hopes remain high that somewhere down there is the man who kept me up all night.

Down the second floor hallway, wearing these impossibly painful high heels, I try to channel my sister and strut. I've calculated that strutting is my best chance at not falling on my stupid heavily-made-up face. Let's hope my math's right.

It takes me a few seconds before I realize my mother's no longer at my side. She's hanging back, and probably going to head down using a different stairwell. I glance back at her, worry likely seeping into my gaze. She gives me only a single nod, alluding to the man in the tux, waiting for me up ahead with his broad back tucked against a marble column.

Gianfrancesco. *Frankie.*

Damn, I forgot about this part.

Ciro wants us to make an entrance. A *dramatic* entrance.

I wonder if me falling down the stairs would be dramatic enough for him.

Impatient and sulking, Frankie scowls at his watch until the sound of my approaching footsteps carries to his ears over the noise below us. He lifts his thick head in my direction and drags his gaze over my body, which sends a small wave of anxiety through me.

"What took you so long?" He grumbles.

I shrug. "Couldn't figure out what to wear."

He gives me a smug half-smirk, and for a moment, he's the spitting image of his father. "Trying to pick out something I'd like, were you?"

I want to scream a laugh in his face, but instead I smile through gritted teeth. "Dream on, asshole."

His smirk melts off, much to my satisfaction, but instead he fits another glare on his face. "You will not speak to me that way when I'm your husband."

Wanna bet?

He cocks his elbow toward me, offering me his arm.

"Of course I won't." I agree, reluctantly taking it. "I won't speak to you *at all.*"

Frankie's head jerks in my direction like he has more to say, but his voice is cut off by the roaring applause of family, friends, and other guests and associates, who've spotted us on the top stair.

We descend to this deafening, horribly uncomfortable crescendo of clapping hands and ogling eyeballs, taking the grand staircase slowly, step by step.

This is already way too much human interaction for me at one time.

Wow. How the hell am I going to make it through an entire night of this?

To keep the panic down, I distract myself, eyes anxiously scanning the crowd.

I barely know a single person here.

And then I spot him among the faces gazing up at me.

It's like picking out a king in a crowd of peasants.

Rocco stands near the back of a large group, looking like a million bucks in a designer Italian suit, hair pressed back, and freshly shaven. His syrup brown eyes are all over me, and as soon as our gazes touch, I can feel his presence in every corner of my body.

The look on his absurdly handsome face says it all.

Heat, desire, and admiration glimmer in his eyes. I feel the weight of them from here. I want him. So badly, I have to resist every impulse in my body crying out for me to run to him, fly to him, swim to him, whatever I have to do.

But I can't. Not yet.

Instead, I have a role to play. At least for a little while.

The dutiful bride-to-be.

Yuck.

After we've safely descended into the crowd of our guests, members of the estate serving staff usher us, followed by everyone else, into what used to be a ballroom. I can't keep my mouth closed as we journey beneath an arch, and find ourselves in a bountifully decorated marble auditorium.

The room is at least the size of an NBA basketball court, and so tall, banisters of the upper floors of the mansion look down on it.

Silk banners braided with nature hang along the walls. Flower arrangements as tall as I am sit at equidistant intervals on an excessively large dining table that bisects the room, cutting it in half. Delicate place settings, elegant name cards labeling each one...Tall chairs with freshly steamed, decadently red upholstery.

I don't want to marry into their family, but no one will ever say the Calzavarras don't know how to entertain.

Damn, this place looks incredible.

Two attendants lead us to the head of the table, where we're the first to be seated, and slowly, everyone else in attendance follows suit.

This wide imposing table is so long and so ornately adorned that I cannot even see the other end of it, where Don Sabatini sits, the Dalla Porta underboss and caporegime on either sides of him, followed by Donna, Ciro, and my mother. Technically, we're sitting across from our parents, but the distance feels significant.

Especially when the chatter filling up the room is enough that I can't even hear myself think. It takes everything in me not to look for Rocco, though I know he's nearby. I'll find him, surely, once everyone sits down for the meal, but until then, I know I'm not to look as though there's anything more important about tonight than what I'm currently doing.

Spending quality time with the Dalla Porta's one and only prince, cruel and unusual though he may be.

Soon, the servers return to serve us a gourmet five course meal. More juicy seafood. Seared flank steak. Exquisite pasta. Bread and butter that taste fresh from the motherland. It's a foodie's paradise in here.

Too bad I'm too amped to fully enjoy it.

What I should be enjoying is the delightful *silence* coming from the man beside me. But instead, I'm hardly breathing in this dress.

The real reason my heart's palpitating is because I can feel Rocco's eyes on my face from further down the table. He was seated on the left side about eight seats down from me.

I can't sneak too many glances in his direction, or my interest will be obvious, especially when I'm sitting so close to my betrothed, and all the many members of our families.

But pretending like Rocco's presence doesn't mean anything to me is fruitless. Joy and excitement have my heart rejoicing.

He came, I comfort myself. *He really came.*

When I'm not finding subtle, easily misread opportunities to glance at Rocco, I subtly watch Ciro Calzavarra, chatting eagerly with my still-despondent mother.

After everything I learned yesterday about the Red Years, I can't help but wonder how he fits into all of it. His oldest brother was stolen by the family's sworn enemy. His middle brother was killed by the same mafia—or so people think.

In a matter of just a few years, the man went from being the youngest son to the only one. What sticks out to me is that he doesn't carry himself like a man who's been unduly burdened by these tragic turns of fate.

Unlike his father.

I always thought Don Saba's demeanor was due to the harshness and cruelty of the world he commands, but now that I know more about all that he's suffered and lost, it's obvious to me that the man's dark, stoic demeanor is also a container for pain that runs fathoms deep.

Whereas Ciro seems awfully at home as the heir of this mafia, for someone who was never supposed to have that title in the first place...

After we've been stuffed full of dinner, it's time for dancing.

Why God?

Guests rise from their places, taking each other's hands and gliding toward the other half of this enormous room, where a large space has been left clear, precisely for this purpose.

Anxious, I watch to see if Rocco leaves the table and whether any of the single women here try to coax him out onto the floor.

But before I can lay my eyes to him, a classy orchestral melody begins to swell through the room. I'm admiring it, until Frankie crushes his man hand around mine.

My eyes snap to his face, except his head isn't where I expected it to be. He's standing up now, instead of sitting down, yanking my hand like he expects me to go out and there and...

I look to the dance floor, then back up to his impatient face. "No."

"Yes." He uses his strength to hoist me out of my seat.

"I hate dancing."

"I don't care what you hate." He gives me a wicked smile.

No, no, no, no.

I can't stop it as he all but drags me out onto the floor for a slow dance.

Frankie doesn't spare his strength, yanking me firmly into his meaty embrace. My back arches involuntarily away from his touch, trying to keep our faces far enough apart that he won't get any disgusting ideas.

But the more I pull back from him, the more he tightens his

grip, until his mouth hovers right next to my ear, and I'm eye to eye with his thick, massive shoulder.

All of my attention is eaten up by the danger of being in the literal clutches of a man I loathe. Almost every part of me seems in danger of being touched by him.

"That's it," Frankie chuckles darkly, sending a quiver of fear through me. "Quit resisting me, *Eleanora*."

"Never."

"We're not children anymore." He goads me with mock maturity in his voice. "In two weeks, we will be married, you and I. Isn't it time we started acting like it?"

The song we're dancing to FINALLY winds to a close, but Frankie doesn't loosen his grip on my body even a bit.

"*There*. You've had your dance. Now let me go." I spit the words at his shoulder with all the malice I have inside me.

Then he roughens his grip, like he's trying to piss me off. "I'll do whatever I like *for as long as like* with my own wife."

I hate the way he has the lines of our bodies crushed together with his might.

I'm having enough trouble breathing as it is without his awful cologne choking me like this. Fear thunders inside me, hard and crackling.

What if Frankie forces me to do this for the next hour? What if he doesn't take his big horrible hands off me until the night is over? What if he doesn't release me, even then? What if this sleaze-ball expects a preview of the honeymoon night?

My mind fractures into terrifying imaginations of what might await me at the hands of Gianfrancesco, and the images don't stop coming, not until our dance is interrupted by the authoritative edge of a deep, warm voice.

"May I cut in?" It's Rocco. *My hero.*

Gianfrancesco jerks us to a stop, acknowledging him with a darkly suspicious glare. "Excuse me?"

"If you don't mind…" The edge in Rocco's tone is sharp enough to cut meat. "I'd like to ask your fiancée to dance."

CHAPTER 20

Rocco

OBVIOUSLY, coming over here was risky and reckless as all fuck.

But I couldn't just stand by while Nora's prick of a fiancé got carried away.

I clocked the fear in her bright brown eyes from across the room.

Something needed to be done, so I did it.

I cut in, and here I am, face to face in a vicious staring match with the grandson of Don Sabatini Calzavarra, one of the deadliest and most powerful men in New York City.

"I don't share what's mine," Gianfrancesco replies, still with one grubby hand dangerously close to Nora's ass, and the other squeezing the life out of her hand.

"And once you're married, you'll never have to." I try for a polite smile, though I'm *aching* to rip my pen from my pocket and stab this jackass in the face. "Won't you be so kind as to make an exception tonight?"

"Get lost, you fucking geezer." He stabs me with the words.

Now, this little brat is *really* starting to piss me off.

"As much as you'd like that," I smile through murderous intent. "I'm not going anywhere."

Gianfrancesco releases Nora, so he can face me head on.

As soon as he removes his hands from her body, I relax on the inside. That's all I wanted him to do.

The man is seconds away from some snarled remark when his mother joins our trio of discontent, wearing a long pink frock with her dirty blond hair piled high on her head. Donna Calzavarra only has eyes for her son.

"Dance with your mother and stop frowning like that," she interjects, touching his cheek with her hand. "You'll get lines."

It's clear young Frankie has a soft spot for his mother. Whatever feathers I bristled relax, his confrontational posture deflates a few notches, and he holds out his hand to her without protest. She takes it and leads him away, and that's the last we hear from him. He does throw me one last glare before I settle my hands on Nora's body and begin to spin us in the opposite direction.

"I can't believe you did that." Nora's awed tone barely hides a giggle underneath. "My sister's the only one with the balls to stand up to *him.*"

I can't believe I'm really here, and that this exquisite woman is actually in my arms. As soon as I look down at her smiling face, I'm struck all over again by how stunning she is. Seeing her walk down those red carpet stairs on the arm of another man about gave me an ulcer.

"Has anyone told you how beautiful you look tonight?"

Her eyebrows hop, her painted lips pulling up into the first genuine smile I've seen her wear all night. "You clean up pretty well yourself."

"You don't have to sound so surprised," I say to cover for the way her simplest flattery creates pandemonium in my core.

"I'm not." Her smile warms even more.

Jesus, I want to kiss her right here in front of all these people. Not a single one of them matters to me. She's the only thing in this whole palace worth looking at.

"Are you all right?" I nod in the direction of Prince Charming. "He didn't hurt you, did he?"

"My hand hurts a little," she owns. "But I'm sure his ego hurts *worse*."

"What can I say?" Grinning, I lead her into a new rotation and pull her a little closer to me in the process. "He wants there to be something between you, and so do I. A crowbar."

She laughs. "A continent, if I had my way."

"I like your way better."

For a song, we simply spin in victorious delight. Here we are, in plain sight, doing what we each want to do most. Keep Nora away from her horrible fiancé...and perhaps, be together.

I wouldn't even consider flirtatious banter a strong suit of mine, but somehow, with her...my personality works. Instead of being the ghoulish shadow in the back of the room the way I am with the Balbonis, I'm front and center, fitting in for once.

Nora and I seem on the same page about one thing at least.

We're both trying to mask the rampant attraction running back and forth between us, like a happy dog.

With every circle we make, the desire to devour her grows stronger.

I've got to get back to making small talk or she may not get through this dance without a good tonguing from me.

Glancing over her head at the other guests, I spot Frankie and his mother.

As though reading my mind, Nora murmurs. "Can you see him?"

"Yes."

"Is he watching us?"

"No. He and Mrs. Calzavarra have stopped dancing though." I meet Nora's inquisitive gaze. "Seems they're doing a bit of networking."

"Spin me around," she suggests, amusement bouncing in her eyes.

I rotate us as she suggests, and watch as she gazes past me toward the far side of the room. The way she breaks into a smile and a little laugh briefly stops my heart.

"She's doing it again." Nora shakes her head.

"What?"

"Donna's showing him off to all the other eligible women she'd rather he marry."

Ah. That would explain the cold interruption she made while her son was in the middle of dancing with his fiancee.

"You're not her top choice?" I arch an eyebrow.

This question sends Nora into another laugh. "Oh, I'm definitely her top choice. For a guillotine, maybe. Or exile on a deserted island."

Now, I'm laughing. "Why's that?"

She gives me another adorable little shrug. "Would any woman be good enough for a mother who loves her son that much? Donna thinks the sun shines out of his ass."

"She's not the only one…" I mutter, glancing back over at them. The elegant women being introduced to Frankie seem quite happy to fall all over him. He's entirely occupied by their undivided attention.

So occupied in fact that he's not watching us.

Which gives me and Nora a bit of privacy.

Some much needed cover.

Which emboldens me to pull her even closer to me, as the next slow song blooms through the room. The hand of hers I'm holding, I lift up onto my shoulder. Soon her forearms rest on either side of my neck, and both my hands have found a place on the small of her back.

Her eyes and lips are just below my own, the temptation to kiss her reaches an apex so high, I can barely remember to keep turning us in small circles.

But of course, allowing myself to hold her so intimately sends guilt and dread running through me. Faster with every passing second.

This morning, Jaco, Vito and the others ordered me to kidnap Nora from this party.

How exactly to do the job undetected is a detail that Vito purposefully left out.

That's just like him to send me behind enemy lines without a plan or clear instructions. If I survive, I'm praised for being quick on my feet, which only pisses Vito off more. If I get shot or someday die, Vito throws a fucking party.

But even if my employers had given me a clear exit strategy and lots of backup, how would I begin to harm Nora when I feel this way about her?

Fiero mentioned in the debriefing earlier that they planned to take the Dalla Porta security cameras offline for the evening, but left out all the specifics. And honestly, in a room full of as many people as there are guns, cameras are the least of my worries.

"Rocco." Nora cuts through my doom spiral with just the sound of her sweet voice.

"Yes, sweetheart," I reply involuntarily. What the fuck kind of kidnapper am I?

She lowers her voice, giving me an intent look. "Meet me upstairs?"

I gape at her a little.

"My room's on the fourth floor." Her gaze drifts down to my mouth a moment, and I swear to God I almost take her right then. "We can talk there…"

CHAPTER 21

Nora

INTO ROCCO'S EAR, I whisper the best way to get upstairs unnoticed, and try to not get carried away by his delicious scent.

He waits until this song ends, and then slips away from me, leaving me a little chilly in the absence of his insane warmth, glancing anxiously around the room for any signs of an overbearing fiancé.

Thankfully, Frankie seems perfectly happy with the more suitable wife contestants Donna's picked out for him. He's not paying me any attention which is excellent.

All that's left for me to do is find my perfect window of opportunity to disappear.

Maybe, heading for one of the several downstairs bathrooms is my best bet. I begin to migrate toward the arch that leads out of the grand ballroom, but before I get anywhere near the exit, I'm caught by the scathing expression on my mother's face.

Shit.

Mothers have the uncanny ability to tell you exactly what you've done wrong with just one withering look. She's clearly displeased about my dancing with Rocco, and as if that weren't clear enough, she jabs her finger in my direction and then sticks it toward the hallway beyond the ballroom.

The universal gesture for *get your ass outside, now.*

I can only brace myself.

Whatever comes next is definitely going to be painful.

But it is also one hundred percent my best chance to get away from this party and sneak upstairs.

So I buckle up and follow her lead.

I swivel between party guests until I've made it to the arch. When I duck under it, I don't see my mother. It's her snapping fingers that catches my attention. She's standing, halfway hidden in a circular alcove around the corner at the end of this magnificent hall. I walk her way until the alcove is in full view.

Two benches, a small fireplace, and an armchair set into a large cutout in the wall.

As soon as we're both out of sight of the hallway, a searing, blinding pain cracks into the side of my face. I'm so caught off guard the force of my mother's slap sends me down onto the bench.

I cup my blaring, stinging cheek, startled tears brimming my eyes before I've even convinced myself that she just did that.

My mother. A woman who has never raised a hand to either of her children once in her life... She just struck me.

"What the hell did you think you were doing back there?" Her voice is serpentine and cold, as she snaps at me. "How dare you shun your fiancé like that?"

"Donna wanted to dance with him—"

"Shut your mouth this instant."

I can't even look at her, I'm in such denial that our relationship has gotten as bad as this. All I'm looking at is her arms by her side, her delicate mothering hands coiled to shaking, furious fists.

"You dare openly disrespect the man you're about to marry? *Flirting*—No. *Throwing yourself* at that family associate?"

That makes me look up at her, now furious myself.

"Disgracing yourself and me. Not to mention your father." Her eyes are wide and wild with rage I've never known her to be capable of. "This isn't how we brought you up, Eleanora."

"No." I rise to my full height, like we're about to go head to head. "This *isn't* how you brought me up. You didn't raise me to marry a man I *hate* just to protect ourselves. You didn't raise me to lie about what I feel or what I think, just to please other people!"

"Everyone is watching your behavior!" She erupts. "Especially Ciro and Saba. Don't you understand that?"

"What I *understand* is that your new in-laws matter more to you than I do."

My mother closes her mouth like I've hurt her.

Good.

"Just tell me who he is and how long this has been going on." Voice low, she folds her arms tight across her chest.

"*Who?*"

"Give me a little credit, Nora." She narrows her eyes. "Don't tell me you're in love with him."

Turns out my mother can slap me without using her hands, too.

I about choke down my own tongue. *In love?*

With one sentence I find myself waking the hell up, like an alarm clock's blaring where my heart should be.

Me? In love with Rocco?

I've never considered the idea until this moment, and the way it does something to me on the inside is more than a little concerning.

"Well?" Now, she's angrily tapping her foot.

"Well, nothing." I brush down my dress, hating how guilty I sound. "There's nothing going on between me and that man."

I don't sound convincing at all, and my mother makes no secret of it.

"Stop *lying*," she seethes. "Where did you meet him?"

"Dad's funeral." I blurt out the truth. "He's an old friend of his."

My mother's eyes widen in confusion, before rolling closed. She affixes her fingers to her forehead. "Nora, you cannot be so stupid."

"Apparently, I can."

Her head snaps up, horror stricken. "What do you mean?"

"What does it matter?" It hurts to shrug now, my shoulders are so tight with tension. "All you care about is your precious son-in-law to be."

Her eyebrows fly up her forehead, a new wave of rage charging out of her mouth. "You cannot begin to understand the sacrifices I've made for this family. I haven't spent all these years playing the role of dutiful wife, so that you could get knocked up by some whoremonger who met your father once!"

I've never heard such harsh cutting words from my mother.

More proof that the woman I once knew is gone.

She's turned into someone entirely unrecognizable from the warm, loving woman who raised me. Maybe, never to return.

I'm sure as fuck not going to wait on it.

Not after this.

Even though it kills me to let her go.

"You don't even know him!" I spit back at her, defensive and spinning out of control. "And I'm not pregnant. And there's nothing going on between us. It was just a dance."

It still doesn't sound like I'm telling the truth, but in my defense, I don't exactly know what the truth is.

I don't know how to answer these horrifying, hurtful questions because I don't know what's going on between me and Rocco.

Until two weeks ago, I didn't even know the man existed.

How can everything be so different after just a few days?

A few chance encounters...

"Whatever it is, *end it,* Nora. End it now." The edge in her voice chills me to my core. "You're someone else's bride, and nothing you do is going to change that."

We'll see about that, I don't say.

My mother storms off after those parting shots, but what she doesn't realize is that she's left me with a renewed sense of determination to find out what happened to Dad.

Why he was murdered...

And after I get that closure from this whole experience, I'm going to disappear from this awful mafia. For good.

It only takes me a few moments to navigate to the restrooms. I choose the set nearest to the kitchens, which are still bustling with activity, even an hour after that giant scrumptious meal was served.

I slip inside the enormous single stall room and splash ice water on my face.

There's a faint redness on my slightly-swollen cheek.

I hope Rocco won't notice.

Tears drift down my face, but I swipe them away and sniff hard to keep the sobs at bay. There's no time to linger on these feelings now.

I've got work to do.

When I slip out of the bathroom, I leave the light on to create the appearance that the room is occupied, even after I'm done and gone.

Afterward, I slip past the kitchen and zip down darkened, cool, cavernous hallways until I reach the stairwell on the backside of the Dalla Porta property, equally enormous, but less grand.

Then I flit upstairs beneath everyone's notice.

I need to find Rocco.

CHAPTER 22

Rocco

I FOUND the private staircase Nora mentioned, but the higher up I climb, the stranger I begin to feel. The upper floors of this estate give me a hazy, head-achy kind of deja vu which just might be the worst thing to happen to me all day.

Worse than Zia accusing me of being in love.

Worse than my employers ordering me to kidnap a woman I've come to care for.

A random flashback coming on, here, now, where that woman might see me... If she finds out how defective I am, there's no way she'll trust me to protect her. There's no way that she'll still be interested in me.

Why is the idea of *that* more devastating than the reality that I've got to hurt her or face the consequences for my defiance?

Splitting cranial sensation attacks as I climb the final step and find myself on the upstairs landing of the fourth floor. I can see that the case continues up to a final floor above, but tilting my head back sends on a fresh wave of pain so intense, I fall against the bannister, dizzy and nauseous.

Fuck me, I hate it when this happens.

Sometimes, certain places trigger physiological responses in my body, even if I don't know why. Might be that the place or orientation of it reminds me of somewhere I can't remember.

I've never figured out what this feeling is or why it happens.

Neither did the doctors in Sicily when I was just a teenager struggling with these massive migraines.

All I know is that they've been happening as long as I can remember, and they always happen more or less the same way.

Without warning, I find myself caught in the throes of some kind of flashback.

Voices from the past warp my hearing, gnawing at the frayed edges of my consciousness. Featureless faces from the past that I can't remember float through my mind, while my skull pounds and my pulse speeds beneath my skin.

No. I grip the bannister hard, dragging myself up. *She'll be here any minute. Please, no. Don't let me fall apart here and now.*

Not in front of Nora.

Fighting off flashbacks only leads back to the awful reality of my mission tonight.

Despite all the warring guilt, lust, and now pain I'm experiencing, I'll have to find a way to abduct Nora tonight. Or else. The Balboni administration is agitated that it's even taken this long.

Any idiot could see that now is the perfect chance to subdue her and haul her off.

I have to find the strength to do that. I can't let my brain get in the way.

Not again.

Not tonight.

I force myself upward until I'm standing at my full height. The dizziness has yet to subside, my gait isn't surefooted, I'm swaying.

My gaze blurs and clears out of step with my racing heartbeat.

Come this way. I want to show you—

DAD! The shout of a little boy.

Not now, Lio.

I slap my palms over my ears, as though that might lessen the volume of the voices echoing in my own head.

In this red-carpet hallway with marble floors and ceilings, I stagger into a nearby chair which faces a larger than life oil painting. A masterpiece.

Breathing deeply, I cling to the mindfulness practice years of meditation has given me. I pour my willpower into my eyes, working with difficulty to focus on the painting and the details. The dark shadows, the strokes of light and color. People depicted in curious positions, beckoning around animals in distress

Slowly, the overwhelming head pain lessens, funneling out like debris-filled water through a big storm grate.

My pulse slows down to its regular pace, and my head starts to feel its normal weight again, instead of the insanely heavy feeling I get when I'm caught in an attack, like my brain weighs ten times more than usual.

Amazingly, wondrously, miraculously, I'm starting to feel more like myself, and Nora didn't arrive to discover anything to the contrary.

In fact, I don't perceive the sound of her footsteps coming up the staircase until several minutes later. When she does finally appear before me, her expression is excited and victorious, if a smidgen crestfallen. It's barely perceptible but her cheek...

Her right cheek seems pinker than the other.

It wasn't that way when we danced downstairs, but before I can say a single word, about anything, she strides right up to me and slides her fingers through mine.

"Come on." She flashes a dazzling smile, but I don't let it get to me.

Hardness solidifies in my chest.

I'll do it in her bedroom.

As soon as we're alone together, I'll take the pen from my breast pocket and jab her in the neck with a tranquilizer. She'll be out before she realizes what's happening. I'll decide how to transport her once she's under and I'm alone with my thoughts to formulate the next part of this plan.

I already despise myself for what I'm about to do.

It's not an unfamiliar sensation. I've done more than my fair share of gruesome, bloody, despicable things. But my self-hatred has never been quite this strong before.

Maybe that's because I've never cared this much about anyone I've ever been assigned to handle, hurt, or terminate.

Despite the learned apathy I've honed so well over the past two decades spreading through me like an ice layer, Nora's hand in mine is warm. The coldness I feel doesn't reach my fingertips, which eagerly curl around hers. Clinging to her.

She may not know it, but these are our last moments together.

Like this anyway.

Once I get her to the safe house the Balbonis have picked out, I've been ordered to leave her there and return to the warehouse.

Whatever happens after that...

A knot forms in my throat.

My brain knows what I'm supposed to tell myself.

It's not your concern, Rocco.

I know how this works.

I didn't just become an enforcer yesterday.

But even my many years of experience don't make this easy.

Why can't this be easy?

Mind racing, body on high alert, I follow Nora the length of this hallway and then to the left, down another double wide corridor.

It's deadly quiet up here. Anyone who lives on this floor must be downstairs at the festivities. Smuggling her out of here should be simple enough.

There's no one milling about to see or stop me.

And if Fiero and the others really were successful in jamming the security cameras stationed every few feet, all the better.

Finally, Nora stops to let us through a set of heavy wooden double doors.

We step inside what appears to be a multi-bedroom suite.

A luxurious seating group in the center, a large fireplace on the far wall. A full kitchen. A bedroom off to the right, and…

"This way." Nora pulls me again to the left.

This is it. My heart pounds hard and painful in my chest. I can't put this off any longer. It has to be tonight. There won't be any forgiveness if I fail a second time.

Through a nearby doorway, I follow her—as I'm starting to believe I might do anywhere—into a large, old world bedroom. It looks like something from the palace at Versailles. Red walls, curtains, drapes, and carpets greet me, as Nora locks the door behind us.

It's a room certainly fit for a queen, but it doesn't suit Nora.

Too stuffy, regal, and old, when she's a breath of fresh mountain air.

Only one question remains.

How will I muster the courage to hurt the only woman who's managed to truly captivate me in all my life?

CHAPTER 23

Nora

I TURN THE LOCK, securing my bedroom door.

And the moment I turn around and see Rocco there, gazing at me with that severe, heart-meltingly sexy look on his face, it hits me.

I have a dangerous, deadly, unbearably gorgeous man alone in my bedroom.

With a locked door behind me.

We're free to do whatever we want. Am I really going to waste this precious opportunity with talking?

Lust sandbags me so hard, I can't move.

For fear that my panties are going to fly off.

Which is an overwhelming feeling because…this is the first time I've felt this way about someone before. I've never wanted a man so much in my life. No man has ever made me weak in the knees. Literally.

And my mother's damning words from earlier are still on my mind. *Don't tell me you're in love with him.*

Could it be possible that I actually feel that way about someone I just met a few weeks ago? A man I barely know, at that.

I'm so turned around—so *mesmerized*—by the sight of Rocco in that designer suit, eating me one bite at a time with his eyes, that I start babbling almost immediately.

"I just got into a fight with my mom."

His eyes immediately lower to my cheek. "What about?"

"Our dance." The tears aren't far off. "She scolded me for... flirting with another man in front of my fiancé. She thinks I'm in love with you."

Whatever mask Rocco wears falls away when I say those words. His nostrils flare, his chest swells up. Eyes widening, he clenches his fists. Almost like he's working hard to hold something back. Meanwhile, there might as well be a construction site in my chest, my heart's jackhammering around so hard.

"Well." Rocco takes a single step toward me, voice rough with an emotion I can't name. "What do *you* think?" He shunts his eyes closed like he's angry with himself, and then opens them again. "I mean, what did you tell her?"

"It doesn't matter what I told her." Rocco comes at me this time, unreservedly. Reaching for him with my last breath, I say, "*So what if I am?*"

My lips melt into his, as he claims my body with his big, strong hands, another growl in his throat. Rocco crushes us to the door behind me, his tall, thick frame covering every part of me.

All notions of talking to Rocco about what I discovered in my father's office yesterday evaporate into the air, while I lose myself in the kiss of my life.

My head rocks back into the wood of the door as Rocco angles his hot, hungry mouth at mine, pressing my lips further open with every deep, seductive kiss.

Rocco awakens my body with his hands, letting them rove all

over the soft luxurious material of this dress. He paws at me until I'm breathless, his right hand roaming from my waist up over my breasts, drifting across my collarbone up my neck until his long fingers are balanced against my jaw.

He slides his tongue into my mouth and lust douses me through and through, creating humidity between my thighs. We tangle our tongues together until my whole body seems to be made of lust and lightning, and when he pulls his mouth away, he rests his forehead on mine.

"Before I came here tonight," he pants. "Someone accused *me* of being in love with *you*."

"Really?" I try not to sound as eager to hear more as I actually am.

He nods, his silky soft hair grazing my face.

"What did you say to them?" Murmuring to him in this heat we've made, I lock my hands a little tighter around his neck.

"I didn't know what to say." His admission makes my heart sink ever so slightly.

Does that mean…whatever's happening here is different for him than it is for me?

"What should I have said?" His long fingers come back to my jaw. He tips my mouth up to his. *"She's all I've been able to think about since I first laid eyes on her'?"* He sticks a wild kiss to my mouth. I'm so hot for it, I moan against his lips. "That I'm obsessed with the idea of *making her mine?*"

I can't breathe.

"It's not love, I just dream of her touch'?" Somehow, he drags me even tighter against him, deepening his irresistible kiss. "How could I know what to say? I've never felt this way about a woman before."

My eyes spring open at those words. "You haven't?"

He shakes his head against mine. "No, Nora." When he can see the utter surprise on my face, he draws back to look at me. "What did you think?"

"I thought..." I'm too stunned to tell him what I thought.

Rocco's so much older than I am and far more experienced. I just assumed that he'd been in love and done all of this at least a few times by now.

He exhales hard, looking a bit... well, embarrassed. Self conscious? So am I.

"It's all new to me." He tucks a tendril of hair behind my left ear. "Can't you tell?"

"Not at all." I touch his marvelous face, bringing his eyes back to mine. "Because it's the same for me."

His eyebrows hop. "You mean..."

"I've never felt this way about anyone before either."

He gives me a wild-eyed stare before letting his eyes fall closed completely. When he opens them again, his lids only rise halfway, and the lust brewing underneath is tenfold. "I don't think you understand what I'm saying, Eleanora." He bends his head into my neck and gives my throat a good bite.

God, that sprinkle of pain is heavenly.

"You are the only woman who's ever been able to capture me." He kisses up my jaw. "My attention. My thoughts. My...hopes."

To find out that I'm the only one who does this to him is insane... I barely know how to believe it, let alone what to do about it.

"I'm serious, Rocco." I drop my head to his chest, turning inward so my forehead rests against his sternum. "You're the only man who's ever... moved me." My face broils in the flames of vulnerability. "Since you barged into my life, I haven't been the same person that I was before."

He squeezes me tight, and I squeeze him back, burying my face against him, eagerly drinking in his scent.

How can this be?

I'm in his arms and nothing has ever felt so right before. I'm mystified by it, overwhelmed by the desire I feel for him. The urgency of it.

And how words don't do it justice.

I want to tell him how I feel with every part of me.

Wishing there was some way to show him this fire he starts and stokes within my heart. The intensity of all these feelings overflows, making me feel helpless and enamored, until the magic words arrive in my mind.

I pull back to find his eyes, in a similar state of chaos as my own. "Nora…"

"Make love to me."

That's all it takes.

Rocco's eyes fly wide, milliseconds before he rips me up into his arms with enormous strength. Lifting me by my waist, my legs fold around his on instinct.

For once, I'm finally up high enough to reach his mouth without any difficulty. I ply my lips to his, while he spins us away from my bedroom door and marches over to my bed. He lays me on the giant thing with surprising gentleness and grace.

Next, he rips off his suit jacket, tearing at his cuff links and shirt collar.

His face is so mottled with lust, he looks angry as he prowls onto my bed, climbing over me like a lion in his den.

He seals his mouth onto mine.

I can't help feeling that we're like converging streams of rushing river rapids, gushing toward a magnificent waterfall.

CHAPTER 24

Rocco

WELL, fuck. She's done it now…

My cock aches for me to rip every inch of clothing off her body, but I'm already careening helplessly through my attraction to her. If I see her naked, laying here for me, I know whatever thinning threads of self control I have left will tear away altogether, never to be regained.

It's already not looking good.

My tranquilizer pen is in my suit jacket.

The one I just took off and dropped onto the floor because all I can focus on right now is Nora and that crazy spell she hexed me with the moment her lips spoke the words *make love to me.*

Why did she have to start talking about love?

After all we've confessed to each other, I…

Fuck, I can't take it anymore.

On this enormous bed, fit for a queen, I stand on my knees a moment, undressing Nora with my eyes.

I won't get her naked. Not tonight.

But that doesn't stop my wild, hungry imagination from feasting on the fantasy that is her body.

"You're so fucking beautiful." My hands go to the hem of her royal blue dress and push the fabric up, revealing the soft skin of her thighs.

I keep going until my fingertips meet cotton and lace.

Leaving her dress in place, I strip her underwear down her thighs, drawing them away until her feet are free and I can toss them on the floor.

"Open those legs for me." I can't stop staring at the beginning of her cute little cunt, curls of her dark hair standing against her smooth skin.

"Rocco…" An ounce of concern tremors in her voice.

With difficulty, I tear my eyes from her body and meet her worried gaze.

"What is it?" My hands fall to her calves, stroking them gently.

I'm holding back a tidal wave of my own lust, and I don't know how much longer I can do it.

"I haven't…" She shakes her head, self conscious. "No one's ever done this with me before."

I blink at her, feeling as though I've been nailed between the eyes. This insanely alluring woman is… She's a…

No. That can't be right.

"Nora, you're not a virgin," the words fall out accusatory and disbelieving.

Her chest rises and falls faster, like her breathing is out of sync. "I've done a little bit here and there, but a very little. I've never gone quite *all* the way."

That nervous sheen in her hazy eyes only tantalizes me further.

My voice drops into a rough, dry, growl. "Oh, let me have the honor."

Fingertips clamping around her shins, I pull her legs apart myself. And then I'm staring at her pussy, swollen with need, her untouched folds ripe and ready for my hot, hungry tongue.

I descend on her with relish, savoring the moisture that meets my tongue, every sound Nora makes, and each twitch of her smooth, tone legs on either side of my face. Digging my hands beneath her ass, I pull myself deeper into her folds.

Sucking her clit between my lips, I bully it with my tongue, and then with the stubble bristling my face. I drag my chin over it and back, delighting in the way she jumps from pleasure, long arduous moans unfurling from her sexy mouth.

Trailing my tongue down to her hole, I torpedo inside.

Nodding my head up and down, my tongue slides inside and out, my nose wet as a pit bull's. Her hands fly to my hair, combing through it, and then holding on for dear life as I christen her pretty pussy with my ravenous mouth.

I flatten my tongue against her folds and travel the length of her, all the way back up to her clit, swirling my tongue around and around while I grab at her bare ass and pull it apart. I do this over and over again, until she bucks, yanking at my hair, while her hips shake. In the aftershocks, she grinds her entire pelvis forward and back across my face.

"*Ugh,*" I grouse, my fingers digging into her flesh while she gasps against this mattress from the orgasm I sucked right out of her clit. "You taste amazing."

"Holy fuck..." She murmurs, out of breath. "You're...*way too good* at that."

A chuckle rumbles in my chest, as I rise from my place of honor, face damp from her body. I go for my zipper, freeing my stiff cock from its enclosure. Nora's eyes drop straight to it, and the gratification I feel when I see the look on her face... Mmm.

The *is he really going to fit that inside me* look.

It's my fucking favorite.

Next, I climb onto her, pointing my cock at her sopping wet

pussy. Her knees rise on either side of my waist, and my left hand pushes in under her knee.

I drop my mouth to hers, and she circles her arms around my neck, pulling me in tight. Fire and desire rip through me, hot and scorching, like the lust animating my limbs. "You going to give me that pussy?" I growl against her mouth.

She nods, whispering. "Yes, yes—"

Then, I'm inside her, both of us groaning in unison.

"Mmm!" Nora's voice teeters up, alarm mixing into her sows of pleasure, as I ease all the way in as deep as her tight fucking pussy'll let me.

Heat melts me from the inside out. "Oh, fuck."

I'm in to the hilt, and her body's squeezing my cock so hard, she's going to push me right out without any help from my hips.

Rolling them against her, slow, I revel her in her depths, only pulling out an inch at a time before spearing her all the way through.

"*Oh, God.*" A heated sigh snakes out of her, as her head hits the duvet beneath.

"Yeah…"

Sweet Jesus, she feels so good, it makes me angry.

What the fuck have I been doing with my life up until now?

Why couldn't I have found her sooner?

I draw further out and my eyes slam shut, the sensation takes me over so fast.

"*Rocco,*" she whines my name, and I already know she's going to make me come. As if there was ever any doubt.

But before I let that happen, I'm going to put her pussy to *work*.

Gradually, I increase the tempo, pulling farther and farther out, and entering her with more force, hardening my long strokes until her voice becomes a spastic noise maker, moans, curses, and small shrieks bouncing between her lips while I give her sweet, delicious cunt a good pounding.

It's so intense, I can barely think.

It's so mind-blowingly amazing that the thought of anyone else getting to touch her like this makes me murderously angry, drilling her pussy even harder.

All of a sudden, I see my life for what it is.

An endless merry-go-round of bullshit.

Before I met Nora, I was going through the motions, awarding my allegiance and loyalty to the people who took me in. But not because I care about them, or because they care about me.

Jaco's always approved of me, but that's because I'm smart and capable. An asset he can use. I'm just the useful, pathetic, pitiful orphaned son of a Balboni associate that wound up dead.

I'm not his kid. He's not my father. As for his real children, Vito despises me. And Anunziata wants me. But all for what? None of them know who I am or see me for it. They don't appreciate me for it. And yet, I've dedicated my life to protecting them and all that their family stands for.

Out of nowhere, it hits me.

If I want to have a family, a real one where I love and belong somewhere, I'm going to have to make it myself.

The same way I'm making love to this woman right now.

"Fuck, Nora." I drop my head, planting my heavy palms on either side of her face.

Her hands are hooked beneath her knees, while I nail her in plank position, slamming my waist against hers.

Up into my eyes, she gazes at me, lost in this same pleasure scape that's changing my life right now, one hard thrust at a time.

I don't know how I'll give this feeling up.

Being inside her's just too good.

With our gazes locked on each other, my whole world opens up. I can feel my chest expanding.

"Run away with me," I tell her, voice strong and clear.

The words are out before I can stop them. These words I've never said or imagined before...But the crazy thing is that they're true.

I realize it, balls deep inside this woman, that I really would throw away everything to be with her. There's no way I'm going to hurt her like Vito wants.

The idea of taking Nora away from here and this life she's trapped in—even if it means protecting her from my mafia family and hers—fills me with a blinding, crackling light inside.

Hope. Anticipation. Excitement.

I want Eleanora Di Rienzo as I have never wanted anyone else.

As far as I'm concerned, she's already mine, and no one anywhere is allowed to touch her ever again.

Nora's hazy eyelids rise, as she takes my meaning.

"I will," she moans, nodding and starry-eyed. "I'll run away with you."

"Nora— " Just those five words and I lose it.

The pleasure destroys me, and I bust, my cock firing a load deep into her hot, wet pussy. Our hips grind together as orgasm overtakes me, hard and raw.

After several frozen seconds of post-ecstasy, I collapse on her, crushing her to the bed with the full heft of my body.

Fucking hell, I can't remember the last time I came that hard...

We lay there in silence, our mutual heat gradually easing, our hard breaths softening inhale by inhale.

Nora wraps her arms around my back, squeezing the fabric of my button down. One of my hands cups the back of her skull, while I feel her heart slamming against mine, even through the barriers of our party clothes.

But then, into the quiet darkness of my post-climax mind, without warning, doubt slices through me like a samurai's blade.

Once we're far away from here, of course I'll sit her down and tell her the truth, the whole truth of how we met, why I was there that night... But if she finds out the role I played in her father's murder, will she still want to be with me then?

When she finds out that I was only able to save her that night because I'd been preparing to abduct her on the orders of her family's arch enemy, will she still hold me like this?

Another major revelation charges through my mind.

If I don't tell Nora the truth before we elope, I could lose her forever when I bring it up later…

No. I can't risk that.

I won't.

Which means no more lies.

I don't want to trick her into being with me. She deserves far better than that.

She deserves far better than *me.*

"Rocco?" Nora's soft, satisfied voice cuts through my bleak thoughts before I can broach the subject.

"Yes, sweetheart." I drop another kiss to her mouth, her fingers sliding up my back and over my shoulders to again wind through my hair.

"Do you smell smoke?"

I freeze in place looking down at her, sniffing the air as concern rearranges her features. The crazy part is that when I draw in a deep breath… mixing in with Nora's immaculate scent, I do catch a whiff of smoke.

"Stay here." Climbing off of her, I tuck my cock back into these pants, zip up and head for her bedroom door. I listen first for voices.

Nothing.

Unlocking it, I throw one more glance her way. She sits up.

"I'll check the hall and be right back."

She nods, and I'm gone.

I navigate into the living area of her suite and sure enough, the whole place is filled with a faint haziness in the air.

What the fuck is going on?

I head out the door into the grand hallway, and the noise of a commotion several floors below drifts up into my ears. My eyes skate back and forth down the upstairs corridor as I jog back to the private staircase. When I get to the bannister and look down, I see them.

Smoky black clouds drifting up the stairwell, and beneath them, bright orange flames licking up the walls, casting shadows from the first floor.

The Dalla Porta estate is on fire.

And we need to escape.

CHAPTER 25

Nora

As soon as Rocco's gone, I climb off my mattress and pad over to the window on the far side of the room.

I glance down at the boulevard below, and—Holy shit.

Outside, party guests spill out onto the Dalla Porta's block.

Everyone.

Evacuating.

Standing off to one side, in a circle of security guards, are my mother and my in-laws to be. I spot my fiancé first, and his mother next to him.

Everyone's safe, but...

Yeah, the house must really be on fire.

Which means...

My limbs jump into action. I race around my bed into my palatial bathroom. Snatching a fresh pair of underwear and clean socks from a drawer, I rip them on and dig around for my favorite pair of black Converse high tops. I'd love to get out of this dress, but there's no time now.

This is our perfect opportunity to get away clean, to run away together like we just agreed to do… I'm not going to miss it over a pair of cargo pants—A glint of silver catches my eyes from the vanity counter.

Dad's keys. The ones that open all the doors to his secret office.

"Nora!" It's Rocco, calling from my bedroom. Swiping for the keys and dropping them in my bra, I jog back out and find him grabbing his suit jacket off the floor. "There you are. We've got to go. The first floor is—"

"Burning, I know."

"Why are you smiling?"

"Dreams do come true." I grab his hand, and without a single look back, I ditch this horrible place forever.

Out in the fourth floor hallway, there's even more smoke than I thought there'd be, but still we're okay.

"Come on. This way." I tug Rocco in the opposite direction from which we came, and we half-speedwalk, half-jog down the hallway toward the central staircase.

Even though I've only been living here for a few weeks, I know my way around this estate better than most.

"You're not thinking we're going to walk out the front door, hand in hand, are you?" His eyes are alight with humor, even though…I guess, we're technically running for our lives.

I throw a grin his way. "Absolutely not. I have a better idea."

We reach the main staircase, and hurry down the giant stairs toward the third level of this estate.

"Lead the way then." Rocco squeezes my hand.

"I know a shortcut out of here." I take him down the curving third floor hallway. When we get to the right door, I hold my arm out. "Give me a second to disable the alarm."

"What is this place?"

"My father's old office."

Once I've disabled the silent alarm and the booby traps, we're in. I hold a finger up to my mouth, so Rocco won't say anymore.

"Hugo?" I call up through the room.

Nothing. *Good.*

I doubt even Hugo knows the shortcut we're about to take and there's no reason to change any of that now.

"Coast's clear. Let's boogie." I zip across my father's office, Rocco right on my heels. We head straight for the bookshelves on the far side of the room.

"Who's Hugo?"

"My father's apprentice." I touch my finger to the spines on the middle shelf and drag it across the section of books whose titles start with S.

"Let me guess. A dog?"

That makes me laugh. "Close enough."

S-L, S-M, S-N, S-O...

"Here it is." I chirp, my finger falling on the dark green spine of a worn old tome. "Under SP. For secret passageway."

"Secret passageway?"

I pull the book from its place and a doorway reveals itself to our right, half a bookcase opening into a short, well lit hallway.

Rocco's eyebrows raise when he turns to give me a look. "You weren't kidding."

"My dad's idea. Come on."

As soon as we're in the passageway, we get the bookshelf door closed and locked behind us. The cool, untouched air in here refreshes us. As well as the relative quiet.

"This is a hell of a shortcut." His warm voice above my head makes me smile, even while nostalgia stabs me through the heart. The last time I walked this hallway, I was with Dad.

"My dad didn't want us to live on the Dalla Porta estate, but he also wasn't a fan of a long commute, so..." Tangling my fingers with Rocco's once again, we stride down the hall, only about a hundred feet.

Flagstone tiles cover the floor overlayed with a long Persian runner.

"You're saying…" Rocco's voice trails off as we come to a halt in front of the blue door. This is the one that leads into my childhood home.

I press down on the handle, and it opens easily into the darkened rooms of the townhouse I've shared with my parents since I was a child.

"We used to live here. Next door." I reach for the light switch on the wall, but Rocco stops me.

"Don't," he whispers. "We don't want anyone to know how we escaped."

We get the passage door shut behind us, and soon, there's no light whatsoever. Just the darkened floor plan of my childhood home brightened only by the street lamps outside and the murky copper glow of the flames people can see from the road.

"There." I sigh. "Safe, sound, and undetected."

"For now."

I don't like the ominous way that sounds, so I don't waste a second dwelling on it. Instead, I allow the familiar scents of home to calm me down. It's painful, remembering the way things used to be, and how they'll never be that way again.

But on the bright side, at least I got to say farewell.

"There's a fire escape we can use on the backside of the building," I sniff, my voice wobbling a little.

"Nora?"

"I'm okay." I swallow down a lump of emotion. "It's just been a big day."

Rocco squeezes my hand reassuringly, while we roam through my darkened house, finding our way down the hall to my old bedroom. The walls are covered with Switzerland posters and taped up pictures of me, my sister, and my mom from when we lived there during my childhood. There's a bookcase in one corner, beyond max capacity with novels and comics coming out of every crevice.

Next to my bed is the big window, the one with the fire escape, just outside.

I haven't opened this window in several months, and it sticks.

Takes me and Rocco to drag it open, lively sounds of a New York City night wafting in with the late April breeze.

We both climb out onto the escape, and get the window shut.

Down about eight flights of wiry metal stairs, we make it to the alley below that runs along the backside of the Dalla Porta block. This way, we won't be spotted by all the party guests out front, gawking at the fire engulfing the first floor of the estate. Hand in hand, Rocco and I take the alley by storm, jogging from there the few streets over to where Rocco parked his car.

In a few minutes, we're gone, basking in victory from the front seat of Rocco's Jaguar, purring down the darkened Manhattan city streets. He drives us in a happy, awed sort of quiet, until we're several neighborhoods from where we started.

He dives into a parallel parking space, cuts the engine and the headlights, and we look each other in the eye.

And then, we laugh.

Because we…

"We're really doing it," I marvel.

"We really *did* it." Rocco shoves a triumphant kiss to my mouth.

"Running away together," I muse when he lets me breathe. "Wait a minute. Rocco, does this mean we're a…couple?"

Rocco blinks at me, like he's doing the math for the first time too. Then he grins. "You better believe it."

"So, doesn't that make this our first night together as a couple?"

"It certainly does." He kisses my cheek and down into the curve of my neck. "What do you think we should do about that?"

How can just one question send such lewd fantasies stampeding through my mind? My face is hot all over again, visions of what we were doing just an hour ago, sparkling behind my eyes in hot, sexual glory…

As soon as the effusions of lust die down though, my mind really attaches itself to his question, and something does come to mind.

Something I've always wanted to do.

"Rocco, I want to go on a date." I've never said anything that made me feel so bubbly before.

He pulls back from me with a warm, yet wicked smile on his face. "Name it. Where do you want to do?"

Unfamiliar excitement animates me on the inside. "Let's paint the town."

CHAPTER 26

Nora

EVEN THOUGH I'VE been largely unconnected from the world of romance for...ever really, I surprisingly do know exactly where I want to go with Rocco on our first night together as a couple.

I have my sister to thank for it.

After about half an hour of driving, we pull up to a curb in Hell's Kitchen, and hop out onto a crowded curb.

"Where exactly is this place?" Rocco asks, hovering close to me as I maneuver through a throng of people toward a narrow side street with a hanging wine barrel above it.

"She said it's this way." I point at the barrel, and he grabs my hand.

We check both ways, then jaywalk toward it.

"Who?" Rocco gives me a curious glance.

"I'll tell you in a minute." I smile, as a warm doorway, leading down to a basement comes into view. "We're here."

Rocco and I duck through the opening in the brick wall, and descend down a long curve of small wooden steps until we arrive on a stone floor in the most beautiful place I've ever seen.

I have to cover my mouth.

"It's even more beautiful than she described," I whisper.

We're standing in a vintage wine cellar that a pair of gourmet chefs converted into a cozy, intimate, *gorgeous* little Italian restaurant.

"Welcome to *Annata*." A hostess steps up to us wearing jeans, a black t-shirt, and a patterned black apron with outlines of wine barrels all over it. Her shining blond hair falls halfway down her back, even while in that high ponytail. "I'll be serving you this evening. My name is Sam." Clear-eyed and smiling, she picks up two small menus. "Two for dinner?"

I nod eagerly, still taking the place in.

"Yes, thank you," Rocco answers, since I'm still without the power of speech.

Annata is small, only about eight tables in all.

All the tables are for two or four, and none of them any bigger than you might find in a modest cottage someplace in the Italian countryside. Two small candles light every table, and a mixture of vintage candelabra sconces and repurposed iron wine racks turned into hanging light fixtures give the rest of the restaurant its golden glow.

I feel like we've been transported into a glimmering Christmas ornament, while Sam leads us to a small table against the back wall of this adorable place. We slide down into comfy, worn-in wooden seats.

"Okay..." Rocco clears his throat, as soon as we're alone with our table and our menus. "Nora, this place is incredible. Now, I've really got to know how you found it."

"I didn't." I give him an unreserved grin. "Nico did." When he gives me a puzzled look, I add, "Nicoletta. My sister."

"Ah." He nods. "For a second there, I thought we were talking about the Velvet Underground."

"*You* listen to the Velvet Underground?" I can't hide my shock.

"Why? Can't I?"

"You don't strike me as a sixties experimental art rock fan."

"Well, I'm not." With a mischievous smile on his face, he turns his attention to the small rectangular menu cards Sam gave us. "But I still know who they are."

I pick up my menu—same as him, hiding a laugh in my throat —but still, I can't make myself focus on the words. This place is too magnificent.

All the walls are unrestored exposed brick. The ceiling is covered in rows and rows of hanging wine racks. Reds lay in lines above us, back and forth. Wine crates are stacked high along the walls, stamped with years and logos from all over Italy. Cross-hatched storage shelves peek out from different corners of the place.

The decor in here is so fantastic, I want to take out my phone and snap some pictures. I gasp.

Rocco's head snaps up. "What is it?"

"I forgot my phone," I realize. In my haste to get the fuck off the Dalla Porta estate, I didn't bring anything but myself. "I don't have my wallet either." My eyes go wide. I suggested we paint the town and I don't have so much as a dime on me. Fuck, this is embarrassing. "We got out of there so fast, I didn't even think to grab it, I—"

"You don't have to think about your wallet ever again, so long as I'm around."

"What?" My eyes meld into Rocco's. I shake my head a little, because I have no idea what that sentence even means.

"You're mine now." Rocco draws my hand to his mouth with such speed and grace, I don't even see it coming. He kisses my knuckles. "It is my privilege and honor to take care of you. Whatever you need, whatever you want, I don't want to see you without it."

Heart *flying,* I stammer at him, open mouthed. "It can't be quite that simple."

"Yes, it can. And *it is,* I assure you."

"Rocco—"

"It's my pleasure, Nora. Honestly. I want to. I wouldn't have it any other way, and I won't. Protest is futile."

"But—"

"*Nora.*"He releases my hand, only to place the menu back into it. "What would you like to eat tonight?"

"Took the words right out of my mouth." Sam's back, smiling down at us with a small notepad in her hand.

"I'll have the lasagna," Rocco orders first, and then looks at me. Sam follows suit, and I'm sitting here gawking like an idiot, so I drop my eyes to the menu instead.

There are only three options on *Annata's* menu.

Lasagna. Carbonara. Vongole.

"I'll have the carbonara, please."

"Excellent." Sam takes our menus. "Every entree comes with a wine of the chef's choice. Shall I bring you all some water in the meantime?"

"Yes, thank you." Rocco gives her a small, debonair smile, the picture of politeness, and she disappears, unscathed. I decide our hostess Sam must not be into men. If he'd smiled at me like that, I would have melted all over him.

I'm still gobsmacked about this whole financial care package he's offering.

My dad left me, my mom, and my sister everything he had, which was a lot. So it's not as though I need Rocco's money, but the fact that he's so willing to spend it on me is unexpectedly meaningful.

When Sam comes back with our waters, I down mine almost in a single gulp just to cover for how affected I am by it. Can't think about that right now.

Gotta change the subject.

"Anyway, so...my sister and I exchange letters," I blurt out without warning. "She writes to me about her life and adventures abroad."

"Where is she again?" Rocco sips from his water glass.

"Right now, she lives in Milan. She works in the fashion industry." I gesture with my hand as if to say, *she works in outer space.* "She's not allowed to come back to New York City without the express permission of the Dalla Porta, but her friends come here for work all the time, and they told her about this place. And in her last letter, she wrote to me about it."

I glance around, wishing bitterly for a moment that Nico could be here to see it herself...When she was cleared to come home for Dad's funeral, I actually hoped we might check this place out together to get away from the doom and gloom of everything happening at home. But Mom sent her home right away after announcing my engagement, so it wasn't to be.

I certainly never imagined I'd be experiencing it like *this,* just a few weeks later.

Rocco's deep voice brings me back to the moment. "What do you mean she's not allowed to come back to the city?"

I stare at him, pain reverberating deep in the emptiest place of my heart. Do I really want to tell him about the worst time of my life on a night like this?

Before I decide what to do, Sam returns with two large plates of the most mouth-watering food I've seen...well, since earlier tonight at my engagement party, at least. Then, she places two enormous glasses of wine before us.

The difference this time is that I actually enjoy it.

For the first time since my dad died, I can actually feel the force of my appetite revving back to life. This is the first meal I've been able to enjoy, whole heartedly and without reservation in a long time.

Twirling pasta around my fork, I take my first bite while Rocco cuts into his lasagna. The flavors explode in my mouth like a culinary fireworks display. I feel like the animated rat in that Pixar film about cooking and France.

We eat, and enjoy ourselves, and it is the most magical *date*— the most magical time I've ever experienced with another human being ever. Time drifts by beyond my notice, and before I know it, Rocco and I are splitting a fat square of scrumptious tiramisu, eagerly digging into it with antique silver spoons.

I keep catching his eyes on me, while I chew happily. Like I'm some kind of movie he's watching. It makes my heart skip every single time. I honestly...didn't know there was pleasure to be found on earth like this.

Not for me, anyway.

Rocco takes care of the check without even opening the little leather book with our bill tucked inside. It's like he refuses to take his eyes off me.

"Where to next?" He murmurs.

"I picked dinner. You pick next," I shrug.

Rocco opens his mouth, but before another word falls out, the clatter of shattering glass disrupts the whole restaurant. My head snaps in the direction of the noise. A patron tripped and fell right into a waiter carrying a tray of wine glasses, it appears, but the sudden noise of it was enough to send my heart galloping.

And when I look back at Rocco—*Rocco!*

He's hunched over in his chair, looking positively sick, both his hands buried in his hair like his head's been struck by something.

"Rocco, what is it?" My rock-climbing instructor first-aid skills kick in. "Are you in pain?" But there's something so wrong with him that he doesn't seem able to talk to me. I get up, moving closer to him, but as soon as I reach for his arm, he jerks it at me. Batting me away.

"*Go...*" His voice is a tortured, ragged rasp. "*Wait...outside...I don't...want you to...see...me...like this.*"

What the hell is happening?

Sam reappears with Rocco's card, and the receipt, concern in her voice. "Is everything all right over here?"

"I'm not sure." I take Rocco's card, drop it in his suit pocket, and try again to grab his arm. "I think he's having some kind of migraine. A seizure maybe."

"Should I call an ambulance?"

"*No...*" Rocco manages a strangled growl, even while obviously in serious pain. I've never seen him like this before. My hand brushes his skin, and he's burning up. Veins protrude from his usually smooth skin. His eyes are bulging and bloodshot, though he's doing his best to keep them closed.

I don't know what's going on, but I know we should get out of here. "He'll be all right with some air," I say, just to get Sam to leave us alone, and then I get my arm around his and work to get him upright and out of his seat.

He doesn't fight me this time, and I can see why.

The minute he's standing, he sways into me, like he's going to fall.

I hook his big arm around my shoulder, thanking God for all those long nights I spent at the gym. Supporting half the weight of a man as big as him would be impossible right now otherwise.

Heart still hammering, brain scrambling for what else to do, I walk him step by step toward *Annata's* exit. Patrons throw up puzzled looks, but I ignore them all. I keep looking at Rocco, but his eyes are pinched closed, and he's breathing hard and labored like he's under attack on the inside.

It takes several minutes, and I worry more than once that we're going to fall, but I get Rocco all the way up the restaurant's stairs and back out into the air of the city. He's still not back to normal, and I still don't know what's wrong. My heart's bumbling around my chest, thoughts passing through my mind, errant and frazzled.

Outside seemed like a good idea a few minutes ago, but now that we're out here, it seems worse. The blaring noise of the city at night. The jumpy energy of restaurants and bars, all of it seems to be making whatever's wrong with him worse.

Rocco staggers against the narrow alley's wall, a groan escaping him.

I need to get him someplace he can sit down. Somewhere quiet.

Those are the only two thoughts in my head that make any sense, as I get his arm over my shoulder again, and tug him the opposite way we came.

"Let's go," I grunt, using my quad and core strength to support his slightly shaking unsteady frame. "You're going to be okay. Let's get out of here."

On foot, we walk the length of the narrow alley, come out on the other side, and find ourselves on a quieter street than before. *Good.*

Rocco's still a bit out of it, though I can tell some of his balance is returning.

We keep moving, until the bright shopfronts disappear, and we're walking down residential neighborhood streets. We've almost reached another street corner when a twelve-foot tall wrought iron gate fence appears on our left.

I glance in that direction, and through it, in the distance glimpse a stone bench seated amongst the serenity of a private city garden...

That would be a perfect place to rest.

For both of us.

The only issue is that the garden seems to have just one access point and it's through a locked gate. I analyze the locking mechanism, sliding my hand as far as it'll go between the bars. It won't reach all the way. It's designed so that it can't be unlocked from the outside without a key, but that doesn't mean I couldn't unlock it from the inside, if I just...

When I stop walking, Rocco stops too. Still clutching his head with one hand.

"I'm...sorry...about this..." He grumbles, voice still distorted and strained.

"Shh." Gently I remove his arm from around my shoulder. "Hold onto this fence."

I guide his hand to the thin wrought iron bars, and make sure he's got a steady grip on it before I decide to do something wild.

Glancing up and down the sleepy Manhattan avenue, I check for cars, pedestrians, or...any cops patrolling on foot. But by all accounts, we seem to be pretty alone.

I hope we stay that way.

At least for the next five minutes.

"Nora..." He groans my name, pulling his eyelids back only a bit. "What—"

"Don't speak," I tell him. "I need to focus. Just hang on."

And then, using all my professional rock-climbing experience, I scale the twelve-foot gate in my converse, grabbing the bars, plying my sneakers to them, and hoisting myself up into the night air. Scaling vertical bars feels mostly like climbing, but a little bit like walking too. It's certainly not more challenging than free-climbing a rock's face or getting up the advanced wall at the gym.

Once I've topped it, I realize I can see the whole street from up here.

I can also tell what we've stumbled upon here is more than some private residential garden. It's more like a secret, pocket-sized botanical garden...It's gorgeous.

So gorgeous I forget myself a moment from this vantage point.

Then I hear Rocco grouse from below. "*Jesus...*" It sounds like a cross between a prayer and wince. Either way, I want to hurry.

Maneuvering myself carefully over the rounded points at the top of the gate, I drop down the rest of the way, landing easily on my feet.

The noise makes Rocco's eyes drag open with difficulty. When he sees me on the other side of the gate, his pained expression twists with confusion.

"How'd you get in there?"

I smile, but don't reply, as I unlock the gate, and carefully pull him through.

Once we're safely inside the secret garden, I get his arm around my shoulder again, and help him down a brick-lined pathway, motion sensor string lights blinking on as we pass. The sparkling white-gold lights woven through various shades of earthen green steals my breath a moment.

"You know..." I rub Rocco's side reassuringly. "This is still the best first date I've ever been on, fire and unexpected health events be damned."

"Ha...ha..." Rocco winces a little, as we make it to the bench I spotted.

To my pleasant surprise, it faces a small stone fountain.

I ease Rocco down onto the bench, using all my quad strength, and there, we settle into comfortable quiet, as the last of whatever he's going through seems to pass through his system and dissipate.

I can tell he's back to normal when he drops his head into his hands, striking the universal pose of shame. Rubbing his back, I wait for him to speak, but when he doesn't, I finally do.

"Hey..." I murmur, eyes on the fountain. "How are you feeling?"

"Mortified." His voice is back to normal and edged with self-directed loathing. "I hate that you saw me like that."

"Yeah," I breathe. "You want to tell me what exactly happened back there?"

He sits up, but doesn't look at me. I don't look at him either. We're sitting side by side, so I just slide my hand through his and give him a squeeze to show I'm here and I'm listening.

"That was PTSD." Slowly, his fingers bend tighter around mine.

"From what?"

"My childhood, funny enough." Though there's nothing funny about this moment. Rocco squeezes my hand back. "When I was thirteen, my parents and I were in an accident. I suffered pretty severe head trauma."

My heart's in my mouth, the weight of his story settling over me. "Oh God, Rocco."

"Don't feel sorry for me," he rushes on. "I'm the lucky one, after all. My parents didn't survive the accident."

The double whammy of lifelong head trauma and being orphaned overnight devastates my imagination. There's nothing I can say that won't sound pitying and stupid, so instead I ask in a small, sorry voice. "What kind of accident?"

Rocco shakes his head. "I don't remember. I don't remember anything before waking up in the hospital afterward, actually."

I can't help but turn to him then, my eyes connecting with his solemn profile. "Nothing?" I whisper.

He nods. "Nothing."

"Like…amnesia?"

"The doctors I saw as a kid weren't really sure what it is. Maybe my hippocampus was impacted by the accident. Or maybe whatever happened was so horrible and traumatic than my brain's simply repressing all the memories, and I'll get them back one day." He shrugs a big shoulder. "Who knows?"

"And in the meantime, you have these…brain attacks?"

He nods again. "They happen randomly for the most part. Unless something triggers them."

"Like what?"

"Shattering glass."

Understanding dawns on me. Back at the restaurant…

"So that's what caused it…"

"Yes."

After that one syllable, we devolve into a heavy quiet.

I'm amazed that Rocco's been through something so horrible, I had no idea. I'm also awed that a man so strong and smart has an insecurity that cuts him this deeply.

And even more confusing, somehow his humanity only makes him more attractive to me. Knowing he's not perfect makes him more approachable…

Not that I want to tell him *that.*

"It's okay, you know…" He interrupts our strange silence. "You can tell me if this changes things for you, I'll understand."

"What do you mean?" I turn to him again, but he still won't look at me.

From high above us in one of the townhouses over looking this garden, old-timey jazz floats through an open window layering these garden grounds with song.

It's beautiful, but it doesn't match the pained look on Rocco's face.

"Rocco." I touch his cheek with my fingers, slowly guiding his gaze to mine. "What are you talking about?"

Doubt shines in his deep brown eyes. "My brain's a loose cannon." I can tell by the edge in his voice how hard these words are to say. "What if when it comes down to it, I fail and I can't protect you?"

What is this painful nonsense coming out his mouth?

"I don't care. So what, you've got crazy shit going on upstairs." I'm so eager to reach him, wherever he is in that broken part of himself, that I'm tripping over my own words. "Listen to me. I care about your mind, and I want you to be okay. But it's not like I'm the poster child for perfect mental health. Who is? You are who you are, and you're okay with me. That's all there is to it. More than okay."

His eyes narrow at my response. He gives his head a shake. "You're not thinking clearly."

"Maybe not. But you're just going to have to deal with it." I rise to my feet, still firmly gripping his hand. "A little while ago, you said you'd give me whatever I want. And right now, I want another dance."

CHAPTER 27

Nora

ROCCO DOESN'T LOOK happy about it, but he stands up, and takes me in his arms the way I want him to. And after a few minutes of spinning in circles to borrowed jazz, he seems lighter on his feet.

I lay my head against his chest and close my eyes, while we rock side to side in an easier quiet. *Maybe*...Maybe I'll be able to put him at ease if I show him he's not the only one with a complicated past.

"Where were you born, Rocco?" I murmur against him.

"Sicily." He exhales deep. "What about you?"

"Here." My eyelids lower. "But we left New York only a few years after I was born."

He seems eager to talk about anything other than himself. "What happened?"

"When Nico and I were five years old, our parents told us that we were going on a vacation with Mama. And that Dad couldn't come because he was too swamped with work...We went to the south of Switzerland to visit Dad's family. We spent the summer there, expecting to leave by the end, but we didn't."

"What do you mean?"

"Every time we asked Mama when we were going home, when we'd get to see Dad, she made some excuse. And we didn't fully understand why. We didn't return to New York for many years. Eight, to be exact."

"But why?" His mouth is near my forehead.

"Our mom told us later on that it was for the safety of our family, since Dad did dangerous work, and we left it at that."

"Was that the truth?" Rocco's question strikes me a little funny. I don't like to think of my mother lying to us, but if the past few weeks have taught me anything, it's that I don't know her as well as I always thought I did...

"Not sure." I nestle my head a little more. "We didn't really question her back then. And besides, as much as we missed Dad, we also loved Switzerland. We grew up swimming, boating, hiking, skiing, and traveling around Europe quite a bit on the train. In fact, by the time it was okay for us to return to New York, aside from getting to see Dad again, I was entirely bummed about moving back to the states."

"How old were you then?"

"Thirteen." My face falls, and so does my voice. "That's when everything fell apart."

Rocco loosens his grip, so he can look down at me. The tenderness in his eyes is what gives me the courage to tell him the story. I've never told anyone before him. It's hard for me to talk about it.

He waits patiently, and finally, I sigh.

"Everything changed when we got back from Europe..." My eyebrows knit together in frustration just thinking about it. "Almost as soon as we got home, we began to hear these rumors that...that I'd been selected as Frankie's bride."

249

"When you were just a child?" Anger underscores Rocco's tone. "That's absurd."

"That's exactly how we all felt about it. My parents hated the idea of it. They resisted entirely, as did I, and they assured me that no such marriage would ever take place."

"I don't understand." Rocco's shaking his head. "If that's true, then...why now?"

I give him a humorless laugh. "Why do you think I was up on that ledge?"

His expression pinches together in anger. "Don't even joke about that, Nora." It's obvious he dislikes it, me making light of my life. I like him the more for it.

"Even though my parents were against it and let that be known, it wasn't long after we got back that Frankie started harassing me."

I feel the muscles in Rocco's body tense around me, once I get the words out.

"And one day, he..." I don't want to tell him how Gianfrancesco shoved me down and went for his belt. "He took it too far."

"Did he hurt you?" The depth of Rocco's rage is palpable. He's giving off heat, he's so angry.

"He might have, but Nico intervened. Thank God. She's..." A flush of love swirls through me, thinking of my sister. "She always had my back. And she was the brave one. Nothing scared her. When she saw him on top of me, she flew at him like a wild cat. I've never seen anything like it. She slapped the shit out of him. Scarred his face."

"Remind me to thank her one day..."

I smile at him for saying at that, but it doesn't last. "That's why she was sent away...She protected me, and in so doing, she harmed a Dalla Porta prince. Exile was my parents' way of protecting her, but it broke our hearts. And we never recovered from that." I hate the way my voice wobbles.

Being forcibly separated from my sister seems nothing

compared to what Rocco's been through, but the pain of that moment is still so acute for me, even now, I can hardly stand it.

"I'm sorry," I whisper, a tear running down my cheek. "I probably seem overdramatic, crying about this."

"Don't be ridiculous." Rocco pulls me tight against him. "I could never think less of you for loving your family."

The sincerity in his voice is real. I feel it, all the way in my toes.

"Going through middle school, high school, college without Nico around...It tore me apart. We write each other all the time, and we talk on the phone when we can, but it's not the same." Telling Rocco this is like yanking thorns from my heart.

I sniff hard. "At least, Nico was able to make something of herself and of the freedom she got out of this awful deal. I just turned into more and more of a wall flower. Without Nico, I didn't belong anywhere. With anyone...Except Dad. He was usually too busy to spend a lot of time with me, but still, next to Nico, he was my best friend."

Rocco's silent for a while. And then, voice thick with more emotion than I can decipher, he says, "I'm so sorry he's gone."

"Me too..." I lower my eyes, but then lift them right up to Rocco's. "Thank you for showing up that night."

"What?"

"I've been meaning to tell you this. I don't know how you ended up there that night or why, but thank you so much for pulling me off that ledge." Rocco looks nothing short of flabbergasted by my gratitude. I rush on. "If you hadn't been there, I would have missed Dad's message. And the thought of that...hurts more than anything else I've been through the past few days."

"Nora, I..." The words don't come to him, so I push up on my tiptoes and press my mouth to his. I kiss him like this until my ankles strain against this position, begging me for rest.

"I promise your scars don't change the way I feel about you." I run my fingers reassuringly through his hair. "Not even a little. I mean it, Rocco. Believe me."

"I wish I deserved you…" Heat comes to his hooded gaze. "But I don't."

Rocco's mouth descends on mine with such impact, my heels hit the ground, and I have to hold tight to him so that he doesn't knock me over with the power of his kiss. He pries my lips open wider, dipping his tongue against mine, while bunching his fingers into a fist around the fabric of my dress.

"I want to take you someplace no one can ever hurt you again," he growls against my mouth. "And fuck you until you remember no name but mine."

Lust slides through me like a serpent, coiling tight in that hot place between my thighs. Rocco's words deliver his desire for me, like a tidal wave floods the earth. Alone in this garden, we're mauling each other like wild animals.

I bend back at the waist, his arm cuffed around my middle to keep me from falling. My fingertips dig into his shoulder blades while Rocco bites into my lower lip like a beast. I moan at him, not for the first time tonight, and it only makes him kiss me harder.

Until a soft noise nearby interrupts us.

I might have ignored it, Rocco's kiss is so potent. But this time he's the one to pull back first, expression hazy with lust, probably mirroring my own.

His eyes flick left then right, like he's listening for the sound again.

"Did you hear that?" His grip on me gradually softens, as he turns his head one way and then another.

There it is again. A tiny cry in the night.

It's a small mewling.

I turn around in Rocco's arms, listening harder for it, and the next time I hear it, I pick up the direction.

"It's coming from over there, I think…" I point toward the other side of the fountain. The crying is hard to hear over the water trickling. Rocco and I stride in that direction, and now, we can hear the cry clearly enough—It's meowing.

Rocco walks ahead of me and drops to the ground, kneeling.

"What is it?" I ask, approaching his shoulder.

But I see it before he responds.

A tiny gray kitten.

Sick, injured, and tangled in the brambles underneath a big hedge in the garden.

Oh no. I can spot an injured animal about as well as the next person, but actually knowing how to engage is another story altogether.

My first instinct is to call the police, but they don't help in situations like these. My second instinct is to start googling, but I don't have my phone, and—

Rocco reaches inside his suit jacket, and with a firm hand rips out some of the silk lining from inside. I don't care, but I know if Nico were here she'd gasp at him for mutilating a designer suit like that.

I'm wowed by the ease with which he does it.

Like it's the natural, correct thing to do.

And then...with the steady, sure hands of surgeon, Rocco carefully gathers the injured baby into his strong palms, wrapping it in the silk.

"Do you mind if we make another stop?" He stands up, the kitten in his arms.

"No. Of course not, let's go."

This time, I follow Rocco. It probably took us forty-five minutes to make it to the garden from *Annata,* but with Rocco back in fighting shape, getting back to his car barely takes ten.

As soon as we slide into the front seats, he gingerly places the silk wrapped kitten into my unprepared lap. "Hold her while I drive?"

He's already turning the engine over and revving away from the curb, by the time I say, "Sure."

The first thing I notice about this tiny silver cat is how thin and cold she is, barely able to keep her little eyes open.

"How do you know it's a she?" I mumble.

I study Rocco's grave expression. "I just know."

It's been a few days since I've seen Rocco like this. Fiercely protective.

But if he can be so up in arms over a hurt little kitten, I doubt I have anything to worry about. I try not to stare too much at him, while he whips his car through Manhattan in these late hours of the night.

When his car does start to slow, I'm shocked to find him pulling into an open parking space on what appears to be the backside of a veterinary clinic.

Surely, they're not open so late, I'm thinking the second before I see 24-Hour Vet Hospital written in small letters on the bricks beside the back door.

Without so much as a word to me, Rocco takes the kitten from my lap and climbs out, jogging up the back steps and sweeping right into the building like he owns the place. This man sure is good at shocking me.

I follow him, several steps behind, but doing my best to keep up.

As soon as I'm inside, the clinical tang of hospital mixed with that musty animal odor slams straight into me. I'm standing in a short tan-carpeted hallway, fluorescent lights buzzing overhead, with windowed white walls on either side of me, both of which look into animal examination rooms.

Rocco's nowhere to be found. He must have disappeared deeper into the hospital.

But soon I hear his voice, headed back this way. He's trading short, staccato sentences with a woman, by the sound of it. When they appear in the hallway, I take the woman in.

She's older than both of us, in her late fifties perhaps, dressed in sky blue scrubs beneath a white doctor's coat, her name sewn above the lapel.

Dr. Tanya Greer, VMD. Her dirty blond hair is flipped up in a clip, and her green eyes look caffeinated and bright. When she sees me, she stops. "Yes, may I help you? If this is an emergency, head down the hall to the front desk and Kiki will check you in. Unless...you're not here to pick up, are you? Our pick-up hours are between seven am and five pm daily. You'll have to come back tomorrow."

"Um," I bleat, glancing at Rocco.

"She's with me, Tanya." Rocco cuts in, still holding the kitten in his hands.

Tanya gapes at him, open mouthed in disbelief. She looks me over, then him, then me again. "Well, this is a surprise."

"We've gotta hurry, doc."

"Right, sorry. Yes. Come in here." Tanya opens the door to the examination room on my right, and she and Rocco I duck into it. She flips on lights as she goes, getting a better look at the injured feline between Rocco's fingers.

I stand in the hallway, watching them convene over the kitten through the giant observation window, feeling out of place and completely curious about Rocco.

He...he's friends with a vet?

The man goes around saving injured animals on nights when he's not pulling strange women off ledges? What?

I don't know how to process this at all.

After a few terse minutes, Rocco comes out into the hallway to tell me what's happening. "Is the kitten okay?"

Rocco's expression is grim. "She's very sick. Tanya needs to check her for any viruses, but she also needs surgery."

"Shit," I blurt out.

"The problem is she's so weak right now, she might not survive the surgery she needs. I've got to go get the nurse on duty, but Tanya asked if you wouldn't mind watching the front of the hospital while the two of them work? I'd do it myself, but I scare people who call. They're understaffed these days, so..."

"Of course." Manage phones? No problem.

R. R. NIGH

"Follow me." He turns away up the hall, and this time, I keep up with him, as he winds his way through this hospital like he's done it a hundred times.

We pass a room full of boarding animals, many of whom are asleep, some of whom watch us pass with alert expressions.

In a minute or so, we reach the small front room waiting area, where a woman, only a few years older than I am probably, sits popping gum and flipping through a magazine. She's got long dark hair that falls down her back, a gorgeous face, and figure to match. Her name tag reads Kiara Escobedo.

She jumps at the sudden appearance of both of us, but mostly Rocco. Her eyes seem glued to him. All of him.

"Kiki. Doc needs you in the back." Rocco gestures to me. "This is Nora. She's going to watch the desk."

"And you are..." She gives me a suspicious look, even though Rocco just told her my name.

"She's my woman." Rocco interjects. "Now hurry, Kiki. Please."

The disappointment on Kiki's face is *titanic*, I've never seen someone look so deeply stricken. And then she forces her polite smile back in place and disappears into the back.

As soon as we're alone in this waiting room with crosshatched wallpaper and an old monitor hung up in the corner, rotating animal care facts drifting past onscreen, I give Rocco a long look.

"*Your woman*?" I drop my hands to my waist.

Rocco actually clams up a little, like he didn't expect me to care about that macho-ass introduction. "Well, you are."

"We need to have a serious discussion about titles."

"Why?" Even through the seriousness of this situation, he cracks a small smile. "What should I have called you?"

"Something a little less *caveman* would have been great, thanks."

"Fine." He guides my hips forward until they're square with his. "Next time, I'll introduce you as my obsession."

"A cologne brand." I playfully shove his chest, so I can head around the desk and take Kiki's place. "What a promotion, wow."

"My treasure."

"Now, you're a pirate?"

Rocco leans against the counter, like he's hoping for a kiss. "Well, I can't call you my wife yet, and *girlfriend* sounds so…prepubescent."

"We'll discuss it later," I assert, pushing Kiara's rolling chair aside.

"Fine." Rocco exhales, reaching for me across the counter. "I am sorry for the detour. It's supposed to be our first date, not an episode of Animal ER."

"It's all right…" I lay a kiss on his cheek. "I like getting to see you in your natural habitat."

"I'm going to go see if Tanya needs any extra help, but when we're done here, I'd like to pick up where we left off…" He yanks me tighter against him, and gives my ear a tantalizing little nip I feel all the way in my knees. "Okay?"

"Okay…" The word comes out a sigh.

It's not until Rocco's gone that I realize he just said *I can't call you my wife **yet**.*

Up front, I sit alone in this quiet animal hospital. No one phones in or walks through the door, thank God. They'd see me sitting here red-faced and winded from the heat Rocco De Carlo puts inside me with just a few words.

I've barely recovered by the time approaching footsteps perk up my ears.

I'm expecting Rocco, but instead it's Tanya.

Dr. Greer, I mean.

"Sorry about the way I acted earlier." Damn, she's just as blunt as I am. She sticks out her hand to me. "Please. Call me Tanya."

"It's all right. My name is Nora."

"Nora…" She smiles at me. "What a beautiful name."

"T-Thank you." I swallow. "How's our patient?"

"Time will tell." She points a thumb toward the back. "Kiki's prepping one of the operation rooms, and Rocco's trying to warm our little girl up the old fashion way."

I don't know what she means until Tanya puts her hands together and rubs.

"Oh. Okay." I feel so awkward. "I hope she makes it."

"I do too…"

It's so surprising meeting Tanya. Rocco hasn't said as much, but I don't get the feeling he's that close with too many people. Tanya may be one of only a few, if not the only one herself…But in some poetic way, their connection makes total sense to me.

Dr. Tanya is great with wounded animals, and Rocco definitely is one.

"I know I acted like a jerk back there. Please forgive me, I was just surprised."

"By me?" I point at myself.

"Rocco's never mentioned you before." She gives me a knowing smile. "He's certainly never brought anybody by before."

"Does he come here a lot?"

"A few times a week at least…For the past seven years."

"*Seven years?*"

She nods. "He's a bit rough around the edges, but he can't stand to see a defenseless creature in harm's way." She gazes toward the back of the hospital, as though she can see him from here. "Rocco's a good guy."

"I know."

I'm so awed by Rocco's capacity for kindness and compassion, I don't know what to do. Like…is it just me or is the strength of my connection to this man growing by the minute?

Just one night with Rocco… This is the most alive I've ever felt.

It takes about two hours, but Dr. Tanya is eventually able to stabilize the sick kitten.

Around 11pm, Rocco and I stand in the recovery room looking at the little gray girl, sleeping hard with a cast around one furry leg.

"Dr. Tanya's really cool," I say after a while.

"She's a terrific doctor."

I bump shoulders with him. "And you're just terrific, all around..."

Rocco sighs hard. I'm starting to think compliments throw him off.

It's really cute.

He grabs my hand. "How would you feel about catching a late movie?"

CHAPTER 28

Rocco

WELL, this has somehow been the best and craziest night of my life.

I feel like I'm walking on air, my fingers intertwined with hers as we stride down a Manhattan street toward the Oasis Theater, another old movie palace—not unlike the one Orazio chose for his secret office.

It's my absolute favorite place in the city. I come here to be alone or on the rare night that I'm in a good mood and want to watch a silver screen masterpiece.

The grand old edifice from the thirties rises before us at the end of the block, all lit up with little white bulbs. Above us, black plastic letters advertise the films being shown tonight and their start times.

We've missed all but one of them, which starts at 11:30.

We're lucky, but I know that, with or without a late night showing of *Roman Holiday*.

I step up to the counter and pay the clerk, a gangly, pimply guy who looks about nineteen, and has for the past five years at least. Trent. He knows me by face and name, and when he sees me holding hands with Nora, he gives me a suspicious look, while printing out our tickets.

That would be because I've never brought someone to my secret place before, and he's probably wondering whether armageddon is at hand.

What I don't say is that I myself am surprised.

By everything. By every part of her.

Why is it that everywhere I go with her, everything we do together, we seem to fit?

Or should I say, Nora...fits into my life. Like a missing component I didn't know I'd been living without all this time.

With anyone else, taking them to my secret spots around the city would feel like an imposition, a stranger trespassing on my sacred grounds. But with Nora, it's natural.

I'm staring to think going anywhere with her might feel this way.

Like she and I belong somehow in this crazy world we were born into...

But doubt still lurks in the back of my defective brain.

Yes, she agreed to run away with me on a whim, and no, she didn't blink at severe neurological challenges, but she still doesn't know the truth.

About me. About her father's death and how I factor into it.

She doesn't know why I was there that night she jumped, that I'd been stalking for her two weeks, waiting for the perfect opportunity to victimize her.

If I tell her the truth and she doesn't want anything more to do with me, or worse—if I fuck up and put her in even more danger than we're currently in, I already know the ghost of her will follow me around for the rest of my days.

That thought seems to get heavier in my mind with every step I take, but I don't slow down. Nora and I navigate through the Oasis to screen number eight, and when we enter the theater, the first thing we notice is that the place is completely empty. We're the only souls in here.

"Let me guess," Nora throws me a smile, before she turns in a wide circle. "This is where you come to be alone."

She's so stunning, I just watch her go, before following her to the seat of her choice. There's no assigned seating in here. There aren't even arm rests and cupholders, just comfy red velvet seats with rounded backs.

We get comfortable in two chairs in the middle of the place, and she leans into me easily, my arm wrapping snug around her shoulder, like we've done this a hundred times before.

I'm amply enjoying the perfection of this moment until Roman Holiday starts up and I realize how like Gregory Peck's character I am. The unscrupulous reporter taking advantage of a charming young princess on the run from the captivity of her family.

The similarity spears me with guilt until I can't even look at the screen anymore, so I just look down at her.

Only to find her already looking up at me.

My heart stumbles in my chest.

Wordlessly, our mouths draw together, like movie magic.

I think she just wants one kiss, but she doesn't let me pull away. Her lips pry at mine until one kiss has turned into five or six, and soon, we're just openly making out to the soundtrack of famous voices from the fifties.

Without an armrest in the way, it's easier to paw at each other.

Her right hand comes to my chest, fingertips digging into my shirt as I ease our tongues together. We're entirely alone, and even if we weren't, I'm not sure I'd be able to stop my hand, wrapping itself around her breasts, one then the other. Kneading them. Pinching for her hard nipples beneath that blue dress.

"*Mm...*"

I'm done for, the *second* she starts moaning against my lips.

My greedy hands drop to her waist, and then I'm dragging her toward my lap, using all the strength in my arms. "Come here, beautiful."

In one maneuver, I pull her and she moves with me until her back's to my chest, and her perfect ass sits snug over my hardening cock, as it rises up in my lap. As soon as I feel her weight against it, lust pummels my self-control to pieces.

It must show. Because Nora starts to flex her hips, rocking against my shaft like she means to massage it with her ass.

One of my arms circles her waist, and the other one climbs up into her hair, pulling it away from her neck so I can bite her.

"Keep this up, and you're going to get us thrown out of here for indecent exposure." She grinds against me so good, my eyes close.

"I can't help it," she swears.

"You want me that much?"

She nods, bracing herself against my thighs, while she moves her hot body along me. My right hand adventures up to her breasts again. The shape of them, the weight...the way they perfectly fit inside my palm.

Fucking mouthwatering.

I can't wait to get my mouth on every part of her.

"My, we've come along way from arguing on a rooftop, haven't we?"

I handle her breasts harder, and nice and clear in this black and white darkness, she moans, "*Yes.*"

Just that one syllable has both my hands reaching for the hem of her dress. One draws it up over her thighs and yanks the soft fabric of her panties aside, and the other dunks into her folds, drawing a circle with my finger tip around her swelling clit.

"Is this what you wanted?" I rub up and down her bare thigh, working my fingers through her wetness with more vigor and speed.

"*Mmm...*" Nora drops her head back, balancing it on my shoulder while she rolls her hips against my steady strumming fingers.

"You want more?" I rasp in her ear, and she nods.

I tighten one arm around her waist, and slip my longest finger into her dripping wet cunt. Right here. In the middle of my favorite movie theater. In the dead of night.

And it gets me so hot beneath the collar, I'm going insane, listening to the music we make. Her wetness slicking my finger as I stuff it in and drag it out, her moaning at the ostentatious ceiling, all while Audrey Hepburn and Gregory Peck slow dance above us, larger than life.

Shit, I'm about to fuck her in here. I'm ten seconds from pulling out my cock and poling into her.

Nora's fingers dig into my arm around her waist, struggling against the pleasure the same way I am, while she moans right into my ear.

I can't take much more of this.

Finally, I pull my hand away from her addictive pussy. Her wetness drips right off my fingers, dotting the floor. I've never wanted to lick my own fingers so badly.

Nora pants, partially exposed, recovering in my lap, and I'm trying to resist every primal instinct inside, demanding I shove her down on these red velvet seats and pump her full of cum all over again.

Dear God, the heat between us is crazy.

We're not even through the whole movie, and I need to get us to a hotel. *Pronto.* Lust gushes through my system with all the force of a flash flood. I need to unload my cock for the second time tonight and if we don't get out of this theater, it's going to happen right here.

Thankfully, I have the perfect place to take Nora. A one-off luxury hotel in the heart of the city. I know the guy who runs the place and we won't be disturbed. More importantly, we'll be able to enter through the staff quarters, avoid security cameras, and pay in cash. We don't want anyone from either of our families to catch us.

We haven't talked about it yet, but since we've decided to run, Nora and I have plans to make. A lot of plans.

But they can wait until tomorrow.

Tonight, I need her in my bed more than I need anything else.

More than California needs rain.

"Let's get out of here." I shove kisses to her neck, and one more bite, before we get up, straightening our clothes, and book it out of the Oasis.

As soon as we're through the door of the suite I reserve for us, I pin her against the wall three steps into the foyer. With one hand, I get back under her dress, ripping her under wear down like some kind of fucking brute, while she sucks my tongue into her mouth.

The second her panties hit the floor, she lifts one of her legs into my waiting hand. I rip my dress pants loose, and she handles my cock like she's hungry for it, guiding it straight into her tight, hot hole.

How we made it from the elevator all the way in here with our clothes on, I'll never fucking know. I balance my forearm above her hand, while her hands grope around my waist, and then I thrust inside her as hard and as far I'll go.

"Do you have any idea how good you feel?" My voice sounds positively livid when I'm having amazing sex. That's what I've learned tonight.

She gasps and shrieks, and whines, "*Oh my god...*"

Her pussy sucks me in, even when I pull out. It's like my cock's being strangled by a small sensuous mouth.

I've had sex many times before now, but not like this.

I've never been so desperate to be inside someone that I

couldn't make it to the bed. She does something to me I can't deny, explain, or escape.

And the worst part is that I don't want to escape her influence. Not at all. I want to drown in it. I *am* drowning it.

I rail her against the wall right next to the hotel room door. Anyone walking by outside must hear the bang of my hips slamming her against this wall, and the way she's crying out for me.

"*Rocco...*" She whimpers, sultry and sweet.

"Fuck," I groan. "You're going to make me come again, you sexy—"

My words are lost as an orgasm tears through me. Unintelligible grousing in Italian follows as my hard breaths echo between us, another load spurting out into her deepest place.

Then, I slowly drag my leaky cock out of her, another groan pouring out of me, both of us breathing hard. Gently, I let her leg down, and we allow the wall behind her to take our weight as we recover from what just happened.

When I regain the strength to look down, I notice that we're both damp with sweat. My seed is dripping down Nora's thighs. We're both flushed, hot, and disheveled.

In other words, we're a mess.

"Why don't we..." I'm still breathing rough.

Nora nods. "Let's shower."

I let my forehead balance against hers. "You can go first."

She shakes her head, her fingers going for the top button of my shirt. "Together."

CHAPTER 29

Nora

I'VE HAD sex with Rocco De Carlo twice already.

Twice and a half, if I count that hot shit that happened at the Oasis. But still, I've yet to see this magnificent man naked, and I'm not about to lose my chance.

I lead him by the hand deeper into this suite.

It's on one of the highest floor of this boutique hotel called the Argyle. I barely spare a glance at the floor plan. That can wait.

As soon as my eyes find the bathroom door, we're headed that way.

I try not to freak out when I glimpse my reflection in the full length mirror the minute we step inside. My dress is half twisted around, Rocco's cum, still fresh, streaks down my inner thighs. And my hair, oh God…

I've never wanted to get out of my clothes and into a shower so badly, but when I turn around and see him standing there, a lazy, deeply satisfied look on his face, I realize that I'm about to get naked in front of the sexiest man I've ever met in real life. In a very brightly lit room.

My nerves are ping-ponging all over the place.

And now that we're alone in here, the gravity of that fact seems to expand between us like a hot air balloon.

"Well?" One of Rocco's eyebrows arches, smug and suggestive. He opens his arms to me. "Aren't you going to pick up where you left off?"

He's talking about the buttons on his shirt, the ones I was just about to undo before we decided to come in here.

My hands rise to his shirt. Rocco looks like he walked into a sauna wearing it.

Jesus, he's gorgeous. I swallow, my fingertips taking his buttons one at a time, revealing the dizzying array of tattoos that decorate his long, chiseled chest. I'm staring big time, like I'm unwrapping a present, as I peel the dress shirt away from his skin...

"Your tattoos..." There are too many to count. All over his chest, his shoulders, his back. He looks like he's still wearing a shirt. Among the designs are objects, animals, nature, dates.

"What?" Rocco flexes, or maybe he's tensing up under my analytic gaze.

I raise my eyes to his. "I love them."

"Yeah, yeah. Now, *strip*." He gives me a wicked smile. "Before I make you."

In minutes, we're tangled around each other enjoying the tropical rainfall setting of this world-class shower. Rocco's giant hands comb through my damp hair, while he samples my mouth with his. Being naked together feels so different from everything else we've done tonight so far...

It's freeing and scarier and definitely more intimate.

Between my legs, Rocco's cock has risen again, pointing straight ahead at the glass bathroom wall behind me. Every time he pulls my body tighter against his or hunches over to graze my neck, I feel the girth of it collide with me.

And wonder washes me all over again.

This beautiful giant thing has been inside me twice already today?

Rocco sucks on my earlobe, sending heat coursing through my veins. There's no where to look but down, and just staring at him, upright like that…It does something to me. Inside, urges pop into existence in bright shimmering color.

Before I know what I'm doing, I'm on my knees, kneeling before him.

No, I've never given a blowjob before. Right now, I'm simultaneously so eager to try it and so nervous to, that I look up at Rocco for encouragement.

But the intensity of the wildfire heat in his eyes is too much for me. I can't do this while looking at him. Not yet.

So instead, I'm eye to eye with his glorious cock.

It dominates my field of vision. Thick, long, veined. When I touch it with my fingers, it feels like he's got titanium beneath his soft, warm skin.

"Open that sexy mouth." Rocco's voice is rough with need. The command in his tone sends a zap of electricity straight to my clit for some reason.

My lips drop apart at his instruction, and then he guides his cock into my mouth.

Oh, God…he barely fits in there. Only about half of him gets into my mouth.

Rocco's hot and throbbing on my tongue. The veins along his shaft twitch against my tastebuds. He groans as soon as he's inside.

I suck him off as best I can, a total amateur out of my mind with lust, but he moans above me, "Yes, sweetheart. Just like that."

His hands lower into my hair, gathering the wet strands into a ponytail, his fist tightening at the back of my skull.

"I love using your perfect mouth." Then, Rocco starts thrusting himself in. Why it turns me on so much, I have no idea.

Moans and burbles escape my drooling mouth as he shoves his cock between my lips as far as he can. My eyes snap open when he rams the back of my throat, tickling my uvula. Gagging, I grab his thick, muscled thighs for support as he uses my face like his own personal sex toy.

It's vigorous and satisfying, somehow. I want him so much that whatever gets him excited about me excites me too.

"*Fuuuck*," he groans deep and guttural, the primal sound bouncing off the bathroom tiles. "I'm going to come again."

"*Umph!*" Nonsensical noise chokes out of my mouth as he continues to drive his cock in and out, hard and staccato.

"*Yeah*, sweetheart. You're such a good girl, making my cock disappear."

Sparks of delicious lust crackle through me when he talks like that. No man's ever spoken to me like this before.

To know that I bring this side out of him fills me with fizzy, heady power. I'm drunk on it, down here on my knees.

My throat aches as he slams all the way to the back once more and rips his cock out, cum spurting from his tip onto my lips, chin, and chest.

"*Ugh.*" It's only a hard exhale, but it comes out a single-syllable growl. "Fuck you for being so goddamn hot."

The water showering us slowly picks up the warm creamy drizzle he defaced me with and carries it down my body to the shower floor.

We're both breathing hard. My vulva pulses hard between my legs. I've never felt it do that before. Maybe Rocco De Carlo's awoken a side of me I didn't know I had either.

In a second, his big hot palms wrap around both my biceps and he pulls me up to my feet. "Come on." The expression on his face is absolutely angry. Fear pings through me, as he throws his hand at the postmodern shower faucet hard enough to break it, turning it off with a vengeance.

"What?" I murmur, as he shoves the glass door open and yanks me out. "What's wrong?"

He tows me across this spacious bathroom to the giant granite sink, and before I know what's happening, he grabs me around the waist and lifts me onto the counter top. It's ice cold beneath my wet skin and slippery, but Rocco doesn't care.

He's on *his* knees now, tossing my soapy legs over his shoulders.

"What are you—*Ah!*" A cry of pleasure flies from my mouth when Rocco crushes his angry face right into my folds.

"Payback time," he growls against them, sending a new flush of heat up through my waist into my chest.

"Wait—" I say, but he sucks my pussy into his mouth with such force that it knocks the top of me backwards. "*Mm!*" My hands connect with the countertop just in time to stop my head from bonking the tap.

He's done this to me once before, just a few hours ago, but it feels entirely different now. The first time was reverent and passionate…This time, he's eating me up like it's his life's purpose. Like he was made to do this to me.

The rippling slurps and squelches echo through the room, beneath the bound of my moans and sows.

"*Oh, oh, oh…*" He swipes his whole face through my pussy, his stubble tantalizing every part of my vulva, the outer lips, the inner folds, my clit. It feels so off-the-charts amazing that the muscles inside me start to twitch.

Rocco pulls back and tilts his head up, a hungry, devilish look on his face.

"You like it when I tongue-fuck your sweet, juicy cunt?"

All I can do is nod, helplessly. I've never seen him look so demonic. It somehow scares, excites, and leaves me speechless all at once.

Then he slides two of his long thick fingers through my entrance.

My head drops back.

"*Oh God,*" I whimper.

"Did you like it when I finger-fucked you in that theater?" His rough, smug voice is like lewd velvet. "Anyone could have walked in and seen your pussy being played with. Would you have liked that?"

"No…" I whine as he curls his fingers inside, reaching new depths. "*Ah!*"

"But it got you so wet, just like you are now." Rocco drills me harder with his fingers. The pleasure radiating through my body multiplies, sending tremors quaking through my core. "I don't know what to believe, Nora."

"Stop…teasing…me," I rasp. My whole body's burning up.

A dark chuckle eases from Rocco's mouth.

"But it's so fun." He slides his fingers out, letting me breathe. "I could do it for hours."

Rocco lets my legs down, rising from his place. Then he flips me over in one act of strength. Now, he has me bent over the counter top, balancing on my elbows, while he gets an eyeful of my backside.

This position is compromising enough as it is. Self-consciousness blooms around the edges of my mind, but all remnants of it disappear the second Rocco drops his hands on my ass, spreads my cheeks apart, and presses his hot mouth to my unprepared asshole.

My eyes jump wide at the unexpected contact, and the even more unexpected pleasure of it. "*Hmm!*" The cry escapes, even as I roll my lips together to stop it.

Rocco licks my asshole with the flat of his tongue, and the feeling it gives me is nothing short of sinful. So good my eyelids flutter and my eyes roll all the way back.

"*Fuck,*" I pant at the granite beneath my face. "Oh—"

Rocco goes around and around my anus with the tip of his powerful tongue.

"See how fun it is to be teased?" The arrogance in his tone makes me think he's smirking. He's removed his mouth, but he leaves his thumb over my bud, pressing down hard on it so that there's no escaping the pleasure.

"*Oh, fuck!*" I drop my forehead to the cool stone countertop as Rocco slides his thumb into my asshole. "Rocco, please..."

"Please what?"

"I can't take this," I whine at him, breathless and twitching. Even though the heat is amazing, it's somehow unbearable at the same time.

"Then beg me to fuck you again," he orders with that vain edge in his voice. "I know you want me to."

"I want you to..." My words are lost as he jams his thumb further in, a stinging, burning, robust pleasure settling over me in ripples.

"*Yes?*" He leads, dropping another heavy hand on my ass.

"Please fuck me again..." I drag the words out of my throat, face down on the counter, the embarrassment only barely kept at bay by the rampant arousal driving my thoughts and actions.

"Thank me for playing with your ass first." He adds, changing his terms all of a sudden. Who is this domineering sex fiend and why am I going along with this insanely hot power trip of his?

"Thank you for—*Ah...*" He gives my ass another good slap, still with his thumb jammed inside. "Thank you for playing with my ass."

"You like it when I tease your asshole, don't you?" The smile in his voice is obvious, even though I can't see it like this.

"*Mhmm...*" I nod despite myself, like my body's determined to be honest with him.

He supplies another dark chuckle, deep in his throat. "I knew you would, sweetheart."

Ugh. The way he calls me sweetheart melts me down to my bones.

"*Please* fuck me again..." I groan at him, my pussy wet and warbling for him.

"Fine." Rocco pulls his thumb out, then brings the rest of me upright until I'm facing him again. Lust boils in his deep brown eyes. "*Race you to the bed.*"

Those words make something childish and competitive break open in my chest. With damp excited feet, I all but sprint out of the bathroom back out into this gorgeous suite.

The place is a giant rectangle, with half the walls made from floor-to-ceiling glass panels, overlooking Manhattan. Corporate office building scrape the night sky, their lights creating an urban sea of starlight. And with a gentle rain drizzling down over New York, a curtain of water drops clings to the glass.

It's dazzlingly beautiful.

I'm so taken by the sight of it, I completely forget about getting to the king bed on the far side of the room.

I drift toward the window, body completely bare. "This view is... stunning."

Behind me, Rocco emerges from the bathroom. "I know exactly what you mean."

When I look over my shoulder, my heart leaps up into my throat. Rocco's eyes glow with a dark, possessive lust. He looks positively incensed as he strides over to me, standing by the rainy window panes.

His big hands are all over my body in seconds. Everywhere Rocco touches me with his fingers, *his mouth...* Oh, god, it's like he marks me forever.

"Give me that perfect ass," he rumbles, gripping my waist so he can spin me toward the windows. I press my face to the glass, my hands on either side, as he rips my ass square against his waist, his reawakened cock already standing between my legs.

He releases my hips, both his hands sliding up and around my torso to grab my breasts. Groping and squeezing them, he begins to rock his cock through my wet folds. *Ugh*…The stimulation from just these two actions has my knees weak and wobbly.

"Oh, sweetheart, I'm going to fuck you until every single part of you belongs to me." He growls against my neck, taking a huge bite. "Understand?"

I nod hard. "*Yes.*"

"Good." Rocco slaps my breasts with his right hand, while his left takes hold of his cock and jimmies it against my entrance, making that wet sound echo through the room, and sending me lurching against the glass.

"*Unh!*" My eyes drop closed, it's so good. "*God, I want you so much.*" The words fall right out of my mouth, nothing but pure, honest sluttishness.

"Yeah?" He jams his cock into me again, all the way, but he doesn't make another move. "You want it?"

"Yeah," I pant, my hot breaths making bits of fog on the glass.

"You want me to add some stretch to your pussy?"

"*Please, Rocco…*" I whine, like the wanton whore I never knew I was until this moment. Rocco seems satisfied, reeling his cock out of me before he drives it back in.

How can this position feel so completely different from all the others we've done so far? Bent over with my hands against the glass, Rocco rails me, making my legs shake with every rough thrust.

He grabs a handful of my hair again, coiling his fist like a pony-tail holder while he slings his cock inside me, hard, steady, and deliberate.

The pleasure is unreal.

My body buzzes like a lightbulb that's been on too long.

On the inside, I've begun to tingle. It's a new sensation, mysterious and hard to describe, but I know exactly what it means.

"*Ugh, you're going to make me come…*" My voice is unrecognizable in this strange sex-fueled state of consciousness Rocco's fucked me into. I sound drunk, feverish, like I'm losing my voice all at once.

Fuck, I don't remember which way is up, he's doing me so good.

"You gonna come for me, sweetheart?" He grunts out the words, his rough fingertips digging into my waist as he hits that spot inside me, over and over.

"*Rocco.*" I moan his name, like some devoted worshiper. "*Right there, oh, fuck.*"

The pleasure's eating me alive, devouring all my consciousness.

I squeeze my eyes shut.

"Be a good girl and come all over my dick." Cuffing one of his thick hands around the back of my neck, he rams me harder.

And that's when it's all over for me.

My moans turn to shrieks as his cock hits deep inside my writhing body.

Three more hard thrusts and I'm flung over the edge of ecstasy.

A strangled cry unfurls from my throat, as my hips buck and shake around Rocco's length. My muscles contract hard and release, euphoria spreading through my body like I've been dunked into a pool of ultimate release.

All the strength leaves my limbs. My knees bend, and in a second, I'm half crumpled against the glass. The only thing holding me up is Rocco's hands, circling my middle, while he drops kisses in my hair.

I don't remember much after that.

Only Rocco's heat, as he takes me in his arms. The softness of a giant bed appearing beneath my body and the steady drumbeat of this man's heart near my ear, as I slip away into deep, exhausted rest.

CHAPTER 30

Rocco

DAYBREAK PRIES my eyes open like a crowbar.

Or is it the horrifying amount of guilt?

Nora's sleeping form tangled around mine, both of us naked in this California king bed is a dream. It doesn't seem possible that I could ever have a morning so nice as this, and I've only been awake thirty seconds.

But I can't enjoy it.

Because I haven't told Nora the truth yet.

The truth is the only thing that could ruin everything we have. The truth could pry this wonderful woman from my grasp and out of my reach forever, and there's nothing I can do about that.

I was sent to betray her.

I *had* betrayed her, before I even knew who she was.

Whether she could or will forgive me for that is in God's hands.

All that is in my hands is how deeply I want to hurt her by keeping it a secret.

The longer I wait, the deeper the wound will be when she does learn the truth, and she will. These things have a way of coming out sooner or later...

I have to do it today.

Before we make our plans and get the hell out of town.

If I don't do it before then, I'll have tricked her into this.

She doesn't deserve that. I won't trick her.

I won't.

"What are you thinking so hard about so early in the morning?" Nora mumbles against my chest. When I peer down into her bright sleepy eyes, I can see that she's been watching me for a few minutes probably, and I've been too stricken by my guilt-ridden thoughts to notice.

"There's something I need to tell you." I brush a curl from her face. "Something very important."

She sits up a little, blinking. "Can it wait until I'm coherent?"

"I don't think so."

"Come to think of it..." She sits all the way up, maneuvering herself so that she's sitting beside me. "There's something important I need to tell you too."

"Nora—"

"Have you ever heard of a time period called the Red Years?" She pulls her knees to her bare chest, like she's shy to be naked before me in the morning light after everything we did last night.

Against my best judgement, I don't redirect this conversation back to where it needs to go. And the reason why is because I *have* heard of the Red Years. It was a time of slaughter for the Balboni family at the hands of the Dalla Porta. I was a child in Sicily at the time, but I've heard it spoken of many times with bitterness and with a spirit of vengeance.

I don't like that Nora knows about it.

"Yes. I've heard of them." Concern ticks faster inside me, when

Nora's expression darkens. "It was a time of great bloodshed. Why do you ask?"

"I found a file in my father's office about it. There was a report on what started it all, and how everything...played out."

Just when I thought nothing could distract me from the task at hand...

"What do you mean?" I cannot hold back my own inquisitive curiosity on this one. "What did the report say?"

The Red Years is exactly the kind of history that I've never been briefed on during my time with the Balboni. Even though I made it all the way into Jaco's inner circle, even though he praises almost everything I do, the man still has lines.

And this is one I've never been permitted to cross.

Even Vito with his loose-cannon ass knows more about the Red Years than I do.

I shouldn't be curious about this right now, and I certainly shouldn't be taking the story of my mafia's mortal enemies as the true account of what happened, but this may be the closest I ever come to learning more about what happened.

Since I'm an outcast within the Balboni.

Nora's father's face comes to my already addled mind.

He seemed a good man. A bad man couldn't have raised a daughter this excellent. There has to be something of the truth in the report, if not all of it.

"The report said...a lot." Nora blows out a breath.

"Did it have something to do with that picture we found at his secret office?" The one neither of us could understand. Don Sabatini Calzavarra and three sons...

Nora nods, and then she tells me a story I never could have imagined.

Sicily. Rossana. Jaco's bride who ran away and fell in love with Sabatini.

How the feud started, family against family.

Nora shakes her head, like she's seeing the awful tale play out behind her eyes. "Jacopo Balboni apparently avenged himself on the Calzavarras by murdering Saba's wife, and abducting his oldest son...as payment for what happened with Rossana's pregnancy and the marriage and everything."

"You mean he *executed* Saba's wife?" The weight of it crashes through me, like a bowling ball through glass.

That's the man I've been working for all this time? The man who took me in?

"He hunted his ex-fiancée down for rejecting him and shot her to death?" It's so demented, so disgustingly weak, so *sick*, that I have to clarify.

Nora looks a little green, but she nods. "That's what the report said. He killed her and stole Quirino, Saba's oldest. Yes."

"And that's how the Red Years began?"

"Isn't it awful?" She drops her gaze to the bedsheets between us. "Unspeakable."

"Makes me wonder what's going to happen to me if Frankie finds out..."

Irrational anger surges through me at the idea.

"Nothing, Nora," I assure her with strength in my voice. "I'm not going to let anything happen to you. I would burn down New York City before I let that dipshit get his hands on you again, understand?"

She gives me an appreciative look, but the gloom remains in place in her eyes. She falls to a plaintive silence.

"There's more, isn't there?" It's a guess, but the way she reacts tells me it's the right one.

"It's the part I understand the least," she admits, before she explains. "The report went onto say that in retaliation for all the killings Saba committed against the Balboni to avenge Rossana and find Quirino, that the Balboni infiltrated a Dalla Porta property and killed his middle son, Azeglio."

My face scrunches together in confusion.

In a moment, I'd like to know what's confusing about this for

Nora. But the first thing that strikes me about it is the fact I've never heard any of this before.

The Balbonis are a lot of things but subtle isn't one of them, and humble isn't another. If they had pulled off a coup of this magnitude—offing the wife of their arch nemesis, abducting one of his sons, and killing another—they'd be bragging about that shit openly. For a century at least.

It's the way they are.

Accomplishments are for bragging about.

So why have I never heard a word about this before in the twenty long years I've worked for them?

No, my brain resists.

It can't be true that all of this happened and I've really never heard a fucking word of it anywhere from anyone. Not so much as a peep.

But on the other hand, in an official report organized by the legendary Dalla Porta spymaster, why would he lie about these events in his enemy's favor? Nobody lies to make their greatest opponents seem formidable. What reason would he have to make up these claims?

That makes even less sense than the Balbonis keeping secrets.

So...it seems more likely that Orazio wrote the truth, despite the way I'm confounded and blindsided by it all.

"When was this?" is all I can manage.

"Nineteen-eighty-six."

"How was the report compiled?" I probe her like she knows everything about what's going on. "I mean...could you tell whether the report was written by one person or many people?"

"My dad wrote it," she says.

"How can you be sure?" I question, hoping my voice doesn't sound too suspicious.

"His signature was on every page. He also annotated it, and I'd know his handwriting anywhere." She rests her head on top of her knees. "The craziest part is that I think he transcribed most of it from interviews he did directly with Saba."

"Interviews?" Fuck. It doesn't get much more official than that... "You mean, like first person retellings of everything?"

She nods. "Dad was Saba's oldest friend, so it makes sense that he would have confided in him about it. But this is the part I really don't get—" Nora lifts her head, as though an idea's just struck her. "The report clearly says that the Balboni were behind the middle son's murder, but my dad didn't believe that."

I sit up straighter and give her a hard look. "You just said he compiled the reports from interviews he did with Sabatini."

"Exactly." She begins to climb out of bed, swathing herself in a sheet. She looks like she's wearing the longest wedding dress in the world. "But he'd annotated that section a lot."

"What did his notes say?"

"Not much, but there were question marks and underlines and circles around different parts of the report, as though he had doubts about whether what was written in there really happened the way it happened." She paces back and forth. "You know what I mean?"

"You think he was skeptical about the circumstances surrounding the middle son's murder." Now I finally understand what she's saying... "You think he might have been investigating."

"What if that's what got him killed?" She gives me a helpless little shrug. "What if he uncovered something about it that he wasn't supposed to know and..."

All I was ever told about the feud between the Balboni and the Dalla Porta was that they once stole something precious from the family. That's all I ever knew.

And to think now, maybe all of this began over a woman...

A woman Jaco coveted and assaulted and hunted down to the ends of the earth?

I don't know what to believe.

Killing one of Sabatini's sons would be a feather in Jaco's cap, but...

"Nora, your father was an extremely smart man." I exhale hard. "If he was suspicious, I guarantee there was a reason."

Then, she climbs back onto the bed, practically right into my lap, looking up at me with those pleading, pretty eyes. "Rocco, I want to run away with you. That hasn't changed. I know we've got a ton to figure out, but...the last thing I want to do before we get the hell out of here is make one last stop at Dad's secret office."

I can tell she's uncertain whether it's the right thing to do.

"There's something there he wanted me to find, and he said it mattered for our family. Not just the Dalla Porta. *My family.* Him, me, Mama, and Nico." She rests her hands on either side of my face. "Now, I know I'm no Sherlock Holmes, but that's why I've got you."

God, she's got my heart strings in a knot around her tiniest finger.

"I want to at least take a good look around and figure out what he was working on. He sent me that package from beyond the grave, and I want to find out why. If for no other reason than... closure."

I press her lips hard. What else can I do when I care so deeply about her?

"You don't even have to ask, sweetheart."

We dress, order up breakfast, feast on enough food for ten people to regain our strength after a night of the best sex either of us has ever had, and then we head back to the Purple Palace.

It's the least I can do for her, after everything I've destroyed.

CHAPTER 31

Nora

JUST AFTER NOON, we make it back to Dad's secret office.

Rocco and I slept in until about 10:30, which was glorious.

It took awhile to eat all of our hunger pains away but we didn't give up. We left no scone, pancake, breakfast potato, sausage, bacon, or egg uneaten.

But the mood between us today is decidedly less jovial. Rocco seems lost in his own mind. Or maybe he's pondering everything I told him about the Red Years. I was amazed he'd heard of them at all. But then again, he is older and he knows my dad from a long time ago.

Dad's secret office is exactly the way we left it.

A morbid excitement buzzes through me.

Without my phone or any attachments to the place I used to call home, I can relax into this vintage screening room that still smells so much like my dad.

Rocco doesn't crowd me. Instead, he roams around looking at this and that, while I take a seat at my father's desk and really try to get my bearings. There are so many folders, files, drawers and dossiers, I don't know where to lay my hand first.

So I grab the first stack of things I find and begin to go through his notes, unhurried and at ease, without a time limit bearing down on me.

Paranoia about my mother's wrath still pings in the back of my mind.

But there's no way for her to reach me now or ever again…

It hurts me, the foot we left things on. I can still feel the ghost of her hand crashing into my face…*How could she?*

Bitterness, resentment, and self-judgement tear at me, and looking through Dad's stuff is the only thing that keeps my mind off the pain.

I take my time, going through everything methodically as I search for clues about Dad's final assignment.

A lot of the paperwork in here seems to be about tracking down people connected to the Balboni family. Down to minor associates. He has records of favors people did for the Balboni family dating back to the sixties and seventies, labeled and recorded. "It's like he was tracing the Balboni family tree or something," I muse aloud.

"What makes you say that?" Rocco's deep voice appears over my shoulder.

"All these records." I thumb through a stack full of seventies photographs of Balboni soldiers. "I don't get why."

"Could have been to help Saba during the Red Years," Rocco suggests. "During those years, as I understand it, he systematically wiped out about eighty percent of the Balboni's workforce.

"*Eighty percent?*" My jaw about hits the desk. "How do you know that?"

"Everyone does." Rocco's eye seems tangled in all the red threads Dad pinned to the walls. "It's what earned Sabatini his brutal reputation. The Dalla Porta is not to be crossed. The Balboni family is a cautionary tale. He wanted to make an example out of them and he did."

Turns my stomach, thinking about that much violence, but Rocco could be right. The files I've looked through up until this point have all been old. In all likelihood, they probably don't have much to do with what he was working on a few weeks ago.

I keep digging, opening his drawers. There are three to my right and four to my left. In the bottom drawer on the right hand side, I find an old tape recorder and an even older set of headphones attached to it.

Was Dad listening to music up here?

I pull them out and beneath the recorder, I see a slew of old tapes covering the bottom of the drawer. Every single tape is labeled. But they're not music, I realize with a start. They're interviews.

"Rocco, look at this!" He comes over and together we begin to pull all the tapes out from the bottom drawer.

"What are they?" He turns them over in his hand. "Wait a minute, are these…"

"I think they are."

"You think the recordings he made with Sabatini are in here?"

I nod. "Probably, but that's not what interests me most." I pick up the recorder again, hoping against hope that… *"Yes!"*

"What?"

"Dad left a tape in here." I point to it. "There's no way to know how recently he listened to this, but whichever one it is, this is the last tape he listened to. It might give me a clue about what he was working on last."

"Good thinking."

I grab the headphones and slide them over my ears. The tape's label is different from all the others. Most of them have names and the dates they were recorded. This one only has a date. And it's from the early 2000s.

Nico and I would have been just kids when Dad recorded it.

My curiosity heightens, as I work the player buttons, rewinding it all the way to the beginning. Rocco stands next to my chair, looking through the tapes and ordering them chronologically.

I press play.

The recording judders and snaps, and then I hear a soft gentle sobbing.

A woman. Someone's crying.

"Breathe, *vita mia* ...I'm here." My father's voice.

I gasp.

"What is it?" At the same time Rocco glances down at me, I glance up.

"This is... It's a recording of my parents."

Has to be. *Vita mia* is what Dad always called Mama.

Her sobs continue, one hiccup and then another. What is going on? My mind is racing, as I sit still, enraptured by this small piece of history I've just discovered.

"I know it's hard, Tati." The warmth in my father's voice rips tears to my eyes. "This is the last time you'll ever have to tell this story, I promise."

The *swip* of tissues being plucked from the box.

My mother blows her nose.

"It was a few weeks after Easter Sunday. He was waiting for me upstairs after dinner. He'd been drinking. He was angry about something Ciro said. They'd had a fight earlier that night."

Who? Who is she talking about?

"I was tired and I wanted to go to bed, but he flew into a rage, demanding I give him a child. I told him we would try again soon, but he hit me." My mother's voice wobbles. I've never heard her sound so small. "He told me that we would try again now. I didn't want to. I hated him. He was an animal. Always...So I told him no. And he..."

Her voice cuts out as she bursts into another wave of sobs. I

287

can tell Dad's hugging her, the shuffling, the sound he makes as he rubs her back. Her muffled cries, probably into his shoulder.

I'm frozen, listening to this, at absolute attention.

But I still have no idea what they're talking about...? Someone was abusing Mama? While she and Dad were married? When we were small? There's no way Dad would have stood for that. It doesn't make sense.

Someone who was fighting with Ciro?

"He was going to rape me again." My mother asserts, anger and grief warring in her tone. "And I knew it. But I was fed up. I was scared, but I didn't want to be harmed by him again so I...I grabbed a vase off the mantle, and when he came at me, I...hit him with it...so hard it *shattered*."

"What happened then?" I've never heard my father's voice so deeply angry, like he'd snap a man's neck as easily as snapping his fingers.

"Azeglio fell to the floor unconscious and bleeding from his head."

"Azeglio!" I nearly shout aloud when she says his name. Rocco's looking at me like I'm nuts, but he doesn't say anything because I'm clearly in the middle of something important.

Whoa, whoa. Mom and Dad are talking about *Azeglio Calzavarra?* Saba's second son? Ciro's older brother. The one who was murdered by...

Holy fuck.

"I cried," my mother continues. "I knew that he was hurt very badly and that if I didn't do anything, he'd die. And if he died, I'd be killed. Harming a prince of the Dalla Porta mafia is an offense punishable by death, and I..."

Another shuffle as my father holds her. I can just tell. "I know, *vita mia*."

"But then Ciro came in. He must have heard me crying, and when he saw his brother on the ground, and realized what I'd done, he...said he would save me. He said he wouldn't let anything happen to me."

"What did Ciro do?" My father's question is urgent, like he needs to know.

"He pulled out his gun and shot Azeglio through the head..." she whimpers. "He destroyed the room and told everyone the Balboni snuck in and attacked him, but he only did to protect me." My mother's voice is shaking. I'm barely breathing. "I'm the one who killed him. It was me...*Oh God*," she weeps. "And if I don't do what Ciro wants now, he'll tell everyone. Orazi, I'll be killed. You and the girls will—"

"Sh, sh, sh," my father calms her, the way he calmed me and Nico about a million times. "I will protect you. All of you. As long as I breathe, Ciro won't lay a hand on you. I promise on my soul, *vita mia*. Put your trust in me."

"But what about—" *Click.*

Just like that.

The tape ends, cutting off my mother's question in the middle, leaving me shellshocked in breathless, reeling silence.

Oh God, my head is spinning so fast, I can't...

I slide the headphones off, and Rocco's hand settles on my shoulder.

"Nora? What did you hear?" He turns my father's spinning office chair around and kneels before me, looking up into my eyes. "Talk to me, sweetheart. What did your parents say?"

Tears roll down my face once again, but my mouth won't move. I don't know how to make sense of what I just heard.

Rocco shakes me a little. "Hey. What's wrong?"

"It's my mom," I finally croak.

"What about your mom?"

"She..." The truth is so intense I can't even babble about it incoherently.

And then the missing piece flies to my mind. A few tiny words I read straight over in Dad's report on the Red Years.

*Only a few months after Azeglio's marriage to **a protected daughter
of the Dalla Porta mafia**...*

"My mom was Azeglio Calzavarra's wife..." The words fall
from my mouth, and they're true. I don't want them to be true, but
they must be.

"What are you talking about?" He pulls us both to our feet.

"Listen for yourself." I hand him the tape recorder and the
headphones. "The report said that shortly after Azeglio was
married to a protected daughter, he was killed. And this recording... It proves that protected daughter was my mom."

"You're saying that your mother was married to the heir of the
Dalla Porta mafia before he was killed?" Rocco's incredulous. "And
she never told you about it?"

"She didn't want me to know." The pieces fall together, hard
and damning, like anvils falling from the sky. "Azeglio was abusive.
He...hurt her, and to defend herself, she did what she had to do,
but Azeglio got really hurt, so Ciro shot him and blamed the
Balboni to cover it up."

The muscles in Rocco's chest tense and tighten. He can see how
disturbed I am, so he slides the headphones on and replays the
tape.

I drop back into the chair, mind still racing.

I'm overwhelmed by this bombshell, so much so that I almost
miss the most devastating part of all. The ending.

Rocco removes the headphones a minute later, similarly
stunned. "Ciro Calzavarra was trying to blackmail your mother?
Over his brother's death?"

I don't have any curse words strong enough to describe that
evil, wicked, disgusting man. "What could he have wanted that he
chose to torture her like that?"

"I think, the more important question is...why is this the tape
your father last listened to?"

"You're right." Rocco's onto something. "I highly doubt this tape
has been sitting in this recorder for the past fifteen years. On the

chance Dad listened to it recently, that means it might still be relevant."

"I'm so sorry, Nora." Rocco's solemn apology falls on deaf ears. I'm too mad.

"Come on." I yank more of Dad's drawers open. "Let's get to the bottom of this. Before I start planning a homicide."

Rocco and I keep digging, and the mystery unravels itself, revealing the truth to us bit by bit. We find old photographs from the eighties. A wedding picture of my mother and Azeglio from January 1986. He's three times her size, tall, with a nick in his hairline. His dark hair is buzzed short, just like in that picture of him as a kid. He wears a smug, triumphant looking frown, and his eyes are a murky sort of blue.

On the back of his left hand is the viper tattoo, the same one all the made men of the Dalla Porta wear. And next to him, despondent, empty-eyed, and impossibly young, is my mother.

Looking at them together, knowing that man raped my mother. More than once.

It makes me murderously furious. I want to rip the photograph to shreds and raze a building to the ground, I'm so combustibly angry.

Rocco and I keep digging. We look through my father's notes and listen to further recordings, and it isn't long before we discover that Ciro, my would-be father-in-law, has been attempting to blackmail my mother for *years* now.

I can't imagine why.

What could that man possibly have to gain?

But the more pieces we find, the clearer the picture becomes in my head.

"Azeglio was murdered under mysterious circumstances not long after the wedding." I point to the picture of the man. Rocco and I have laid out several photographs on a collapsible work table we found between a row of seats. "The official report in Dad's office said that the Balboni were behind it, but he doubted this."

"And he's been investigating ever since," Rocco concludes, setting down a few pieces of evidence I haven't seen yet. "Wait a minute. Nora, look at this coroner's report. It specifies the cause of death as the bullet to the brain."

"So?"

"So your mother thought she was the one who killed Azeglio."

"He would have died from the head injury she gave him," I remember my mother's strained words. But Rocco shakes his head.

"That's just what Ciro *wanted her* to think." Rocco points to a line further down the coroner's report. "They acknowledge here that Azeglio suffered contusions from blunt force trauma to the head, but if that vase killed him, the bullet wouldn't have been listed as the official COD. They would have written that the blunt force trauma killed him, that the bullet fired afterward was secondary. Overkill. Literally."

Rocco De Carlo just blew my fucking mind.

"*Ciro* killed his brother, but he's been blackmailing my mom to keep quiet all these years by threatening to tell everyone that it was her fault?"

Rocco nods. "That's what I'm thinking."

"But what does he want from her? She's traumatized as it is. What could he be after that she has?"

"A very important question," Rocco agrees. "It's not clear from your father's notes, but what is clear is that he was looking for *this* a long time."

Rocco holds up the coroner's report.

"What do you mean?"

"This isn't just any coroner's report, this is the *original one.* This —" In Rocco's other hand, he has a shorter stack of papers with the same cover page, like several sections of it were taken out. "—is the official one. The one on file with the state."

"You think Ciro tampered with the report to cover his own ass?"

"I know he did. I would've. Any man in that situation with the

292

amount of power and connections he had would have tried at least." Rocco flips through the original report, laying it on the table between us. "Look here."

We're staring at several photographs attached as appendixes to the document and the most damning of them is a close-up of the bullet that was removed from Azeglio's skull. The proof of Ciro's guilt is on it.

The Dalla Porta emblem is still visible in the metal. A viper's fang.

And on the other side of bullet are the initials CC.

Ciro Calzavarra.

That custom bullet is a Dalla Porta tradition. A rite of passage within the mafia. When a member of the ruling family comes of age, he's given the gift of a custom gun and bullets.

So, Ciro signed his name on his brother's murder, and to protect himself, he had the coroner's report doctored to leave these details out.

"I think this could be what your father was looking for all this time..." Rocco thinks aloud. "What if he was working behind the scenes to protect your mother from Ciro and died before this evidence was brought to light?"

"Rocco, what if Ciro had my dad killed *because* he found this evidence?"

We lock eyes.

Holy shit, this changes everything.

Once the question's out of my mouth, I can't imagine the truth any other way.

In a minute, I'm crying again, a teary, flushed mess. "No wonder I don't recognize her..." I whisper to myself. "She's afraid. My dad has always been around to protect her, but now that he's gone...Ciro can manipulate her all he wants."

Rocco pulls me into his embrace, and not a moment too soon.

I feel panicked inside, like I'm one hard reverberation away from the shattering.

"I'm so sorry, sweetheart." Rocco whispers into my hair. "What can I do?"

After a minute, all my grief begins to harden into a dark, bitter resignation.

"Rocco, you have to take me back."

He pulls away to meet my grim gaze.

"I want to run away with you, and I will, but first I need to go back." I know he understands me. "I've got to do what my father couldn't, and save my mom."

CHAPTER 32

Rocco

Nora and I drive back to the hotel around four p.m. that afternoon. The drive from the Purple Palace is ominously quiet. Her words echo in my mind.

You have to take me back.

I can't think of anything I want to do less than separate from her.

And send her straight back into the lion's den, no less.

I squeeze the steering wheel so hard, my knuckles go white thinking about it. About what her mother suffered, marrying into that godforsaken family. What Nora's suffered being engaged to that prick, Gianfrancesco.

Everything inside me hates it. I'm fully resistant. Every few seconds, I yearn to open my mouth and refuse her.

I won't take you back. Over and over again, I rehearse my arguments, about why this is a terrible idea, why we shouldn't separate, but I don't speak a word.

Why?

Nora deserves the chance to save her mother.

I wish I could save mine. The least I can do is preserve Nora's opportunity to help the woman that raised her, even if it means throwing herself back into the clutches of the same danger threatening them in the first place.

All I can hold onto is the fact that she still wants to be with me.

She didn't call things off with me.

We're simply making one last stop on the road to our happiness.

That's what I tell myself, as I park my car in the hotel's underground garage and she and I jog for the service entry and head up to our room.

We've got plans to make and plenty of them.

An hour later, over another in-room feast, we discuss everything we know and everything we need to figure out.

Nora now has the evidence she needs to free her mother from Ciro's continued manipulation, but she needs to give her that information in person. I still hate the sound of it, but I don't have any better ideas.

She can't ship it to her mother. The package could be intercepted, screened, or thrown away well before it ever reaches her mother's hands. If she's going to do this, she has to do it herself.

Doubt still knocks at the back door of my mind.

"Nora, if you want go back...for good, that's okay too." I sound like a robot the words come out so cold and unfeeling. The thought of her doing that sends my emotions free-falling inside. But she has a family to go back to, and that's worth something. I should know.

Nora touches my face to reassure me. *"Please.* Don't even say that. I definitely don't want to go back. There's hell and high water waiting for me, since I disappeared after the fire without a trace..."

Bitterness contorts her features, but she manages to rein it in. "I'm willing to brave the family elements though, if it means getting my mom out from under Ciro's thumb."

"Are you sure?" I ask her for the thousandth time in sixty minutes.

She nods. "I can do it, Rocco. I know I can. I have you in my corner, and you'll be waiting for me on the other side."

The trust she puts in me murders my heart.

Jesus Christ, I'm crazy about her.

I know that now with every molecule of my being, and there's nothing I can do about it.

"We're running away together..." I murmur against her lips, tasting her mouth on mine. She nods, her nose brushing mine.

"And nothing on this earth is going to change my mind."

With just a sentence, she fills me with radical strength of will.

I know I'd cross any ocean, traverse any mountain for this woman. And I will help her get back to her family.

And most importantly, I will come back for her, exactly as we've planned. I don't care what it takes. Yes, Vito's going to be pissed when I return empty-handed, but I couldn't give a flying fuck.

What Nora and I have is more important than any assignment from Vito Balboni.

"So I'm going to drop you off near the Dalla Porta's estate line downtown."

She nods. "I don't have any idea what's happened what with the fire and all, but I do know that they'll have security on the ground. And they'll likely be searching for me. If I step foot on that block, they'll clock me in seconds, and they'll take me straight to wherever my mom is."

"Where do you think the Calzavarras will be staying?"

"No idea. But wherever it is, it's temporary. The wedding is scheduled for May second, and it's happening at the country house upstate."

"The country house?"

Nora pulls up a map of New York State on the smart Tv in our room. "We've been up there a few times over the years. I'm not totally sure of the exact address, but I know for sure it's up the hill, set far back on a few acres, about fifteen minutes from this town here." She points at tiny unassuming town.

When I get back to my computer at home, I'll pull up estate records tied to Sabatini Calzavarra and cross-reference what I find with her rough location.

"Got it."

"Can you come for me the night beforehand?" Her next question throws me off.

"Why so long?" I blurt out. May 2nd is ten days from now. "It'll take a whole week to talk to your mom about everything we've found?"

"Talking to Mom should be the easy part." Her eyes fall to her hands. "I know it's a long time, but I'll probably need that long to leave a trail for Nico."

"How does Nico factor into all of this?"

Nora looses a long breath, like she doesn't want to face what she's about to say.

"There's more going on here than I ever imagined, Rocco...I can feel it. It's bigger than just this wedding, or my dad or my mom. It's bigger than Azeglio's murder, I just know it. If we had more time, I'd hole up in my dad's office until I got to the bottom of everything, but we don't have that luxury."

"But Nico will?"

She gives me a helpless half-shrug. "Someone's got to figure out what the fuck it all means, and there's no one I trust more than Nico. She's got all of Dad's natural sleuthing ability too. If anyone can pick up where we've left off, and find out what really happened to Dad, it's her. The letter he sent me said so. He said Nico and I are the only ones who could do this."

Even so, the idea of spending ten days away from Nora with no way to contact her or make sure she's okay alarms me.

There's no way for me to feel comfortable with it.

But I trust her. I'd do anything for her.

I'll have to find some way to believe that we'll make it out of this okay.

Finally, I nod. "I've got the plan."

She nods too, giving me a somber smile.

All the details she's given me about the wedding will help me make my excuses to Vito, Jaco, and the others too.

After an hour of strategizing, there's nothing more for us to figure out.

Instead, we just settle into the reality that we'll be apart for almost two weeks, and it feels like shit.

Nora wants me to drop her home tonight.

I begged her to let me do it tomorrow, but she held firm. Time is of the essence. Any idiot can see that. I'm just the idiot that doesn't want to let her go.

Not now. Not for anything.

The *last* thing I want to do is say goodbye to her, even temporarily, but this is her only chance to help her mother. There's nothing I can do for either of my parents now. The least I can do is not stand in Nora's way when she wants to try.

"Rocco?" Nora circles her arms around my chest all of a sudden. "I think you should know that...I'm in love with you."

She bowls me right over with that confession.

I almost fall off the bed, she knocks me so off kilter.

"I don't want to separate from you, and I just realized the reason why is because I love you so much, and I..."

I rip her mouth to mine, extracting the words right from her beautiful lips.

Intense, burning, rippling affection destroys me inside. I've pushed her down on this massive bed, yet again, in mere seconds.

"I love and adore you, Eleanora Di Rienzo." She blinks up at me, all of her affection clear as daylight in her eyes. "I'd go blind for your touch."

I anchor her body with mine, greedily devouring her lips.

A passionate goodbye, it is.

I'm going to need it to get through our separation.

Doesn't take long for us to get naked between these hotel bedsheets.

I'm inside her again, her legs folded around my waist. I haven't done missionary like this in decades.

Fuck, I didn't know anything could feel this right.

My forehead rests on hers.

With her arms over my shoulders, she pulls at my hair while I bury my cock inside her. I'm so over the moon for this woman, all kinds of confessions tumble from my lips.

"I want to wake up next to you every day."

Tears pearl in the corners of her eyes and drip down over her temples.

"I want that too," she mumbles, opening the way for desperate affection to ravage me on the inside.

"*Nora...*" Now, I'm pounding her.

She pulls me down until her head slides over my shoulder.

"*Rocco, I love you.*" She says the words right in my ear, and a new flood of heat overtakes me.

Every time she says those words, my heart takes flight in my chest.

If she weren't holding onto me for dear life, I'd float up to the ceiling. I'm sure of it.

Eleanora Di Rienzo is the best thing that's ever happened to me.

And I'm about to let her go...

CHAPTER 33

Nora

LEAVING Rocco De Carlo is the hardest thing I've ever had to do.

Harder even than burying my dad.

When Dad died, I had no choice.

Rocco and I were free, and I could have run away with him. By now, we could have been in another state, happily ensconced in romantic bliss.

But I chose *this* instead.

Hustling down a New York City block in the dark, closing the distance between me and the Dalla Porta estate. I have nothing to my name. No phone. No wallet. Just the keys to my father's secret office, and a folded-up picture of the bullet that killed Azeglio tucked beneath the lining of this dress.

I'm on a mission. A noble one. These two thoughts are the only defense I have to stop my feet from racing back to the curb where Rocco left me, praying that he's still there...

No. I've got to keep moving forward. For the love of my parents.

As soon as the boulevard comes into view, I can see much of it has been cordoned off while authorities deal with the fire damage.

I hate the sight of it.

When I left here last night, I was fully prepared to never return.

What I'm facing instead, I'm nowhere near prepared for.

As I walk, all I can think about is Rocco.

His hands, his heat, his smile, his mind...

Without Rocco, I wouldn't even be alive right now. I truly am a different person since we met. I know that without a shadow of a doubt.

Almost as soon as I step foot onto the family block, security personnel dressed in street clothes step into my path, obscuring my view. Three of them.

Big guys I've never seen before.

But each of them have their viper tattoos. They're all Dalla Porta soldiers.

"Tell them we've found her," the one in the center orders the others. To me, he says, "Right this way."

None of them ask me if I'm all right, if I need any help. They just usher me to the nearest available cage—I mean, *SUV*, talking hurriedly into earpieces and cellphones alerting the whole mafioso phone tree that I've been located.

I guess they're calling off the city-wide manhunt. Jesus, am I in trouble...

This is way worse than the day I snuck away from my security detail.

I've been gone a whole twenty-four hours at this point.

Who knows what manner of hell awaits me... Which reminds me.

I lean forward on this plush leather seat, hoping the driver will hear me.

"Where are you taking me?"

"The country estate, ma'am." The driver calls back. "Your family's already there."

I sit back, rolling my eyes. Oh, perfect.

They're taking me to the wedding venue.

I knew I was going to end up at that house sooner or later, so this is convenient.

But on the other hand, staying in a house alone with my mother, Don Saba, Ciro, Donna, and Frankie and almost no one else around? Especially knowing now what I know about the horrible history between our families?

It might as well be one of the circles of hell.

In the backseat, I close my eyes and try to summon Rocco to me through my senses. The intoxicating scent of his cologne, the pressure of his hands pressing against my skin...

My hand flies over my mouth, the tears come on so unexpectedly.

Oh God, why did I do this? Why did I come back here?

I had heaven in my hands and I let it go. What if something goes wrong? What if Rocco and I can't find our way back to each other? What if by some sadistic twist of fate, these horrible people really get me down the aisle with Frankie Calzavarra?

How will I live with myself for choosing this path?

You have to help Dad save Mom. I'm doing this for Daddy, I remind myself. He can't do it. He was ripped away from this world before he could. It's up to me.

Despite all the painfully strong emotions battling inside my brain, I try to enjoy the hour and a half drive up to the country house. I know it'll probably be the last vestige of peace and quiet I get before Rocco busts me out of this horrible life I was born into.

Finally, the transport I'm in exits the highway and winds through the darkened sleepy shopfronts of the small town nearest to the country house. We climb a long narrow road to the crest of a hill, then turn left in between two fat, tall brick piers with lanterns hanging from the tops.

Attached to one of thick square pillars is an intercom. The driver rolls his window down to converse with the security squad here on the property. Their chat is short, and then the SUV is granted entry through a pair of tall wrought iron gates.

Heart drumming in my chest, I begin to bobble in my seat as the concrete below the car transitions into bumpy cobblestone. We pull around toward the enormous mansion house with a circular backlit fountain anchoring the round driveway.

Multiple lights in the mansion are on, despite my highest hopes that I might not have to see or speak to anyone tonight. When the caravan finally pulls to a stop, there's a man in a suit I've never seen before standing at the ready to open my door, and yank me out onto the pavement.

"Ms. Di Rienzo." His tone is sharp, his distinguished features drawn tight over protruding, striking bone structure. "I've been instructed to deliver you to your mother."

"Thank you," I exercise good manners, though this man is hardly giving me a choice, with his long-fingered hand cuffed tight around my bicep.

He walks me into the lavish, lofty foyer. Or, I'm sure it's lavish. I can't quite tell because the place is resplendent with flower arrangements and expensively-wrapped gift boxes.

Don't tell me these are wedding presents!

I don't have time to wonder. The pushy butler drags me down a hallway on the left to the first set of parlor doors we come to, and inside another spacious suite, decorated with far too much beige, is my horror-stricken mother.

As soon as the butler leaves us, she unleashes her livid voice on me, charging right up and into my face.

"Where the fuck have you been?" To my surprise, tears spring from her eyes like she cares more about me than whatever punishment may await us at the hands of the Calzavarras. "I went hysterical when I thought you'd been killed in the fire back at the main house. And then when they didn't find any bodies, to find out that you ran away. Again!"

I wish I had the energy to fight with her, but I don't.

After everything I learned today about my mother's life, I don't think I'll have the energy to fight with her about anything ever again.

Instead, I stand there, pitying her, taking all of her verbal retribution in stride.

This is the first time I've seen her since learning the truth, that she used to be married to Ciro's abusive older brother, and that she's been the victim of Ciro's blackmail attempts more than once over the years.

Knowing this information entirely changes my perspective on my mother's behavior... I feel so sorry for all that she's been through, all that she must still be going through, that I can't offer a single rejoinder to all of her criticisms and disdain for my actions.

Before this sad and angry reunion can stretch on too long, the pushy butler reappears with a message.

"Miss Di Rienzo has been summoned."

"Where?" My mother demands. "She just got here."

"To her fiancé's quarters."

My mother and I share a fearful look.

If I've got this butler right, then...

Sounds like, now I'll have to face Frankie over my unexplained absence.

Fuck.

CHAPTER 34

Rocco

"WELL?" Vito's the first to speak when I finally get back to the warehouse and get through the door to the conference room. Everyone's waiting there, almost like they haven't moved since the last time I was in here. "What the fuck took you so long? Were you successful? Did you deliver the target to the holding facility?"

"The building went up in flames, I heard," Fiero moves a bishop to a new square, while Lancini looks on with interest.

"There was a fire," I confirm. "It wasn't my doing. By that time, I'd already captured the target."

"So, the mission was a success," Lancini concludes too soon.

"If you got her there, why the fuck didn't you tell anyone?" Vito fumes.

"Because I didn't take the target to the holding facility."

The room comes to a halt, eight eyeballs in total flicking in my direction.

Jaco is the first to speak after I drop that first bombshell. "Rocco. We told you to nab that girl and take her to the gulch."

The gulch is how we refer to Holding Facility A, an abandoned shopping plaza basement about three hours outside of the city.

"Are you telling us that you disobeyed that order?"

"The girl started to sing, and promised us an even bigger prize, if I let her run home to her in-laws." The carefully rehearsed explanation I've planned is in progress, and by the darkly intrigued look on Jaco's face, I feel optimistic that it's going okay.

Until Vito goes fucking nuclear.

He roars, like a volcano erupting, ripping a laptop off the lectern to his right, and chucking it at my face with the force of a hall-of-fame pitcher.

The thing revolves through the air like a throwing star, hurtling to the wall behind me, only an inch over from my left cheek. It explodes against the exposed brick, silicon, steel, and plastic raining down onto the hardwood floor, he threw it so hard.

"You fuck-up!" Vito kicks over the nearest chair, shoves the lectern into the brick wall hard enough to break the wooden panels apart. He stomps the shit out of a metal trashcan that he obviously wishes was my head, yelling, "You insolent, useless, cock-brained bastard!"

I've seen the kid act out, but this is Tony-award-winning.

Even for him.

Vito does everything short of pull another weapon on me, out of respect for his father, though it's clear the temptation is great.

Jaco makes it all worse by not sharing his son's frustration, but instead folding his fingers over the conference table and nodding at me. "Go on."

"Once I had the target alone in captivity, she began to rapidly reveal information to me that not only makes abducting her closer to the wedding day a more desirable option for us, but also ensures that we'll have quite the ammunition stock against the Dalla Porta going forward."

"What kind of ammunition?" Fiero removes his cigar from his mouth, like this meeting just got interesting.

"Dirt on Sabatini."

A hush swells through the room.

The secrets of Sabatini Calzavarra are morsels too delectable for these hyenas to resist, even in imagination. Just the *possibility* of having the upper hand on that man would be an irresistible proposition for Jaco.

Especially now that I know how deep his twisted, jealous hatred runs...

It takes serious effort on my part to keep up the pretense of respect, even though I lost my loyalty to this man and his mafia the minute I heard about what he did to Rossana Facci.

I've done many dark deeds. Killing. Maiming. Interrogating with knives and gasoline. But hunting down a woman over her rejection?

Murdering her, stealing her child?

Turns out even my sorry excuse for a conscience has its limits.

"What would she know?!" Vito demands, hoping to steer everyone back toward rage. "She's just a cunt with a meal ticket!"

The only person he succeeds in angering is me.

Trying to keep my rage at bay is like trying to control Cerberus with a leash.

But if I break down here and deck that shithead in the mouth, I'll lose more than my opportunity to run away with Nora.

"How do you know she wasn't bluffing?" Lancini swivels his thick scarred face in my direction.

"Her father was Sabatini's oldest friend." I answer, having prepared myself for this question. "In his office on the Dalla Porta estate, there are tapes. Hundreds of them. Interviews he did with Sabatini. Talking about everything from business practices and transaction records to his dirtiest secrets, the ones her father was responsible for making go away."

"And she gave you the tapes in exchange for letting her go?" Fiero presses.

I nod. "Every. Single. One."

A dark excitement takes over the room.

Jaco actually smiles. "You've done it again, Rocco."

"Bring the tapes to my office at once," Fiero orders, taking a victorious puff from his cigar. I give him a nod, knowing I'll be long gone by the time he realizes I'm bluffing.

"She, of course, thinks that was the end of it. But she's wrong. I say we ambush the reception and rip her from them, right as they're cutting the cake. It'll be a red reception, and if we're lucky, we may even get a clear shot at her in-laws."

"There's much to prepare." Lancini shoots out of his seat, glee bouncing in his frenzied, black eyes. The thought of getting to plan a murder excites him and always has. "Let's go, Fiero."

Fiero and Lancini rise from their seats and exit the conference room first. I ache to follow them out, but I haven't been dismissed by Jaco yet, and this is no time to forget my manners. They're the only thing protecting my façade.

Vito remains beside himself with ire. I've never seen him so pissed.

Jaco holds up a hand as if to dismiss me, but then, the doors behind me swing open and in walks...

Sweet Jesus Christ.

It's Anunziata.

Fuck, fuck, fuck.

I feel like I've been shoved off a cliff, the minute I see her sharp, irritated expression. The past forty-eight hours have been such a whirlwind that I've all but forgotten our last encounter.

The one where she left in tears after accusing me of being in love with someone else. I couldn't even muster enough bullshit to deny her, and now, she's walking into this conference room with vengeance in her eyes?

R. R. NIGH

If Zia mentions to her father her suspicion that I'm cheating on her with someone else, even though she can't prove it, my entire plan goes to shit.

Disastrous would be the polite term for it.

No amount of well-planned words would save me from Jaco's wrath then.

"Daddy," she addresses Jaco, like any brat anywhere, crossing the room to his side with the careful, yet self-assured grace of a spoiled, pretty house cat.

"Precious, I'm in a meeting."

"I saw Fiero and Lancini leave. Isn't it over?"

"What is it?" Jaco motions for her to go on.

Meanwhile, Vito's walking an angry little track into the floor, since he's run out of things to throw.

"I want to set a date," she says, capturing the full and complete attention of all of us in the room.

Huh? I try not to gape at her.

"Can Rocco and I be married when he's done with this assignment?" She throws a haughty glance in my direction before pouring the full force of her puppy dog eyes on her father. "I want to pick out a dress already—"

"I'd rather marry you to a STRAY DOG than that dumb fucker!" Vito jabs an angry finger at me, growling at his sister. Before any of us can say anymore, Vito storms off, the conference room doors slamming so hard behind him, they shake in their frames.

In his wake, he leaves carnage and on my part, confusion.

If anyone's an expert on pissing Vito off, it's me.

And that's how I know that something's going on here that runs deeper than the usual animosities alive and well between us.

Nora's words return to my mind in sudden stunning clarity. *There's more going on here than I ever imagined, Rocco...I can feel it.*

Her words alter my perspective on what just happened, like a filter bringing new contrast to an image.

Why does Vito Balboni personally care so much about when and how Nora is abducted? *What's riding on this?*

I was going to need a distraction for the next ten days anyway, something to keep me busy during this horrid stretch of time when I can't see or spend time with the only woman I love.

And I think I just found my new time-kill.

It's time to do a little reconnaissance on Vito.

CHAPTER 35

Nora

THE PUSHY BUTLER escorts me up to the third floor of this sprawling country residence and foists me into an expansive master bedroom without another word. Four large curtained windows dominate the far wall. Twin chaise lounges face a square black coffee table in the center of the room, and to the left of the seating group, an enormous bed sucks up all the focus in this spacious suite.

I guess I expected the place to look like a replica of Frankie's suite back at the Dalla Porta estate but this room is completely different. It's actually nice. If he weren't standing inside, half naked, furious, and clearly on his nth finger of whiskey, I'd think this room were quite lovely in fact.

I'm barely inside the door and already frozen in fear.

Gianfrancesco watches me like a jungle cat preparing to pounce.

"Come here," he commands, voice rough, low and impatient.

I take two steps forward and stop again.

His face pinches up with bitterness and irritation, as he takes another long swig from his too-full whiskey glass.

We haven't been this alone together since the *last time* I ran away, and the sensation is even more eerie than before.

My muscles are tensed tight, like they're preparing for something.

For what though, I don't want to imagine.

Frankie drops onto the chaise lounge that faces me, his massive arm draped over the back of it, like a lazy boa constrictor, ready to strangle the life out of me. "What the hell happened last night, Nora?"

Again, I find myself in his crosshairs without a ready response. I'll have to find a good lie, while telling the truth.

"I left the party to go to the restroom..." Flashes of our engagement party slowly return to my memory. "Then I started to smell smoke. When I came out, the house was on fire, so I got out through the back door. By the kitchens."

"Why didn't you rendezvous with the rest of us after you escaped?" His gravelly voice almost sounds unbothered. That's how pissed he is. His fury's reached such a high pitch, my ears can't even pick up the frequency anymore.

"I wanted some air." I mean to swallow, but it sounds like a great big gulp.

Frankie squeezes his whiskey glass so hard, I can't hear his skin straining against the crystal. "I thought I told you that you were *forbidden* to leave the estate without my permission."

Bringing that up only creates a bloom of resentment in my chest. "You may find this hard to believe, but being treated like your personal prisoner doesn't really work for me."

Frankie flicks his arm, and the whiskey glass goes flying. It shatters against an egg-shell colored wall, brown liquor and glass shards cascading to the floor.

The sudden noise makes me jump, I'm so high strung right now.

"Sass me again and you'll regret it, Nora."

"I already regret it." The words are out before I can stop them.

Fuck. Now, he's giving me that raging bull look.

He shoots up from his seat, nostrils flared and fists coiled so tight that the veins along his hands and forearms stand and twitch against his skin.

"Not as much as you will, if I find out you've been whoring yourself behind my back," he snarls with a scowl so deep, I can feel it in the back of my head.

What am I supposed to say to *that*?

"I'm not seeing anyone, Gianfrancesco."

"You expect me to believe you were out all night *alone?*"

I exhale slowly, trying to ease some of the upset in my chest. "I just wanted to enjoy one last hurrah in the city with my friends from work before beginning my married life."

"Did you set the fire?" Frankie's green and brown eyes dig into me like surgical tools. "Just to get away from me?"

Now, there's a brilliant idea I've never thought of.

"Of course not." I keep my voice calm. "Arson isn't for me."

"You think this is a fucking joke?" He roars, marching in my direction.

I want to back up, but then he'll have me cornered against the door and unable to actually leave, if I need to.

"No." I keep my tone level, even as he stamps right into my personal space. His whisky-tinged scent is next to unbearable.

"*I don't believe you.*" Frankie growls at me, like he wants to tear my flesh from my bones. Like I've angered the animal inside of him. "Which is why I've decided that you're going to fuck me tonight."

"What?" I can't keep the terrified wobble out of my voice.

Dear God, please no.

"You should be thanking me." A wicked smile spreads across his face. "I'm giving you a chance to prove your fealty and devotion to our marriage."

"No, Gianfrancesco, please."

"*No?*" His eyebrows push down into a glare. "You defy me?"

My hand flies to the cross around my neck, terror swelling at the base of my spine. "God wouldn't want it."

"I AM YOUR GOD," he explodes at me.

"I'll be yours in just a few days," I plead, shaking my head.

"Wrong." He snatches my chin between his rough fingers. "You're already mine."

I can't tell if I'm arguing with him or the whiskey polluting his blood, but it doesn't matter when he grabs my wrist hard enough to snap it and drags me deeper into his bedroom.

Before I can protest, he flings me toward his massive bed and shoves me down onto it, pinning me to the mattress with his fists tight around my wrists. His thick knees dig into the duvet on either side of my waist, but then he picks one up and shoves it down against my pubic bone, until I yelp from the pain and unwillingly part my legs enough that he can position both his legs between mine.

Panic floods my body.

Oh God. Am I doomed to follow in my mother's footsteps? To be raped by a member of the Calzavarra clan?

Frankie's thick head hovers above mine, his eyelids low, lustful, and uncaring. He moves slowly, almost like he thinks this situation qualifies as anything remotely consensual. He drops his head lower to mine, as though he expects a kiss.

I yank my head aside before our faces connect, hyperventilating from the terror tearing through me from head to toe. I could scream, but no one would hear me. Even if they did, they wouldn't dare try and stop him.

Frankie lifts his head, and when I glance back at his face, he's scowling at me.

His expression blurs as tears fill my eyes. "Please, Frankie. Please don't do this. You're hurting me."

Something about this pitiful display—me begging him to spare me—it seems to sink in that he'll have to rape me to make this sexual encounter take place.

And whether it's his pride or self respect or his highest self or the straight-up grace of God kicking in, I don't know, but he abruptly shoves off of me, releasing my wrists.

Even angrier than before, he grabs the quarter-full bottle of whiskey off the coffee table and staggers toward his bedroom door. Before he pulls it open, he stops.

"*Don't* be here when I get back."

And then he's gone, leaving me panting, shocked, and untouched on his bed—Spiraling through flashbacks of almost the same crime that happened the last time he pushed me down, when I was thirteen years old.

I don't know how long I lay there alone, half dissociating, but at some delayed point, my limbs spring into action and I get the fuck out of his room, my heart flying.

This close...

I came this close to being assaulted by my fiancé.

Like Rossana Facci. Like my mother. *Oh God.*

Hurrying back through this dizzyingly large house to the quarters allocated to me on the first floor, I think of my mom. And how she horribly knows exactly what it's like to be forced by a man she was arranged to marry.

When I burst back into our suite, I expect to find her in the den where she was when I left, but she's not. I don't know where she is, and right now, I don't care. I duck into the first open bedroom I find, lock the door, turn on all the lights in the room, and climb into the clean, warm bed and try to sleep.

I want to do everything in my power to leave the dark shadows of this horrible night behind me. But sleep doesn't come easily. I have to talk myself into it, slowly, over many hours of reassuring myself with the same truth, *If I can survive this place for ten days, I'll be free of it forever. And Rocco will be my reward.*

When daybreak finally comes, I shower and throw on a pair of clean clothes I retrieve from a dresser in yet another palatial walk in closet full of fashions I'd never pick out for myself. Today, and every day until Rocco comes for me, I've got to work.

And the first thing I need to do is talk to my mom.

When I exit my bedroom into the suite's communal living space, I find my mother in another dress that doesn't suit her, slowly putting earrings through her lobes with slightly shaking hands.

"Mama, are you okay?" The tremble beneath her skin continues to draw my focus, but she ignores my question altogether.

"There you are. I was just about to wake you. It's time for breakfast." She gives herself a blank unreadable look in the mirror and then turns to me, but she doesn't meet my eyes.

There's never going to be a good moment for this, so I just come out with it.

I'm past the point of caring about why we're here in this huge house and how we're supposed to be acting.

"Why didn't you ever tell us that you were married before you and Daddy got together?" I submit the question softly, but she stops dead in her tracks.

It's like I can see her shutting down, like windows shuttering closed all over her body. "Stop talking nonsense. We'll be late."

"Mama."

"You don't know what you're talking about." Cagey. Defensive.

"I do know what I'm talking about."

Her head snaps in my direction, but she doesn't speak.

"Why didn't you ever tell us that you were married to Azeglio Calzavarra?" I swallow down the lump of emotion in my throat. "Or that he even existed in the first place?"

"Who told you…"

"I found a tape. Daddy interviewing you about the night that Azeglio was killed." I set my jaw, bracing for the full force of my mother's shock. "I know everything."

If she was shaking before, now she's shaking worse. "Eleanora. It's best to leave the past alone."

"No!" I bark at her. "Not if Ciro's still trying to blackmail you, even now."

She covers her mouth with a hand, muffling a ripping sob that tears out.

I close the distance between us, laying my hands to her hopping shoulders.

"Mama, listen to me. Daddy found the original coroner's report from the night of Azeglio's murder. *You didn't kill him,* Ciro did. He wouldn't have died from the head injury caused by the vase. The coroner said the bullet is what killed him. And Ciro had the report altered to leave that part out. I have the proof with me, Mama—"

"Destroy it!" She bursts at me, voice rasping and tortured. "Get rid of it right now, don't let anyone ever see it, and don't speak of this anyone ever again—"

"What are you talking about, Mama?" I squeeze her shoulders. "Don't you understand? Having this proof means that you don't need to live in fear of Ciro's retribution anymore. As soon as you tell him what you have, you'll have the upper hand, he—"

"You're wrong!" She shrieks at me. "Why can't I make you understand that it's *over?* Your father has been fighting Ciro over this for years, and look what happened to him. Who do you think got him killed?"

She glares at me through red watery eyes, stabbing a knife into my heart.

"You think Ciro did it?"

"I know he did." Her voice gets low. "He's been threatening to do it for years. And he finally did. Do you really think he's going to back off now just because you have a sheet of paper with his name on it?"

"But Mama..." Now, my own tears are shaking me. "What are you saying? You aren't even going to *try* to stop him? You really think he killed Daddy, and you're just going to do nothing about it?"

"What would it change?" She chokes on a sob. "The love of my life is gone, and there's nothing else I can do. He's won."

I can see it now, what I've been seeing the past few weeks but been too afraid to face. The truth.

My mother's spirit is broken. She has no more will to fight.

"The best way forward is to give him what he wants and leave it at that." She swipes at her swollen face. "At least if we give him his way, he'll see that we're taken care of. That no harm comes to us."

"Ciro Calzavarra *is* harm to us."

"That doesn't matter now." She straightens her dress, wipes her teary face once more, and strides toward the door. "Now, come on. You're making us late."

She doesn't wait for me. Just goes, while my heart crumbles to pieces in my chest.

I was free and I came all the way back here to unlock the prison door for my mom, all to learn that she has no intention of ever being free again. She's chosen a path of submission and self-abandonment, and I can't do anything to change her mind.

I have to let myself cry. There's nothing else to be done and no one to turn to.

Desperation for Rocco's embrace bursts open inside me, but I'll have to embrace myself. I'm on my own in this wilderness, and I'll have to find my way out alone.

Without being able to get through to my mom, my only hope to save her is to leave clues for Nico. She'll be in town for the wedding, if nothing's changed, and now, I know with all certainty —it'll be up to Nico to unravel the rest of this mystery.

I just can't. I've got to get away from this place and all these horrible people before my sanity is ripped right out of my hands.

Again, I soothe myself with hopes of my future.

My time in this hellhole is winding down. The only thought that stops my tears is imagining how good it will feel to be back in the arms of the man I love.

CHAPTER 36

Rocco

IT HAS BEEN NINE DAYS, eight hours, and fifty-two minutes since I last saw Eleanora Di Rienzo, and it has been the longest, most grueling, achingly painful week and two days of my life.

Time crawls past, and every second of it I'm anxious, not knowing where she is or what she's doing. She left her phone on the Dalla Porta estate the night of the fire, but it's obvious the main family isn't staying there right now in the aftermath.

I'd be lying if I said I hadn't stealthily been monitoring that block for any signs of her, but the tapped security footage I have of the place has been the same, day in and day out. No new news.

The Balboni warehouse has been abuzz with energy and excitement about the plan to bust up the wedding reception of Nora and Gianfrancesco. In hallways and meeting rooms, I field a mix of impressed and resentful glances from people excited for carnage to come and displeased that such a large operation has come out of an unpunished act of defiance on my part.

I don't even want to imagine what this place will be like on Sunday night when they get back here, after my true betrayal has taken place. As they will soon discover, I gave them the wrong Dalla Porta property—a different country house owned by Sabatini Calzavarra—as the intended destination of the wedding.

On Sunday afternoon when they storm the place and find themselves with nothing but their dicks to hold onto and the Calzavarras, Nora, and myself nowhere to be found, their miscalculations will be clear.

And I'll already be a few states away, Nora in tow, on our way to a better life.

Acting otherwise takes up most of my strength, and believe me, I've been giving the performance of my life.

When I'm not in meetings or war rooms, discussing plans, I'm being hounded by Anunziata. She follows me around the estate like a shadow while I'm home.

If my cellphone pings, she shoots me threatening glances, as if to say, *I haven't told my father about your other woman, but I will, if you so much as answer her call.*

I ache to tell her that the woman I love can't call me these days, even if she wants to as desperately as I want to call her.

And when I'm not roasting under the microscope lens of Anunziata, I'm doing everything I can to figure out what Vito's hiding.

But maybe I'm losing my edge.

Because even after nine days of turning over stones and sniffing behind him, I've still got nothing.

Vito's definitely hiding something. I know it.

The issue is that this time, he's actually doing a good job of keeping it a secret. His usual amount of sloppiness is absent, which must mean that he's not alone in whatever he's hiding *or* that whatever it is means so much to him that he's neatened up his messy MO in order to protect it.

Either way, it's a puzzle I'm determined to solve, and it's clear I'm going to have to rely more heavily on my investigative talents to crack this one.

Combed through his phone records and his laptop contents, but I haven't found anything out of the ordinary. I even got my hands on the enforcers assignment log—had to sneak into Lancini's office for it—to see what he's been working on lately, and everything appears to be as it always is.

I've lurked in the shadows of his favorite haunts and watched him drink himself into oblivion, but other than that, I haven't seen, heard, or found anything of merit, and that's not good.

I'm running out of time.

As happy as I would be to let this go and never give Vito Balboni another thought ever again, figuring out what he's up to matters to me because of Nora. There's a reason he's so personally hellbent on abducting her, and that reason might be strong enough to motivate him to hunt us down after I take her far away from here.

If that's going on in the background, I need to know about it.

I won't be blindsided.

I will end him if it comes down to it. The future I want with Nora is worth any price I have to pay. Even if I tell her the truth and she never wants to see me again, I've decided that's fine. I'll spend the rest of my life trying to make it up to her.

Whatever it takes.

I won't let her go.

After all that I've lost, after being brought into the Balboni family only to be singled out and ostracized, she...is the only place I belong.

She is the only source of joy I've found in forty-five years and I refuse to be without her. Anything and anyone who gets in my way will be eliminated, it's as simple as that.

Vito's no exception.

I know what I have to do where he's concerned: Tail him.

If I follow him, I'll find out exactly where he's been going and what he's been up to. The challenge is that Vito's security detail would recognize my car. Or any of the other cars normally parked in the garage downstairs.

I'll need another way.

Hence where I am right now in the underbelly of the Balboni's garage. There's an auto mechanic's area underneath where we keep the equipment to service our cars when need be, and next to the equipment storage is a private staff lounge of sorts where members of the Balboni family's security detail play cards.

I'm looking for one member in particular.

Tommaso. Vito's chauffeur.

He's a round man in his sixties with a bearded face and dark, beady eyes. The guy's a real crook, I hear. He cheats at everything, and settles petty debts by breaking fingers. I'm sure Vito picked him since they have such similarly charming personalities, but that doesn't matter now.

In the dark of the under-garage hallway, I lean against one wall with a cigarette and wait. It's almost nine am, and I overheard Vito tell Tommaso to be ready to go this morning around this time.

What the fuck does the prince of hangovers need to do this early in the morning? I intend to find out.

After a few minutes of waiting in the dark echoey hallway, blowing smoke trails up to the cement ceiling, the door to the staff lounge squeals open and out steps Tommaso, grumbling about a loss he just took.

He passes me by without looking up, and I doubt he notices that I'm following him. He definitely doesn't see it coming when I jab him hard in the neck with my tranquilizing pen. Tommaso releases a grunt of pain, but the chemicals are so potent he's lost control of his tongue halfway through the reaction.

Meanwhile, I grab two fistfuls of his suit jacket, shove his giant ass a few more steps, then stuff him in a triple wide storage locker at the end of the hall. *Fuck,* the man's heavy, especially, as he loses control of his limbs, turning slowly into the world's heaviest rag doll in my grip.

Once he's put away, I have a matter of minutes to fish a pair of car keys from his pocket, find Vito's usual SUV in the garage above, get behind the wheel, and whip the car around to the street side entrance of the Balboni warehouse.

My heart's pounding by the time I get it all done, but still, I've succeeded in beating Vito to the front door, even though time wasn't on my side.

When the security guards pull the doors open, and Vito appears, looking sharp and fresh, despite his usual morning stupor, I know I've made the right decision.

Something's definitely up.

Without a word, Vito climbs into the backseat of the SUV separated from me by an opaque, pitch-black partition. Even though it took some effort to get to this point, this part of my mission is actually easy.

Vito's such an unobservant asshole that he doesn't even bother to put the partition down. I'm driving him, and he hasn't the faintest idea. Which is perfect.

I doubt he'll even notice the difference between my voice and Tommaso's.

After he's inside, I press the intercom button which allows me to hear what's going on in the backseat and vice versa. "Where to, sir?"

"Same place as last time," Vito replies. "And hurry the fuck up."

Shit. No address.

"Yes, sir." I ease onto the gas pedal, even though I have no idea where we're going. That's when I notice the SUV's monitor. There's bound to be GPS history somewhere in this thing. Tapping rapidly with my pointer finger, I toggle to a screen with the last known directions Tommaso took and select the address they visited most recently, *praying* it's the right place.

But after half an hour of driving and no complaints from the backseat, I assume I'm headed in the right direction. The real confirmation comes several minutes later.

The most important thing I'm getting away with here is leaving the intercom engaged, so I hear it loud and clear when Vito's phone rings and he answers.

"Yeah, it's me. I'm almost there."

Of course, he's meeting someone. Vito hardly strikes me as the kind of person who takes long drives at nine in the morning just to clear his pistachio-sized mind.

The navigation ends, and that's how I find myself parked on an isolated strip of concrete near the water, all the majesty of the Brooklyn bridge stretched overhead in the midday sunlight.

I put the car in park and wait. We're alone so far.

And then, movement in my periphery makes me turn my head.

Striding across the street to where we are, carrying a sleek black clutch under one arm is a well-dressed woman, who—Wait.

What the fuck? I balk at her.

It's Donna Calzavarra, hastening this way in a pair of death-defying high heels. Sunglasses hide her green eyes, the same ones her son has. A colorful silk headscarf covers her dark blond waves, but I can still pick her out.

The last time I saw her up close was at the engagement party.

What the fuck is she doing here? Meeting Vito in the middle of the morning?

How do the two of them even know each other?

Is this a trap? Did Vito lure her here under false pretenses the same way he did with Orazio? Questions race through my mind. If he can't kidnap Ciro's coveted daughter in law, his plan is to snatch Ciro's wife? But what would she be doing *here*? What could he have possibly lured her here with?

I expect Vito to get out or call in a few Balboni soldiers who are hidden someplace unbeknownst to me, but all he does is throw open the back door, so she can climb in.

My ears tune for a tense conversation, so I'm nothing short of *baffled* by the unmistakable sound of...kissing. I stare at the intercom like it's lying to me.

"You are so sexy," Vito groans, followed by a smack which can only be Vito's hand on Donna's ass. "Why did you make me wait?"

"Things have been crazy since the fire," Donna sighs.

"My little arsonist." The way Vito purrs turns my stomach in every way, but I barely have the brain space to register nausea, before an entire onslaught of horrifying audio porn fills the front seat of this car.

Vito's repulsive dirty talk follows the noise of their joined lips and tongues, just minutes before the entire car starts to bounce. Donna moaning his name like that is almost enough to make me turn the intercom off, but I can't risk it.

I can't risk missing a single word these coconspirators say to each other, even if I'm about to hurl up breakfast.

The truth crushes me flatter than a rockslide.

Vito Balboni and Donna Calzavarra are having an affair.

No wonder he was so easily able to infiltrate the Dalla Porta... I knew he had an in somewhere. A mole on Jaco's payroll was to be expected, but not Donna Calzavarra...

I mean, Don Sabatini's daughter-in-law? How? Why?

There's no way Jaco knows about *this,* that Vito's been getting sex and suggestions on the side from an integral member of the Calzavarra family. *Dirty little secret* is an understatement here.

"Setting the fire took so much work," she fusses in between kisses. "And all for what? She made it out."

Wait a fucking minute.

She was the one who set the fire on the estate?

And she was...trying to kill *Nora* with it?

But then I remember something Nora said that night when we were dancing. I asked if Donna liked her, and she made some joke about a guillotine. About no woman being good enough for—

Fuck.

Donna is the one who wants Nora out of the way.

Her husband wants the match between Nora and their son, and she's against it. Always has been.

I've never heard of a woman being so against a marriage that she was willing to betray her husband by having an affair with his greatest rival, and team up with them to kidnap her son's fiancée, but then again, I've never been married to Ciro Calzavarra...That awful fuck.

The wheels of my mind won't stop turning.

If Donna was willing to involve her family's greatest enemy to get one defenseless woman like Nora out of the way, she's capable of anything.

Betrayal. Sabotage. Arson.

Maybe even murder.

Nora.

She's in far more danger than I thought. I have to get to her before Donna takes matters into her own hands.

Everything in me wants to jump out of this car, run for it, and not stop until Nora and I are together again, but I can't.

I have to take Vito home to the Balboni warehouse. Or else, he'll realize what's going on. And I'll be shot, long before I make it back to the love of my life.

CHAPTER 37

Nora

AFTER THE WORST, emptiest ten days of my life, the night before the wedding finally comes. All the wedding preparations are complete. I've played the part of a willing sacrifice. My mother and I have hardly spoken a word since I confronted her about everything, and I've never felt more alone in all my life.

I've thought of Rocco every minute, *ached* for him, begging this night to come faster, and now that it's finally here, I'm a bundle of anxiety and anticipation. All day, I've hardly been able to keep still, and for the life of me, I don't know *how* I'm going to get through another of these horrible family dinners.

When the house staff serves the meal, everyone is present.

Don Saba, Ciro, Frankie, Donna, Mama, and me.

It's awkward to say the least.

Ciro looks triumphant, as though some private good fortune is lighting him up from the inside out. Donna, beside him, actually has a pleasant look on her face, unlike the usual thinly-veiled glare she reserves for me and my mother.

Beside me, Mama remains distant and checked out, eating vegetables off her plate like nothing in the whole world will ever matter again.

Don Saba maintains his typical silence. I don't think I've ever heard him say more than ten words in a single day, and even that's a lot for him. He speaks more to business associates and members of the Dalla Porta administration, I'm sure, but for his family and family-to-be, he is a quiet and deeply reserved man.

Even on the eve of such a happy occasion as his only grand-child's marriage, he seems about as enthusiastic as I am.

My body's bound so tightly from nerves that I've hardly been able to eat a thing all day. All through dinner, I push carrots around my plate and spear bits of mashed potato on my fork to pretend.

Despite my better judgement, I can't help sneaking looks at Frankie, who hasn't spoken one word to me or thrown me so much as a *glance* since the night he demanded I sleep with him…

I'm glad to have been left alone all this time, but in the pit of my stomach, I brace for something worse coming around the mountain.

I keep quiet while we eat. Almost all of us do.

It's strange for me that this is the last time I'm going to see any of these people in my lifetime. What a bland, lopsided goodbye.

After dinner, Mama and I retire to our rooms.

Everything inside me is dying to give her one last hug. After all, by the time she wakes up in the morning, Rocco and I will be gone. But the woman disappears into her bedroom without even saying goodnight.

The bitter emptiness of this non-goodbye is going to haunt me. I can already feel it.

Inside me, the guilt over leaving my mother alone in this

ungodly mess is considerable. But so is the hurt she gave me, leaving *me* alone with all of this shit. I'm so sorry, but I also can't apologize for trying to take care of myself.

Especially knowing Dad would have been on my side, all the way.

Everything could have worked out so differently, if only he were still alive...

After the light in her bedroom clicks off and I'm safely tucked away in mine, I dress for my escape, pulling on pants and my converse. It took some digging through that massive closet, but I was able to find a dark mauve hoodie. Something that will blend into the night.

All that's left to do is wait for Rocco to get me out of here.

The unknown of it all terrifies me.

I don't know how he's going to get onto the property or how he'll contact me. My cellphone's back in Manhattan, not that my mother or the Calzavarras would have let me keep it after the stunt I pulled.

I don't even know when tonight to expect him, I just—

A knock comes at my bedroom door.

I shoot up from where I sit on the bed, a few clothes packed into a small bag I found buried deep within the closet.

My heart pounds out a hard jagged beat, as I move to the door, unlock it, and pull it open. I half-expect Rocco to be standing there, but it's the pushy butler again.

That only makes this moment more ominous.

"Miss Di Rienzo, I have a message. Your fiancé is outside and he wants to speak with you. Now."

Shit. Cold tendrils of fear coil around my heart.

After what happened last time he wanted to talk, I...

But he wants to meet outside. Someplace without beds. Not that that stopped him the first time he ever pushed me down and tried to force me.

"It's bad luck for the groom to see the bride the night before the wedding," I blurt out. The butler is unamused, looking down his nose at me.

"It's bad luck to defy the men of this house."

More importantly, what if my not being in my room causes problems for Rocco when he comes looking for me?

What if we miss each other in passing and miss our opportunity to escape together, in the process?

"Where is Gianfrancesco?" I swallow hard.

"In the greenhouse," the butler informs me. "I'll take you there."

The greenhouse...okay. Plants. Benches. Glass. *No beds.*

But also no one to hear me scream for help.

Ugh. For fuck's sake, I just want to run away, but the heavy irritated gaze of the butler feels like claws in my face. And I'm already dressed for the outdoors, and I've run out of excuses.

So as not to arouse suspicion, I go with him. It's a struggle to keep up with his long strides as he leads me through the sleepy first floor of the house, out onto a brick-tiled patio and down three flights of stairs separated by square landings set into the grassy slope of the property's back lawn.

On the bottom landing, the butler stops and motions toward the green house down a short curving path off to the right. "He's waiting for you over there."

The butler doesn't wait for a reply before hastening back up the steps and into the house. I'm alone out here with the crickets, hoping for the best, even if everything inside me wants to run back to my room right now.

He just wants to speak with you, Nora... I chant inside, trying to make myself believe that everything's going to be okay.

I start down the path, motion-sensor lawn lights flicking on as I go.

Lights outside the greenhouse cast warm shadows on the old curving glass structure. From here, it looks like a humongous counter-top cake display case.

I coil my hands and release them rapidly, trying to make the clammy feeling dissipate, as I find myself steps from the front door.

A shadow moves inside.

He's definitely here all right.

Grabbing the handle, I pull the door open and let myself in.

Once inside, I find the greenhouse is far less lovely than it looks from the outside. It's obvious as soon as I enter, stepping carefully over debris and overgrown vines, that the place hasn't been used in years. Flower pots lay discarded, and English ivy has overrun most of the rectangular flower beds.

The place is in a state of dilapidation.

Why in the world would Frankie want to meet out here when there's plenty of privacy back at the house?

"Gianfrancesco?" I call out, when I don't see him.

To ease my nerves, I promise myself I'll make this conversation go by as quickly as possible and get back to my room to wait for Rocco.

Not that I have the slightest idea what Frankie wants to talk about—

Sudden impact knocks me off my feet.

Bright, sharp pain cracks into my cranium, as a heavy terracotta flower pot connects with the back of my skull, sending me scrabbling onto the dimly lit greenhouse floor. I scrape my arm on the way down, my vision blurring.

The pain blooms and spreads through me, immobilizing and overwhelming.

Lightheaded. Blurry. Pain pounding.

My hair feels sticky, heavy with the cold-hot sensation that assures me I'm bleeding. Maybe badly.

I'm blacking out, my vision getting farther and farther from me, like I'm staring down a mile-long corridor. Still, my eyes twitch from side to side, searching this dizzy darkness for my attacker.

But I find no one before I pass out.

As I swirl into unconsciousness, cruel words crawl into my ears. *"You're not going to marry my son."*

CHAPTER 38

Rocco

IT TOOK ALMOST an entire sixty minutes to implement, but I did it.

I temporarily bugged the estate's security feeds, so they won't transmit any live footage, for the next half an hour. That's all the time I'll have to infiltrate the property and grab Nora. Before it's too late.

Over the past ten days, I've planned and replanned everything multiple times. I spent my long lonely nights memorizing every step of this process. Now that I know how dangerous Donna Calzavarra is, I have even less time to waste.

According to the blueprints of the grounds I was able to get, the country house is old enough that it still has formal servant quarters and back hallways, entirely separate from the main house.

I manage to get onto the property by cutting a fence near the east woods. A short jog through the underbrush, and I find myself standing along the darkened perimeter of the old servants wing of the house.

As I suspected, this part of the house is dusty and dark, full of antique furniture covered in sheets... Thank God the Dalla Porta haven't had this place renovated in years. Using the servant hallways, I make my way upstairs undetected.

The second floor is where I think they're keeping Nora.

I'd bet my life on it. Scratch that. I *am* betting my life on it.

Managing my footfalls carefully, I find the door that opens from the servants hallway into the main part of the house, where everyone staying here will be.

I slip through the door into a small alcove and inch forward, hand ready to pull my gun at a moment's notice.

Approaching the perpendicular hallway slowly, I listen for noise—

"Frankie." The deep, bone-chilling voice of the one and only Sabatini Calzavarra.

Fuck! I flatten myself against the wall to my left, nearly fucking caught.

I almost popped out right into their path!

Gianfrancesco walks past my hiding place first, one peripheral glance away from finding me here, Sabatini right on his heels. The groom-to-be and his grandfather walk like they're headed to their rooms.

"Yes, *nonno.*"

"Go talk to your bride."

Nora? My whole body bristles, on high alert.

The expression on Gianfrancesco's face is sour and dark. "Isn't it bad luck to see the bride the night before the wedding?"

"Make your own luck." Sabatini's hand falls on his grandson's shoulder. "Tomorrow, you two will start your life together... Don't start on a bad note."

"But she—" Gianfrancesco starts to argue, sees the expression on his grandfather's face, and softens. "Yes, *nonno.*"

"Good." Sabatini stops in front of a door up the hall. *"Buona notte."*

"Night," Gianfrancesco stands there while his grandfather disappears. Then he runs a rough hand through his hair and starts for the staircase at the end of the hall.

Is he really going to Nora's room?

Gianfrancesco heads back down to the first floor.

Shit. I miscalculated.

Doubling back through the servant's hall, I get back to the first floor and slip out into the mansion with more caution this time. I manage to do it fast enough that I beat Gianfrancesco only by a few seconds. He arrives on the downstairs landing and immediately heads down a long hallway to his right.

I follow from the shadows, keeping an eye out for any security personnel.

Gianfrancesco reaches a set of double doors, lifts his fist to knock, but freezes. He glares at the door, bitter and angry before dropping his hand back to his side, turning on his heel and stalking back toward the staircase.

Perfect.

Once the coast is clear, I make my move, taking this expansive hallway with long strides, headed toward what must be Nora's room. But as I cross to the door, searing white-hot pain sneaks up on my skull.

Another fucking flashback.

No.

Head-splitting pain tears into my head, voices from the past echoing through my mind, overwhelming my senses, destabilizing my balance.

Fuck, not now!

At the worst possible time for my body to betray me, my balance and vision warp, when I'm only a few steps from Nora's door.

I fall against the smooth wood, weight collapsing on the handle.

The door swings open. I'm inside the living room of a suite, struggling through pain.

The first bedroom door I find, I push through it.

Empty. The first thing I see through my blurring vision is a packed bag sitting on a massive bed. This is definitely Nora's room, but…why isn't she here?

Where is she?

No, no, no, no, no.

I stagger toward the desk on the far side of the room by the window, the throes of the flashback and devastating migraine still tearing me apart.

Through the haze of my pain, panic builds inside me.

This is wrong. Nora should be here.

Something's wrong.

Donna Calzavarra got to her first. I just have this awful feeling.

She wants Nora out of the way, and after two failed attempts, she's likely looking to take matters into her own hands.

Fuck.

This property's huge, and there are only fifteen minutes left of security camera cover. As soon as the bug I planted wears off, the feeds will revert to normal functioning, and I'll be spotted faster than I can pull out my gun and shoot somebody.

Where would Donna have taken Nora?

Hunched against the desk and reeling from the volume of the pain, I lift my heavy head, getting a view of the golf-course like grounds, unfurling down a long gradual incline from the base of this enormous house.

There's a pond down the hill, a short dock, a boathouse, gardens, a greenhouse, an indoor tennis court—Wait.

A shaft of white in the greenhouse captures my heavy eyes. A flashlight.

With all the strength I have left, I race for the door.

It's just a hunch. I could be all wrong. It could already be too late, but I won't give up even the ghost of a chance to save the woman I love.

CHAPTER 39

Nora

STINGING, burning pain drags me back over the surface of consciousness.

My hand tries to go to the place where it hurts, but I can't move it.

Something's wrong. Something's on me. Something tight, painful, and sticky—

My eyes open to slits. Just opening them a crack sends fresh pain through my already tingling, aching head.

Alertness returns to my consciousness slowly, layering itself inside me until I can feel every jagged edge of fear puncturing my pounding heart.

Where am I?

Ahead of me is a murky wall of glass, dusty panes that haven't been cleaned in years, translucent with dirt.

The air smells of blood, old soil, and rotting wood.

*The greenhouse...*I remember slow and painful.

I was on my way to the greenhouse to meet Frankie when...

Someone attacked me. I heard a woman's voice.

Where is she?

Why can't I move?! Panic peals through me like whaling emergency sirens. *What did she do to me?*

The back of my head feels sticky with dirt and my own blood.

Cautiously, I tilt my head forward and look down at myself. In the dimness of this decrepit place, I've been strapped to a rusting metal chair. Duct tape binds my caves to the chair leg, and my thighs to the seat.

Behind the chair is a rusted iron trellis. The chair seems to be attached to it. When I shift in my seat, what little I can move, the trellis moves with me.

My right arm is bound to the chair's arm, and my shoulders have been fastened to the chair's back. But when I look left, I don't find my other arm.

Instead, my dizzy, heavy head brushes the end of a cold metal cylinder—

It's the barrel of a gun, positioned at my temple.

Panic sends me hyperventilating. My muscles spasm, and that's when I realize what's happening. My left arm is duct taped to the trellis, bent at my elbow, and the palm of my hand...

Oh God.

My palm has been duct-taped around the grip of a gun.

A whimper of terror escapes, as my predicament washes over me.

"Waking up, are we?" The unmistakable voice of Donna Calzavarra travels to my ears. She's behind me somewhere.

Desperate relief bursts in my chest. Thank God my mother-in-law found me. She'll be able help.

"Donna—" I bleat.

"Quiet, you dumb bitch."

My clipped racing breaths hitch, as my eyes widen. All my momentary relief converts back to fear.

The cutting edge in Donna's tone...

Awful realization swallows me whole.

Donna Calzavarra isn't here to help me.

She's... the one who attacked me in the first place. Isn't she?

Over my shoulder, I find her reflection in the dark glass, standing beside a long wooden table with a hand on her hip. She cracks her neck before striding this way in a dark jumpsuit.

"I think it's time we had a moment of silence to honor the end of your pathetic life."

Her Jimmy Choos click over cement, wood and shards of ceramic tile, as she approaches me, slow and unbothered.

Who the hell wears stilettos to a murder scene?

Someone who's going to get away with it.

Horror swallows me again and again.

"I should thank you really." She trills a laugh. "Suicide was your idea first, after all."

Shock jumps through my chest. "H-How do you know about that?"

"If only you'd had the fucking guts to go through with it, there'd be no need for *all this*." Finally, Donna saunters past the trellis, allowing me to look upon the face of the woman who intends to kill me. "Or you could have done me a favor and died in the fire, but *no.*"

Donna's words cook me alive. She's been wanting me dead for weeks, and now...It's almost too awful for words.

Now, she's going to stage my suicide.

"But why?" Tears wells in my eyes.

I don't know how to believe what's happening right now. I always knew Donna disliked me and my family, but to the point of *murder*?

"What did I ever do to you?" My head shakes a little, but as soon as I brush up against the barrel again, I freeze, fresh terror icing my blood.

She smirks at me, humorless and wicked. Her green eyes look black in this semi-darkness. Hair pulled up into a tightly coiled bun on top of her head, she gives me an apathetic glare. "Nothing, little Eleanora. You've done nothing wrong.

"Then why are you doing this?" I croak. *Fuck, it hurts to speak.*

Her voice is a low growl. "Because I hate that loose cunt mother of yours."

"My mother...?" Even with my head pounding and my heart sprinting from fear, I try to keep Donna talking.

Anything to keep her from pulling the trigger and ending my life.

How wild. The irony isn't lost on me, not at all.

Just a few weeks ago, I was ready to jump off a building, and now, I want to cling to life with everything I have.

Because...

Rocco's face flashes through my mind.

I want a future with him. A real one.

And the sliver of hope that I'll get that future exists, but only if I manage to survive this horror film my life has turned into.

"My mother's miserable, Donna." Another round of tears spill down my dirt-caked cheeks. "She died inside the moment my father left this earth. There's nothing else left to take away from her, I swear—"

"Except *you*." Her smile brightens, like this opportunity to hurt me delights her. "Her prized daughter."

"Is this about Frankie?" I'm trembling beneath my getaway clothes. The excitement on Donna's face melts off into cold, hard rage. "I won't marry him. I'll disappear. Tonight. For good, I promise."

A clap of pain rebounds through my whole head when she strikes me across the face with her acrylic-clawed hands. The force shoves my head to the right.

"Oh, you'll disappear all right," she agrees, anger coating her bitter words. "I'll make sure of that."

"No. No, please," I whimper as she grabs my left forearm, the gun shuddering in my quaking palm.

"I won't let Frankie marry some stuck-up whore's daughter," she snarls, her fingers digging into my flesh. "Over my dead body."

"Donna, *please—*"

"Enough, you little brat." She gets her hand around my mine, forcefully rips one of my fingers back, and carefully, tucks it around the gun's trigger.

Oh God.

This is it.

It's over. I know it is.

I'm going to die without ever seeing Rocco again. I'll never get to tell him how much I wanted a future with him.

This is a fate worse than death—

A giant shadow falls over us both.

Donna's head snaps up. Her eyes jump wide, but I can't see what she's staring at. "*You...*" Her voice becomes meek with fear.

Then, something happens so fast, I hardly catch it.

A long arm above my head swipes out from behind the trellis and delivers a swift shank to Donna's neck. She cries out in pained surprise, but the sound is cut off unnaturally, as her taught panicked expression slackens, quickly swirling into a queasy, shade of dizziness.

She staggers a single step backward before collapsing, unconscious onto the grimy floor of this old greenhouse.

Leaving me alone with the one responsible.

"Who's there?" I cry, frozen, shaken, and still unable to see who's standing over me. I hear the *shink* of what can only be a knife's blade flicking out.

The man sweeps around the side of the trellis, bending down to one knee, showing me his face. "Me, sweetheart."

344

"Rocco!" I wail, choked up with wondrous relief. "You...you came."

"Of course, I came." He eases his utility knife between my skin and the duct tape restraining my legs and jerks his arm up, slicing with deft skill clean through it.

I kick my legs free, as he starts to free my left arm. "I can't believe you made it."

"Hold still." His voice is heavy with emotion as he surgically removes the tape binding my hand to the gun. "Don't move, baby."

I freeze, still shaking inside, as he retracts the firearm carefully, pulling it away from my temple and tucking it inside his suit jacket. He cuts the rest of my left arm free, then my right, and finally, my shoulders, and the second I can move my whole body, I leap up from my seat and throw my arms around his neck.

"I thought I'd never see you again," I sob into his shoulder, as he squeezes the life out of me.

"I was scared too." He kisses my hair, my neck, my bedraggled face.

As soon as I meet his gaze—full of concern, his deep brown eyes rimmed with moisture like he's on the verge of crying too—I crush my lips to his. He kisses me hard, but only for a moment before he pulls back, urgency in his tone.

"We've got to go, sweetheart. Right now."

I'm already nodding. "Let's get the hell out of here."

He grabs my hand, and tugs me through the wreckage of this greenhouse toward a back door on the far end of the room. "I temporarily jammed the security cameras and bugged the alarm system. If we don't leave now, we'll be caught."

"How did you find me?" I shake my head in awe.

"The grace of God." Rocco halts us, sticking his head through the open greenhouse door to make sure all's clear outside.

"Thank you," I sniff hard, wiping my face with the back of my hoodie's sleeve.

"Don't thank me yet." He throws me a smile despite this crazy moment we're in. "We've still got to get through the woods."

"I love the woods." I grin at him.

Hand in hand, we sprint the three hundred feet between the greenhouse and the woods that surround the country estate's main grounds. Rocco has a small navigation device that points us in the right direction once we find ourselves in the pitch black underbrush, he's also brought a pair of infrared shades for both of us, so we can traverse the terrain out here without too much difficulty.

After a few minutes we make it to the security fence, the one that borders the total acreage of the property. Rocco leads me straight to the spot where he cut into it, creating a metal curtain he can push back, allowing us both to maneuver through onto the darkened black road beyond.

With my infrared shades, I clock the outline of a car across the street, stashed beneath a small copse of trees. Not his Jaguar. A different car. He leads me toward it, and as we cross the pavement, Rocco suddenly asks me, "Nora. Are you sure you want to do this?"

His question startles me. I'm shaken by all that's happened tonight, but my answer's still yes. I'm going with him as we planned. It's the best and only choice.

"Of course, I do. Anything would be better than staying here..." I tug on his arm when he doesn't reply. "Rocco, getting to be with you is the best case scenario. Better than anything I could have imagined or foreseen."

"I'm going to protect you with every ounce of strength I have." He pulls my hand to his lips and kisses the back of my palm, without slowing down. "But if it's not enough...if danger comes and finds us..."

"Then we'll face it together."

"I don't have anything to go back to, but you do. You're choosing to leave everything and everyone you know behind..."

"Rocco, my mother-in-law just tried to kill me. Getting the fuck away from these people is my top priority."

"What about your mother? Were you able to help her?"

The thought of her weighs down my spirit. I shake my head no. "She wouldn't listen to me, but…I left proof of Ciro's treachery for Nico to find. She'll be able to help Mama use it to get away from him, if that's what she wants. Or not."

"What about your father's death?" Rocco's grip on my hand strengthens as he helps me down a small embankment toward the getaway car below. "We didn't find out for sure what happened to him. Are you really going to be okay leaving New York for good without the answers you wanted?"

"I left a trail for Nico. She'll pick up the thread of all this craziness," I reassure him. "She's a better sleuth than I ever was. God only knows how long it would take me to get to the bottom of everything, even if I had all the time in the world."

"I'm in love with you." Rocco opens the passenger side door and gives me a hard look, pulling the infrareds off his face and mine. "You know that, right?"

I nod. My beleaguered heart flutters back to life in my chest. "And I love you."

"I just need you to understand that if you come with me, I'm never letting you go." His words are darkly possessive. The threat of danger underlies his tone. Deep inside me, a small bud of doubt blooms, but I ignore it, a monsoon of affection flooding my system.

"That's absolutely fine by me."

He crashes his mouth into mine, revitalizing me with a hot, desperate, primal kiss.

"Get in," he growls, the second he lets me breathe. "We're out of here."

I slide inside, he's just a moment behind, and hand in hand, Rocco De Carlo and I flee to a new life.

EPILOGUE

Rocco

THE ROAD STRETCHES OUT before us, a perfect May morning unfolding overhead.

After her ordeal, Nora lays reclined and asleep in my passenger seat with an ice pack positioned under part of her head.

We stopped at an emergency clinic on the way out of town just to make sure she wasn't concussed, but left before anyone could phone the police or realize that we weren't using our real names.

While there, I also managed to grab her a fresh pair of clothes, so she could change out of what she was wearing when Donna Calzavarra came at her in that greenhouse.

My knuckles ache, I'm squeezing them so tight around the steering wheel of this Ioniq I bought in cash several days ago. Utilizing my Jaguar for our escape was out of the question. It's safely parked at the Balboni warehouse, and when my former colleagues tear it apart looking for clues at to what happened to me or where I went after pulling a fast one on them, they'll find it spotless.

I made sure not to leave anything in there.

Not so much as single finger print is left.

We've been driving for about three hours now, and in another two, we'll arrive at my personal safe house.

One the Balboni family doesn't know about.

I bought it a few years back so that on the rare occasions when I had time off from work, I'd have somewhere other than the Balboni warehouse to be.

It sits on about an acre of land out in Pennsylvania.

The closest town to it is Meryton.

Which is in Dimikov territory.

The Dimikov syndicate is the most powerful bratva on US soil and has been for a two decades at least. I chose to buy a house so close to their enclave because I knew the Balboni would never look for me there. And most of them wouldn't have the guts to try. Not when they might risk pissing off the bratva.

I, on the other hand, know how to be subtle and keep to myself.

I've never run across anyone, and no one's ever run across me.

It's the perfect place to take Nora while we figure out our next steps.

The amount of joy and relief I feel to be with her again weighs more than a whole family of whales. Whenever I think what might have happened if I'd been even a few seconds late, my whole body blanches on the inside.

Thank God she's okay.

But beneath the relief, there's also guilt and gloom.

I haven't told her the truth yet, and no matter what she thinks, learning who I really am could change everything for her.

That's another reason I'm taking her to my safe house.

From there we can decide where we're going.

I'll tell her the truth and if she doesn't want anything more to do with me, I'll make sure she gets someplace safe, somewhere she wants to be. I'll send her to a new life with money and any other resources she might need.

And then...I'd follow her there and spend the rest of my life making sure she lives undisturbed by my kind again, if only from the shadows.

That's what I tell myself, but the primal beast inside me howls in deadly pain at the thought of never touching her again.

Deep down, I know it's a lie.

Even if she begged me to let her go, I wouldn't be able to.

Not when I feel this way about her.

My real plan? Tell Nora the truth *after* I marry her.

Once we've committed our lives to each other, nothing and no one will come between us. I'll make sure of it.

I promise myself. Once she's mine, fully and completely bound to me, nothing will tear me away from the woman I love.

TO BE CONTINUED...

The *Endangered Brides* series continues.

Book 2: The Replacement Bride follows Nico and Gianfrancesco. Nora and Rocco's story picks up in **Book 3: The Captive Bride**.

ABOUT THE AUTHOR

R. R. Nigh is a reluctant romance writer who fell into the genre by happenstance after a lifetime of writing young adult and fantasy books under her real name.

Branching into darker, dangerous territory, she ventures to write love stories that never let your heart go for a second. Nigh brings a cinematic edge to romance, blending emotional depth with high-voltage tension.

When not plotting betrayals, kidnappings, or steamy encounters on the page, R. R. can usually be found researching actors on Wikipedia, bingeing 90s sitcoms, or dreaming up new ways to make fictional couples suffer (and fall in love, of course).

The Target Bride is the first book in the *Endangered Brides* series and marks the beginning of a bold new voice in dark romance.

Subscribe to *The Nightingale*, R. R. Nigh's newsletter, for exclusive content, behind-the-scenes looks, and early access to future books.

For series information, release dates, exclusive content and more, visit www.rrnigh.com.